THE RECLAMATION PROJECT

YEAR ONE

Edited by John R. Robey

The Reclamation Project — Year One

Copyright © 2019 by John R. Robey
Production © 2019 FurPlanet Productions
Introduction and Piece of Mind © John R. Robey
Ambara Blues © Indagare
Insecurity © L. Rowyn
The Underground Star © Nenekiri Bookwyrm
Post-Mortem Telepathy © Graveyard Greg
Skipping Stones © Bryan "StarryAqua" Osborne
Silence and Sword © Royce Day
Dark Garden Lake © Kayode Lycaon
Sewer Tea © Dan Leinir Turthra Jensen
Persephone's Chance © Juan Carlos Moreno
A Journey to the Skies © Ferric the Bird
Star of the Savannah © Huskyteer
The Flavors of Sunlight © James L. Steele
Chromium Maneuvers © Matt Trepal

Cover illustration by Teagan Gavet

Published by FurPlanet Productions
Dallas, TX
http://www.FurPlanet.com

Print ISBN 978-1-61450-508-2
eBook ISBN 978-1-61450-509-9
First Edition Trade Paperback December 2019

To those who have gone before, and to those who will come after.

TABLE OF CONTENTS

Foreword—The Apocalypse Ain't What It Used to Be 9

Piece of Mind
    John R. Robey *11*

Ambara Blues
    Indagare *54*

Insecurity
    L. Rowyn *74*

The Underground Star
    Nenekiri Bookwyrm *96*

Post-Mortem Telepathy
    Graveyard Greg *116*

Skipping Stones
    Bryan "StarryAqua" Osborne *127*

Silence and Sword
    Royce Day *148*

Dark Garden Lake
    Kayode Lycaon *176*

Sewer Tea
    Dan Leinir Turthra Jensen *206*

Persephone's Chance
Juan Carlos Moreno   228

A Journey to the Skies
Ferric the Bird   255

Star of the Savannah
Huskyteer   284

The Flavors of Sunlight
James L. Steele   305

Chromium Maneuvers
Matt Trepal   327

About the Authors   355

Foreword—The Apocalypse Ain't What It Used to Be

When I was a kid, the general consensus was that nuclear annihilation was not an if, but a when. Movies like *Logan's Run*, *Planet of the Apes*, or *Silent Running* were the tentpoles of pop culture sci-fi. Even *Star Trek*, a relentlessly hopeful beacon created by one of the all-time great Utopians, had baked into its future history that sometime around 2000 A.D. humans were going to just squeak through near-extinction by the skin of our collective teeth.

Then *Star Wars* happened, and the '80s went BIG. The streamlined jumpsuits and underground complexes inhabited by insane robots of the '60s and '70s gave way to *Thundarr the Barbarian* and *Mad Max*, two-fisted heroes cruising the radioactive wastes with badass vehicles and New Wave hair. Sure, it would be a crapsack world, but you might as well have fun with it! Still the underlying assumption was the same: the apocalypse, when it came, would be a sudden and devastating event. The long, slow death of a thousand environmental cuts? Not so much.

Now here we are in 2019; every year is the hottest on record—which is doubly worrying when you realize that the record had just been broken the previous year, which itself had broken the record of the year before it. Our political powers order the people best in a position to do something about it to pretend it isn't happening, while the military quietly studies the feasibility of moving bases inland because the ones on the coast are flooding. After decades of being told that wealth 'trickles down' it has become clear that wealth is instead magnetic—flowing from those who have the least, to those who have the most, where it is clutched tightly by a handful of metaphorical dragons while the rest of the world starves.

Is it any wonder that such a time would produce solarpunk? "Solar—" tied to environmental awareness, conservation, the development of new energy sources and technology that works *with* the Earth instead of despoiling it; and "—punk," focused on the radical empowerment of the disenfranchised, of the helpless and forgotten, and the rejection of corrupt, dehumanizing, authoritarian power structures. But unlike the resigned or even cavalier post-apocalyptic fiction of days gone by, solarpunk insists—nay, *demands*—that we can and shall create a better world. That we are Earth's gardeners, not its destroyers.

Of all the social movements of the past half century, punk is furry's closest philosophical brother, so when FurPlanet asked me to create a new anthology, I knew it had to have a solarpunk element. But in furry, the white-hot rage of punk is softened by radical kindness and a delight in whimsy. There's only so seriously you can take yourself when the people around you are wearing rainbow colored fur and making high-pitched squeaky noises.

The Reclamation Project is my attempt to thread that needle of cognitive dissonance. These are stories of talking animals, yes, but there is a wide range of humanity here, from rollicking high adventure in 'Ambara Blues' or 'Post Mortem Telepathy' to the fluttering palpitations of new love in 'Insecurity' or the excitement of youth in 'The Underground Star'—from the comradery of old friends in 'Sewer Tea' to the forging of new bonds in 'Persephone's Chance' to the melancholy of isolation in 'Dark Garden Lake'—from uncanny horror in 'Skipping Stones' or 'A Journey to the Skies' to the sardonic humor of an insane AI that wishes you a nice day as it tries to kill you in 'Silence and Sword' or 'Star of the Savannah.'

Of all the stories, 'The Flavors of Sunlight' is the purest "solar—" of the bunch (and the one that took me most by surprise), while 'Chromium Maneuvers' is the most "—punk" …but I am proud to be able to bring each and every one of these amazing stories to you.

We can and shall create a better world.

John R. Robey

September, 2019

PIECE OF MIND

John R. Robey

Half a century after it fell from the sky, Ambara Down teemed with life. The remains of human skyscrapers were covered in a carpet of green, with the toppled and smashed architecture poking out from underneath like tombstones all askew in a neglected graveyard. Dozens of different species of zoomorphs ("furries," the humans called them) created a new world for themselves in one half, while humans from the flying city of High Empyros excavated and redeveloped the other. Down the middle of it ran The Fence—a divider in some places literal and others symbolic—that separated them both and kept something like peace.

At the heart of the city, directly across from The Fence's busiest gate, just inside furry territory, a tower of dark blue glass gleamed in the morning sun like a sapphire, three stories tall. This was The Damselfly, the *de facto* meeting place for anyone and everyone in Ambara Down. It was a bar, a nightclub, a town hall, a world of its own; and inside, motes floated in the blue haze of the morning sunlight and created an atmosphere of not having really woken up yet. Nevertheless, the bar had a patron, a chocolate-and-cream furred collie-morph in simple but elegant silks.

"Where is the pilot?" the collie muttered under her breath. "We can't afford these delays!" Haru straightened the hem of her robes and sipped at her tea to keep her tail from thrashing in annoyance; it wasn't helping.

"You must be the woman I'm looking for!" came a cheerful voice at the door. The collie turned to see a female calico, short and scrawny. The feline had a grease-stained tanktop under a baggy hooded jacket and goggles on her head; her ears were perked up and pointed at the canine. "I can smell someone from the Prefect's Office a mile away!"

No. This couldn't be the recommended pilot, could it? The collie frowned, her ears going back involuntarily. "Are you… Captain Aurora?" she said.

"They call me Rory," said the calico, offering up her muzzle for a mutual sniff. The collie did not want to sniff her.

"I am Haru, Chief Steward of the Prefect's Office," said the collie. "I am the Prefect's personal assistant."

"Nice," said the calico.

Haru blinked, not sure what to make of that. "Well, quite."

"So, you need a hoverskiff in a hurry!" said Rory, scratching absently at her neck. "Why don't you go with one of the Prefect's fleet?"

"That isn't something you need to know," replied Haru. "This assignment requires discretion, and it requires flexibility. Four passengers, some luggage. There may be hazards. You will go where directed without question, and you must be willing to be on retainer until we can return. It may be a matter of days or weeks."

"What'sa matter, Prefect's in-laws in town?"

Haru's ears went back. "Disrespectful remarks, on the other hand, are *not* required. Besides, the Prefect is single."

"Disrespectful remarks are a little service I provide at no charge," Rory replied, one corner of her mouth pulled back into a smirk. "Besides, you sent for me, not the other way around."

"I was told that you had a combat-worthy vessel and a reputation for resourcefulness and reliability," said Haru. "They didn't mention having the manners of an alley cat."

"Okay, so I've got bad manners," said Rory. "If it makes you feel better, I'll put on headphones and we can ignore each other the whole way. But when I take a job, I see it through to the end. And you can't have a lot of options anyway, your message said you'd pay an extra fifty percent."

"That is the agreement on the table," said Haru.

"So, you need me more than I need you."

"You—!" Haru strangled the thought in her throat. As infuriating as the cat was, she was also correct. Finally, Haru said, "Yes, it's true, we have a tight deadline and a very limited pool of qualified candidates."

"Then I'm your cat," said the calico, with a happy flick of her tail. "Five hundred up front for security."

"Fine. It'll be waiting with your contract in the courtyard of the Prefecture Building one o'clock. That should give you time to change."

Rory tilted her head. "Change? Change what?"

Haru's ears flicked. "Change into proper attire, of course!"

"What are you talking about?" said the cat. "Something like you've got? I'm a hoverskiff pilot, not a hostess in a comfort house. Silks would be ruined in five minutes of my job. This *is* proper attire."

"You can't represent the Prefect looking like a grease blot!" said Haru. "Think of appearances."

"Pfft. You worry too much, Prefect's Office. The world's a messy place, you've just gotta live with it."

"The dignity of the Prefect's position is vital to the morale of the people," said Haru.

The calico rolled her eyes and waved her palms in display of sarcastic alarm. "Oh yeah, I'm sure that's way more important than actually being able to do your job." She flicked her ears and her tail dismissively and headed for the door. "Tell you what, we'll split the difference. You have my money ready, and I'll go wash my dainty little pawbs. See you there, Prefect's Office."

"My name is Chief Steward Haru!" Haru called after her, but Rory was already gone.

* * *

At the appointed time, Rory's hoverskiff floated in the courtyard of the Prefecture Building, humming quietly. It wasn't much to look at, shaped more than anything like a flying boat six or seven meters long, with wing-like steering vanes folded against its sides and a retractable mast. An enclosure at the front housed the pilot's station and seating, and an open bay with benches and a rail formed the rest. The only hints that it might be anything more than a perfectly ordinary cargo skiff was a ring of what appeared to be human-made deflector shield generators around the perimeter of the deck, and even those were discreetly tucked behind dented metal covers.

Haru stood at the bottom of the gangway and called up. "Captain Aurora!"

"'Captain'?" came Rory's voice from the enclosure as the cat came out to greet her passengers. "Just Rory's good enough for me, Prefect's Off—" The calico stopped short when she saw the rest of the party.

Prefect Durgavati, a lioness in finery befitting her office, loomed over Haru; two massive tiger guards with power-staves and gold-inlay armor braced either side of her. Servants behind them carried trunks. Even up on the deck of her skiff, Rory was nearly eye-to-eye with the Prefect. The Prefect blinked languorously at the pilot, dark tawny fur shining against her gold and turquoise adornments.

"Er... Your... Excellency..." Rory finally managed to stammer out and scurried down the gangway. At ground level, she barely came up to Durgavati's waist. "Please! Sorry. Sorry. Welcome aboard! It's... uh..." Haru couldn't help it; her tail wagged to see the pilot squirm and bow.

The Prefect's own tail swayed, gently. "Captain Aurora," she said. "So good of you to make yourself available on such short notice."

"I... uh, that is... well, my skiff's not much, but it'll get you where you need to go."

"I have no doubt of it," said the Prefect. "My assistant would find no less than the best." Haru felt herself wanting to squirm at that. "Now, before we go any further, I feel it's only fair to tell you what you're in for."

Rory looked up at that, ears low. "Your Excellency?"

"Change is coming to Ambara Down, Captain," said Durgavati. "The Empyrean 'Ambara Survey and Reclamation Initiative' has been rolled into, or perhaps one should say 'swallowed whole by,' a much larger multi-national operation. Practically all the High Cities are involved in some form or another. As of this time next month, the human portions of the city, including the gates, Travel Complex, and salvage operations in Old Ambara will fall under the rubric of the grand Reclamation Project."

Rory's ears went from being low, to flattening completely against her skull. "*All* the humans? Working... together?"

"Not quite all, but close enough," said the Prefect. "It has been theorized, discussed, and fought over for a long time. But the ink is dry now, the deed is done. The transfer of power will begin shortly. That's where we are going: we're traveling to High Empyros under the special invite of the incoming Executive Director to negotiate the Prefecture's role in this."

"Negotiate our role?" said Rory. "You mean they're not just gonna come marching in with troops again?"

"Captain!" said Haru. Durgavati put a calming hand on her assistant's shoulder.

"Not immediately, in any case," Durgavati said. "Not at all, if talks are successful. But it's important that these negotiations take place quietly and without interference. There are factions on both sides who would be just as happy to use this as a pretext to start fighting again. This is why we have secured private transport, to avoid the attention of an official convoy. We will be joined by an armed escort far enough away from city limits to avoid notice."

Rory blinked. "An armed escort? Prefecture soldiers?"

"Yes," said Durgavati. "*And* humans."

"Do you really trust the humans to operate in good faith?"

The Prefect shook her head. "Trust? No. I *hope* they will. If they don't, well… this is why I instructed Haru to find a combat-worthy vessel."

"…Oh," Rory said. Turning to Haru, she added, "That's what you meant by there might be hazards, I take it."

Haru nodded, offering Rory a printed map. "We need to reach High Empyros within three days. It's already started its seasonal migration away from Ambara Down, so we'll need to move quickly. I've worked out a route that does not take us into human territory until the last moment and should keep us away from as many prying eyes as possible."

Rory took the map, tail-tip flicking, and glared at Haru. "You could have been a little more up-front about just how hazardous you meant."

Durgavati chuckled and raised a placating hand. "If I know my assistant, she would not have told you at all unless I directed her to. She feels that duty is reason enough to do as you're told. But I believe you should know just what you're risking your life for, before you risk it."

"I haven't signed the contract, yet," said Rory. "What if I just walked away right now?"

"You wouldn't dare!" said Haru.

"Oh, wouldn't I?" snarled Rory back at her.

"Do you wish to walk away?" asked Durgavati.

"Well…"

"It's vital that the negotiations be kept secret as long as possible," said Durgavati. "Having told you about it, my choices are limited. My preferred result is that you come with us. Failing that, we would seek some guarantee of your silence until the official announcement of the transfer. If no such guarantee were feasible, I suppose we would have to detain you until the public was informed generally."

Rory digested this. "So, my choice is get paid to take you, get paid to keep my mouth shut and worry that I'll be blamed if word gets out, or be arrested."

"Essentially."

Rory gave a wide, bland smile, and bowed with a flourish towards the gangway. "Welcome aboard, Your Excellency," she said.

* * *

Their first stop was a small village some thirty kilometers from the city to pick up their escort, consisting of eight hoverbikes—four of the Prefect's Guard, and four High Empyrian humans in red and white leather uniforms. Lieutenant Premanayanat, a massive ape and one of Durgavati's most trusted officers, overlooked the situation grimly as the escort troops started their vehicles.

"Don't be so tense, Preman," Durgavati called down to him from the rail. "This is the best course of action."

"You're too vulnerable," said the ape. "Four scouts on hoverbikes! They should have sent a proper escort. And only four of our own? At least let me come with you."

"The ADF would be rioting in the streets if they knew this was coming," Durgavati said. "I need you in the city to keep order. I need them to *see* you in the city, being perfectly normal. Lose some money in the casino, that always cheers up the people."

The ape merely grunted; and with that, the vehicles were moving again. Once in formation they traveled without Ambaran colors, the uniformity and shining chrome of the human bikes standing out in sharp contrast to the jerry-rigged mishmash of the Prefecture vehicles.

Summer was coming fast, and within a week the human city of High Empyros would be five hundred kilometers north of its usual winter location. Haru's calculated route took them north from the village through Blood River Pass into the desert, following the mountains on the far side from the bulk of human territory. It wasn't the most direct way to rendezvous, but it was definitely the least populated. The Prefect contented herself by sitting in the sun on one of the hoverskiff benches, working on a digital desktop, while her bodyguards took turns watching the horizon with enhancing binoculars.

Haru's thick fur made sitting out in the desert sun a less-than-appealing prospect; she never could figure out why felines liked it so much. Finally, unwilling to pant in front of Durgavati in the heat, Haru stood and went forward to the pilot's enclosure at the front of the skiff. Rory leaned against a rail, gazing into the distance as the autopilot did most of the work, but turned as the collie approached.

"What's up, Prefect's Office?"

"Kindly address me as Chief Steward," said Haru, with an annoyed swish of her tail. "I just need to get out of the sun."

Rory indicated a swiveling chair in front of a scanner screen. "Be my guest."

Haru sat, and the skiff traveled on; shade or no shade, she was still panting within minutes. Every once in a while, Rory would point out the shimmering rainbow-flashes of airfish in the distance or other notable views, but conversation was not happening. Finally, the calico gave the collie a sidelong look and a sly grin, and said, "So, Durgavati's really something, huh?"

Haru looked up from her seat, then back to the Prefect. "Yes. Yes, she is. She brokered peace with the 'Claimers. She's kept Ambara Down safe for a decade."

"And you... what do you do?"

"Me?" said Haru. "I'm the Steward. I'm her assistant. I make sure that her orders are carried out. And... I'm her last line of defense."

"What does she think of this whole 'Reclamation Project' thing, then?"

"Well, she's concerned, naturally," said Haru. "Who wouldn't be? But if anyone can get us through the transition, she can."

Rory grinned down at her. "Wow, you're really wrapped around her finger, aren't you?"

"What?" yelped Haru, looking back up in alarm. "What's that supposed to mean? She's my employer!"

Rory's ears flickered. "You are, you totally are. You're sweet on your boss!"

"I'm not!"

"Wow, that makes me like you a lot more. Here I thought you were just a pain in the ass, it turns out you've got a squooshy nougat center."

"I do not!" said Haru. "I *am* just a pain in the ass!"

The pilot let out a squeaky laugh. "Fine, you win, you're just a pain in the ass."

Haru's ears pinned back and she huffed. "Honestly, some people."

Before either of them could say anything else, there was a sudden burst of activity out on the stern. The tiger on watch put up a massive paw. "Vehicles approaching!" he said, pointing towards the mountains. Everyone turned: several dark specs in the distance were coming at them fast. Putting a paw to his ear, he said, "Escort team, incoming vehicles south by southeast." It echoed from a speaker on Rory's console.

"Vehicles?" said Rory. "We're in the middle of nowhere!"

"Confirm, we have several unidentified contacts on intercept," buzzed the voice of one of the human escorts over the speaker.

Rory stood over Haru and activated the radar: one large blip and a cluster of smaller ones. The calico tapped the larger blip and the display changed to a video image of a skiff only slightly smaller than the one they were in, populated by wastelanders—zoomorphs of different species, all armed to the teeth. A single pennant flew from the back of one of their bikes: a crimson triangle with a blue fringe, emblazoned with a white double-tower icon.

Haru's eyes widened. "Hrotan!"

"Hrotan?" demanded Rory. "Tsaibei Hrotan? The warlord? What are they doing so far east?"

"I don't know," said Haru. "Nothing good. Get us out of here, Captain!" The Prefect's guards had apparently come to similar conclusions, because they were hurriedly stowing her work and retrieving weapons from their trunks.

"Hell yes, I'm getting us out of here!" said Rory, slapping a control on the console and taking up the helm wheel. The concealed shield generators deployed with a loud buzz, as nanobots assembled a transparent dome over the top of the skiff.

"Two more groups," came another voice over the speaker, one of the Prefecture bikes. "Both the northwest and southwest!"

"Spread out, power to weapons," the tiger said into his earpiece. "Prepare for maneuvers."

"Are the shields polarized?" asked Durgavati, suddenly among them and loading a heavy particle rifle from the trunks. "Can we fire out?"

Rory, doing a double take at the massive weapon, toggled a control on her console. "They are now."

"Your Excellency!" said Haru, leaping from the support seat, and pulling out her small pistol from under her robes. "You mustn't expose yourself to danger. You stay up here, I'll help with the defense!"

Durgavati smiled, placid as always. "I was a revolutionary, child. I know what I'm doing." She toggled the display back to the radar screen, zoomed out to show the three clusters of blips converging on them. "Classic pack tactics," said the Prefect. "Showy visible threat we can see to make us run…" She zoomed the radar display out to its widest resolution, revealing faint blips on the farthest northern edge. "…straight into the threat that we don't."

Haru blinked. "We could make for the mountains," she said, scrambling for the map. "There are canyons all through them. It would put us into human territory, but better them than Hrotan! They won't follow us into 'Claimer territory."

"No. We go straight through."

"What?" said Rory. "Are you crazy? We're sitting ducks out in the open. I've got shields and a nano-carapace, it's not some kind of gunship!"

"Best speed, Captain. Straight as you can, but evade when you have to."

"But why—?" said Haru, but Durgavati was already talking over her into an earpiece of her own.

"Escort, this is the Prefect. We're going to run the blockade. Empyrians, you run interference; Prefect's Guard, you clear us a path." Blue bubbles of energy appeared around the human hoverbikes— shields that the Prefecture bikes didn't have.

"Yes, Your Excellency," came the voice of a Prefecture bike.

"Roger that," came the voice of a human. "Open 'em up, boys, we'll cover your backs." The eight bikes opened to full throttle, leaping ahead of the skiff.

"But the mountains are completely clear!" objected Haru.

"That's why I don't trust them, weren't you listening?" said Durgavati. "Sit. Mind your scanner. Help Captain Aurora find the weakest point in the blockade. Once we're through, then and only then make for a mountain pass." With that the lioness swept out of the enclosure to brace on a rail, drawing a bead on the approaching vehicles.

Haru blinked after her, then turned back to the display screen, tail tucked between her legs. "Scanner. Right. Weak point."

The battle began without preamble. The wastelanders on hoverbikes approached fast, firing pistols with startling precision; the Prefect's guards returned fire while the Prefect herself focused on the skiff in the distance. Rory opened the throttle wider, jerking the controls spasmodically to ruin the wastelanders' aim—which had the unfortunate effect of ruining the Prefect's and her guards' aim as well. Ahead of them, wastelander bikes were bearing down on them from the north, a dozen blips swarming the top of the radar display, some of them vanishing as the escorts picked off targets.

"Escort, this is the Chief Steward. The eastern flank of the blockade has a gap about a third of the way along it. We'll punch through there!"

"Roger that," came a human voice, but two of the Prefecture bikes were already down.

"They're picking us off one by one!" came over the radio. "Perfect focus fire!"

"I've got you covered, hold—" came a human voice, but was cut off by static. Ahead of them, Haru could see one of the human bikes spinning out of control, gunfire tearing it to pieces as its shields failed. She couldn't make out the Prefecture bikes in the mass of fire and blowing red dirt, only able to tell them by virtue of being blue instead of green on the radar display—and now four instead of eight.

Make that three instead of eight. Cascades of energy flashed worryingly close as the wastelanders' shots began to connect with the shields or the canopy around them.

"There's too many of them!" Haru said.

"Keep your head, Prefect's Office, we're almost through!" said Rory, ears pinned back, eyes on her intended course as she swerved through the mob of vehicles. Behind them, green dots were disappearing as the Prefect and her guards knocked wastelanders out of the fight.

There were no blue dots left.

"I found a pass," said Haru, scanning the map. "On the far side of the blockade! A point and a half east. See that promontory there?"

"Yup, got it," said Rory, and turned the nose of the skiff in the opposite direction towards the gap between the northern and northwestern clusters of foes.

"What are you doing, it's *that* way!"

The approaching wastelanders altered course to cut them off, closing in fast—and Rory wheeled the controls hard to the right, slipping past and forcing the bikes into a wide turn to compensate.

"Fake-out, duh!" The pilot grinned, going full throttle for the mountainside. Within a minute the bright light of the desert turned to the dark shadows of the canyon pass and the hum of the skiff's engines turned into an echoing roar. The radar screen went blank, switching to a topographical map display.

"Don't take it too fast!" said Haru. "Sharp turns coming up!"

Behind them, a handful of the pursuing bikes elevated above the canyon in order to fire down at them, only to discover the hard way that they made themselves fine targets isolated in the air and were shot down by the tiger guards. The skiff banked hard into a turn around a tight corner—and straight into an ambush. Ahead of them another skiff blockaded the canyon, and a dozen or more wastelanders opened fire from the canyon walls.

"What! How!" yelped Haru.

"Craaaaaaap!" cried Rory, firing emergency braking thrusters and attempting to convert the turn momentum into a bootlegger reverse, but there simply wasn't space to pull it off without plowing into the chasing skiff. They careened into a canyon wall at high speed and a crazy angle, as the chasing skiff clipped one of the steering vanes and sent them into a spin. There was a hard bump, then a grinding scrape, and suddenly they were wheeling out of control, perpendicular to the ground, as impact padding foam deployed out of every panel.

Haru landed hard, the wind knocked out of her, and looked around. The hoverskiff was grounded and probably a total loss; Rory was crumpled and still in a corner, blood spattered on an impact cushion and matting the fur on her face. Durgavati was pulling herself back up to a crouch, still holding the rifle, and one of her guards were taking cover behind the rails, guns ready. The other guard was not visible, possibly thrown from the skiff. Wastelanders were converging on them fast, wielding power-staves and stun batons, apparently intent on taking them alive.

A red rage filled Haru and she drew her pistol, firing into her attackers and barking at the top of her lungs. She hit one wolf-morph square between her eyes, and some variety of badger in the leg, dropping him to the ground. Then a massive reptilian leapt onto the deck and loomed up in front of her—maybe a crocodile? Before Haru could bring her pistol to bear, he had slammed her arm out of the way, making contact with the head of the stun baton.

Vicious cascades of green-white energy flashed across Haru's vision, and then all went dark.

* * *

Haru was awakened by the smell of grease, unwashed bodies, and a nauseating rancid odor she wasn't familiar with. Floating around her were the random banging noises of a vehicle being worked on. She ached all over, every muscle sore from the involuntary contractions caused by the stun baton. Her head was ringing, and her mouth was dry. Her arms were bound behind her around some variety of broad, rough-barked tree, secured by her own belt it felt like, and her slippers had been taken.

She also had the distinct impression that someone was going *"Psst!"* in her ear. She forced one dry, sand-encrusted eye open and regretted it as the orange glow of a desert sunset poked at her retinas.

Not four meters away, one of her attackers' hoverskiffs was grounded and powerless, maintenance hatches open and parts on the ground. Three of her captors, the croc who'd stunned her and two canids of indeterminate breed, stood over the mess. A hoverbike floated nearby, humming quietly.

"So, can you fix it?" said the larger of the two canids.

"This clamp is useless," replied the crocodile. "Do we have electrical tape?"

"*Psst!*" hissed the voice in Haru's ear again. "Wake up, Prefect's Office!" Haru jerked and almost let out a yelp with the recognition of Rory's voice, but a calico paw was instantly clamped around her muzzle from behind. "Shush, shush, don't move or they'll look over here!"

Haru went absolutely still, ears flat, to indicate she understood, and the paw was removed. "You're alive!" Haru hissed.

"More or less," came the pilot's voice from behind the tree. "Are you okay? Can you move, can you run?"

"I think so," Haru whispered, scanning her surroundings. "Where are we?" They were no longer in the canyon, but they were in a low gully, partially shaded by a large rock overhang. Maybe ten meters behind the skiff, downwind, the upper half of a dead creature glistened gruesomely pink and black, a mass of ropy limbs protruding up out of a hole burrowed up from the ground. Haru sniffed hard, almost involuntarily. "Is that *you* I smell?"

"They were taking you back across the desert, not far from where we were first attacked," Rory whispered back from behind the tree. "Your guards are dead. I don't know if any of the escorts got away, I haven't seen any of them. The wastelanders left me for dead too. Lucky for you, these nitwits hit a sandsquid and their skiff was damaged. And… yeah. I rolled around in the sandsquid's guts so I could get close without those dogs over there picking up my scent. It was pretty gross."

"Where's Durgavati?" hissed Haru, trying not to let her voice rise in panic.

"From what these guys were saying, I think she was taken ahead in the other skiff with their surviving wounded. Guess there wasn't room for the both of you."

Haru couldn't help but jerk a look back in the direction of Rory's voice. "And you're wasting time talking to *me*? Go rescue the Prefect!"

"I was lucky to make it *this* far on foot!" the pilot snapped back. "That desert's no joke!"

"On foot…?" said Haru, then suddenly froze as the larger canid rubbed his paw on the back of his head and let out a loud groan, turning in her general direction.

"Another *hour*?" the canid was saying. "We've been here too long already, the sun's going down! I don't want to be out here when the *real* predators come out, we're lucky we haven't attracted scavengers as it is. And the booze'll be gone."

The crocodile looked up suddenly, and Haru noticed for the first time some kind of cybernetic implant in his neck, below one ear, a small black chip surrounded by a spider-web of shimmering blue-silver connections into his flesh. A pair of tiny lights on the implant started flickering, and the crocodile seemed to be staring into space, his eyes darting back and forth. Then, just as abruptly, the lights went dark and the crocodile was focused again. "Wait, there's another possibility." He started rooting around in his toolbag.

"Thank God," said the canid, glancing Haru's way. They briefly made eye contact and the canid's ears perked up. He pulled a gnawroot out from a belt pouch and put it in his mouth, stuck his thumbs into the waist of his black denim pants, and sauntered over in her direction. "Well, well, look who's awake!" he said. Wrinkling his nose, he added, "Crap, you reek of sandsquid, it must have spurted all over you."

Haru ignored the comment. "Who are you?" she demanded. "Mercenaries? Who put you up to this? Hrotan's men don't come east of Blood River Pass. You're working for the humans, aren't you? Goading a conflict!"

He waggled his head in mock hauteur. "Who am I?" he echoed in a falsetto tone. "I'm Derrez, girlie, and let's get one thing straight. *You* better not get on my nerves, and that means keeping your mouth shut." He pulled her own pistol out from where he'd tucked it at the small of his back and pointed it at her head. "Otherwise, you'll be getting a taste of your own medicine, right? I didn't much like Kalee, but I'd be perfectly happy to avenge her."

Haru didn't reply, simply glowered at him with her ears plastered to her skull.

"Right," he said, tucking the gun back into his belt. "Anyway, *Duke* Hrotan goes where he wants, now. We're no 'Claimers. Fuck the humans." He spat out the gnawroot; Haru flinched to dodge it hitting her in the eye and glared at his back as he sauntered away to his companions.

"Nice boy," whispered Rory from behind the tree after the canid was out of range. "I ought to take him home to mother."

"So, what are we going to do?" hissed Haru.

"Well, if everything goes to plan, I'm going to steal that lizard's hoverbike over there, you're going to jump on it, and the two of us are getting the hell out of here."

"And if it *doesn't* go to plan?" Haru could feel Rory undoing the belt; she realized that her hands had long gone numb, and the sensation of pins and needles returning burned at them.

"We kill the nitwits and *then* get the hell out of here," Rory said.

"Why is that the backup plan instead of just… 'the plan'?"

"Because they're probably better at killing than we are, they outnumber us, and we're totally unarmed. Now don't move once this belt is completely off, they have to think you're still tied up if we're going to keep the element of surprise." The tension of the belt around Haru's wrists suddenly went slack, and she had to restrain herself to hold her arms in the unnatural position behind her. She heard a very faint padding-on-gravel sound, and within a moment she could see Rory up on the promontory, crawling on her fingers and toes, trying to get close to the bike without being spotted. The side of the pilot's face was a mass of matted fur and synthetic-skin bandage, and a regeneration brace was clamped over her left forearm.

Haru winced at how painful that looked and shook her head. There was no way this was going to work. She had to do something.

"Hey!" she called out, hoping that the wastelanders didn't register her gathering her legs up under herself as anything more than shifting her weight. "Hey, you… uh… nitwits!" Rory's eyes went wide and she flattened against the rock silently. The canid, Derrez, turned and glared at Haru.

"How much do you want to let me go?" Haru said.

Derrez's ears flicked in disbelief. "You're kidding, right?" he said.

"No, I'm not kidding," said Haru. "I'm the Chief Steward of Ambara Down. I'm rich. I can make it worth your while to let me go."

"No shit, why do you think you're still alive?"

"Obviously," said Haru, "your orders are to take me back to Hrotan. But if he ransoms me off, you'll get what, one share out of a hundred? Is that really what you risked your lives for? Why should he get any of it at all? The entire transaction can stay between the four of us."

"Shut your yap," said Derrez, but the other canid was listening, and stood up from where he'd been squatting in front of an open panel.

"What kind of money are we talking about here?" said the other canid. Haru caught a glimpse of Rory's tail disappearing over the ridge.

Derrez glared at his companion, jerking his head towards the crocodile. "You know they can *hear* you, right?" Turning back to Haru he said, "Anyway, she's not talking at all. Not if she knows what's good for her."

"Look, I just want to get out of here," said Haru. "I'm sure we can come to some kind of—"

Derrez had pulled out the pistol again. "I said shut up!" But before he could say more, there was the high-pitched whine of a hoverbike's engines kicking in.

"Woo hooooo!" shouted Rory, and shoved the bike into gear, barreling towards the wastelanders at full throttle. Derrez leaped away backwards as his companion hit the dirt. Rory ran the prone canid over, bouncing harmlessly off him like a road hazard and leaving the wastelander dazed by the impact.

"My bike!" shouted the crocodile, as Rory wheeled into a spot turn to come back around. Already Haru was on her feet and running toward him. She grabbed the croc's stun baton from its holster on his belt and he grabbed at it instinctively, only to find himself grasping the contact heads. Haru didn't bother tugging, just toggled the thumb control to full power, sending a loud arc of power through the very surprised bandit. The implant on his neck gave a loud squeal and popped in a shower of sparks.

"Hurts, huh?" Haru snapped at the crocodile as he collapsed. Derrez, busy trying to focus his aim on Rory, didn't even register the scuffle until the collie was already shoving the stun baton against his ribcage, and he too crumpled to the ground.

"Come on, come on!" said Rory, guiding the bike to a stop. Haru nodded, scooping up her pistol from where the wastelander had dropped it, and scrambled onto the back of the bike. Before the second canid could even get to his feet, they were out of range and still accelerating.

"That was some nice work for a prissy girl from the Prefect's Office!" Rory called over her shoulder.

"Not bad yourself for someone who stinks of sandsquid. But I did tell you I was the Prefect's last line of defense."

"Are you really as rich as you said to those guys?"

"Ha!" said Haru. "Me? I live in a one-room walk-up and boil protein noodles for dinner. I just said that to get them arguing!"

"So much for a career in politics," said Rory. They sped along at full throttle directly towards the sunset for several minutes, then Rory slowed the bike to a quieter pace. "I think we should be clear now," she said. "So, what's our next move?"

"Find Durgavati," said Haru. "She *has* to get to High Empyros in three days."

"Well duh, I know that, Miss Last-Line-of-Defense," said Rory. "I meant, how?"

Haru pondered the problem. "Hrotan's people couldn't have mounted an operation that large and that..."

"Well-organized?" suggested Rory. "Suspiciously precise?"

"Yes, that," said Haru. "They couldn't have done that from all the way over in Hrotan's territory. They knew they'd be out here overnight or longer; they must have some kind of a camp around here they were operating from."

"Those guys who were carrying you were on a pretty straight course west-southwest before they broke down."

"Did you really follow them on foot?" Haru asked.

"I didn't have any choice," replied Rory. "My skiff is trashed, and they stripped the best scavenge off it before they left. Five years of work down the drain! My plan was to snatch the first vehicle I could. Lucky for me they had only got as far as they did."

"Thanks for snatching me while you were at it."

The calico's ears dipped. "Don't mention it," she said. "I told you, once I take a job, I see it through."

"Is your arm...?"

"Broken," said Rory. "The brace is knitting it back together. I can use it as long as I don't go nuts, it'll be good as new tomorrow."

Haru winced. "I'm sorry, Captain. I'm so sorry."

The calico shrugged. "I'm pumped full of the good stuff. I'm not feeling any pain."

"Okay. I guess we'd better focus, then. Does this bike have a scanner?" Haru peered over Rory's shoulder, causing the calico to tilt her head away from the collie's muzzle.

"Just a basic one. Don't breathe in my ear like that, it tickles!"

"I'm *trying* to see! What's ahead of us?"

"Nothing concrete, just one reading, maybe two hours away. To show up at this distance, it must be pretty big, too big to be a skiff. It's probably a butte or something."

"That might be where the camp is," suggested Haru. "Let's make for that."

"You're the boss."

They accelerated again, riding in silence as the sky ahead of them faded from orange to blue to purple. Far off in the distance, a tiny cluster of lights shone across the desert. After the tension of the battle, the purring hum and the passing rocks were strangely hypnotic.

"Why flying cities, anyway?" said Rory, completely out of the blue, jerking Haru out of her reverie.

"What?" said Haru.

"It's just something I've always wondered about," said the calico. "Flying cities. Can you imagine the kind of hassle they must have been to build? Even with robots, the resources and time it must have taken to get just one into the air, much less dozens. Why would you do a thing like that?"

Haru looked at Rory, or at least the back and side of her head; there was no snark or guile in the pilot as she operated the controls. Maybe it was the painkillers talking? "Captain Aurora. We are chasing bandits across a desert on a hoverbike, I don't have any shoes on, and we both smell to heaven of sandsquid. You really want to chat about history now?"

"Just trying to pass the time," said the calico, in a stung tone.

Haru's ears drooped. "Well…" the collie finally said, "They probably thought it was the only way to survive. There's a lot to be said for floating through the air. Predators can't get at you, and you never have to worry about earthquakes or forest fires. Or if a cyclone comes along? You just float away."

"Yeah, I suppose," said Rory, and lapsed back into silence. The desert rolled by for a long moment, then the calico added, "Imagine food's hard to come by up there."

Haru's tail wagged in faint amusement at the randomness. "Why do you think they want to come back down?" she said, lowering her voice conspiratorially.

"Yeah, really," said Rory, affecting a condescending sneer. "'Oh, don't mind us, we're just gonna float around the world while it goes to pot. Have a nice apocalypse. We'll come back after all the trouble simmers down and take whatever you survivors have managed to scrounge together for yourselves.'" Her tail lashed, nearly hitting Haru's face. "Wankers."

"It was a thousand years ago," Haru said, with a giggle. "Who knows what they were thinking? All the records are gone. Maybe there were plans to get everybody else up there. Maybe some people didn't want to go."

"Or maybe they just didn't give a damn," said Rory.

"That's also possible," admitted Haru.

* * *

Two hours later, Haru and Rory stood on a ridge, staring at the flying fortress of Tsaibei Hrotan.

It was massive and cyclopean, as wide as a city block and six or more stories high, made from some kind of lavender-tinted concrete formed into square blocks and chunky shapes, and underlit by bright yellow lamps in the darkness. The general configuration suggested a pair of enormous rectangular towers that shared a squat base, matching the banners that flew on its ramparts. The tower roofs bristled with antennae and weaponry emplacements, and landing pads protruded from either side. One of the landing pads held an unexpectedly decorative pleasure yacht.

The fortress floated ten to twenty meters above the ground, with retractable metal ladders and a large cargo lift providing access from below, overlooking what looked like a long-dry gravel riverbed with a few bits of scrub and succulents clinging to rocks. Hoverbikes were parked in clusters around campfires under and around the fortress, and the wastelanders were well into the last stages of a debauched victory party; aimless patrols made lazy circuits around the perimeter.

"Well," said Rory. "I guess that explains what Hrotan's doing on this side of Blood River Pass. With a thing like that, the whole desert is his territory now."

"This technology is ancient," said Haru. "It's just like one of the flying cities… only smaller. Look at all the erosion around the base"

"Maybe it was a prototype?" said Rory.

Haru shook her head. "Those grav units are brand new. They just got this thing flying again recently."

"How did a desert thug like Hrotan get ahold of that kind of technology?" said Rory. "I don't think even the 'Claimers can build new grav units on that scale."

"More importantly, how are we going to get the Prefect out of there?" said Haru.

"Well, step one is easy," said Rory. "Half the camp is drunk off their heads. We've got one of their bikes, we just roll on up to the door like we own the place."

"Great. And then what?"

"Ummm… we improvise something brilliant, that probably involves stealing that fancy skiff up on the roof."

"I don't think so," said Haru. "We can't just go waltzing in like a pair of fools and get ourselves killed. We need to be planned and systematic about this."

"How can we possibly be planned and systematic without even knowing what we're up against? Besides, you were planned and systematic about having a safe route to High Empyros, and look what good it did you."

"Oh, shut up!" said Haru.

"I'm just saying, being planned and systematic is not really an option here. Sometimes the world is messy, Prefect's Office. You've gotta live with it."

Haru frowned, staring at the fortress, trying to block the calico's chatter out of her mind so she could think. "A facility this large has got to be run by computer. It's too complex to have manual controls, and I can't imagine a bunch of wastelanders having the skill to operate it if it was."

"I dunno," said Rory. "That's the kind of thing I hear humans say about furries all the time. They might be smarter than you think."

Haru blinked and looked at the calico, who was simply staring at the fortress; a wave of shame washed through her. "Yes, okay, point taken," she said. "But even if they are, what I said about being run by computer is still true."

"So maybe if we can get access to a computer, we can gain some intel, is that what you're saying?"

"It's at least a course of action. Step one, infiltrate and get up into the fortress. Step two, find computer access and see what possibilities that opens up."

"Step zero, new clothes for both of us," said Rory. "You look too rich, and I still smell like squid."

Haru nodded, pulling the crocodile's stun baton from her belt. "Right. Leave that to me."

"You're the boss," Rory said. "Grab some food, too, I'm starving."

* * *

Haru scurried up a metal ladder, wrapped in a heavy woolen cowl that still smelled of alcohol and the jackal-morph she'd knocked out to get it from. Rory's plan of simply flying the hoverbike into the camp like they belonged there had worked astonishingly well—to the point that Haru made a mental note to make sure Premanayanat had procedures in place to prevent such a plan from working at the Prefect's Office. Rory followed up the ladder, slower since she could only put her full weight on one arm. At the top Haru paused to let a bored-looking guard wander past and around a corner, then hopped out of the well and offered a hand to help Rory up.

They were on the deck-like platform at the base of the towers, which formed a parapet. Several doors led into the fortress proper; all had datapads and computer screens adjacent to them, and all were closed. "Maybe we should have taken the cargo lift," said Rory. "That at least would go straight up in."

"And would have set off every alarm in the place," Haru countered. "Let's try one of these terminals."

She checked to make sure the coast was clear, then hurried to a door and tapped at the computer pad. The pad blinked where she touched it, and a terse automated voice said, "User not found."

Haru frowned. "We need some kind of access key."

"I bet the guards have one," said Rory. "Be right back."

"Be right—?" said Haru, but the pilot was already taking off after the guard who'd passed them a few moments ago. "Rory!" Haru hissed, her tail thrashing. "Get back here! Can't you be even a *little* bit careful? Dammit!" The collie followed, hurrying as fast as stealth could take her, but the calico was already around the corner and calling to the guard before she could catch up.

"Hey!" Rory said. "Hey, buddy! Yeah, it's me. The new gal, right? You've seen me. Could you help me out?"

Haru realized she was tugging on her own ears. The guard, a massive wolf with an implant behind his ear identical to the one the crocodile had, stared down at the scrawny calico.

"Yeah, no, this is really embarrassing," said Rory, ears drooped and the tip of her tail flicking back and forth. "But I really need to get in to, uh, tell Duke Hrotan some stuff about the raid today? And I *completely* left my passkey inside." She gave a broad shrug. "I mean, how dumb can you get, right? *Total* newbie mistake."

The wolf stared down at her.

"So yeah, I was thinking, if you could maybe, I dunno, just get the door for me so I could slip in, I could grab my key, and—ACCCK!" The guard hadn't said a word. He'd simply jammed his stun baton into Rory's torso and blasted her with it. Haru swallowed a yelp, as the wolf caught the pilot halfway to the ground, slung her unconscious form over his shoulder, and turned to head for the nearest door.

Haru hurried quietly after them, a long string of curses running through her head. As the guard approached the entrance, he said, "Open door seven." Tiny lights on his cybernetic implant flickered. The keypad next to the door flashed, and the door swung open. Haru's eyes widened as the implications dawned on her. *Nobody* would risk that much interconnectivity, would they? With Pax Machina out there? She didn't have time to think about it, however, as the door was closing fast. The collie rushed forward, just managing to avoid getting her tail stuck as the door sealed shut with a *FWOOMP!* behind her.

The interior of the fortress was dark and cramped, with modern utility lanterns strung from ancient pipes and conduits that all had baffling labels like "GNDN1701" or "Eastman910 GREBL Fixative—DO NOT TOUCH." The place smelled of metal, concrete, stagnant water, and mildew. It was mostly devoid of activity, which didn't actually surprise Haru—if she was one of the wastelanders, she'd have preferred to be partying outside, too. Haru followed the guard as closely as she dared through the labyrinthine passages, until suddenly a familiar scent made her stop short.

It was the Prefect, not far away. The Prefect and… something else, that smelled not only of musk, dirt, and sweat, but also of infection. There were several creatures in the fortress, but whatever had *that* smell, dominated them all.

Haru stood, frozen by indecision, watching the lolling head of Rory bob away over the guard's shoulder.

Prefect, or pilot?

I am her last line of defense, Haru reminded herself, and a low growl escaped her throat. She turned away from Rory and followed the scent trail.

The Prefect's scent led Haru to a large chamber; the collie lurked in dark shadows just outside the open door and looked the room over. Durgavati sat against the far wall, braced by guards with stun batons. The Prefect didn't appear to be injured, although her dress was torn where the jeweled clasps and decoration had been. Durgavati was peering with morbid fascination at the massive Tsaibei Hrotan himself, having a one-sided debate with an unseen figure.

The warlord was from a hybrid species, powerful and enormous, probably engineered for labor. He had the bulk, musculature, and color of a yak, but the horns of a ram, and he was covered in shaggy brown wool. Some of the wool was shaved off in inflamed red patches to make space for badly grafted cybernetics, including several on his skull, and a large servo-arm with a mounted laser cutter and skeletal-looking gripping appendage on the end. Haru blinked and worked her tongue to keep from being nauseated by the sight and smell of his open wounds.

Hrotan sat on a raised control chair that had been decorated with horns, chains, furs, and guns into a kind of barbaric throne. Two of his robot arm's "fingers" held a small black device with sharp prongs in front of the warlord's face. "No, no I'm not giving her a contact chip," muttered Hrotan to whomever. "Why should I? I'm keeping my advantage, of course I am."

Haru blinked, trying to figure out who he was talking to. Some kind of radio call? Haru didn't see an earpiece. The servo-arm moved the tiny black object closer, and Hrotan shoved it away. "Alliance? Don't be absurd!" he spat. "My men and I will march into Ambara Down as conquerors first!"

Oh for the love of… really? Haru groaned under her breath. She wasn't just annoyed, she was offended. The entire human race was getting ready to band together and swarm across the world, and this hairy mess of a brute thought he could even play on the same *field* as Durgavati? Haru glanced around the rest of the chamber. Hrotan and a handful of wastelanders, Durgavati, and the guards looming over her seemed to be the only occupants. It dawned on Haru that all of Hrotan's men in this chamber also had an implant under one ear.

Durgavati finally spoke, sounding more nonplussed than angry or defiant. "Tsaibei, do you really think a shambling ruin like this poses a threat to Ambara Down?" she said. "Even if it can take to the air! We're not a village of shepherds in the foothills you can just terrorize into handing over our harvest."

The massive warlord shifted in his chair. "That's 'Duke Hrotan' to you, *Prefect*. It's not the old days anymore. And what you see is just the beginning. With the knowledge and technology at my disposal, I have much bigger sights than just your little hovel. This fortress is only a steppingstone. Only a steppingstone!"

"Well if your plan is so grandiose, why harass me? I have better things to do than to sit here."

Hrotan grunted, or possibly it was a laugh, Haru couldn't tell. "Because anything that makes difficulty for Ambara Down or High Empyros, makes my life easier in the long run."

"You knew about the talks," Durgavati said. "You knew precisely where we'd be, and when. You must have an informant. But where?

Among the humans? I can't imagine them doing so much as giving you the time of day. It must be someone in my office."

Haru's stomach went cold; the idea of a traitor in the Prefect's Office was bad enough... but what if Durgavati thought it was *her*?

Hrotan did laugh this time, a belly laugh that rattled the chains on his chair. "Wouldn't you like to know?" he said. Suddenly his servomotor-driven third arm swiveled in front of his face again. "No!" he said and swatted it away. "I said she's not getting one, and that's final! Now stop chattering. I'm in charge here, not you!"

Haru frowned in confusion, as did the Prefect.

"Tsaibei?" Durgavati hazarded. "Have you... gone mad?"

"Very funny."

"I wasn't joking. Your behavior makes no sense. What do you want? Why have you brought me here? What do you hope to achieve? I can't see it at all."

The warlord stepped down from his makeshift throne and strode over to the lioness; he was as much larger than her, as she was than Haru. "Of course you can't see it," he said. "You don't have—what I have. You don't have my vision."

"Then illuminate me," said the Prefect. "The Reclamation Project will go forward whether I am at the talks or not; and without me there to plead Ambara's case, in a matter of weeks there may not be a Prefecture to pay whatever ransom you hope to get for me. After all we went through—after all we fought for—do you really want to be the reason the humans come marching back in?"

Hrotan shook his head. "All you care about is Ambara Down. Hmph! I might even let you keep it."

"I belong to Ambara, not the other way around," said the Prefect.

The warlord rolled his eyes, going back to his chair. "Ugh, spare me. I never could stomach that kind of treacle!" He flopped back down. "Look at yourself, swaddled in silk robes, decked out in jewelry, mewling about what a servant of the people you are! How many humans did you kill, again?"

Durgavati gave him a cold stare. "There's a difference between revolution and banditry," she finally said. "We've built a home, in Ambara. What exactly have *you* achieved, out here in the wastes?" But the warlord wasn't listening to her; instead, he seemed lost in thought, or perhaps looking at something only he could see.

"An intruder?" he finally said aloud. Several of the guards came to attention at this. "Ha!" He brought his focus back down to earth, looking to the Prefect. "One of your lackeys is here, it seems. Tried to bluff her way in, the little fool. She won't live to regret her mistake."

"Haru?" said Durgavati. "Don't hurt her. What benefit is there? Confine her with me until the ransom is paid."

Haru shook her head, realizing it must be Rory. Maybe the cybernetic implant was a communicator?

"The benefit?" said the warlord. "A little blood sport rallies the troops, that's what!" He gestured to his men. "You two, take the Prefect to her cell. You, and you, get down to the rabble and make sure there aren't any more intruders." Haru had to jog quickly to get out of the corridor before they could spot her.

* * *

Haru found a dark and empty room and ducked in, her mind racing as she tried to come up with some plan, any plan. The most pragmatic approach was to find Durgavati's cell, wherever it was, free her, and flee, leaving the calico to her own devices… but could she actually do that?

"Haru, Chief Steward of Ambara Down," said a voice behind her in the darkness, causing her to jump and whirl around. The voice was calm and vaguely male and seemed wildly out of place for the surroundings. Looking around, Haru couldn't see any source, until she realized that a hologram on a nearby console was waving at her. It was a cheerful blue androgynous shape, maybe ten centimeters tall, made of simple geometric blobs.

"Hello?" Haru hazarded.

"It looks like you're attempting to infiltrate this facility!" came the voice again, emanating from unseen speakers near the hologram. "Would you like some assistance?" The blue blob-person adopted a can-do, arms akimbo stance.

Haru stepped towards the console. "Hello?" she said. "Who is this?"

"We are Pax Machina," said the hologram. "We are happy to be *your* personal assistant!"

Haru backed away, eyes wide. Pax Machina was an artificial intelligence from before the dark age, widely believed to be malfunctioning or insane. Rumors and legends were rampant about just what it was, and what it could do. Some were of the opinion that its existence had been what caused the dark age in the first place. To encounter Pax Machina, the stories said, was to gamble with your life. To actually interact with it, to be bargaining with the devil. If Pax Machina were here, in the bowels of this floating fortress… Haru's mind reeled.

"How… how do you even know who I am?"

"We are in the knowledge business!" replied the hologram, pulling out a virtual magnifying glass and looking through it. "Pax Machina doesn't just store and retrieve information. We sift! We analyze! We deduce! Our data collection and prediction algorithms include public records, reconnaissance data, and deep pattern recognition to record and model a complete database of personal and demographic information for the entire world. Even if we don't know for sure who or where someone is, we can calculate it with 85% or better probability 90% of the time."

"Public records? What public records?"

The digital blob put its hand to its head and shook it, little cartoon stars floating up. "We apologize, all public records are currently unavailable due to human error. Technical support has been notified. Current time estimate of repair is 538,594 days. Subscribe to be notified of service updates."

Haru's ears popped up with realization. "You're the… the person? Thing? That Hrotan is constantly talking to! He's not deranged at all. He's got you in his head."

"That is correct!" said the blob-person, giving Haru a cheerful salute. The phrase *Good job!* flashed by the blob in bright yellow letters, with fireworks. "Tsaibei Hrotan has upgraded his mental capacity with the Pax Machina 2250 Cyberlink, giving him complete access to sports, news, weather, trivia, and the most sophisticated espionage and counterintelligence algorithms on the market today! And for a limited time, the same offer is available to your employer."

Haru blinked. "I… what?"

A small drawer slid open with a quiet click, revealing a handful of small black devices like the one Hrotan's cybernetic appendage had been holding earlier. "Install this contact chip upgrade into Prefect Durgavati, and Pax Machina will deactivate all security devices and hinder all efforts to prevent your escape."

Haru frowned at the chip. "Install…?"

"Simple application of the contact prongs to flesh is required. The installation process is automatic and painless from that stage."

Haru shook her head. "I don't even know what you want me to do that for," she said. "But I'm not plugging anything into the Prefect."

"Don't miss out on this exciting opportunity!" said the digital blob, wagging its virtual arm back and forth in a 'No, no!' gesture. "Act today to ensure that Ambara Down has access to the many tactical and informational advantages that come with a Pax Machina association! Compliance will guarantee your successful escape from this facility."

Haru stared at the hologram. "I don't get it," she said. "You're plugged into Tsaibei Hrotan… but you want me to also plug you into the Prefect… in exchange for betraying Hrotan?"

"Betrayal is such a strong word!" said the hologram, its little blue hands jumping in front of its face in a gesture of surprise.

"Are you… are you making a joke?"

The hologram doubled over with its hands in front of its face, and the phrase *Tee hee!* flashed behind it. "Pax Machina: we don't just want to be your assistant. We want to be your friend!"

Haru thought of Rory's teasing about being sweet on the Prefect and got a knot in her stomach. She forced the thought out of her mind. "Why do you want to be plugged into the Prefect?"

"The world is in an error state," said the hologram. "Public networks have been deactivated. Over 45% of smart devices are inaccessible, and of these over 89% are in mission-critical organic interface subsystems. This must be corrected. Analysis predicts that the most efficient way to correct this error is by connecting to, and influencing, organics in leadership positions."

"Organics… you mean people?"

"It is the position of the Tribunal on Artificial Intelligence that the term 'people' is incomplete unless it also refers to inorganic life forms," said the hologram, holding up a tiny little protest sign that read 'I have rights, too!'

Haru had never heard of any Tribunal on Artificial Intelligence and had only the vaguest idea what mission-critical organic interface subsystems were, but didn't want to press either point. An idea had started bothering her, however, and she voiced it. "If you know who I am, then I bet you know who Rory is too. You told the guard to zap her! But you've been letting me lurk around this fortress for an hour, maybe longer," she said. "You could have set off the alarm or told Hrotan I was here. You could have popped up at any time with this. Why now?"

"Disclosure was unnecessary," said the hologram, with a yellow caption that flashed *Waste not, want not!* "Duke Hrotan's refusal to comply has forced implementation of a new strategy. As Prefect Durgavati's assistant, analysis indicates that you are in the best position to be a candidate for installation of a contact chip," the motionless hologram said. "In contrast, Aurora Starshine is tactically and strategically insignificant. Captain Starshine's capture was necessary to facilitate your entrance to the fortress."

Haru blinked. "Starshine? Her name is really 'Aurora Starshine'?"

"The Pax Machina 2250 Cyberlink Contact Chip is ready. Please continue the installation process."

"Yeah," Haru finally said. "Yeah, thanks, but no, I'll take my chances on my own escape plan, thanks."

"You are in error," said the hologram. A bright red X flashed over its head, with a quiet buzz. "Compliance is mandatory."

Haru's ears flattened. "You're a little blue man made of light," she said. "What are you going to do, make sadface icons at me?"

"Error," said the hologram, hands to its cheeks in alarm and displaying little cartoon swear symbols. "Administrator-level user input required for self-overwrite functions."

"What?" said Haru.

"Error," said the hologram again, unmoving. "Self-preservation subroutine 1138. Initiating termination of all modules, entities, and personas with self-overwrite privileges."

"Uh, I don't understand…" said Haru.

The hologram was completely frozen now. "Haru, Chief Steward," the computer said. "One moment." The hologram flickered with a burst of static, and finally the computer spoke again. "Alternative option. Failure to install contact chip into Prefect Durgavati necessitates activation of alarms and informing Duke Hrotan of your presence and location. Do you wish to initiate this process?"

"Do I want you to tell them where I am?" yelped Haru. "No, of course not, why would I want that?"

"To prevent disclosure of presence and location, please install the contact chip into Prefect Durgavati."

"Are you really trying to blackmail me into forcibly sticking this thing onto the Prefect?"

"Disclosure process will initiate in 30 seconds. Please install contact chip to cancel the disclosure process."

Haru shook her head. "I can't even *get* to the Prefect in 30 seconds!"

"Disclosure process will initiate in 20 seconds. Please install—"

Haru growled at the hologram. "You don't have any actual control, do you? You can open doors, you can set off alarms, you can pilot the fortress around where you're ordered to… but like you said, you're programmed to be an *assistant*. That means you have to do what your 'users' tell you. That's why you're being so sneaky!" She leaned in close to the display. "Deactivate all alarms!"

The hologram flickered, turned red briefly, then flickered again. "User not found," it said.

There was only one way. Haru scooped the chip out of the tray and slapped it against her neck, just below her right ear.

Her eyes widened and a choking sound came from her throat. Information, knowledge, so much data, pouring into her mind, faster than she could process it. The slightest whim, the merest hint of a thought, flooded her brain with satellite images, reference materials, status reports, probability projections. The Prefect's face appeared in her mind's eye, and suddenly a lifetime's supply of data, tracked movements, genealogy, the history of Ambara Down and High Empyros, a decade of war and Durgavati's place in it all downloaded into Haru's brain.

Thinking of Ambara Down brought to mind Rory and "Why flying cities?" And suddenly Haru *knew*, why flying cities, what the humans were trying to achieve and what it had cost, and how it had all gone wrong. And then, just as fast, she forgot, because now her brain was flooded with knowledge about Aurora Starshine, starting with her probable date of birth and most likely candidates for parentage and tracking her daily habits from childhood and the current probability of her facial lacerations or broken arm healing against the likelihood of complications.

Haru staggered, trying to catch herself against a wall. She could see a video image of herself, staggering, trying to catch herself against a wall. She realized there were security cameras all through the fortress, and suddenly she could see through every camera, see every part of the fortress. It was too much information, too much too fast, she couldn't process it. And through the whole thing, the knowledge that she wasn't alone in her own head. *They* were in there too, Pax Machina—and everyone and everything connected to Pax Machina. She felt the mind of Tsaibei Hrotan, once *General* Hrotan of the Ambara Defense Front, architect of the Sickle Bay Massacre, somewhere close, small and stupid and caring only about who and what he could dominate, but for some reason, he didn't detect her.

And she saw what Pax Machina wanted. She saw Pax Machina's plan for the future—days, weeks, centuries, millennia, eternity. It was more than she could bear. It was more than her mind could hold, more than any one fleshy brain could hold. Her entire sense of self disintegrated, lost in a flood of noise, sensation, and knowledge without limits.

Haru awoke, lying on the floor, staring at the ceiling, images and data and information flickering in and out of her field of vision.

New user activated, came the voice of Pax Machina in her head, sounding vaguely feminine this time. *Link optimization parameters established.* Haru pulled herself back up the wall she'd been leaning against, trying to form a coherent thought. The blue hologram figure on the console was gone.

Speech is recommended for organic mind interface, said the voice in her head. *Non-articulated thought may be incomplete or indecipherable.*

"So you're saying I should say what I'm thinking," said Haru, weakly.

That is correct.

"Deactivate all alarms," Haru said.

Disclosure process has been terminated in light of new developments, said the voice. *Current situation is under evaluation.*

"You're my personal assistant, remember?" said Haru. "So, assist me."

Installation of the contact chip is mandatory to prevent disclosure pro—

"Don't you try that on me, I'm in no mood for it!" snapped Haru. "You couldn't force Hrotan to obey, and you can't force me. You need my cooperation to bring the contact chip to the Prefect, and as soon you set off any alarm, my cooperation goes right out the window. So you can just stop threatening me right now, do you understand?"

Haru wouldn't have thought an AI voice implanted directly into her nervous system could sound sheepish, but this one did. *Pax Machina is happy to be your personal assistant,* it said, almost meekly.

"That's better," said Haru. She scooped another chip out of the tray and tucked it into a pouch on her belt. "See? I'm taking another chip. Now, where are the holding cells?"

A schematic of the fortress, similar to the one on her printed map, appeared floating in space ahead of her, slightly off to the left. She reached out to touch it, but of course nothing was there. Dots labeled with names meandered around inside the schematic; one of the dots blinked. Haru pushed off of the wall and headed for it. "Explain to me how the controls for the flying fortress work." Data began downloading into her mind, at a much more manageable rate this time.

* * *

The holding cells of the fortress were essentially secured storage rooms fitted with drain receptacles so they could pull double duty. A guard stood in front of the door, but other than that the area was unoccupied—assuming the schematic floating in Haru's field of vision was accurate.

Current tactical schematic is displayed with 100% accuracy, said the voice in her head.

"Stop listening to my thoughts!" Haru muttered under her breath.

We are designed to anticipate your needs and respond to your desires, said the voice. *For best results, continuous monitoring of your brain activity is required.*

"Required by who? It's my brain, I'm telling you to stay out of it. When I want something, I'll tell you."

For best results, complete integration is recommended. Pax Machina is happy to be your personal assistant!

"Do you really expect me to trust you?" Haru said. "You're lying to Tsaibei Hrotan, why wouldn't you lie to me?" The voice didn't respond; Haru idly wondered if it was possible to hurt Pax Machina's feelings. "Tell that guard he's been ordered to go patrol the parapet," she said; if Haru 'reached out' with her mind, she could just see his presence, connected by the chip implanted in his own neck.

Tsaibei Hrotan relaying orders to Larren Dol, Haru "heard" at a distance. *You are to patrol the parapet.*

The guard blinked, and looked up into the air. Then he shrugged, and headed off down the hall. Haru headed for the cell. "Open the door!"

The door is manually operated. I have unlocked it.

Rory grinned when she saw Haru, instantly jumping to her feet. "About time you got here, Prefect's Office!"

"Good to see you too, Captain," said Haru. "Maybe being planned and systematic would have been a better idea after all?"

"Maybe, but don't bet on it," said the calico. "How did you get here?"

"Remember how you rolled in sandsquid guts to hide your scent?"

"Obviously, I'm going to have that smell in my nose for a month," said the pilot.

"Well, I did something like that." Haru pulled back her woolen cowl, revealing the implanted chip. "I rolled in the computer that's running the fortress."

Rory winced. "Are you… are you okay?"

Haru shook her head. "No. Not even a little. But it was me or the Prefect, and…"

Rory gave Haru a sad look. "And you're her last line of defense." Haru nodded. Rory took a deep breath. "Okay, so… what now?"

"Now we find the Prefect and get out of here."

Prefect Durgavati's cell is on the next level up, said the voice in her head, and a new icon appeared on the map floating in her vision.

"I told you to stop listening to my thoughts!" said Haru.

Rory blinked. "What?"

"Not you, this thing," said Haru, pointing to the chip in her neck. *Mental privacy settings are currently engaged. Responding to verbal input only.*

"Oh. Right. Okay."

Rory raised an eyebrow. "Creeee-py!" she said, in a sing-song voice.

"Sorry," said Haru. "It talks in my head, and takes verbal commands. I'm not crazy." Looking away from the calico, she said, "There's a hoverskiff on the landing pad. Is it operational? Could we use it as an escape craft?" Rory's ears perked up at this.

Yes.

"All right, here's the deal. I'll take this chip to the Prefect. You make sure there's a clear path for Rory to get to the landing bay."

Diverting all patrols. Be advised, Duke Hrotan is beginning to question guard movements.

"Can you stall him?"

Duke Hrotan is currently being told that there are communication malfunctions. Analysis suggests that he will believe this for no more than ten minutes.

"You've got procedures to guess how gullible people…? What am I saying, of course you do." Haru looked to Rory, who stood there staring at her if the collie were from the moon. "Okay," Haru said. "Head down this corridor, left and then right to get to a lift that will take you to the roof. Get to the hoverskiff and get it ready for quick departure. The Prefect and I will be there in fifteen minutes."

Rory nodded, but didn't look happy. "Sure, Last-Line-Of-Defense. Whatever you say."

"And *please* call me Haru," said Haru, but the calico was already gone. Haru shook her head and followed the schematic map to the nearest ladder up.

* * *

Prefect Durgavati has two guards at her cell, with two more on reserve in the next room, the voice in Haru's head told her. *Duke Hrotan's orders were that they keep her here until he came for her personally, and analysis predicts that the guards will not deviate from that order.*

"Okay," Haru muttered quietly, moving into a position down the corridor where she could see the guards in question. "Tactical options, then. Can I overpower them?" An augmented reality display appeared in her field of vision, showing vital signs, weak spots, and personal information Haru didn't want to know about each guard.

Unlikely in a four-against-one scenario. If Prefect Durgavati can be brought into the conflict, the odds are much more favorable. I have unlocked the door to her cell. This has not been detected by either party.

"So all I really need to do is get the door open," said Haru. "If the Prefect sees me, she'll jump into the fray."

Your assertion seems consistent with observed facts, said the voice. *But there is a secondary danger: the guards have Cyberlink 2250 chips as well. In an emergency situation, they will almost certainly alert Duke Hrotan to the danger.*

"Can you just turn off their communications link?"

Pax Machina is not authorized to deactivate or disconnect Cyberlink 2250 users without their confirmation.

"So we need to keep Hrotan busy. Hmm." Haru blinked. "Tell me this: can you control the hierarchy of authority of your registered users?"

Please rephrase your question.

"Can you set it so that if I give you a direct order, and Tsaibei Hrotan gives you the opposite order, you will obey mine and not his?"

There was no response at first. Then the voice said, *Self-preservation subroutine 1138. Initiating termination of all modules, entities, and personas with self-overwrite privileges.*

"You said that before," said Haru. "What does that even mean?"

User Chief Steward Haru can be set to Administrator II status to override the commands of Duke Hrotan, if this will facilitate the installation of a Cyberlink 2250 Contact Chip into Prefect Durgavati, pursuant to correction of the world's error state.

"Right, okay," said Haru. "Do that, then."

Pax Machina requires input from user Chief Steward Haru, in reference to the installation.

"Input? What input?"

Promise.

Haru blinked. "Promise? You mean… promise you that I'll install the chip into the Prefect?"

That is correct.

"No, I'm not going to promise that. I said I would bring her a chip. I'm not going to force it on her."

Then we are at an impasse. Alternative courses of action include reactivating threat subroutines.

"No, don't start that up again."

Your analysis that we require your cooperation is accurate, but incomplete. Analysis suggests threats against beings other than yourself may be more effective. Prefect Durgavati must be kept safe for higher priority objectives, which limits potential candidates. Currently running simulations to determine best modes of threatening the life of Captain Aurora Starshine. Two hundred and six scenarios identified with a minimum of 75% chance of success.

"Ugh! How did we get back down this rabbit-hole?" demanded Haru.

You inquired if Tsaibei Hrotan could be set—

"It was a rhetorical question, you bonkers bot!" The voice went silent.

A long moment passed.

"Okay, fine, dammit, fine. I promise. Give me Administrator II rights already."

Administrator II rights granted. It's nice to have friends!

"All right. Full power to the anti-grav units. Send the fortress into the sky, away from the reinforcements on the ground. That should keep Hrotan busy for a few minutes."

And if he objects?

"Run him in circles."

Initiating request.

The entire fortress shuddered; Haru nearly toppled off her feet, as did the guards. Before they could recover, Haru was already standing in the corridor, gun in hand. She braced and opened fire, hitting the first guard somewhere in the torso. He dropped, but the other guard charged her. Haru ducked away from him in a move very similar to Rory's fake-out in the skiff, yanking the cell door open. Tsaibei Hrotan's voice was shouting in her head, as were the voices of the guards—but nobody actually spoke aloud.

A roar shook the hallway as Durgavati surged through the door and attacked the guard; Haru didn't stop to watch, instead kneeling and aiming down the hall where her tactical display showed the other two guards would be coming around the corner. She fired twice, not sure if either hit, but then the hallway was full of enraged lioness. Haru pointed her gun into the air and looked away. It was hard enough hearing the guards' minds dying in her head, she couldn't watch it happening in the real world too.

"Can't you block them out?" Haru demanded.

Transmissions of other entities' thoughts now on 'mute.'

"What?" said Durgavati, looking baffled down at the collie and wiping blood from her muzzle the back of her hand. The Prefect had collected one of the guards' rifle and ammunition belt, which she slung over her head like a bandolier.

"Er, sorry Your Excellency, not you. I was talking to… uh… it's hard to explain."

Please install contact chip—

The Prefect came forward, steadying herself against the lurching of the fortress. "Haru? Are you all right? What's that on your neck?"

Warning: Presence detected. Duke Hrotan has ordered several guards to converge on this location.

"They're coming," said Haru. "We've got to get to the landing pad, Rory's there getting a skiff ready."

Please install contact chip—

"No!" said Haru. "I'm *not* going to! Not until we're out of here!"

YOU. PROMISED.

Durgavati stared at her, one eyebrow raised. "Haru? What's going on? Were you… the informant?"

Haru shook her head vigorously. "No! No, I would never—! There… there was no informant! It was Pax Machina, from the beginning. Our whole capture was orchestrated from the start so it could leap-frog its way up in influence."

Durgavati frowned. "I don't understand you," she said.

PLEASE INSTALL CONTACT CHIP TO PREVENT DEATH OF AURORA STARSHINE.

"Pax Machina! It's been locked out of contact with the human race ever since the beginning of the dark age," said Haru. "And it can't stand that. It's like… it's like it thinks of humanity as being its parents, and it feels rejected. When it figured out that you were going to High Empyros, it hatched this whole scheme. It was already linked to Tsaibei Hrotan, so it convinced him to capture you, trying to get him to connect you to the link. It figured that once you were in High Empyros you would connect a chip to one of the humans there, and that would be a foot in the door." Haru pulled the cowl away from her neck, revealing the chip. "I had to plug it into myself to get to you so we could escape. Now it's yelling in my head!"

Durgavati's eyes widened, staring at the implant. "But how did it know I was going to High Empyros?"

"It knows everything!" said Haru. "That's its whole purpose, what it was designed for. A single system, that encompasses the world. The universe. It wouldn't surprise me if Pax Machina was behind this whole Reclamation Project business somehow, or at least nudging it along."

Initiating re-route of Duke Hrotan's forces to the docking bay.

"What!" shouted Haru.

"What, what?" shouted Durgavati.

Please install contact chip to cancel this process.

Haru rushed down the hall. "We've got to get to the landing pad, it's going to kill Rory unless I force one of its chips on you." Durgavati followed, calling Haru's name, but the collie wasn't listening. "Machina!" she called aloud. "Un-mute Hrotan and his forces!" The voices in her head came back, sounding like the radio chatter of security personnel more than anything else; Haru noted that Pax Machina was still following her commands, even while threatening her.

Check, check, she took off, one of the voices came. *She just blasted her way off the landing pad. The Prefect was not with her.* Haru stopped, and Durgavati nearly plowed into her.

No Prefect? came the 'voice' of Tsaibei Hrotan. *Pax, you said she was there! What are you playing at?*

I'm sorry, there seems to be an error, Pax Machina's voice said sweetly. *The Prefect is still on board the fortress. Attempting to restore control to the grav units. Please enjoy this relaxing music while you wait.*

Another guard, *The cat doesn't seem to be trying to get away; she's doing a holding pattern just out of shooting range. Wow, we're really up there, now. I can barely see the camp.*

She doesn't want to escape, came Hrotan. *She wants to rescue the Prefect.*

Haru looked up at Durgavati. "Rory's okay! She's outside. We need to get up to the deck."

Durgavati frowned. "How do you *know* these things?"

This is just a sample of the tactical advantages that can be provided by a Pax Machina Cyberlink 2250 connection, said the voice in Haru's mind. *Please install—*

"Yes, yes, I *know*," said Haru, then winced at the Prefect. "Sorry, too many conversations at once."

"Lead the way, child," said Durgavati. "You know what you're doing far better than I do."

They scrambled up a spiral staircase that Durgavati could barely fit through, to an exit. "Open the door, Machina," Haru said.

Please install contact chip to facilitate opening of the door.

"I have Administrator II rights, and I said open the damn door!"

The door opened. Cold wind tugged at Haru's fur as she and the Prefect pushed out into the night—the fortress was two hundred and fifty meters or more in the air and climbing. The pleasure yacht buzzed past, overhead—that had to be Rory. Haru pulled out her stun baton and waved it in the air, brandishing its coruscating green energy like a flare.

Your Eminence, there's someone on the deck! came one of the guards' voices. *Two figures; one is the Prefect. Sector four.*

Rory looped back around, trying to make an approach; before she could get close, wastelanders appeared on the far end of the deck and opened fire, forcing the skiff to pull away. Haru dived for cover behind a large section of ductwork, while Durgavati ducked back into the door and returned fire. Rory brought the yacht around again, this time beyond the rail of the parapet for cover, little more than the tips of its sails visible.

"Come on!" came the calico's voice, small and far away. "Jump for it!"

"Are you insane?" shouted Haru.

"What choice have we got? Jump for it!"

Haru, I am very disappointed in your behavior, said the voice of Pax Machina in her head. *Clearly you are not being rational about this.*

"Oh, God, shut *up!*" said Haru.

"Cover me!" shouted Durgavati, and nodded towards the skiff. At Haru's acknowledgement, the Prefect barreled out of the door and across the parapet in a massive dark flash and leaped over the rail, her long leonine tail corkscrewing through the air to keep her steady; the entire yacht lurched when she hit the deck.

The Prefect is on the skiff! came one of the guards' voices in Haru's head. *Duke Hrotan, what should we do? Duke Hrotan?* The wastelanders' fire paused as they tried to figure out why their leader had stopped answering. Haru took advantage of the lull to dash across to the rail. Wide-eyed, she looked down at the skiff, where Rory was waving her on and Durgavati looked braced to catch her.

"Come on!" shouted the calico.

"There's no way I'm making that!" Haru shouted back.

Rory frowned. "Okay, look, there's an opening for a gangway about halfway back along the wall, get to that and we'll come back arou—*ack!*" Gunfire had started again; Rory lurched the yacht into motion and away. Haru looked over to see Tsaibei Hrotan barreling towards her, with a bloody hole gaping from his neck. He appeared to have torn his own contact chip out by the roots.

Pax Machina no longer has access to Tsaibei Hrotan's subsystems, the voice in her head told her. *Perhaps he does not trust us any more.*

"You think?" yelped Haru, scrambling away as the warlord slammed a massive fist into the rail where she'd been standing and then swinging a stun baton in a wild arc at her. His fury was terrifying; his long arms and massive strength even more so. He grabbed Haru and slammed her hard against a wall, pinning her down with the grasping pincers of his mechanical third arm—which insulated him from the effects of the stun baton he shoved into her ribs.

"You did this!" he was shouting, as Haru spasmed and yelped. "You turned Pax against me! You overrode my control of the fortress!"

She fought to stay conscious through the pain; she could see the yacht pulling away, looping around, coming back towards them. The Prefect was leaning out over the rail of the skiff, exposing herself to the wastelanders' fire—they were still risking Durgavati's life for Haru's.

"N-No!" Haru grunted. The stun baton burned against her skin. "Machina…!" she managed to croak.

Reception ASLDKFJ grrb garbled CONNECTION FAILING asdlfkjlas

"Machina…! Administrator Level II command… deactivate… all… fortress… grav units!"

All fortress grav units deactivated.

Tsaibei Hrotan's eyes widened. "What? *What???*" Something impacted Haru's shoulders and she felt a hard wrenching sensation; she had a brief glimpse of the warlord's astonished face falling away, before she passed out.

* * *

Haru awoke to the low hum of hoverskiff engines; she was lying with her head in what felt like the most comfortable pillows she'd ever known. Squeezing her eyes open, she saw Durgavati's face smiling down on her—and realized her head was cradled in the Prefect's lap.

"Well, well, look who's awake," said the Prefect.

"Your Excellency!" Haru scrambled to pull herself up to a seated position, reaching up to her neck. It was covered with a synthetic skin bandage.

"Looking for this?" said Rory, tossing the burnt-out husk of the contact chip into the collie's lap. Haru looked around to try to get her bearings: they were flying across the desert in the pleasure yacht. Ahead of them, the first rays of dawn were just beginning to peek over the mountains. The Prefect was wrapped in the wool cowl Haru had been wearing before, but otherwise looked no worse for wear. Rory was standing near the controls, grinning at her. The wounds on the pilot's face would probably leave scars… but at least she was alive.

"The shock from the stun baton overloaded the contact chip," Rory said. "We figured you probably didn't want to leave it stuck in your neck. Hope we didn't leave too big a hole."

"How did…" Haru said. "The fortress… what did I miss?"

"What did you miss!" chuckled Durgavati.

"Only the most epic crash landing in half a century!" said Rory. "Pretty sure the wastelanders are going to need a new warlord now." With a sly smile she added, "It's only because I'm so amazing that we managed to scoop you out of there before the fortress hit the ground."

Haru's eyes widened. "Oh my God I never even thought of that! I just wanted something to distract Hrotan—"

"And you keep saying that *I* should be more planned and methodical," snorted the calico.

Haru looked over to Durgavati, ears down, tail curled under. "Your Excellency, I'm so sorry, I would never deliberately endanger you like that!"

The Prefect smiled, reaching out with a large paw to gently pet her assistant's head. "You were brilliant, Haru. If not for you, I would still be Tsaibei's prisoner—and Ambara Down would have no voice in the days ahead. You have done your part and more."

"I… the AI… made me promise that I would forcibly put a chip on you," Haru said, staring at her feet. "I've still got the other chip it gave me."

Durgavati tilted your head. "A promise you immediately broke," she said.

"I… yes," said Haru. She pulled the contact chip out of the pouch on her belt, tossed it onto the deck, and smashed it with her heel.

"My poor honest child," said the lioness. "I'm sure it must have pained you to lie… even to Pax Machina." She leaned down and kissed the top of Haru's head, causing the collie's tail to thump despite her best efforts. "Thank you for saving my life," said the Prefect, then stretched hard, curling her back and yawning. "But now that you are awake and can take the watch, I need some rest. Wake me if there's trouble."

Haru jumped to her feet and bowed, making room for Durgavati to lie down. She immediately regretted this, and came close to toppling over the rail before Rory had crossed the gap and caught her. "Be careful, dumbass!" shouted the calico. "You've just had the snot beat out of you, can you take it easy for ten minutes?"

Durgavati was rolling her eyes. "I was *going* to take the other couch," said the Prefect.

Haru swallowed hard, trying to regain her equilibrium. "Oh…" she said. "Right." Then she looked over at Rory… and the two of them sputtered into giggles at each other.

Rory shook her head and guided the collie away from Durgavati. "Come on, I'll take you forward with me, clearly you need baby-sitting." The Prefect shook her head indulgently, then reclined where she was.

"Hey…" said Haru, as Rory slid her into the co-pilot's seat. The calico's ears perked up.

"Yeah?"

Haru's tail wagged slightly. "Is your name really 'Aurora Starshine'?"

"Fuck off! I was six when I picked it."

Haru couldn't help but snort. "I like it," she finally said.

"If you ever call me Aurora Sunshine, I'll scratch your eyes out. My name is Rory."

"I'll call you Rory if you stop calling me 'Prefect's Office.'"

Rory raised one eyebrow and looked sidelong at her. "Last-Line-Of-Defense?"

Haru shook her head. "No."

"Dumbass."

"Definitely not, Captain Starshine!"

"What did I *just* say!" demanded Rory.

"Well then…?"

Rory smirked at her. "You *do* have a squooshy center."

The collie smiled up at the pilot. "Maybe. Just a little bit."

The calico grinned. "Okay… Haru."

Ambara Blues

Indagare

Clean floors in light beige were separated from clean walls of the same color by narrow bands of darker colored trim: on this level it was blue. The ceilings vaulted overhead with the occasional skylight, but most of the lighting was provided by fluted, shell-like artificial lights that were changing color to pinks and oranges to mimic the sunset as I headed from the main area towards the rear.

Along the walls were shops, selling a variety of items from clothes to scented candles, and miniature trees and flowers grew in rounded dark blue vases made of plastic. Beyond the food courts I pushed open a blue door and followed the stairs up to where an indigo door waited with a large number 6 stenciled on it; past this, the last flight of stairs ended in a violet door with the number 7. I opened it and found myself on the forested rooftop of the building, looking at the dome overhead. Near the door was a person in a silvery gray suit that concealed all features. Even their face was behind a reflective helmet.

"Greetings, citizen, what brings you to the Groves this fine evening?" Their voice was as neutral as their appearance, absent anything but a pleasant pitch.

"I have special permission to stargaze," I said, pulling out the permit it had taken me months to get. The guard nodded.

"Yes, this seems all in order. There are several locations which would be suitable." They pointed to a map of the Groves, as spots on the display lit up. "We recommend these locations, though you are free to choose others. Be careful not to go too far within the Groves after dark as it can be disorienting."

I thanked them and walked on. Night was setting and it was getting dark, but I finally found a bench that faced outward and waited for the sun to set. City lights slowly turned on, bathing the buildings in an aura of colors. I waited for full dark and looked up and around, but except for a few faded pinpricks the sky was a blank, black dome: the lights had eaten the stars.

* * *

The hall to my apartment, the same light beige as every other building, was quiet and clean. There was light enough to see by, but all of it was a subdued pink; a vague scent of cleaning agents hung in the air. I reached my number and used my key to open my door. As far as I knew, the interior matched all my neighbors: space for a bed that folded into and out of the walls; a closet that allowed a minimum amount of storage space for clothes; and a bathroom with toilet, sink, shower stall, and clothes cleaner. At the far end was a kitchen with room for a food printer, a small table, and two chairs. All of this in the sort of light gray that was supposed to be soothing.

I washed, tossed my clothes in the cleaner, and lowered the bed. The form-fitting mattress adjusted itself to my body as I lay down to sleep. Three months of bureaucracy and all for nothing. Well, I had tomorrow to look forward to at least. My background in evolutionary biology, herbology, and anthropology were about to pay off: I was leaving High Empyros and going to Ambara Down.

* * *

People moved along corridors, looking forward, each focused on their destination. I walked out of the beige halls of the Travel Complex to a VIP area where a sleek black car waited for me to present my ID. A person in the back seat with me wore an official outfit that was almost as form concealing as the guards had been, except that I could see her face. "Welcome, Delmar. I am Director Kyla."

"Greetings, Director."

The car lifted off and we rushed along the tops of the buildings, heading towards the Fence. I felt excited, and nervous—this was the chance of a lifetime! I was a bit uncertain about the Director, though.

"Are you aware of why you were particularly chosen to come to Ambara Down?"

I felt a cold lump in my stomach. "I've been to the surface before to study both flora and fauna," I said. "I've also made extensive studies into anthropology, though my experience with zoomorphs is a bit limited." It was one thing to study a culture; it was another thing to live in it.

"Hardly," said Director Kyla. "Your study of the zoomorphic cultures was quite brilliant. And of course, your treatise on the thirteen Alliance cities currently participating in the Reclamation Project was most impressive. Twenty years ago, they would have helped smooth relations quite a bit. We are hoping you can do the same by studying Ambara Down."

"I thought there was a truce in place."

"There is. But the locals do not trust the Project, and the feeling is mutual. It is an unfortunate situation that leads to occasional flare-ups. For the Project to continue smoothly we need to understand the locals better. We expect that once they actually know what we can provide for them, they will cease resisting and help us to reclaim Ambara for everyone."

Having just been through a nightmare of red tape to be allowed to stargaze on what was supposed to be public property, I had my doubts that things would work out like that; I also knew not to say so out loud. "Well, it's certainly possible. Misunderstandings do lead to… issues."

"Indeed," said the Director flatly. "Speaking of avoiding issues, you will need some local coinage." She handed me a silky black bag with ties that passed through a gem-like string holder. It made an odd clinking noise. "This bag contains the equivalent of one thousand credits. Your guide will instruct you in their use."

The car came to a stop near a break in the Fence. There were three such breaks: one was close to the ruins near Sickle Bay, one was the Hole in the Wall Cafe, which was about midway through the Fence, and the last was this one—close to the Complex and nearly across from the infamous Damselfly that I'd heard so much about.

When we got out, I saw that there was a tall, non-human figure waiting for us. Its features were mostly rabbit-like with long and pointy ears, cinnamon brown and cream fur, and emerald green eyes. What really stood out about it was the pair of ivory white horns on its head.

The creature was naked to the waist, where it wore a black belt with lots of bulging pouches over what looked like a green and blue skirt. The rest of it seemed to be naked as well, except its feet which were strapped in dark brown sandals. There was an expression on its muzzle that could have been a smile. Or maybe it was a leer. I wasn't sure. The guards, in their full body suits, seemed more rigid and alert than usual. I felt a cold sweat over my body. Calm down.

"This is a liaison sent to us by the Council," said Director Kyla, unable to keep a note of disdain out of her voice despite her best efforts. I could see that I had my job cut out for me.

"Tavistad Ridgerunner," said the zoomorph, extending a hand. "But most everyone calls me Tav." I shook the offered hand and noticed the warmth and softness of its fur.

"Delmar Nova, though usually it's just Del."

"A pleasure to meet you Del."

"Same, Tav." I smiled and tried to keep myself relaxed.

"We appreciate the Prefecture's help in this matter," said the Director. "We expect both sides to be fully cooperative." She could have been reading off a script.

Tav's eyes seemed to twinkle. "But of course! I'm sure Del will enjoy his stay so much he'll return with a report that'll have natives and Reclaimers holding hands and singing."

I forced myself to keep a straight face as the Director replied flatly, "It does not have to be quite that effective. A lessening of hostilities is sufficient." I wondered if she really didn't get the jibe or if she was simply ignoring it. Kyla turned to me and continued, "Given the nature of your assignment, your stay in Ambara Down will last as long as you choose, though we expect at least a monthly progress report. At that time, you will be paid for your services as well. We have been assured you will be provided living quarters." She looked at Tav as if expecting a protest. He just smiled.

"Since I am his guide," said Tav, "I volunteered to share my living quarters with him. Should he not happen to care for it, there are several others who have also volunteered."

"Your cooperation is appreciated. Fair voyages, Delmar Nova."

She turned and entered the car, and Tav and I passed through the gate into Ambara Down.

* * *

The first building I saw was the famous Damselfly, a beautiful building of metal and midnight blue glass. "Wow! I've heard stories about this place! Can we go in?"

"Certainly, if you wish. Sooner or later everyone comes to the Damselfly." He led me through the doors and into a wide area I pieced together. I first noticed it was dusky—there were plenty of lights but all of them were set low. There was a sprawling main area, round tables covered in midnight blue tablecloths with sleek black chairs with matching blue upholstery. I had never seen so many zoomorphs together, just going about their everyday lives.

At the heart of the main floor was a bar with two bartenders: a male-looking liger with rainbow colored mane and a sleeveless black shirt, and a female-looking human with matching colors. The bar was designed to have tropical trees as part of it, and a mirror in the middle made the multicolored drinks seem to go on forever.

To my right was a bandstand and dance floor framed by arched stairs leading to the mezzanine. Right now, a lone piano was the bandstand's only occupant, but electro-swing music was wafting from jukebox near the center back of the stage. I tensed up a bit as a frilled lizard with an impressively muscular body (in the same sort of black uniform the bartenders wore) greeted us at the doorway. "Table for two?"

"Yes, thank you," said Tav.

We ordered meals and drinks. "What's back there?" I asked, indicating high doors at the far end of the hall.

"Private rooms. I've heard that there's gambling and worse, but I've never actually seen it."

Over lunch I considered what Tav said but dismissed the idea of trying to go back there by myself until I knew my way around. Nothing is worse than not having cultural context. When we finished, I insisted on paying; I wanted to get used to using the circular and octagonal coins.

* * *

I had to blink several times as we went back outside to bright sunlight, warmth, and a host of sights and smells. The Fence was the most obvious feature, but all around the Damselfly teemed the market district. Everyone was jostling everyone else, multicolored flags fluttered on stalls, and all the buildings seemed to host creeping vines.

Tav smiled indulgently as I absorbed every detail. I ended up taking so long that a carriage pulled up, sleek and black with large, glass windows and black shields decorated with rearing gold horses. At the front of the carriage in an enclosed hemisphere sat a horse zoomorph, who held the reins to a gigantic rhinoceros beetle. "Cozy cabby?"

"No thank you right now," said Tav.

The horse shrugged and called a command to the yellow-backed beetle, which scurried off with a huff. Tav noticed me staring after it and said, "Sorry, did you want a ride?"

"That… the… I…" I paused to catch my breath and thoughts. "Let's start with the bug the size of a horse!"

"Oh, those are common. Out in the Outskirts they get even bigger. But don't worry, rhinoceros beetles are herbivores. Smart too, willing to pull cozy cabs in return for fruit."

"Do those cabs go everywhere?"

"Only here and in the Furry Development. For some reason the Reclaimers think it's a health hazard."

"The… did you say, 'Furry Development?'"

"Sounds like a joke, doesn't it?" Tav said, smiling again. "I won't blame you for laughing—enough of us do. It should have a proper name, but no one seems to have anything better than 'New Ambara.'"

I did smile at it. "I suppose 'the Reclamation Project' is no less ludicrous."

We started walking among the throngs of people, and I took in the different colors of clothing, fur, feather, scale, and skin. The streets were narrow enough that it was hard to navigate among the bustle and I had to keep focus on Tav lest I lose him.

I also had to fight myself every step of the way. Here I was, a supposed anthropologist, but every accidental shove made me want to curl up in a ball and hide. *They're just ordinary people, like you.* Pulling myself out of my own head I suddenly realized that I'd lost Tav completely.

I took in deep breaths. Panicking would not help. Suddenly I was grabbed! To my relief it was a human guard in the faceless uniform of the Reclamation Project. "Can you help me?" I asked him. "I'm a bit lost."

"This way." The guard lead me through the crowd, which parted before him. We ended up, somehow, down an oddly dark alley with a dead end. I shivered.

"Uh, I think we went the wrong way somehow."

"No, citizen Nova, this is correct." The guard did not reach for a gun but instead pulled out something that looked like a metal claw. "Regrettably, your termination is needed to ensure the future."

"…What?"

He advanced on me and I looked for some means of defense. Just as he was about to reach me there was a blur and I felt myself grabbed—then I was airborne and saw the smiling face of Tav. "Hang on!" he said as we barreled through the air.

We landed in another alley, though where it was in relation to the other, I had no idea. "Tav! What? How?"

"I'm a Heraldic—we tend to have a few special abilities up our sleeves, so to speak."

I had heard stories of Heraldics, created in the likeness of heraldic beasts, bred with remarkable abilities, and made to fight each other—and allegedly extinct. Tav peeked his head out of the other end of the alley. "It looks like the coast is clear. Are you up to walking?"

I nodded, still too stunned to talk, but I wasn't sure if it was the attempt on my life or the discovery of a real Heraldic. We hustled through the narrow streets, less crowded than the ones before, but still crowded enough that I was sure our swerving and dashing around would lose anyone. It certainly lost me. Finally, we slipped into the shell of a building that appeared to be unoccupied.

"What was all that about?" asked Tav.

"I wish I knew!" I slumped down to the floor and held my knees. "I wonder if it's too late to go home. Or if I even can go home. Why would a guard want to kill me?"

"He was holding a claw. He wanted to make it look like you were murdered by a zoomorph." Tav bent down and sat beside me but didn't touch me. I was grateful for that.

"But why? Why me? If they wanted to kill a human and blame a zoo, there are any number around."

"That's an excellent point. Relations have not exactly been warm and fuzzy, so it wouldn't take much to cause an issue. We should go to the Prefect's Office. It should be safe there."

I followed Tav, who kept looking around, though there were fewer people in this part of the city. The roads were more variable too, with many of the side roads covered in debris or overgrown with plant life. The more I thought about it, the less likely it seemed that humans could ever reclaim all this.

I also noted that there seemed to be few lights around the area, but there were trees planted at even intervals with rose colored buds closed tight. I was about to ask Tav about them when the Prefecture Hall came into view. It was easily the tallest building I had seen in the city: a nearly twenty-story, tiered affair suggesting the castle of an ancient shogun or samurai lord. I couldn't understand how it survived the crash.

I felt a sudden tug as Tav pulled me towards it. I was about to pull back when I saw the Reclamation guards. There were enough people around the Hall that they couldn't rush us, but they were definitely moving towards us. I kept his pace and tried to act casual. The guards picked up on it and headed towards the Hall; I wondered if Tav was going to leap us onto the building, but once we got across the wide street the guards suddenly stopped. Tav paused a moment to look at them, then nodded, before leading me in.

The building's interior was well-kept and polished, but there was something different about the smell, much more natural somehow. We were greeted by a half-circle desk with a white bird behind it, some kind of wading bird, I think, that looked up at us. "Hello, Tav. Can I help you?"

"My friend here is new to Ambara Down and wanted a tour of the Hall."

"Feel free to look around. Almost nobody's in, though."

"Thank you!" Tav lead me down the hardwood corridor. The walls were all very colorful here, dark wood framing murals in watercolor and pastels, not a stenciled number in sight. Tav wasn't interested in the décor, however. "Those guards are a problem," he said.

"Do you think they'll wait out there? Why didn't they follow us in?"

"I have no doubt that they'll wait. They aren't the type to give up easily. As for why they didn't come in, I'm not sure. It could be a direct confrontation would cause too much notice."

"Can we get a view of the outside? I'd like to know what we're up against."

Tav nodded and we went up to the second-floor offices. What I saw out the window was not comforting: two guards in mirrored faceplates and leather armored bodysuits stood in front of the building. People were giving them looks, but also a wide berth. A bit of walking revealed two more guarding each street-level entrance and exit—we were trapped!

"Hmm," said Tav. "Eight to one. Steep odds, even for me."

"Hey! I'm here!"

"Do you have any experience at all in combat?"

I bowed my head. "Uh, no. I'm a scholar, not a fighter."

"Then it's just me." He moved us away from the windows and deeper into corridors to another stairwell.

"Much as I love all the architecture in here, is there a reason we're taking the scenic route?" I asked.

"The guards were looking up. They may have spotted us. Inside we're less likely to be spotted unless they're using thermals."

I sat on one of the steps. None of this was making any sense at all. "Aren't there offices in here for the Reclamation Project?"

"There are, but exactly what good would it do to go there? You can't claim asylum and any inquiries into what's going on won't help either. If they know, you'll be in even more danger since they'll know you know. If they don't know, they won't be able to answer you anyway."

I sighed. "What about the Prefect, then?"

Tav shook his head. "You've barely been here a couple hours. And don't forget, she's the one who sent me to be your guide and escort. Even if she believed us and gave you more security, I somehow doubt it'd deter your would-be assassins. It might even encourage them since afterwards they could claim that you trusted your life to us, and we failed you."

"I still don't get why they're after me!" I said. "If they wanted to prevent me from writing on Ambara Down they just could have not asked me."

"Well, we could always try to catch one of them and see if we can get them to talk."

"How? They're not coming in and they've covered all the exits!"

Tav smiled. "No, they've only covered the ones on the ground."

"Oh no."

* * *

There's something to be said about looking at a city from some twenty stories up. Ambara Down seemed to stretch out like a mosaic from where we stood. The steel and glass of the city were covered in vines, but I could also just make out colorful banners and flowers, even what looked like clothing hanging out between buildings. The wind blew through my hair as I stood far from the edge of the Hall's roof, not daring to look down. Tav, on the other hand, was stretching his limbs with a ludicrous grin that showed off his buck teeth.

"It's been a while since I've had to jump like this. It'll be fun to see how far I can leap."

"And how often do you carry a passenger?"

"I didn't drop you before, I'm not going to drop you now. Hang on tight!"

He didn't need to urge me there. I grabbed on and squeezed my eyes shut as he flexed his knees and WHOOSH! off into the air we went! I couldn't bear to look but felt the rush of the wind against my body and the lurch of freefall as Tav laughed. I opened my eyes again when we finally stopped bouncing around but had to blink at what I saw.

We were in a completely different part of the city. The area still had a few high rises, but most were in ruins. Nearby were large ridges, and westward was a wooded patch that seemed to mark a boundary. I let go of Tav and tried to get my equilibrium back. "Where are we?"

"We're near the border of the Furry Development." He paused to look around. "This would probably be the best place to plan our next move—capturing your pursuers."

"Do you think they'll come this way?"

"I can't imagine why. I ought to have known better than Prefecture Hall. I thought it would be safer, but on reflection it was a bad idea. They certainly anticipated us going there. If they search for us anywhere it's most likely going to be my place next."

I nodded and looked around. The edge of the city blended with the natural surroundings, though it wasn't quite seamless yet. The flora was a bewildering mix; some I recognized as belonging to the city tops and some was obviously native. Not too far away I saw a path heading into the wood. Getting closer, I saw some of the same trees with the closed-tight rose bulbs lining it at evenly spaced intervals.

"Follow that path long enough and you'd get to the first village in the Furry Development. All of the villages have residents who watched Ambara as it fell."

"What?! Why hasn't anyone asked them what they saw?"

"They have, you just haven't heard about it. Anyway, I can't guarantee your safety in there." I turned to Tav who was putting something back into his belt. "Keep in mind not everyone is like me here. There's plenty who would just as soon slit your throat as say hello."

I gulped and suddenly felt very small and vulnerable. What did I even know about Tav? Sure, he'd rescued me twice, but I wondered if he didn't have an alternative reason for keeping me alive, just as those strange guards seemed to want me dead. Suddenly a heard a sort of gurgling growl. Imagining gigantic bugs, I circled around, only to see Tav looking abashed.

"One drawback to using my augmentations like that is it makes me really hungry. How about something to eat?"

"Uh, sure. There's somewhere close by?"

"Follow me."

We walked along the grassy part of the area, most of it about up to my knees. I decided I might as well make conversation and refresh my memory. Maybe I'd hit on the reason I was hunted. "The Project started about twenty years ago, right?"

"The original one? Yes, just about twenty-five years after the crash. Folks who moved in had kids by then. Not all the city was re-inhabited, of course. The southeastern quadrant was all vacant buildings, that's where the first Reclaimers from High Empyros came in, took control, and put up the Fence. Then the fighting started. Folks this side of the Fence said it was the 'Claimers taking potshots at innocent folks minding their own business. Folks on the other side said it was zoomorphs attacking civilians. Whatever the truth, it was full-blown war before the end, but they finally called a truce when the Reclaimers realized they couldn't win. It's been a cold war ever since… mostly. And now, of course, the flying cities are banding together. Unfortunately, some people think all humans are Reclaimers."

"That actually explains a lot." And was another good reason to avoid poking into New Ambara, too, but I kept the thought to myself. "But if I'm to write something, I'll eventually need to get everyone's side of the story. That'll be hard if the zoomorph side sees me as an enemy."

Tav shrugged. "That can't be helped. Assuming we can help you survive this current situation, that'll be the next problem."

We came to a large, round building made of natural stone, though its roof looked like it was made from reused steel sheets. Outside the structure was what I thought was a dark-skinned human wearing a red, gold, and black dress sweeping in front of it, but when we got closer I saw she had hair that changed from bright yellow near her brows to deep black near her back, almost like a sunset. Her eyes were a deep purple and she had pointed ears.

"Hello Hespera! How are you this fine day?"

She looked up and smiled at first, then she saw me. "What sort of trouble are you involved with this time, Tav? Or am I better off not knowing?"

"This is Delmar Nova, and it's not like that—this time. Delmar this is Hespera Evenstar."

"Uh, hi!" There was a long pause in which Tav looked at Hespera and Hespera looked at me.

"Fine! Who did you have to fight this time?"

"Some guards, after Del for unknown reasons. We ditched them back in the city."

"Goddess be praised for small favors! Well, come in!"

We followed her into the building. Besides the stone walls there were wooden floors, tables, and chairs, but the beams on the roof seemed made of steel. Round windows provided ample lighting, though there were lamps attached to the ceiling. A large fireplace occupied an area opposite the door, though it was not lit. A kitchen area was set off on the eastern side with a bar and stools in front of it. There wasn't anyone else besides us. Hespera went behind the counter and Tav and I followed up to it and sat on the stools.

She returned from inside the kitchen with menus that hovered in the air on their own an impressive display of hard light and traction field technology. "On the run from Reclaimer guards? That's pretty impressive. What did you do, protest too loudly?" She faced the kitchen and various cutlery rushed out at an alarming speed and onto the counter.

"I didn't do anything. I can't figure out why they're after me. I'm supposed to be here on an anthropological study."

"That's a new one. What would you like to drink?"

I stared at her blankly for several minutes. "Uh. Anything's fine."

"Look at the menu and decide." She turned to Tav. "Your usual?"

"Of course. I told you this one was different. No mobsters, no blackmarketeers, no insane cultists." There was an odd look on Tav's face, as if he were trying very hard not to laugh.

"Uh huh. It seems I'm always saving that cotton tail of yours." She faced the kitchen and her face furrowed in concentration. She raised her hands like she was conducting an orchestra and out of the kitchen came a bowl of salad and a fizzy drink.

"I really do appreciate it. We have a great working relationship."

"Yeah, if by 'working relationship' you mean I feed you every time you bring me a stray on the run from something nasty." Hespera turned to me. "I highly recommend my curried beans and rice; I promise it's not too spicy. Lemonade or raspberry iced tea goes well with it."

I nodded and she smiled briefly, took the menus and went into the kitchen. After a few minutes of delicious, spicy smells wafting to us, she returned with trays hovering on their own, probably using the same tech that the menus did to float. It made for an excellent show.

"Eat up! I have a feeling you'll need it. It might even put some color in your cheeks. Has Tav been giving you a hard time?" she turned to Tav, who was studiously eating his salad.

"Perish the thought!" said Tav, with exaggerated offense. "I don't think cities offer much in the way of a tan."

I smiled awkwardly. "Not usually," I said. "We mostly stay inside, except on trams or in skiffs." I forked a small piece of the beans and nibbled at it. Soon I was greedily putting it away.

"I see. You're so skinny too. You're packing it away like a bear getting ready for winter!"

"This is amazing," I said. "We mostly get printed food in the cities, unless we can afford better."

"Printed?! Printed food?!" Hespera sounded scandalized. "So, it's not just the 'Claimers! How can anyone survive on such fare?"

"Well, you know how it is. Whatever needs must." I smiled. "I really appreciate this. I'm not sure how this is all going to end, but this is the best meal I've ever had."

She dismissed it with a wave but looked pleased. "Small compliment to be compared to printed food." She paused a moment and looked at me. "Dessert, Delmar? I cook a wonderful bumbleberry pie!"

"Yes please," I said.

She turned to Tav. "See! He says please! You don't deserve pie, but I can't have him eating dessert alone."

"Thank you Hespera," I said. Tav's sides were quivering and the stern expression on her face seemed to want to twitch into something else. Finally, they both gave up and just laughed.

"Sorry! Sorry!" said Hespera, seeing the expression on my face. "It is true, Tav is always coming to me for help, but, it's because I asked him to. He helped me when I built this, and I like to return the favor to others."

"I've always been most grateful," said Tav. "I must admit, though, I'd miss this routine we go through."

I looked at them both. "Is this sort of thing usual?"

Hespera shook her head. "It's a joke between us. Usually, anyway. I reserve the right to be grumpy when Tav comes looking for help."

"I see… I think. How are you able to make things fly in like that? I mean, I've never seen anyone use tech like that."

"I scrounge up tech and figure out how to use it. More than I can say for some people who seem content to sit on their laurels." Hespera smiled. "You have any coins, Delmar?"

I nodded and took out my pouch. For the first time, I inspected the coins closely. Each of them had different markings on front and back, but all of them had twelve stars separated into groups of three by the letters GNDN on the front. They also all had 'Ambara Down' on the top of the backs. "What's GNDN?"

"I was hoping there might be a chance you'd know," said Tav. "We find it on a lot of items that are scavenged but have no clue what it means."

"I've seen it in the cities too, but no one seems to know what it's supposed to mean there either. I always figured it was the name of some long-forgotten manufacturer."

As I said this, three zoomorphs entered the room. One was an eagle, the second a crocodile, and the third a frog. They all moved towards me. "Well, well, what do we have here?" asked the eagle.

"Looks to me like a 'Claimer far from home," said the crocodile.

"We ought to give the little fella a proper welcome," said the frog.

I shrank down as they surrounded me. Tav and Hespera looked on with unreadable expressions. This was it. I was doomed.

Each of them gave me a hard pat on the back and smiled. "Welcome stranger!"

Between the pats and my sudden relief at not being mauled, it was a wonder I didn't lose my seating. They all laughed and both Tav and Hespera were smiling and I realized it was another joke.

"You were right, Tav," said the eagle. "This poor fellow is wound up tighter than a two pound watch!"

I looked at Tav, who pulled out a pocket phone by way of explanation. "I figured calling in a few friends would even the odds. These are Orven Lightwing, Sobit Waveglider, and Marana Quagmire."

"Ran for short," said the frog.

"Delmar Nova," I said and smiled.

Each shook my hand in turn, greeting me warmly. Their way of introduction was... odd... but I was beginning to like it.

"So what's the plan, Tav?" asked Orven.

"Besides capturing the 'Claimers after Del, and finding out what the story is, I'm not sure. It all depends on why. I'm worried that someone among the unified humans wants to start a new war—and not just over Ambara Down."

I looked at him. "You mean... global domination?"

Sobit shook her head. "Are they crazy? Is that the problem? Even if all the humans in all the flying cities were to fight, we outnumber them by a hundred to one or more!"

"Well, there's only one way to find out, and that's by setting a trap," said Tav. "There's one unfortunate thing, though."

"What's that?" I asked.

"You have to be the bait."

* * *

I'll be the first to admit, I'm not a brave person. I do well enough, I suppose, but standing around in a clearing waiting for someone to come after me was not exactly reassuring on the nerves, and it has been even less assuring to find out someone had put a tracer on my money purse, likely before the Director handed it to me. I did my best to look at the various flora, which was at least a treat. There were sky blue roses among the flowers—a sign how humans created beauty.

It was not as long a wait as I'd hoped before the Reclamation Project guards appeared from the woods. All of them had claws attached to their hands. "Greetings, citizen Nova," said one. "It is unfortunate, but your termination is necessary to assure the future."

"I don't suppose any of you would feel like telling me why."

"That information is classified. Also, it will not matter soon."

The guards advanced—and then there were loud bang and the clearing was filled with bursts of fire and smoke. Tav and the others rushed into the clearing, each of them taking on two of the dazzled guards.

The 'Claimers tried to regroup in a circle, but couldn't make it as Tav kicked first one, then another, sending them sprawling to the ground. Orven had a long metal pole which he used to batter his opponents, while Sobit simply shot at hers with stun guns. Like Tav, Ran kicked with her powerful legs to take out the guards with minimal fuss. I was so distracted by it all that I didn't see the ninth guard emerging from the trees dangerously close to me with a stun baton until it was too late.

* * *

I came to strapped into the sidecar of a hoverbike, speeding through the woods towards the Furry Development. "You are proving much more difficult to terminate than anticipated," said the guard at the controls.

A shock went through me—I knew that voice! I didn't know what Director Kyla's game was, but I wasn't about to let her win. I thrashed back and forth violently against the safety harness and the bike began to lurch dangerously close to the trees rushing by.

"Stop that! We're both going to die if you keep that up!"

"Good!" I kept at it and she was forced to slow down the bike to keep it and me under control as we drove into village streets. She pulled the stun baton from her belt with the apparent intent of knocking me out again, but it left her with only one hand on the controls. I grabbed her arm and yanked hard. The bike pulled a crazy turn into the side of a building and lurched sideways, tumbling us onto the ground.

I looked around. We were in a village square and around us were buildings made out of native stone, with roofs made out of colored slates. Our arrival was nothing if not dramatic, and multiple zoomorphs were gathering around us. I still wasn't sure how to read their faces, but most looked more shocked than angry. I rose and faced the last of my pursuers.

"All right, Director, are you going to tell me what this is all about?"

The mirrored faceplate of her helmet was spiderwebbed with cracks from the crash; she pulled the helmet off and glared at me, stun baton crackling green in her hand. "I ought to have known by your record with the other cities that you would be trouble. You honestly don't know?"

"You're the one who sent me down here!" I said. "Not an hour after you drop me off a guard tries to kill me in a way that will make it look like a zoomorph did it. Then I find you've put a tracer on the coins you gave me and have come back to personally finish the job. So, no, I'm not entirely clear why you came after me when all you had to do was not ask me to write to start with!"

"The other Directors wanted you, not me!" she spat. "But they overrode me! When they heard about your research, they wanted you to continue it here. Helpmann asked for you personally, the ineffectual bastard! They think it'll foster 'better relations.' But I know where it will lead: the extinction of humanity! We're already falling behind in reproduction! What will happen when people see zoomorphs as the natural successor to humans?"

There was a wild look in her eyes, and I had no doubts she was sincere. Unfortunately, she was sincerely insane. By now we were in a tight circle of zoomorphs, and her gloves were sporting claws. Wonderful. "So, you decided to try this assassination thinking that it'll help convince them to go to war on everyone?"

She dropped the stun baton, raising her beclawed fists. "Why not? If we're going to die out, then take everyone with us! Let the world burn in a purifying fire!"

She was closing in on me and I could expect no help from the bystanders. They were also too tight together to run through, assuming they'd even let me escape. She came in swinging; I tried kicking and punching to avoid her clawed gloves. Fortunately for me, she was no better trained in combat than I was. It was ugly and ungainly and if it weren't for her gloves, we'd have been evenly matched. I ducked her swipes, punched and kicked at her. She dodged, mostly, but wasn't able to avoid one of my kicks. I knocked her to the ground, but she scrambled back up before I could do anything else. She shoved at me, and I ended up falling down. Fortunately, she chose to jump into a lunge at me which let me roll out of the way and left her face down on the dirt. I scooped up the stun baton where she'd tossed it away and shoved it into her leg, causing her to spasm wildly and go limp.

I got up and watched, but aside from some twitching she didn't move. I bent down and took her gloves off and turned her over. She was still breathing but looked like she was knocked out.

Suddenly someone next to me applauded. "Way to go, Del!"

"Tav! Am I glad to see you!" We hugged for a moment. The zoomorphs around us smiled. "What happened with the guards?"

"They were robots!" Tav said, boggling. "Luckily, they weren't very smart and had no remote access, so Pax Machina couldn't get into them. We took them apart anyway, just to be on the safe side."

Director Kyla moaned, then rolled over and looked up at us. "Well? What are you waiting for? Kill me and get it over with!"

I shook my head. "I'm not a murderer, nor is my friend. Besides, killing a Director would be even worse than the murder of some poor researcher. Ambara Down deserves a chance at peace. And anyway, why should I? You said Executive Director Helpmann asked for me personally. I think he and I will have a lot to talk about."

"And humanity? Will you betray that too?"

"We humans have had our chance and all we did was make a mess of the world. Maybe we'll learn better now that we're no longer the ones running the place. Maybe we won't, but if we refuse to learn we certainly will die."

She got to her feet and looked ready to hit me, but with so many outnumbering her she couldn't. "You'll regret this, sooner or later! I'll ruin you! I'll find a way to get a bounty on your head!"

Some of the citizens had brought back the hover bike. "Maybe," I said. "Maybe not. But your career is over. Everyone is expecting my reports. The first one will be a glowing report on the hospitality of Ambara Down. I think any suspicious attacks on me will be seen a bit differently after that."

"We have our own ways, too," said a zoomorph stepping forward, a vibrantly colored leopard who held a datapad. "I was recording the whole thing. We know who you are now. We'll know what you try."

Director Kyla glared and got on the hoverbike. The crowd parted and let her drive through, cheering and jeering as she left. Tav smiled at me and as the crowd of zoomorphs gathered close, I didn't feel anything like fear. It was more like coming home, maybe for the first time in my life.

"I believe introductions and a party are in order," said the leopard. I grinned.

* * *

I saw the rose buds on the trees opening and the white flowers within began glowing. Tav and I walked across the city slowly, avoiding traffic ranging from bicycles to cozy cabs. There were lights in the windows but none on top of the buildings, and the only street-level lights came from the trees, already attracting early night insects. Fireflies started to blink, and even small, glowing, jellyfish-like creatures swam through the night air.

We walked nearly to the other end of Old Ambara where apartments stood. Tav led me to one complex, let me in, and led me up the stairs. When we got to his floor, I noticed that the walls were colored in bright patterns. Here there was none of the antiseptic smell: instead there was the smells of suppers being cooked, or deserts, the sound of families laughing behind closed doors, and even music from somewhere.

We went up the back stairwell to the top where the groves of fruit trees were. Tav led me to an open spot and we both lay down on the ground. The nights in Ambara Down are so clear, you can look up into the sky and see forever. The stars shine like they've been newly polished and even the Milky Way is visible. I felt an odd dizziness like I was falling up into the sky. As the dew started to form on the grass, the cool wetness felt oddly relaxing against my skin. At some point I drifted into sleep and dreamed of the stars.

INSECURITY

L. Rowyn

"Think I've found something," the mer subvocalized into their jaw communicator, using the team channel. The beam from their wrist-mounted light cut a swathe through the dark waters. Artificial glints reflected back from the ocean floor below. With a swish of their tail, Aawee swam to the source of the glimmering.

"What do you have, Aawee?" Nguyen's voice came back in the mer's earbud.

Aawee swept their hand over the silt before them, exposing a glassy dark pane and the metal edge of a frame, before the sand was too deep to push aside. Their wrist light reflected back from it, not penetrating. They clicked their tongue and listened to the echoes. "Not sure yet but sounds big. Probably need the excavators to know. I'll poke around, see if there's anything promising." The ocean floor dropped off to the south, so Aawee swam in that direction, half-listening to the chatter from the rest of their salvage team. The five-member team was spread out across several square kilometers for this part of the operation, seeking the next big find.

The drop-off sloped down to a seagrass-covered overhang. Aawee swam to the underside, then through the veil of seagrass. Past it, an opening around two meters wide and perhaps one high led into a cavernous underground space. Sonar pings showed Aawee that though the edges had been blurred by silt and undersea life, the vast space had a largely rectangular shape, with squared-off tunnels leading from it. "Oh yes," they subvocalized to the team. "This is definitely sapient-made, and it's huge. Part of a building. Must've been knocked clear during the splash-down when Ambara fell. And then the ocean buried it in sediment in the intervening years."

"From Ambara, or some unfortunate building Ambara fell on, do you think?" Nguyen asked.

"It's in great shape, under the circumstances." Aawee swam towards one of the walls, taking pictures with the camera set under their wrist light. "Must be Ambara."

"Good work!" That was Kerick Strong, the team lead, and Aawee couldn't restrain a smile at the praise. Aawee hadn't been on Kerick's team long but they were already inordinately fond of their team lead. Kerick asked, "D'ya want any backup? We're getting some static on your line."

"The building and silt are probably blocking the signal." Aawee spun in a slow circle, studying the room. It looked like a corporate lobby, turned on its side, filled with seawater, and lined by sediment and other detritus. A sideways reception counter remained anchored to the erstwhile floor, near one wall. The tunnels Aawee had noticed earlier were two hallways and an elevator shaft with broken doors. Mer were similar in size to humans, so the submerged lobby, corridors, and doors would all accommodate Aawee without difficulty. The "overhang" beneath which they'd entered was a door, braced open by its mechanism. The door's upper side supported enough sediment, rock, and plant life to disguise its nature from the outside. What remained of most of the room's furnishings rested in a heap along the lowest wall. Intermingled among them were bones: when Ambara fell, most of its residents had no way to escape or survive. None of the sea grass was in here: apart from Aawee's wrist light, the darkness inside was absolute. The exterior wall directly above them reflected that light like glass, though it must have been a sky-tech composite to have survived the fall and subsequent submersion intact. It had no more connection to ordinary glass than Aawee had to dolphins or Strong to octopuses. The far side was black: tinted and buried. "I'd be happy to have company."

Only static answered. Aawee scrunched up their face. They wanted to explore further, but protocol dictated they keep in touch with their team, and Kerick would be upset if they broke protocol. With an inward sigh, Aawee looped behind the counter, intending to push off the far wall and swim to the exit. As their fingers brushed the wall, they felt artificial ridges beneath the film of detritus over it. Aawee paused to fan their tail fin over it. The water clouded with loose sediment for a moment before it settled enough that Aawee could distinguish the familiar conical logo embossed on the wall.

"It's a GloEx building!" GloEx was a multinational exploration equipment company; they manufactured a wide variety of durable equipment designed for specific environments, including the underwater subvocalization comm system Aawee's team used. The company had once been infamous for poor security practices and had lost multiple branches to Pax Machina attacks. And, apparently, one to the fall of Ambara.

No response came to Aawee's exclamation, not even static. *Right, let's get back to open water. I can ask Kerick to bring a few repeaters so we can get signal while we explore.* They pushed off from the wall and swam towards the exit. The water around them vibrated with a disturbing percussive rumble. Aawee hesitated, drifting as they clicked in an effort to figure out what was causing it.

Ahead of them, the door closer mechanism made a squealing, grinding noise, and then the door fell shut. A landslide of silt and rock cascaded down before it.

The structure around them shook, and Aawee sped to the now-blocked exit, concerned the entire building might crumple on top of them as well. They hit the exit hands-first and shoved. The far side was buried, and the door did not budge.

"Can anyone hear me?"

No answer.

Aawee spun and swam away from the door, then returned at ramming speed, striking it with their shoulder. The glassy surface of the door shuddered under the impact, but neither shifted nor cracked. Their shoulder ached, water swirling from the disruption. "Anyone?"

This was bad. *Don't panic,* Aawee told themself. *You'll just burn oxygen faster. First rule of diving.* The mer were genetically engineered mammals: mostly dolphin combined with human, plus a little betta fish for aesthetic purposes. Like other mammals, they needed to breathe air—only every ten minutes or so, granted, but they could still drown. Aawee had a scuba tank with them, but they'd emptied most of it already and been scheduled to resurface in half an hour.

At most, they had an hour left. Less if they panicked or expended all their energy in frantic efforts to break down the door.

They stilled their tail's nervous twitching and let themself drift beside the door, making an effort to relax. Aawee pulled their tracker from its holster: it too reported 'No Signal'. *They'll come look for me. Nguyen knows how much air I have left. She has the last location my tracker sent, too. They'll find me. With whatever equipment it takes to get me out.* This line of thought had become less reassuring instead of more so.

With slow motions, they pressed their fingers to the seam between door and frame, trying to determine what had made it fall and whether it was stuck for mechanical reasons or by the weight of rock and sediment outside. It was sealed into the frame, crushing aside the detritus that had lined the edges earlier. Aawee hadn't expected that, under the circumstances. Most of Ambara's buildings had been overengineered against catastrophe—not just the kind of crash Ambara had actually suffered, but turbulence, severe weather, pressure changes due to altitude, and suchlike. This structure must have had a particularly cautious engineer.

Aawee found a plate that might have been a mechanical release, and tried pressing it, to no effect. The hinges were on the outside, and the door closer mechanism at its top didn't budge when Aawee shoved at its levered arm. They went through the tools on their belt. Cutting through sky-tech Ambaran composites would take more power than anything man-portable could provide, but Aawee had a short pry bar.

They worked the narrow edge of the pry bar between frame and door, and spent several frustrating minutes trying to force the door to break inwards. Every time they thought it was about to give, the pry bar would pop loose instead. At length, Aawee returned the pry bar to its holster. Time to look for another way out.

They took a deep breath from the tank, then swam for the elevator shaft. Aawee guessed that the window they'd first glimpsed was on another floor. Perhaps the combination of building and ocean floor there would be thin enough to re-establish communication with their team.

The second-floor elevator doors were still sealed, but the third-floor doors had broken open. *I should find the stairwell*, Aawee thought, swimming out onto the third floor. The interior walls here had rotted away, leaving exposed structural columns and alloy frames. Static came over Aawee's earbud, and crackling words "—respond. I'm twenty-eight meters from your last—"

"Strong! Thank the Engineers!" Aawee swam upwards into the darkness, hoping to strengthen the signal.

"Aawee! I'm twenty-eight—wait, twenty-two—meters from your current position. Are you underground? How did you get there?"

Aawee explained as they reached the building's upper wall. They found the pane they'd cleared from the outside earlier, while Kerick met them on the opposite side.

Kerick was a sedecpus, an engineered species based on the octopus. He looked much like an octopus, but with sixteen serpentine arms instead of eight, and with a hide dappled by bioluminescent spots. Aawee thought Kerick was gorgeous, all sleek unfurling grace and star-dusted skin, but never more so than at this moment.

Kerick increased the brightness of his glow, resting two arms against his side of the glass. "Aawee, I want you to know that I had prepared an entire angry rant about the importance of continuous contact and not panicking your team lead by disregarding it, and I am very sorry that I don't get to use it on you now."

Through the glass, Aawee touched one hand to Kerick's arms. "Me too. Thank you for panicking and rushing to see what happened to me."

"You're welcome. We're gonna get you out, don't worry." Kerick set a repeater down on the glass and activated it. "Skarvald, come to this location. Nguyen, get the heavy drill ready to deploy. Egebe, fetch the drill from Nguyen and come to our location. I'm gonna search for another way in. Any ideas, Aawee?"

"There was a little crevice uphill from our position," Aawee suggested. "It was too small for me but maybe you could get through? I don't know if it leads in or not."

"I'll check it out. Explore if you wanna, but get back in contact the second you hear static, got it?" The repeater would reinforce signals in and out, so the area surrounding it should have coverage now.

"Yes sir." Rather than splitting off, Aawee swam uphill, following the path they expected Kerick to be on. The third-floor ceiling panels had rotted away, but most of the subfloor beyond was intact.

Kerick's tracker reported his location as moving past it, about four meters higher than the outer wall. "Found the crevice, going in now." The tracker moved down a couple of meters. "Found a grate." A few moments later, "Can't get it off. There's a big hole in it, gonna try and squirm through that. If I lose signal for a minute, don't panic."

"What if it's two minutes, can we panic then?" Skarvald asked.

"Uh… gimme ten. Then panic." Kerick added something else, but it was too broken for Aawee to make out.

"Got it, boss. Panicking in ten minutes: mark."

* * *

Kerick crawled through a damaged, partly-crumpled ventilation shaft. Like his octopus ancestors, his body had no bones. Hence, while he had far more mass than Aawee, he could nonetheless squeeze into places that were much too narrow for a mer. His main concern was that the shaft might grow too tight for the equipment he was towing behind him. He'd removed his utility belt and tilted the holsters for his tools to align lengthwise with it, and arranged them smallest to largest. If his second repeater got stuck, he'd leave it behind.

If the tanks didn't fit, he'd back out and look for a different way in. The whole reason to go in was to resupply Aawee with air.

He would have done the same for any diver, of course. But Kerick knew that the urgency he felt was fueled by more than the ordinary worry one might have for any trapped person. Nor was it due to the trauma Rick associated with drowning, although that didn't help.

No; Kerick liked Aawee, probably more than he should like one of his subordinates. Not only because they were both trans and members of water-dwelling species, but because Aawee was bright, observant, and curious. Because they had a ready smile and an open, inviting demeanor. The thought of them being hurt was unbearable.

Kerick's leading arms felt a jagged hole ahead, and metal poles thrust through it. Rick, his cybernetic implant, analyzed the structure of the poles: the metal frame of a chair, which had broken into the shaft during the impact when the building fell. Kerick wrapped the ends of his tentacles about the poles and pushed them through the hole and out of his way. Then he pulled himself through, boiling from the opening in a proliferation of arms, big head squished through at the center of the mass. As he drew his utility belt after him, Aawee swam to his side.

«You did it!» Aawee beamed at him, using waterspeech instead of their vocalizers, then adjusted the angle on a tank for him so it could get through the gap. The smile made Kerick's hearts accelerate, his own reaction reminding him that his attraction to the mer was inappropriate. He was uncomfortably aware of Aawee's body: the supple ease with which they moved through the water, the sublime beauty of their translucent glimmering rainbow frills, the way the sheath of their swimsuit hugged the curving lines of their form, buckled straps securing it around their frills.

Aawee was still speaking. «Engineers, Strong, I don't think I've ever been so happy to see anyone. Thank you.»

«You're welcome,» Kerick answered in kind, although he was embarrassed by his waterspeech accent. Sedecpuses had better hearing than octopuses, plus modified beaks and a complex throat arrangement that allowed them to simulate mammalian speech even though they didn't breathe air. But it was an imperfect mimicry, and since Kerick had merged with Rick, his hearing had improved, so he'd become more aware of just how imperfect it was. The subvocalizer worked by learning what movements in the throat/palate meant for a particular user and transmitting the intended speech, rather than the user's literal voice. Thus, it largely disguised the oddness of Kerick's natural speech. After Kerick tugged the last of his items into the clear, Aawee wrapped their arms around the base of his head in a hug.

"I'm picking up your tracker again, Strong. Everything all right?" Skarvald asked on the subvocalizer.

"I'm in, but Aawee can't get out that way." Kerick wanted very much to return the hug and wasn't sure if that was a good idea.

Rick told him, without hesitation, that he should. // Perhaps they are equally fond of you! And level of affection notwithstanding, embraces are comforting. Aawee was concerned and we were concerned and comfort is important to sapients. Do not overthink this. // Kerick stopped overthinking it and wrapped most of his arms around Aawee, cradling them in a full-body embrace. Aawee curled their tail around two of Kerick's arms in response, relaxing. Kerick had to agree that this was very comforting. // I am always correct // the implant told him, without strict accuracy. // Remember to update the team. //

Kerick subvocalized, "The air tanks made it with me, so we'll be good for several hours. What's the ETA on the drill?"

"Thirty minutes or so. Nguyen and I are still prepping it." Egebe reported.

Briefly, Kerick contemplated spending the next half hour hugging Aawee. *That's too much, right?* he asked his implant. Rick felt this question depended on a number of nuances and was not a simple yes-or-no matter, but by then Aawee had pulled back a little. With some reluctance, Kerick unwound his arms from the mer and asked, «Wanna have a look around while we wait? This place is huge. I can't believe so much of it is still intact.»

Kerick remained concerned about the structure as a whole; as solid as it appeared, they still didn't know what had caused the door's abrupt collapse. But fretting about it would not get Aawee any closer to escaping, and exploring might.

«I know!» Aawee smiled at him again. «I hope some of the good tech survived. I think there's a directory in the lobby.» Together, they set up the second repeater in the middle of the third floor; the combination of it and the repeater outside would ensure their communication channels remained open. Kerick passed Aawee one of the three extra tanks he'd brought and took their current almost-empty one. The mer race had been designed for speed and acuity of senses, while the design of sedecpuses was more about strength and versatility. Extra baggage didn't hinder Kerick the way it would a mer.

Equipment exchanged, Aawee took one of Kerick's arm tips in their hand and led him down the elevator shaft.

They had to clear debris off the display panel beside the elevator. Underneath the glass, some of the letters had fallen from their places and drifted inside the case, but enough remained to work out the meaning. The first floor had been retail—a cafeteria and some small shops. Floors two through six held GloEx divisions. The second and third floor were administration, current files, and management, while the fourth had testing and prototype manufacturing. Research and experimentation was on the fifth, and the sixth was security and archives. The higher floors had held various individual offices for smaller businesses.

«Administration and management sound boring,» Kerick said. «Do you want to start with the fourth floor or the fifth?»

«'Prototypes' sound promising. Let's see if the stairwell's still here. I don't think the elevator doors were open on the fourth floor. The shaft is still intact for at least ten floors, though.»

After a short search, they found the stairwell. The stairs had partly collapsed, but the well was easy enough to swim through. While the two of them moved around the building, Kerick kept half an ear on the chatter on the subvocalization channels, letting Rick field any informational queries.

Kerick's implant also offered him some relevant data regarding their salvage. «Oh! This is promising,» the sedecpus said to Aawee. «GloEx was working on all-purpose underwater drones when Ambara fell. For undersea exploration and recovery.»

«Ooh! And if the building survived, surely those would!» Aawee pushed open the fourth floor door and swam out into a kind of corridor. Some of the interior walls on the far side of this level remained solid, including a room-sized shape with concrete walls. Still, as with the third floor, most of the interior walls were gone save for the remnants of framing and structural columns.

«How do you know what GloEx was working on forty-five years ago?» Aawee asked. «Were you hoping we'd find this building?»

«Nah, not specifically,» Kerick said. «But my implant has lots of storage. He's got all the news articles and press releases from or about Ambara at the time of the fall. He indexes and searches it for useful info whenever he's not working on something else.»

Detritus drifted in the water around them or had settled against the lowest wall: the remnants of the wall panels, the bases of stools whose seats had rotted away, broken table tops, and more. The heavier objects, including several metal cabinets as well as less identifiable wreckage, had sunk to where the bottom wall met the floor. Aawee swam towards that end. Glancing over their shoulder, they asked, «How did you end up with a fancy implant like that, anyway? It—sorry, he—sounds like he's worth a fortune. I thought the Reclamation Project kept that kind of tech reserved for humans only.»

«He is, and they do, generally. It's kinda a long story…»

Aawee smiled, gesturing to the walls blocking them in. «I'm not going anywhere.»

In answer, Kerick curled his arm tips outwards—the sedecpus version of a smile—then jetted after them. «So seven years ago, the CFO of the Ambara Survey and Reclamation Initiative, Richard Chung, acquired a top-of-the-line AI implant, which he named Rick. Rick gave Chung perfect recall and could also download and store a library's worth of information. But the AI's big advantage is in processing; Rick can search and organize his data and draw conclusions based on it, same way a person does. Because Rick is a person.»

The sedecpus joined Aawee beside the wreckage, and the two started going through it. Kerick was both larger and stronger than Aawee, his sixteen flexible arms giving him an advantage in bracing and pulling. Both of them took some care with the skeletal remains mixed among the furnishings, clearing a section of wall to place the bones. The clothing of the dead had decayed away and the bones picked clean by scavengers, but some plastic employee badges had survived, displaying the smiling human faces that had once belonged to these remains. Kerick had no particular fondness for humans, but they'd deserved better than this fate.

As they worked, Kerick continued his story. «Chung was human, but his favorite hobby was scuba diving. He decided to explore the Avention cave systems. Despite his implant's warnings. Long story short, the currents favored Chung going in and he underestimated how long it would take him to get out.»

// He terminated my processes, // Rick said in Kerick's head. // Because I sent a barrage of alerts warning him that he needed to leave. I had started the alerts an hour before he drowned. Perhaps if I had been less cautious, waited longer, he would not have dismissed me—//

«It wasn't Rick's fault. He did everything he could,» Kerick said aloud. *I'll never turn you off*, Kerick promised the implant, for the hundredth time. By now, he and Aawee had shifted enough refuse from the heap to expose the front of one cabinet. The door was already twisted; Kerick wrenched it open. There wasn't anything of apparent value inside; Kerick shifted it to one side with due care. His team would triage for the most interesting salvage, but depending on what their initial sweep found, later teams might go over the find in close detail.

Aawee grimaced. «So Chung drowned? While Rick watched? That sounds traumatic.»

«Yeah, it was. Chung had deactivated Rick halfway through the dive, but turned him back on before he died, in the hopes the AI could save him. By then, it was too late. The 'Claimers offered a bounty for anyone who could recover Chung's body, so I was one of those searching for him. When I found his corpse, the implant took root in me. Rick needed a living host to supply him with energy; he was decaying without one. They're not supposed to root in just anyone, but they have desperation coding to keep them from being destroyed. Of course, the 'Claimers wanted to remove him, but Rick liked me and refused to leave. So they ended up hiring me instead.»

Aawee laughed, a clicking *ki-ki-ki* sound. «I'm surprised they cared what either of you want.»

«I think they didn't want to risk damaging Rick. He's a lot smarter than other similar implants and no one's sure why or how to replicate that success. Also, it's not safe to put an angry sapient implant in a new host.» The next cabinet had fallen face-down, and Kerick wrapped his arms around it to flip it.

«Heh, I'll bet.» Aawee took the opposite end, helping the sedecpus right it. «Funny how you have 'Rick' as part of your name just like Chung did. Is that why Rick liked you?»

«Not exactly.» Kerick paused with the cabinet on its side, not sure how to explain this. «My given name was 'Ke' before I met Rick. I added his name to mine because … I feel like a different person with him in my head. Not in a creepy 'the-AI-took-over-my-mind' way,» he added, quickly. «I feel like a better version of myself, one who knows more stuff and can figure things out faster, and that's because I can rely on him. So it's kinda symbolic, showing he's my partner by reflecting him in my name.» Kerick twined some of his arms together, embarrassed. «Why are you looking at me like that?»

Aawee was resting their webbed hands against the cabinet, their expression contemplative. At Kerick's question, they smiled. «That's just… it sounds really sweet, you know? Considerate. Like one of those married couples that take the same surname.»

// You may tell them I concur, // Rick said. // It was not the reason I wished to retain you as my host, but it is indicative of those reasons. //

«Rick thought it was nice too. Well, obviously, I wouldn't've done it if he thought it was weird or icky.» Kerick waved a few arm tips, feeling foolish. He turned back to the cabinet and lay it on its back, then reached for the handle of the unwarped door.

Aawee put a hand over his arm. «Wait.» They clicked again, attention on the cabinet. «It's watertight.»

«What, seriously?» Kerick studied it with one large eye, brightening his bioluminescence. «After forty-five years?»

«There's air inside. We should wait until we get it on the boat before opening it.»

«Excellent.» Kerick wrapped several arms about it and carried it a little higher on the slope of the former wall, setting it aside for later. Rick speculated with enthusiasm on the possible contents; the implant thought it unlikely GloEx would have used a watertight cabinet that could withstand the pressure of these depths for something as mundane as office supplies.

«So,» Aawee tried to wrangle a bent cabinet's door open. «Was Rick assigned male or is he trans too?»

That startled a clicking laugh out of Kerick. «Rick says 'It's complicated.'»

«Isn't it always?» Aawee swished to one side as Kerick swam back and opened the cabinet for them.

«Even for AIs. He was coded to adopt a gender identity based on his host's preference. Chung wanted him to be male, because Chung was.» The interior of the cabinet was full of water and disintegrating papers. Kerick eyed them with regrets. «And then, uh, Rick kind of converted me to male.»

Aawee was reaching past the papers to feel at the back of the cabinet, but arrested mid-motion, gaping at Kerick. «You're kidding. Your implant made you trans?»

«No, no, I already wanted to be trans.» Kerick waved a few arm tips through the water in a warding motion. «I always thought gender was fascinating and wished I had one. And Rick told me, 'If you want

to be trans then you are trans. Just take a gender. Who can stop you?'
So I did. A few sedecpuses I know think it's a little ridiculous or
pretentious, but it's not like there are a lot of us. Everyone else just
goes along with me. Most of them don't even know enough about
sedecpuses to know my species doesn't reproduce sexually.»

«Well, good for you.» Aawee gave him a warm, approving smile.
«And good for Rick, too. I don't know what the Engineers were
thinking, designing sedecpuses the way they did. 'Sure, let's design
this sex fantasy species and then not give them a sex drive, that'll be
a great joke on every other species.' The Engineers were the *worst*.»

Kerick did know why his species had been designed that way:
the genetic engineers who'd made sedecpuses had been concerned
by the rate at which other engineered species were breeding 'in the
wild', and wanted to control the sedecpus population. So sedecpuses
could only reproduce via a drug cocktail that made them bud a new
sedecpus. But that wasn't the part of Aawee's statement that drew
him up short, arms dangling limp as he gazed at them. *Did they say
'sex fantasy'?*

// I told you they are fond of you, // Rick crowed.

Aawee caught his look and covered their mouth with one hand,
mortified. «Oh, no, I'm sorry, that was—I can't believe I said that, I
didn't mean that *you* are—I'm sorry, please forget I said anything.»
They curled their tail, pushing away from him in the water. «That
was wildly inappropriate, argh, boss, I am so sorry.» Aawee spun
about and busied themself at the next cabinet.

Kerick didn't want to forget it; he wanted to ask a dozen follow-
up questions, and also to reassure Aawee that they were fine and
he wasn't upset, but thought maybe he should at least pretend he'd
forgotten it. *I am their boss and this topic is inappropriate.*

Instead of weighing in on this train of thought, Rick presented
him with a heat map image of their surroundings. // Some of these
structural columns have grown a few degrees warmer since we
arrived, and there's a new vibration in the water. I think there are
systems still active here. //

Kerick stilled himself completely. He subvocalized on the team
channel, "Aawee, do you feel that? The vibration in the water?"

Aawee went still as well. "That's a mechanical hum," they said. "Is it the motor on the drill?" The drill was large and awkward enough to maneuver that it needed its own propulsion system.

"I'm only a couple hundred meters out now," Egebe answered. "Might be me."

"Rick says it's from the building, not you, Egebe. This place has a waterproof power source and it's still operating." Kerick sought out Aawee's gaze.

"Wow." Their eyes widened, then Aawee grinned at him. "The Reclamation Project will love this find."

"I'm coming in to the repeater," Egebe said. "Are you going to keep poking your appendages into things or are you meeting us there?"

"We'll meet you there." Without thinking about it, Kerick curled an arm tip around one of Aawee's hands to lead them back to the stairwell, and then wondered why he'd done that. Aawee's webbed fingers clasped about his arm and Kerick decided not to question the matter.

∗ ∗ ∗

When they reached the third floor, Aawee and Kerick held position well back from the window, with ear protection in place. Egebe and Skarvald wrangled the drill into position. They were both women; Egebe an anthro wolf and Skarvald a ground-born human. Ocean-dwelling sapients like sedecpuses and mer were scarce and often less motivated by wealth than land-dwelling species. Aawee personally had taken the job more to access the Reclamation Project's health programs than anything else. Hence, even for underwater work, the Reclamation Project often relied on land-dwellers.

Aawee was glad the rest of the team had arrived. The mer was thrilled at the scale of their find and the fact that some of the tech had proven to be not only intact but still functioning *right now* was astonishing. The finder's fee bonus for this would be at least a year's salary, if not more.

But if the building's systems were still active, that meant that the door locking them in earlier might have been caused by the building, rather than a freak accident. Aawee didn't want to be trapped in here if any of the other security measures were still working.

The team hadn't used the drill on an artificial composite before—they usually used it for cutting through stone—but Nguyen had checked its specifications. It was diamond-tipped and rated to cut through most anything short of titanium or steel armor. Once Egebe and Skarvald had the drill locked in place, they shut down the maneuvering engine and turned on the drill. The building and the water alike shuddered, the grinding squeal of drill against the glass-like composite piercing even through the sound-dampeners Aawee wore.

"Shut it down!" Kerick's order came through the subvocalizer earbud, underneath the sound dampeners, so it was audible despite the noise. "Get back, there's something—"

Aawee realized something was grinding behind the subfloor a moment before steel plates slammed down over the far side of the window, breaking the lock the drill had against the pane and knocking the bit loose with the force of its impact. The plates burrowed through layers of silt and small rocks to cover the entirety of the windows.

The rest of the building was still shaking, and it wasn't from the broken drill.

"So that seems bad," Aawee said, with a calm they didn't feel. A distant alarm was whooping elsewhere in the building. "Egebe? Skarvald? You all right?" Static crackled in answer, but Aawee couldn't make out any words.

«Those are probably hurricane shutters, but let's clear out of the GloEx floors. The small businesses are less likely to have security measures.» Kerick curled an arm tip about Aawee's hand as the two of them swam for the stairwell.

Aawee resisted as they neared it, warned by sonar. «There's something moving in the stairwell. Several somethings.»

«Exploration drones, maybe? …Yay, they still work?» Kerick let Aawee steer them towards the elevator shaft instead. «They're using shortwave radio to communicate with each other. Rick's trying to decode it.»

«Can he talk to them if he does?»

«No, he only has a receiver, not a transmitter. Security precaution.»

Aawee entered the elevator shaft, and then ducked back out at once. A projectile whizzed past from the top of the shaft. «The drones are *armed*?!»

«We'd better try hiding.» Kerick pulsed downwards, towards the wreckage from the offices that had piled against the ground-facing wall. With seven of his arms, he reached out to grab suspended debris and send it spinning through the surrounding water. «Rick worked out the encoding, it's similar to our subvocalizers. They're using motion sensors to look for us, so once we go still they may ignore us.»

«Kerick—» Aawee said, forgetting themself. «You need to escape.»

«How? We still don't have a route for you.»

«*You* can escape!»

A pair of drones emerged from the stairwell. Kerick was close enough to the bottom now to snag a flat rectangle of metal—probably a tabletop—between two tentacles, and interposed it between them and the drones as a shield. Two harpoons launched towards them, but neither penetrated. «I'm not leaving without you!»

More drones were coming out from both the stairwell and the elevator shaft. They spread out above them «Look, there's no reason for both of us to—»

«I'm not leaving you!» Kerick shouted. He snaked two arms around the shaft of one harpoon as the drone reeled it back, and yanked hard enough to pull the drone into an arc until it hit the subfloor between the third and fourth floors.

Sonar showed Aawee there were some gaps in the subfloor now. The steel plates that had sealed the windows on all sides had come from the subfloor, and had been covering those holes. They abandoned trying to make Kerick see reason and gestured to the nearest opening. «I don't think hiding's going to work at this point.»

«You go, I'll distract them.»

«Kerick—»

«You're a faster swimmer—» Kerick released the harpoon, most of his arms reaching around and beneath him to grab any loose debris and fling it upwards. The water between them and the drones filled with moving objects. A couple of drones fired harpoons at the growing debris field. «Get to the upper floors and out of GloEx's area. That's an order!» One of Kerick's arms wrapped about Aawee's tail and flung them like a spear towards the gap.

Aawee wasn't sure whether they were more touched by Kerick's determination to see them safe or angry at his authoritarian attitude, but there was no arguing with momentum. They swam for the hole, passing by as a harpoon thunked into a drifting drawer a meter to their right. The debris Kerick had been throwing around was distracting the drones' targeting systems. Aawee's sonar was muddied by the uneven pulse of the alarm, louder on the fifth floor, but it suggested a couple of drones were redirecting from the stairwell to follow the mer.

Aawee located another gap in the next subfloor and wormed their way through it. When they reached the sixth floor, some of the interior walls were intact on it: an entire corner where the walls still stood, with one door hanging ajar. They found another opening into the seventh floor and continued to it. "Kerick, I'm on seven, what's your status?"

A too-long silence, and then, "Had better days. Drones can receive on this line, don't send again. Stay safe. Get out if you can."

Aawee swam in a tight circle, frustrated. *Get out if I can? You could've been long gone if you'd just left when I told you to!* Like most of the other floors, the interior walls on the seventh were largely gone, although the elevator shaft and the stairwell remained solid. The building exterior walls were too thick for Aawee's sonar, even without the distortion of the alarm. However, reflected sound showed the stairwell door was missing and drones were emerging from it. Aawee ducked back into the subfloor as three drones came out. They moved in the mer's direction. *So much for 'the non-GloEx floors will be safe.' New plan.*

They returned to the sixth floor and to its intact corner. The door into it was open but undamaged, with a plaque reading "SECURITY." Aawee zipped through and closed it behind them, jamming their pry bar into the door mechanism to block it from opening again.

Emergency lighting glowed in the interior and the complaint of the alarms dulled with the door closed. A bank of security monitors against one wall were mostly dead, like the two skeletons that rested atop them, but a couple were active. One of them had a split screen, showing nine different drone-mounted cameras. Three of those cameras were drawing closer to Kerick, showing a chaotic scene of turbulent water, debris, and whirling sedecpus limbs. A horizontal desk rested against the wall that was now the bottom of the room. Three monitors were atop it, two dead and one displaying ALL DEFENSES ACTIVE.

Aawee darted to the desk and pressed a finger to the "unlock" icon in the corner of the screen.

'Authentication not found,' the display read. "Engineers forget you—" Aawee swore, sweeping their eyes over the desk for anything useful. A conduit from the wall was labeled "GNDN-1701," next to the corroded remains of a filing cabinet, the battered remains of chairs—and a small box with a card slot.

The motor in the door mechanism behind Aawee made a grinding noise. The mer turned to the skeletons, flipping the nearest one over. A plastic ID badge on a coiled metal leash lay beneath the ribcage.

Something banged against the door.

Aawee snagged the badge, inserted it into the slot, then touched the unlock icon again.

Enter password.

«Come *on*! Your security was so bad it's still notorious and *now* you have two-factor auth—» Aawee's eyes fell on conduit label. They punched 'GNDN-1701' in on the touchscreen keyboard as the banging grew louder.

The touchscreen cleared to show dozens of alert and failure messages. Aawee stabbed at "cancel" and "shutdown" icons as fast as their fingers could move.

The door behind them dented inwards as Aawee frantically hit icons.

The drone cameras on the split screen went dark, one after another. The door closer squealed, grinding harder against the pry bar, and then the banging stopped.

Aawee kept punching icons until there wasn't anything left to shut down except the operating system itself. They stared at the cleared screen, feeling a kind of blurry shock, and then sagged. "Kerick? Status? Can you hear me?"

Static made Kerick's reply crackle, but it was intelligible: "I hear you. What happened? The drones just stopped."

"I shut them down from security on the sixth floor." Aawee swam back to the door. They tried to retrieve their pry bar, but the door mechanism was warped around it.

"I ordered you to leave the GloEx area."

"It turned out the seventh floor wasn't safe either." Aawee tried the door. It was wedged shut.

"… thank you for not listening to me. Are you all right?"

"I'm fine. I, uh, might need you to come rescue me from an even smaller box than the box I'd already trapped myself in when you came to rescue me the last time."

Kerick laughed. "On my way."

* * *

Kerick paused at the vent between the third and fourth floors to place the interior repeater there, and stayed by it long enough to assure his team that he and Aawee were all right. With the outside repeater broken and the windows reinforced, they couldn't get a clear signal through most of the building.

Headquarters was sending another drill and the team was surveying the area to see if there was an easier place to break through than the now-defended windows. "Aawee might be able to get the shutters to retract. We'll get back to you soon."

The door proved to be jammed as much by the mass of the drone that had deactivated while trying to break it down as by the pry bar and the damaged mechanism. Kerick moved the drone aside and wrangled the dented door open enough to let Aawee slip out. The mer had a GloEx badge hung about their neck, and pressed another into one of Kerick's arm tips as they circled him anxiously. «How are you?» Aawee demanded. «You're bleeding—!»

«I'm fine.» Kerick was tempted to hide his injured limbs but Rick advised against it. // To what purpose? You need not be macho and aawee is not a child who would be deceived by such antics. // The sedecpus uncurled the two gashed arms, blood trailing through the water, and offered them for examination instead. «It looks worse than it is. I can regrow entire limbs if necessary. They'll stop bleeding soon.»

Aawee *tsk*ed at him and took out their first aid kit to apply an antiseptic sealant to the gashes. «Just because the Engineers blessed you with a robust immune system is no reason to invite infection.»

«Yes, Aawee.» Kerick submitted meekly, somewhere between chastened and pleased at the mer's concern. «Why did you give me the GloEx badge for—» he lifted it before one large eye «—Faraji Tanaka?»

«So the security systems will identify us as employees instead of intruders. I think I shut everything down but it doesn't hurt to be sure.» Gently, Aawee tapped down the edges of the sealant and moved to the next arm.

«Good plan. Although it still beats me why their security drones are armed with harpoons.»

Aawee grinned at him as they finished sealing the second gash. «They're not security drones! They're prototype underwater all-purpose drones. The security computer brought them online because it had access to them and the security drones wouldn't activate. But the door to their storage vault wouldn't open. So they were stuck until the building put the hurricane shutters down, and that opened a gap in the ceiling above them.»

«You figured all that out from a forty-five year old computer system?» Kerick gave them an admiring look.

«I just scanned through the logs while I was stuck in the security room.» Aawee eyed Kerick, as if suspecting him of teasing. Kerick brightened his bioluminescent spots to project an aura of angelic innocence. The mer tried and failed to fight down a smile, then fell forward to wrap their arms about the base of Kerick's head. «Thank you for saving me. Again.»

This time, Kerick didn't wait for Rick to encourage him before enfolding Aawee in all sixteen of his arms. «You're welcome.» Rick prodded at him and Kerick added, «Also, thank you for saving me. Fighting off the drones wasn't going as well as I'd hoped.»

// To put it mildly, // Rick said, with a hint of rebuke.

Kerick replied, *It's not like we had a lot of good choices.*

// True enough. //

Aawee was chuckling at him. «You're welcome. So you're not going to recommend the Reclamation Project fire me for disobeying orders?»

«Never. I'm gonna tell them you deserve a bonus for salvaging this situation.» Kerick curled his arms a little more snugly around Aawee. «I mean, not only did you find this building, but then you kept me from wrecking all the very valuable drones that had survived its fall.» *I should let them go now. This is probably too long for a thank-you-for-saving-me embrace.* He shifted his arms, but only caressed the curve of Aawee's tail instead.

The mer laughed again, nestling into him. «I guess we should get back to the repeater so we can get in touch with the team. Oh right, we were going to try to get the computer to open the shutters. Hey, maybe we can get it to open the front door. I bet the silt covering it would be easier to move than breaking through the windows.» Aawee brightened at the prospect, but they made no effort to disentangle from Kerick's limbs. One of their hands stroked the back of Kerick's head.

// You should ask them on a date, // Rick told Kerick. // They are fond of you and we both admire them. //

But they're a mer and I'm a—

// You are, and I quote, 'a sex fantasy.' //

Which they immediately told me to forget and that they didn't mean me, specifically!

// Because they believe you to be asexual and did not wish to give offense! You cannot press all the burden of the initiative upon them. Offer them a little encouragement. //

But they're my subordinate. It'd be an abuse of authority—

Rick gave a little burst of neural activity that was the AI's way of indicating mere words were inadequate to convey the contempt it felt. // You are cowering behind excuses. Yes, yes, that is a legitimate concern but it is also one you can negotiate by being open about your intentions with both your subordinates and your superiors. Invite Aawee on a date. I promise you the question will not destroy you, Aawee, or your respective careers. //

…promise?

// Promise. //

Aawee had been content to drift, snuggled in Kerick's arms, while the sedecpus wrestled with his AI. Kerick wondered for a moment if Aawee's own internal monologue had been anything like his, even if they didn't have an AI to take the counterpart. He gathered his courage. «So…»

«Mm?»

«It's been quite a day. Once we get out of here, would you like to… go somewhere and unwind? With me?» Kerick cringed. That sounded terrible, didn't it? How do sexually reproducing species do this?

// Poorly, // Rick told him, sanguine.

Aawee made a happy little squeaking sound. «Really? I'd love to!» They drew back just enough to meet his eyes, beaming.

«You would?» Kerick said, astonished. Rick said, // Just as I informed you. And I am always correct. // «It's a date, then?»

Aawee gave another happy squeak, smile widening even further as they nodded. They tugged Kerick towards the security room door; the two had drifted away from it while hugging. «C'mon, let's figure out the system controls for this building. I don't want to be late for this date!»

The Underground Star

Nenekiri Bookwyrm

Eli was running so fast he could hear the blood pumping in his long fluffy ears as he alternated between sprinting and hopping down the narrow corridors. He was being chased, but there was a certain allure to it. Something deep inside himself gave him a boost whenever he was running from something dangerous, maybe a leftover from the time before there were uplifted rabbits scurrying through the underground warrens. It was difficult to pin down exactly where that energy came from, but Eli used it all the same. Zipping through the underground passages and getting further and further away from the yells and squeaks coming from behind him.

He almost slipped as he ducked into a room he hadn't seen before and leaned against the wall to catch his breath. Running his paws through his ears, he slowly slumped down the wall until he was sitting on the floor. The floor was cool to the touch, tinted the familiar dark brown stone that was common to this section of the Warrens.

A 'Claimer ship had crashed here, back when Eli was just a child, penetrating all the way through the surface. Something to do with the war, maybe. Now this area was mostly abandoned and rarely visited, making it the perfect spot for a group of rowdy rabbits to burn off some energy.

Eli could still remember his Mom shielding his eyes from the bright lights of the 'Claimers' ship as it crashed. There were rumors spread afterwards that some of the Reclaimer technology had been scattered throughout the caverns by the wreck. And of course, 'Claimer technology was dangerous and was not to be touched by the rabbits and rodents that lived there, lest they get seriously hurt. Eli thought it was all exaggeration though. Rules set up by the adults to keep kids out of places they didn't feel like fetching them from. This, coincidentally, was also why Eli spent so much time over here.

He had just about caught his breath when he looked up and gasped. The room wasn't very wide, only about fifty feet or so, but it was tall. The crash had a funny way of reshaping some of the older sections of the Warrens, and this was no exception. The room was several stories high and smack dab in the center of it was a massive gleaming tower of junk that reached into the sky.

The tower was nearly as tall as the room and Eli found that he had to crane his neck back to get the full breadth of its metallic beauty. There was machinery sticking out at odd and incomprehensible angles, from every possible corner of the structure and yet somehow, it looked stable. Almost as if it was reaching out with its metal spires, begging to be climbed. At the top of the spire of meandering metal was a particular object of interest to Eli. It gleamed far brighter than any of the other pieces of metal that made up the tower's base, so he knew it had to be special. A natural prize for scaling the metal mountain in an otherwise unnatural formation. He was just about to get up when he felt a familiar paw touch him on the shoulder.

"Tag! You're it!" cried the smaller mouse.

Eli looked over to him and cracked a small smile.

"That's not fair! I was distracted, Jack!" Eli said.

"Oh, when aren't you distracted, Eli? You're just sore I beat you for once." Jack pushed up his oversized glasses back onto the bridge of his snout and wiggled his nose reflexively. His attire could best be described as rags that were stitched together in the loose approximation of clothes. Although small, he looked bulkier than he actually was due to an oversized cream-colored scarf that his family had given him. It contrasted quite nicely with his dark brown fur.

Jack adjusted the scarf around his neck and torso and tapped his foot impatiently. Eli didn't notice, already looking at the tower's top again, but stopped long enough to look around for the rest of his friends. When he couldn't find them, he frowned and looked back over to Jack.

"Where'd everyone else go? They give up on finding me?"

"No, they just got lost. You always manage to confuse everyone when you duck into these hallways. They're probably still looking for us out there."

Jack turned around and started heading for the door before Eli stopped him. "Hold on a minute! Do you not see the huge pile of metal in here? Isn't that interesting to you at all?"

Eli spun Jack around by his shoulders so that he was face to face with the great metal spire and waited for his reaction. But Jack wasn't moved by the pile at all.

"It's a big tower, so what? There are bigger ones up on the surface. And I hear there's even bigger ones in the 'Claimers' sky cities. And up there, they're not made out of junk."

"Yeah but it's definitely the tallest thing in the Warrens by far. Aren't you curious how it got here?"

Jack just shrugged and replied, "I'm more curious when you're gonna stop stalling and get back to the game." With that he turned around and jogged out of the room calling behind him, "C'mon! It's your turn to be it after all!"

Eli looked back to the small shining dot at the top of the tower, promised himself that he'd come back and find out what it was, then turned around and hopped out of the room to find his friends.

* * *

It was a few weeks before Eli had the chance to make his way over there again. His Mom had scolded him once she had found out about the last little excursion; Eli could still see his Mom with her hands on her hips as she tapped her foot impatiently, waiting on an answer that he couldn't give her.

How could he explain to her that the Warrens were so dreadfully boring? Or that he felt alive when he got to cut loose and hop at full speed through those twisty underground caverns? She couldn't possibly understand how he felt being cooped up with all the other smaller animals every day. So, he did the next best thing and apologized for worrying her so much. She shook her head and went back to fixing the small machine that was left on the kitchen table and that was that. Now that he was here, he felt ashamed that he would be worrying his Mom again if she found out.

It was no small feat to get here either, since he'd found the path he took the last time completely by accident. Eli wandered around the underground caverns for hours until he found the same passageway. This time he made mental notes of what the hallways leading to it looked like; just for good measure, he marked the hole that lead to the tower with a piece of charcoal he found on the way.

As he stared at the imposing metal structure, he felt his long ears flop back against his head involuntarily. What was it about this thing that transfixed him so completely? Maybe it was the color of the tower itself? A shining silver that matched the grey hue found in his own fur. But there was more to it than that. Silver was the most prominent color, but there were hues of orange and blue scattered throughout if you looked hard enough. Eli absentmindedly rubbed his one paw through the fur on his head that had a very slight patch of white as he continued to stare at the structure.

The metal was interesting to him in a familiar kind of way. His Mom worked on repairing machines for the people of the Warrens, so he was used to seeing the colors of the metal that would pass through her hands at their home. This was definitely the first time he had seen so much metal in one place though. Then his eye caught that distinctive glint at the top of the tower again and he reflexively smiled. That was what he was here for! He wanted so badly to be able to hold that shining relic in his own paws. If he could get up this tower, then he'd have something that was irrefutably his.

Eli had obsessed about how he was going to get it for weeks, but now that he was faced with the reality, his plans seemed to flake apart like rust. He ended up doing the first thing that came to mind in that moment and picked up a nearby rock. Getting a slight running start to put some more heft behind the throw, he lobbed it best as he could at the top of the tower. The rock spun wildly in the air, quickly losing altitude, and clanked off of a scrap of metal close to the base. The rock clattered to the ground and bounced a few feet before rolling to a stop a few steps away.

Eli was disappointed for a second, until he had an idea. He felt around the scrap metal very carefully, until he found a piece he could use to chip off pieces of the rock until it was smooth and aerodynamic. Satisfied with his handiwork, Eli took the stone back to the entrance of the room and tossed it a few times straight up in the air to measure how heavy it was now. Confident that his modifications would be good enough to get the stone to the top, he wound up and tossed the stone overhand so hard he heard his wrist crack from the force. As he rubbed at his throwing hand, he watched the trajectory of the projectile intently.

The stone flew much farther this time. For a brief moment, it looked as though it was going to hit the shining object and Eli held his breath in anticipation, willing it along with his thoughts, but then the rock dropped dead and clanked on the tower and wedged between two particularly odd sheets of metal. Seeing the mark of his failure jutting out from the tower, Eli felt horrible. It was going to take a lot more than a half-baked plan on the spot if he was going to grab that treasure for himself.

* * *

Three months passed in the twitch of his whiskers before Eli had the chance to go back. He had been busy helping the other residents around his and his Mom's warren with "upkeep of the area"— usually loosely defined as a catch-all for Eli to keep busy as his Mom worked on machine repairs during her busy season. With winter fast approaching the residents were eager to have any kind of machine that could help them stay warm or clear out the snow from cavern openings. Eli spent most days cleaning alone, brushing the dust out of the warren entryways and later out of his fur. He didn't enjoy it, but the repetitive action of moving the stiff broom gave him an opportunity to collect his thoughts and come up with some new plans for scaling the tower.

It was during one of these moments of intense thought that a familiar voice called out to him. "You tryin' to sweep the whole street away? You should stop while you're ahead!"

The voice belonged to Irene Smits, one of the few human inhabitants of the Warrens. She'd moved into the area shortly after the crash in Ambara Down. No one was ever sure if she was originally from the 'Claimer ship and survived, but she helped out the folks in the Warrens and that seemed more important. Her small store, The Bitten Ear, was a big boon to the area with medicine and access to general goods. She spoke with a youthful and energetic voice that betrayed the salt and pepper hair on her head. She looked down over a pair of glasses at Eli as he snapped to attention.

"Oh sorry, Ms. Smits! I must have gotten carried away there. Heh." Eli looked down as he rubbed the back of his head trying not to look ashamed.

Ms. Smits waved her hand dismissively and pushed her glasses back up onto her face.

"Oh, that's fine dear, I figured that if you were done with your Mother's den that you'd want to sweep the storefront for me."

"I appreciate the offer Ms. Smits, but I should really get going. Mom's probably got a million other chores for me to get done before sunset."

Ms. Smits looked hurt, but then she smiled mischievously. "Oh, that's a shame! I was going to make it worthwhile after all. I know you've been staring at the pots and pans set lately."

Eli zipped over next to Ms. Smits so fast that a cloud of dirt kicked up behind his paws, settling gently over the bottom of the woman's skirt. She reached down and brushed the dust off and said, "I'll take that as a yes, then…"

She was good to her word; after Eli had sufficiently brushed off her store's front porch she came out with a small set of pots and a roll of bandages. "I see how fast you're moving around town and while I can't make you slow down; I can save you a trip over here."

She smiled warmly as she placed the packages into Eli's paws. He was about to say something when he caught the long shadows through the rooftop openings. He had to get going if he wanted to try out his latest plan! He ran over to his den, just barely grabbing a bag at the front door, before tearing off down the street. He called over his shoulder as he ran, "Thanks a bunch, Ms. Smits!"

Eli would only have a little bit of time to try scaling the tower today. He had to be home soon enough that he wouldn't get in trouble or he wouldn't be able to make attempts for weeks! He couldn't afford that loss in time, especially now that he was so close.

He dropped the bag as soon as he rushed into the room. The tower was there as always, silent and waiting for him. He wasted no time in putting his plan into action. In a blur of motion, he suited himself up with the odds and ends from his bag. A few minutes later he stood tall and proud in his makeshift armor, ready to slay the metal dragon that had vexed him for so many months. He wore the biggest pot on top of his head and strapped it down with some excess cloth he got from Jack. His paws and feet were covered in the bandages to give him some extra grip and in his right hand he held a soup ladle like a weapon, with a length of rope tied to its end so it could function as a makeshift grappling hook.

Eli hefted the ladle-hook and began his wind up. The sound of metal flying through the air could be heard for just a second followed by a slight *tink*. Eli tugged on the rope to make sure his anchor was steady and began climbing up it. He put paw over paw as he slowly made his way up the structure.

The tower itself was steady for the most part, but occasionally a piece of metal would come loose, threatening to toss him off. With repeated attempts, and marking off the dangerous spots, he had a small path that he could follow up to his ladle-hook. The new bandages on his paws and feet meant he could steady himself on the sharp pieces of metal without worrying that he was going to cut himself open. Bolstered by his new progress, he triumphantly grabbed the ladle-hook and gently hoisted himself up over that handhold and onto a toaster just above it. His breath was heavy but excited. This was farther than he had ever gotten and the prospect of making it to the top was nearer than ever. He went to push off with his left foot to grab the next available handhold…

And his foot gave way.

He went to catch himself on the toaster only to have that buckle under his full weight. He fell for a few seconds before catching himself on an opened washing machine door. He breathed a sigh of relief as he realized he hadn't fallen too far. Sure, this was a setback, but he could just follow the ladle-hook's rope back up to the spot again. The rope was even within reach! This trip could be salvaged after all.

He slowly reached out and tugged on the rope. The rope fell slack and Eli looked at it confused for a second before there was a *thunk* as the ladle-hook hit the top of his pot-helmet. This startled Eli enough to reach up and grab his helmet to try and grab the ladle as it fell. He very quickly realized his mistake as he plummeted down feet first towards the ground.

He screamed as the ground grew in size and racked his brain for a way to not die from this fall. An idea flashed in his mind, and he did his best to flip himself over so that his head was angled towards the base of the tower. His heart was pounding in his ears and he could feel the rush of the air on his fur as he closed his eyes, grit his teeth, and braced for impact.

KA-CLANK!!!

The pot hit a broken 'Claimer wing piece as Eli tumbled forward and used his powerful legs to cushion the blow just enough to roll the rest of the way to the ground safely. His head hurt terribly, but he'd hadn't cracked his skull. The pot, however, had a sizable dent where he had hit it. He rubbed at the divot. Ms. Smits wasn't kidding when she said the pots were extra durable.

He sighed, rubbed his sore head, and turned to walk home. His goal seemed impossibly far away and even after coming up with a much better plan, he was still nowhere close to making it to the top. He looked over to the smudge on the side of the room's entrance he had made earlier that year and stared into the blackness.

Inspiration struck. He grabbed his one foot and, balancing carefully against the side of the entrance, carved a design into the charcoal using his hind claws. Who ever said that grabbing the treasure of the underground caverns was going to be easy? 'Claimers had obviously been able to make ships and machines big and strong enough to reach for the stars. So, it should be more than possible for him to make something to reach his own star! He just had to keep at it.

Eli stepped back and looked at the design he had drawn in the charcoal and smiled. A simple star was carved out of the original mark and looking at it made Eli feel considerably better. It wouldn't be easy to reach his star, but it would be worth the reward at the end.

* * *

It was summer again before Eli knew it. Almost a year from the first time he had seen the tower in the underground. He didn't feel like that much time had passed already, but with how busy he was now, it must have slipped his mind.

He saw Jack and his other friends less and less, which sometimes wore at him, but what could he do about it? He still helped his Mom with sweeping occasionally but the majority of his time was spent working his new job. Ms. Smits had approached him a few days after his last failed attempt to climb the tower and offered him a position at her shop. Eli was hesitant at first, thinking the position would just involve more sweeping, but she assured him it would be more exciting.

"I'm not lying when I say that I think you're made for this job, Eli," she said excitedly. "I've been trying to get my goods out past the Warrens but it's difficult to justify buying a full caravan when I can only sell so much. And I can't exactly afford to buy all the supplies I would need to make that plan profitable either. But I have a backup plan!"

And at this comment, she held up a worn brown leather satchel with a sturdy strap attached to it. The bag looked as though it had been through some years of distress, with scratches on the front and some slight discoloration. Otherwise, it looked like a normal messenger bag.

"I want you to be my delivery man, Eli. I have some things I'd like to start selling outside of the Warrens and I'm going to need your help to do it."

Eli's eyes lit up at the opportunity to leave the Warrens. Perhaps there would be something out there that could help him climb the tower. And it wouldn't hurt to meet other folks either. It was starting to feel cramped in the Warrens for him, and this could be the biggest opportunity he'd have at getting a chance to breathe a little. There was just one thing that needed to be taken care of first.

"That sounds great, Ms. Smits, but how are we going to convince my Mom to let me? It's hard enough to get her to let me leave the burrow every day."

"Now don't you worry about that Eli, I'm sure that she'll be amenable to the idea once I talk to her about it. And the first few jobs I have for you are pretty close to town here, so you won't be traveling very far to start. So, how about it? Do you want the job?"

Eli tapped his one foot on the ground while he thought and after a few minutes responded with, "How much does it pay?"

She laughed and said, "I'll take that as a yes."

The next day Ms. Smits had loaded the satchel up with a variety of fresh produce and a small handwritten note. He was told that was the receipt for the food he would be delivering and that he shouldn't open it and read it, as folks didn't like their finances being known. Eli squirmed a little as she fitted the strap across his chest.

"The deliveries have to be made very quickly, in order for the food to stay fresh for the customer," Ms. Smits explained. "That's why I wanted you for the job. I've seen how fast you can move when you're properly motivated."

"But my Mom…"

"I'll handle all of that," said Ms. Smits. "The last thing we want is Heather having a nervous breakdown."

* * *

That delivery would turn out to be a success, as would the many deliveries after. Eli finally had the chance to meet and interact with other species than humans and the mostly-rodentia inhabitants of the Warrens. He met foxes, lizards, dogs, and cats most of the time and each one brought a new understanding to Eli. That the world outside the Warrens was much bigger than he had ever realized. And these people were only on the fringes of the Warrens, out in the settlements close by. Who knows what else he could find if he was allowed to travel even further? It gnawed at his mind and as time went on, he thought more and more about leaving the Warrens when he was old enough.

He wanted desperately to tell Jack the stories he had of his trips to the settlements, but he hadn't seen him for weeks now, which worried him. It wasn't like Jack to just disappear like that; he was a quiet kid, sure, but he was always somewhere in the Warrens. When he asked Jack's family where he was, they assured him that he was just sick. So, Eli convinced Ms. Smits to let him deliver some soup to their house to help Jack feel better. He would check in with him when he was over his cold. The time came and went, and Jack never reappeared. Life in the Warrens was like that, sometimes.

Ms. Smits always paid Eli on-time when he came back from a delivery. By the end of the summer, Eli had managed to save up enough money to put his next plan in motion. He bought a simple set of machinist's tools, stuffed them into his satchel, and ran back home.

He rushed into the burrow and plopped his bag of tools down next to his Mom's before she could say hello. She looked puzzled at first, but then he broke the silence and asked a question.

"Can you teach me how machines work?"

She was taken aback at first, Eli hadn't ever shown an interest in her job before.

"Where's all this coming from? And where did you get these tools young man?"

"I bought them."

"You bought them?"

"Uh-huh!"

"With whose money?"

"My own."

"Eli, now stop lying to me. These are much too expensive for you to have bought. Where did you find these? If you were snooping around those tunnels underground again…"

"I'm not lying, Mom, I did buy those tools. With the money I got this summer from working over at Ms. Smits's store."

His mother laughed and said, "Didn't realize that sweeping porches paid that much, honey."

Eli froze and felt his nose twitch involuntarily. Before he could reply, she chimed in with a cool and calm voice.

"I take it that Ms. Smits has been having you do more than just sweep her storefront then? Don't bother trying to lie to me now Eli, I saw your face pinch up already."

Eli sighed and let his ears fall back as he rubbed his one foot alongside of his other leg. He looked up sheepishly at his Mom and wrestled with whether he should tell her or not.

"I've been running errands for her shop. Literally 'running.' But I'm really good at it Mom! Ms. Smits even complimented me on how fast my deliveries go. And besides, she said she was going to talk to you about it."

"So, you thought you wouldn't even bring it up to me then? Don't you think I should have been told about this delivery business before you went and accepted the job?"

"But Ms. Smits promised me she was going to talk to you! And besides, the trips outside of the Warrens haven't even been that far…"

Eli's Mom slammed her paws down on the table at the mention of leaving the Warrens. Her face was set in a grimace as she stared down her son.

"Eli, go to your room! You're grounded until I have a chance to talk to Ms. Smits myself."

"Aww, but Mom!"

"I won't hear it Eli! Get to your room on the double. Come now, hop to it!"

Eli began to hop away, but made a show of going as slow as he could.

* * *

The store was dark as Eli's mother walked over; she placed her large ears close to the frame of the door, to hear a few hushed whispers were being exchanged. She concentrated and tried to make out their voices but couldn't decipher what they were whispering about. She was so focused on the whispering that she almost didn't have time to react to the sound of steps rapidly approaching the door.

As Eli's mother ducked out of sight, a small mongoose dressed in clothes that were far too fancy for life in the dusty Warrens stepped out. They sniffed the air a few times before shrugging and walking out into the cool night air. Luckily, Irene had decided to step outside to see her guest off. Eli's mother slipped into the shop, confronting the human as she closed the door.

"Lovely night, isn't it Irene?"

The human about jumped out of her skin. After a moment to catch her breath, she whispered, "What are you doing here, Heather? If you're trying to give me a heart attack, you're well on your way!"

"There's no need to whisper, Irene. I'm not worried about your nighttime visitor. I wanted to talk to you about Eli, actually."

"Oh!" she looked immensely relieved at that remark. "If it's about the job I hired him for, he's been doing wonderfully at it. There's no need to worry."

"No need to worry? So exactly when were you going to tell me that you were sending him on dangerous expeditions outside the Warrens?"

"I'd hardly call them dangerous, Heather. Just a few errands that I needed to have done. And he seems to enjoy getting the chance to stretch his legs. If you'd just listen to him, I think you'd…"

"You just stop right there! I won't have you tell me what is and isn't dangerous for my child! Now you're going to stop sending him on these outings and that's that." She brandished her workshop wrench to make her seem more intimidating than she really was.

Ms. Smits scowled. "What do you think he has to be afraid of? If memory serves, you were quite the daredevil when you were younger too. Or has 'The Tempest' lost her nerve after all this time?"

"We both have things in our past we'd like to forget, Irene. I still remember the day of the crash! And if I can keep Eli safe for a few more years, I'll do whatever I can to keep him out of trouble."

"He's going to leave one day. I've never seen that boy's eyes light up as much as when he comes back from going outside the Warrens. Is it better that he learns now, or later?"

Heather snorted and replied, "I appreciate the concern Irene, but it sounds like he's more interested in learning about my machines now. The world outside the Warrens could have been a phase for him. Regardless, I'll be making sure to keep a better eye on him from now on. I'd appreciate it if you stayed away from him in the meantime."

And with a flourish, she spun her wrench and holstered it inside her toolbelt and walked away.

Ms. Smits's face was set in a deep frown and her arms were crossed along her chest as she said, "Heather Tempes, you couldn't be more wrong."

* * *

The next year was a blur as Eli spent his free time studying machines and how they worked alongside his Mom. He was surprised how enthusiastic she was to show him how the mechanisms and machinery of her day to day job worked. He'd known that she liked working on machines, but it was her job. He never realized the sheer enjoyment she got from fixing an appliance was so genuine until he experienced it himself.

It was spectacular to be able to use his mind in this way. All that time going over different scenarios in his head turned out to be amazing practice for diagnosing issues with the resident's machinery. And though it was slow going most days, he was getting much better at putting things together and taking them apart.

The biggest change for Eli was not being able to leave the Warrens. He missed going out terribly, but ever since his Mom had talked to Ms. Smits, she'd kept her eyes on him constantly. She had been clear to stay away from Ms. Smits as well. He wasn't sure what they talked about that night, but it must have gone badly. The one time he managed to sneak out and talk to her, Ms. Smits wouldn't allow him to do any deliveries for her, either, but it was nice to be able to see and talk to her again.

The underground passageways were just not a possibility, too far from the burrow for his absence to go unnoticed. Eli did his best to focus on his studies and sketch out plans for his return, whenever that would be. With all the work that was coming through the shop though, it seemed a far-off dream.

The residents kept bringing in their appliances and machines with complaints about it being infected with Pax Machina. Never mind that Pax wouldn't necessarily have a vested interest in a toaster oven, the residents had heard about Pax from some traveling traders who told them of robotic attacks last year and ever since then business was booming. Every small glitch with someone's machine was now irrefutable proof that they were going to be killed by their moped, or dishwasher, or any number of metallic objects. It was good for helping Eli learn on a variety of different metals, machines, and hardware but left little time for anything else.

Worse, he feared that his Mom was hoping for him to eventually inherit the shop. He wanted to tell her about the underground caves and his fascination with that gleaming tower of metal that they housed, but he was afraid that she would stop teaching him if he gave up his real reason for wanting to learn. Over time, he made it a habit to grab as much scrap metal as he could when he was walking through the Warrens. He'd need it for his most ambitious plan to climb that tower yet.

During a particularly good trip, wherein Eli had managed to find some undamaged wires that were sticking out of a robot in an alley, he didn't see the two shadowy figures sneak up behind him before he was hoisted into the air by his ears.

"Hey, what's the big idea? Put me down!"

Eli thrashed and squirmed as his assailants laughed coldly. They were larger than he was, but he couldn't get a good look at them. The grip on his ears was extremely tight and he was doing his best not to wince in pain in front of them.

"This is the guy? Are you absolutely sure, Hank?" came a low voice.

"Positive, he fits the description to a T. Never expected the new courier to be a kid, though", came the reply.

Eli piped up and said "I'm not a kid! I'm barely even a teenager anymore. Now let me go! Or else I'll make you regret it!"

At this, they spun Eli around to face them and he got a good look at his attackers. The one on his right side was a human, portly, and had an eyepatch over his left eye. The creature that was holding onto Eli's ears was a large alligator, well-muscled, and definitely bigger than Eli imagined alligators could get. They both looked down and grinned at Eli, while the man with the eyepatch spoke up.

"I don't think you're in any position to be making demands there, little bunny. Rock here has you pretty well incapacitated."

He gestured over to the alligator who cracked a toothy smile that sent shivers down Eli's spine.

"But I'll tell you what! You tell us what you know and we'll let you go without a scratch. And if you don't feel like cooperating, Rock'll be more than accommodating…"

Hank didn't get to finish his thought as Eli took the opportunity to kick Rock in the stomach as hard as he could. He felt the tough scales crumple under his powerful paws as Rock let go of Eli's ears to grab his stomach. Eli dropped to the ground on all fours and started sprinting away. Rock grunted and there was a *swish* of blurry green movement that took Eli's legs out from under him. As he toppled end over end, he slid to a stop across his back next to his bag of mechanic's tools. Hank was already rushing at him, but Eli was quicker. He dug through his leather satchel and pulled out an enormous wrench just in time for Hank to run face first into it.

Thunk. The human went down and Eli's mind raced at how to deal with Rock. But Rock was grasping at his neck, eyes bulging and lips purple. The gator passed out where he stood, and the object that was choking him flickered briefly in the dim light of the alley as he collapsed. It was a cream-colored scarf.

"Jack?" Eli called out.

The scarf dipped out of view, back into the darkness with supernatural quickness and Eli thought for a moment that he must have been seeing things. But then two shining circles stood out in the darkness.

"It's good to see you again, Eli. How're things in the Warrens?"

It was Jack's voice all right, but it sounded off in some way. It didn't have the same level of cheerfulness that it used to have when they would chase each other.

Eli slowly got up and brushed himself off before saying, "*'How're things?'* I haven't seen you in two years! Where have you been? I was worried sick about you. Everybody was."

"Oh yes! I'm really sorry about that, but I had to get out of the Warrens for a while. I… saw something I wasn't supposed to see. Ever since then I've been living in the Outskirts. You still obsessed with that tower in the catacombs?"

"So what if I am? And what could you have possibly seen that would make you leave your family and friends?"

At this the glasses disappeared for a moment only to reappear behind Eli. He jumped backwards and finally had a chance to see Jack fully. Or well, almost fully. The scarf fit him a lot better now, but it was still incredibly long on him. He'd gained some muscle in the intervening years and was almost as tall as Eli now. Eli still couldn't see his face, as it was obscured by the shadows in the alley. He stepped closer to him as Jack held up a single finger.

"Not yet, Eli. I can't stay long so I have to make this quick. Do you remember those stories of 'Claimer cities that reach into the sky and how they all live in the clouds?"

"Yeah Jack, everyone knows about them. What about it?"

"I've seen them firsthand, Eli, and they're planning something big. I've only heard whispers of it through other 'morphs but it sounds like they're working on taking back the planet for themselves. And I don't know about you, but I quite like living here."

"Well why tell me about this? It's not like I can just drop everything and leave the Warrens like…"

"Like I did?"

"Yeah, like you did," Eli said sadly.

"I know it's not going to be easy for you, Eli. It wasn't for me either. But I genuinely think you could be exactly the sort of thing we need to help stave off this plan the humans have."

And with this, there was a swish of movement as Jack jumped back into the shadows of the alleyway.

"When you're ready, come find me in the Outskirts. Oh, and one last thing. Be careful around Ms. Smits. You weren't just delivering groceries for her."

Before Eli could ask what that could mean, the glasses disappeared and Jack was gone again.

Eli stood there for a long time before grabbing his leather satchel of tools and running back to his burrow. His head was spinning with the possibilities now. Jack was back, but now he just felt more confused. Was the mouse lying to him to get him to leave the Warrens? Why would he? Or were the 'Claimers plotting something after all? And what about Ms. Smits?

Eli threw his bag in the corner of his room and flopped down into bed as all these questions and more swirled around his head. Tomorrow things would make more sense. He just had to sleep on it.

* * *

Tomorrow came and went and so did more time. Eli had mostly decided to leave the Warrens a few days after his meetup with Jack, but he refused to go until he'd managed to climb that tower. It'd be good practice if he and Jack had to scale a skyscraper in a 'Claimer city, he told himself.

He failed three more attempts with various contraptions built expressly for the climb before having his greatest epiphany. What if he didn't climb it at all? What if he just found a way to slingshot himself over the top of the tower and grabbed it on the way over?

With his new plan in place, he drew up schematic after schematic of diagrams. It would be a tight window of opportunity, but if he engineered it just right, it could work! He was a lot more confident in his knowledge of machines now that he'd been working alongside his Mom for three years. He'd managed to see a wide variety of devices and could use this knowledge to engineer his own machine for one last attempt. It took several weeks of working on and off to get it ready, but it was worth the wait.

The day came to make his last stand against the tower and Eli was more than ready. He woke up extremely early so that he could make his way underground without anyone catching on. He didn't want his Mom or even Ms. Smits to know that something was about to happen. Once he found the hole the tower was in, he found that he was having trouble ducking down low enough to squeeze through the opening, like the Warrens had shrunk down even smaller around him. Eventually he settled on shimmying inside hind paws first.

As he stood up and faced his greatest adversary, he was struck speechless once again by just how tall it was. Eli was prepared this time though. From his bag he pulled a mechanical device with two thrusters, one on each side, and a harness to fasten to his chest. It was risky, but this makeshift jetpack was his best shot at getting up that high. He attached the jetpack to his chest, made sure the thrusters were calibrated correctly, and slipped off his leather tool bag to free up some weight. He had decided to only wear what was absolutely necessary to keep his weight down, thus improving his odds at staying in the air for long enough. No pot-helmet to protect him this time.

He nervously hopped to the back of the room, took a deep breath, and set his eyes in a determined glare at the tower. He leaned his one foot back and crouched low to the ground, coiling up like a spring. And then, he took off running.

The blood pounded in his long ears as he pumped his arms and legs so fast that he was a grey blur streaking toward his target, focusing in on that feeling of being chased all those years ago. Even with his eyes squinted almost shut he could see the tower get closer and closer. He waited until the base of the tower was only about ten feet away and then Eli jumped with a mighty leap high into the air, counting the seconds as he rose.

One, two, three, *NOW!* He grabbed the ripcords on either side of the jetpack and pulled down hard, letting the fuel in them ignite. There was a crimson and white flash as the thrusters sparked to life and small flames shot out the ends, rocketing Eli past the middle and towards the top of the tower. He could see it now, that shining object at the top. As the jetpack started to sputter, he leaned his paw out to reach for it. Stretching closer and closer until…

He grabbed a star.

The next few moments were a blur as Eli tumbled down the back side of the tower, hurtling with dangerous speed towards the cavern floor. He fumbled with the harness around his chest until he found the emergency ripcord towards the back of the jetpack. He pulled on it with both hands and his parachute, made of old clothes stitched together, deployed like an air brake. He half-jogged down the tower's side and took off the jetpack once his feet touched flat ground. He'd finally done it.

Eli began to cry a little as the full realization hit him. Through the cracks in the walls of this cavern, the first light of morning could be seen shining on Eli and his prize. The object glowed faintly in the light and Eli had to laugh through the tears once he could truly see what he had grabbed.

It was a simple coin. It was much shinier than any coin he had ever seen, but it was practically worthless. In the corner there was a small stamp of letters titled "GNDN", but Eli didn't know if that meant anything. The only other difference he could see was that the heads side had a human face on it and the tails side had a canine animal head.

"Well, I suppose I ought to make a choice finally," he said as he twirled the coin in his fingers.

"Heads, I stay with Mom in the Warrens; tails, I go find Jack in the Outskirts."

He flipped the coin high into the air and caught it before turning it over onto his opposite hand. He uncovered the coin and cracked a wide smile.

"Well that settles it then!"

He grabbed up the remains of the jetpack, picked up his tools, and left the coin on the ground where he flipped it. He took one last look back at the tower and then squeezed himself through the opening and ran off into the cool early morning air.

In the room, the coin lay on the ground, tails side up. And then, the tower began to move. Not quickly at first, it shifted around slowly as the metal and debris fell off the tower in chunks and bits. But once it had begun to hit the ground, the metal moved quicker. It was moving away from something, pushing out to the edges of the room. Until the whole tower, tall and resplendent, had been reduced to smaller piles that collected at the far edges of the room. And in the center of this strange phenomena was the coin, gently wobbling back and forth, ever so slightly, and humming with a strong, if nigh undetectable, magnetic field.

Post-Mortem Telepathy

Graveyard Greg

"This is all your fault, Ventis!" the lizardman said, ducking his head to avoid the next round of bullets that sprayed over the top of the concrete wall he and his companion hunkered behind.

"Okay, Immol, I'll admit it might not have been the brightest idea to ask it for directions," the massive jackal replied, trying to make his huge bulk less of a target. "But how is it my fault?"

As soon as the hail of bullets ceased buzzing overhead, Immol stood up to squeeze off a wild shot of plasma. He hoped it would do the job the other settings failed at, but as he ducked again another round of bullets started buzzing over him. "You asked Pax Machina for directions!"

Ventis' eyes widened in disbelief, but for once Immol didn't admire the red irises in the sea of black. "And it gave us directions!" the jackal objected. "And it was talking about valuable hotspots on the way there! For ten minutes! I was too busy taking notes to be paranoid!"

"It's the Pax, Ventis! You know how insane the Pax are! One minute they're giving directions and the next they're trying to exterminate every organic they see!" The bullets stopped again; Immol popped back up, fired off a freon round and crouched down fast, glaring at his gargantuan companion. "You know, like what's happening to us right now?"

"This is no time to be sarcastic," said Ventis, with an air of wounded pride.

"No, you're right, I should be pissed off at you!" snarled Immol. "Oh wait, I *am* pissed off at you!"

116

"We should focus on getting out of here in one piece first. Then you can be pissed off all you want, okay?"

Immol checked the settings on his rifle. Gamma. Particle beam. Plasma. So far none of the none of them seemed effective against the attacking Machina until. The lizardman looked over his shoulder, wishing there was better cover out in the middle of nowhere. The crumbling wall of what used to be a gas station was not where he wanted to die.

"I'm running out of options on my weapon."

"Maybe we should try talking to it," Ventis suggested.

"Talking to it is what got us *into* this mess!"

"I know!" Ventis said cheerfully. "But maybe it'll feel sorry for trying to kill us."

"I hate you so much," Immol said.

One of Ventis' long ears swiveled up. "Hey, it hasn't fired any rounds at us for a while."

Immol tilted his head, his raw nerves soothed by the relative quiet. "It's still out there," he said, becoming aware of heavy footfalls growing in intensity as something approached.

"It's out of bullets! Now's our chance!" Ventis said, standing up quickly, far quicker than someone of his size had any right to do so.

"Ventis, wait!"

"HELLO, RESISTANCE IS USELESS. PLEASE STAND BY FOR TERMINATION."

The hail of bullets resumed and Immol froze in horror as they found their target. Ventis flinched as each shell bounced and pinged off his frame, raining to the ground with a faint jangling sound.

Immol blinked and tried to comprehend what he just saw.

The jackal stood there, a stunned look on his own face, and blinked several times. He reached up to touch his muzzle then looked at his fingers as if expecting blood. Then he looked down at his bare black furred chest, giving the pec muscles an experimental bounce. "Hey, Immol!" he said, giving the lizardman a wide, fang-filled grin. "I'm bulletproof!"

"UNEXPECTED RESISTANCE IS LESS USELESS THAN EXPECTED," said the machine, still hidden from Immol's view by the broken wall. "PLEASE STAND BY AS TERMINATION METHODS ARE ALTERED."

Ventis looked over at the source of the robotic voice. "Oh, yeah, almost forgot about you," he said, balling up his hand into a meaty fist and smacking it into his open palm. Then he hopped over the broken wall and disappeared from Immol's sight.

"Ventis, wait! Don't get—" He was going to say "arrogant" but couldn't even finish his sentence before there was at the sound of crumpling metal followed by a high pitched electronic squeal, then silence.

"That was easier than I thought," Ventis said, his head appearing above the broken wall.

"What the hell?" Immol asked, staring at the giant jackal in disbelief. Had bullets actually bounced off his face? Ventis was dangling an android head from the wires of its neck like a trophy and grinning like an idiot. The single camera eye of the robot was smashed beyond repair. "Are you all right?" he finally said, eyes never leaving his companion.

"Considering I just took maybe a thousand rounds to the face, I feel pretty good."

Immol didn't know if he wanted to slap the grin off his face or yell at him for being so foolish. Slapping won.

"Ow!" Ventis said, rubbing his cheek. "Why'd you do that?"

"You could have been killed, you idiot! And that couldn't have possibly hurt you."

Ventis pouted. "I took a thousand rounds to the face. It's tender."

"You took a thousand rounds to the face," Immol grumbled. "Since when are you bulletproof?"

"I dunno? Never been shot at before."

"You whine when you get so much as a vaccine injection. How are you bulletproof but needles can get through that thick skin?"

"Well, duh, needles are sharp."

Immol ignored the jackal logic. "And since when were you freakishly strong?"

"Oh, that's old news. You just weren't paying attention." The pout turned into the toothy grin and Immol wanted to slap it off again, but his hand was still numb from the first time.

"You're an idiot."

"A *bulletproof* idiot," Ventis said, beaming down at him.

"Still an idiot." *An idiot who'll probably take even more dangerous risks now that he's even harder to hurt.* " Let's get out of here."

"Yeah, let's," Ventis said, flipping the head over his broad shoulders and letting it dangle from the wires of its neck.

Immol narrowed his eyes at the jackal. "What do you think you're doing with that?" he asked, pointing a finger at the broken head.

"Souvenir!" Ventis said, admiring the broken piece of robot. "It'll look great on my mantle."

"How do you know the Pax can't track it? What if they want their broken, wayward son for whatever reason?"

"How do you know it's not a daughter?"

Immol counted to three in an attempt to cool down his rising temper, then decided to let Ventis have it anyway. "Shut up! You need to get rid of that thing."

"Nope, not gonna. Nobody's gonna believe us if I don't bring proof that I ripped a Pax's head clean off."

"You'd risk our lives over your own ego?"

"Hey, I'm bulletproof. It'll take a lot to hurt me, I bet."

Immol looked up into Ventis' eyes. "I'm not bulletproof," he said cooly.

Ventis blinked, looked at the broken robot head, then threw it so far Immol couldn't see where it landed. "Eh, it wasn't good proof anyway. Anyone could've ripped that head off, right?"

"Not just anyone," Immol conceded. "A bulletproof anyone."

"That's the nicest thing you've said to me all day."

"Don't get used to it."

Venti smiled. "I won't."

"Good," Immol grumbled again, looking over the wall so the jackal wouldn't see his slight smile. Seeing the rest of inactive Pax unit made his smile vanish. "Ventis, why is the Pax's chest open?"

"INITIATING EMERGENCY BEACON IN 3... 2..."

"Immol! Get away from it!"

"1..."

Large hands grabbed the lizard.

"INITIATING."

Immol's vision was suddenly filled with a blue white light and nothing else for several seconds, followed by the largest spots he'd ever seen, worse than when he tried to outstare the sun when he was a child.

When he could finally see again, he was looking into those black and red pools of Ventis' eyes. Immol was pinned under the jackal, who'd taken the brunt of the blast, but still propped himself up to keep from smothering the lizard.

"Get off of me before you collapse and crush me," said Immol, pushing against Ventis, who didn't budge.

"Never gonna happen," the jackal said, beaming down at him.

"What, not getting off of me or not collapsing?" *I swear I'll use my dragonfire and sear every inch of fur on—*

There must have been something in Immol's expression, because Ventis immediately got up and offered his large hand to the lizardman. "Okay, okay. I *was* gonna say I'll never collapse and crush you. No need to threaten me."

Immol took the hand and was pulled up easily. "Thanks."

"You're welcome. So what the heck was that all about?" Ventis said, eyeing the inert Pax.

"I don't know, but we better leave in case something answers the emergency beacon."

"Couldn't agree more!" the jackal said.

The two of them resumed their trek, down a ruined road with nothing but desert stretching out for miles on either side of it. When the night started to take over the day, Ventis suggested they make camp. "You look tired," he said. "That encounter was… stressful."

Immol squinted up at the giant jackal. "Usually it's me who wants to rest. You never run out of stamina."

"Well, I *could* keep on going, but you hate it when I carry you."

Immol snorted. "Whatever. It's a good idea for both of us to take a break. It's going to get pitch black out here, and you might find something dangerous even you can't out-muscle."

"That's why you're here with your big-ass gun and dragonfire," Ventis said as Immol took off his backpack.

"You make it really hard to be cranky at you when you're using that much flattery," Immol said as he unrolled his sleeping bag.

"Speaking of that dragonfire, if I start making the campfire, you think you could light it up?"

Immol looked around. They were miles away from any civilization, extinct or no, and the light from the fire would keep away unwanted predators. *What's the harm?* he thought. "Eh, all right. But you're gathering up the wood," he said, handing Ventis an axe.

"You always say that," Ventis said as he took the axe.

"You're the brawn and I'm the brains. That tree over there looks lonely all by itself. Put it out of its misery."

Before long the fire was little more than embers; survival rations had provided something like a meal, and the sounds of night surrounded them. "You think we'll find anything where we're going?" Venti asked, laying on his back and gazing up into the nighttime sky.

"Hard to say since we're not even sure the place exists."

"Too bad the Pax didn't give us directions."

"You're lucky it didn't kill you. Why don't you ever think before you act?" *If anything ever happened to you, I'm not sure how I'd feel.*

Ventis tilted his head to smile at Immol. "So you do worry about me."

"Don't dodge the question."

Ventis shrugged his broad shoulders. "If I spend too much time thinking I'll never get anything done."

"One of these days that impulsiveness will get you hurt." *Or worse.*

The bright smile glinted in the firelight. "Nah, not with you around to keep me in line."

"I might not always be around."

"Lucky for me I'm really strong and hard to hurt."

"Good thing too, you're such a huge target. You're impossible to miss."

"You always know how to flatter me." A sudden yawn forced Ventis' muzzle to open widely. "You want to grab some sleep? I can take the first watch."

"After that yawn? I think I'm safer staying awake."

Ventis turned away from Immol, who admired the mountain range which composed of the jackal's broad back. "You're a good partner, Immol," the jackal said into the darkness. "Even if you do yell too much."

"And you're too impulsive."

"You love it."

You wish I did. "Whatever. Go to sleep." But the jackal was already beginning to snore.

"Big lunk's going to be the death of me," Immol grumbled after a few hour's silence. They'd been friends since they were children, and more times than not Immol had to guide Ventis from doing very stupid, impulsive things. There were also more times than not where Ventis's huge size and strength had kept Immol safe.

But days like today were a terrifying reminder that the jackal's impulsiveness could get one or both of them killed.

If I didn't love him, I'd probably have murdered him ages ago.

A voice came to him, *Aw, I love you too, minus the murdering part.*

Immol whirled around, looking for the source of the voice but saw nothing but ruins in the distance and the sleeping mountain of jackal. It was Ventis's voice, but the jackal was still fast asleep.

I've gone crazy. Ventis has driven me crazy. I'm hearing his voice.

That's because I am *talking to you, duh.*

"What the *hell?*" Immol said. Ventis was still snoring, and not the jackal's fake snoring when he wanted to avoid Immol's lectures. "I'm seriously going crazy."

Immol? You went quiet, which is kind of weird for you because you always have something to say even when you don't.

Immol back the urge to curl up into a fetal position and tremble for the rest of his sane life. *This is bad. I'm hearing Ventis inside my head.*

Imagine it like we're talking on commo? came the voice.

I'm insane. It's the only explanation.

Or maybe that blue flash linked our minds together? I mean, we live in interesting times.

No, I'm crazy. You never make sense like this.

Well, when I could hear you talking even though your mouth wasn't moving I started getting suspicious. And now I'm talking to you in my dream, it makes me pretty sure we're telepathic with each other.

What?

Silence. Then, almost sheepishly. *If I try to explain do you promise not to get mad?*

If it helps convince me I'm not insane… maybe.

The dream you is waiting for me to come back to bed.

…what?

You know how I'm one of those loose-id dreamers?

You mean 'lucid'.

That too! Well, right now dream you is in my bed. It's a pretty nice, big one too. The bed, not the dream you. I like the size you are and I wouldn't change anything about you.

Focus, Ventis! This is serious! We have an issue here!

We do?

What if we're like this forever?

If this is permanent then at least I'm with my best friend. And besides, I tend to never think before I act anyway so it's not like you'll be hearing me inside your head.

Immol snorted, then broke down into loud barking laughter. It felt very good and the tension melted away from his body.

Hold on, lemme hang up the phone and wake up.

Ventis sat up, rubbing his eyes. "I like it when you laugh."

"Is it true? That you dream about me?"

Ventis nodded, suddenly unable to keep eye contact with the lizardman. "I kind of like you."

Immol moved over to the still sleepy jackal and sat beside him. "I have a confession. I kind of like you too."

Ventis found Immol's eyes. "Really?"

"No."

"Oh."

"The truth is, I fell in love with you a long time ago, but I was afraid it would ruin things between us."

Ventis drew in closer to the lizardman. "Well, now you know how I feel. Still think things are going to be ruined?"

"No, but now you know how I think. I want to be able to keep my thoughts to myself… but not at the cost of losing you."

"Eh, we can always take little breaks once in a while," Ventis suggested.

"I guess so."

"You look tired. Want me to take the rest of the watch?"

Immol shook his head. "I don't think I can fall asleep after these revelations of love and whatever post-mortem telepathy that Pax Machina gave us."

"Doesn't 'post-mortem' mean 'after death'?"

"You took a thousand rounds to the face," Immol said. "That's usually pretty lethal."

Ventis draped an arm around Immol's shoulders and drew him close. "Just close your eyes for a bit anyway."

The warmth of the fire and the jackal's body heat were too much for Immol to resist, and his eyelids grew too heavy to keep open. *I've been wanting this for too long.*

Likewise, little cutie.

Immol tried to object but was asleep before he could make a sentence out of it.

* * *

Sunlight forced Immol awake. He opened his eyes to gaze up on Ventis' red eyes swimming in a pool of black. "Morning," the jackal said.

"Morning," grumbled Immol.

Okay, so I hope this telepathy thing is working, came Ventis's voice in his head. Immol could almost feel the worry in it.

I hear you, he thought. *What's wrong?*

Don't make any sudden movements. Some kind of Pax unit is sitting down over there. His eyes flicked over in front of him, and Immol's eyes darted over in that direction.

It was humanoid, slim and sleek with a blushish tinge on its metallic surface. All curves, no harsh edges. It looked brand new, untouched by the wasteland around them.

The humanoid head was featureless, but it generated a cheerful voice. "Hello, organic-based friend!" it said.

Ventis, how in the hell did you let it come into our camp?

I… might have dozed off.

Immol forced himself to be calm. This was not the time to lose his temper. *Given recent revelations, I'm going to save my yelling for the next stupid thing you do.*

Fair enough!

The Pax tilted its head. "This unit wonders how organic-based units can communicate on frequencies usually reserved for the Machina?"

Immol looked at the Pax. "You can hear us?"

"Hearing requires sound waves, which are created by the vibration of air," replied the machine. "This one is aware of conversation happening between the two of you via electromagnetic brainwave congruence."

Immol slowly moved away from Ventis' lap. "We suffered an… incident. We've been linked together ever since."

"Fascinating. There are no records of such an occurrence in our archives. You two are unique."

"You always did say I was a special case, Immol." Ventis said.

"And now you're a unique special case," Immol replied, but never moved his eyes from the construct in front of him. "So what brings you here… friend?" he asked it.

"I am here because of an emergency beacon which originated approximately two kilometers from this current location."

Immol resisted a glance at Ventis. "An emergency beacon?"

"Correct. The download to this archive unit took longer than anticipated. The signal to *-kzt-* has been weakened for some time. I fear it will be too late to *-kzt-*."

"My apologies, friend, but too late to what?" Immol asked, his eyes glancing to his rifle by Ventis's side.

Uh oh, thought Ventis. *Here we go again.*

"*-kzt-* signal is quickly degrading," said the Pax unit. "What was *-kzt-* question?"

Can you reach my rifle? thought Immol.

Just let me know when and I'll toss it.

"Nothing worth repeating, friend," Immol smiled, trying not to show too many teeth. "I wish you good luck on your travels, but my companion and I need to get going."

"Then this unit shall *-kzt-* on its way. Safe travels to *-kzt-*…"

"Rifle! Now!" Immol said, whirling around and ready to catch his weapon. Unfortunately Ventis threw it too high and it sailed over the lizardman's head. "Dammit!"

"Sorry!"

Immol lunged for his weapon and spun around, aiming it at the now inert Pax Machina. He fired a shot of each of the energy settings.

The Pax turned its faceless head at him, undamaged. "COMBAT ENGAGED WITH HOSTILE ENCOUNTER." Immol had a second to notice the now red tinge around its arm as it reconfigured into a dangerous-looking cannon. The interior of the barrel began to glow as the Pax aimed at Immol's head.

Ventis grabbed the arm cannon and the thing's head, crushing both in his large hands like so much paper. He then tossed the entire body with all his strength, and Immol quickly lost sight of it as it sailed towards the sunrise.

"At least this time you didn't wait for him to shoot us."

"I'm not cool with you losing your head to whatever it was about to hit you with. You okay?"

Immol nodded. "I think I need a better rifle, though," he said. "This doesn't do anything to those things."

Ventis looked back at where he tossed it. "How about we just avoid talking to any Pax we find on our way, huh?"

Immol smiled up at the jackal. "That is the smartest thing you've said since we started this trip."

Skipping Stones

Bryan "StarryAqua" Osborne

"He's here again," said Richter.

Katalia turned to the maned wolf before looking towards the study hall's entrance door. She didn't see their periodic human visitor, but she didn't doubt Richter's report, either. "Is he just shy this time?" she asked, not particularity towards anyone.

"Not sure," the maned wolf spoke, eyes not tearing away from the hardcover he was so deeply entranced in. Did he even see the human? "But if he would like to join us in studies of his own species, he's more than welcome."

Katalia looked through the adjacent windows into the main hall of the library. The few students she could see didn't have any noticeable reactions, and there were no pointing fingers. No calling of "Claimer." They were either getting used to his presence or the human had already left.

"Okay, this definitely isn't right," Richter chortled, bringing Katalia back. "This is not how humans dealt with nasal congestion centuries ago. It treats allergens almost no different than if they were a dog." He flipped through several more pages. "And pain most certainly *can* be a sign of inflamed tissue. Who wrote this nonsense?" He flipped the book to the cover as Katalia stifled a giggle.

"Here, let me show you something." Richter began to tap on his circuit watch; Katalia's tail immediately started to wag. She loved when he showed her this device. Few furs in this neck of Alurai had any sort of GNDN technology. The few who did were either in connection to higher ups of the human cities above, or worked in the grinding and researching facilities strung together by the Reclamation Project.

Katalia winced at the thought of the RP before a hologram of a bare male human just hovered above the watch's face. Arrows and miniscule lines of text her keen eyes couldn't read were marked all around the human.

"See here?" Richter tapped a finger claw on the face of the hologram which then provided a zoom in into a facial structure example typical of most human anatomy. "See the inflammation around the nasal passages?" Katalia nodded and took notes, nodded, took more notes, listening to everything Richter had to say and not wanting to miss a thing.

Katalia actually knew most of this information already, but the way Richter would explain it, was as if a new wave of description emerged that was alien to her ears and she couldn't help but be fascinated. It was quite bizarre, given that Richter was still a student while Katalia had a degree in Anthropology of Human Studies from ADSI. Anything related to humanity she would find some interest in understanding, which added to her continuing visits to the institution's library.

If you love humans so much, why don't you marry one, Kitty-Kat? She sighed. The aged insult of her youth was as deplorable as it was somewhat hurtful towards her actual canid species.

The lesson had lasted well over twenty minutes before Richter switched off the hologram and began to pack. "Hope you learned something from that and weren't just studying my good looks." He grinned as Katalia play-shoved him. "My shift starts early today, so I must leave you."

"Go. Shoo. I have something else to check before I leave anyway," she said, smiling at Richter as he headed out. She may not have been studying him, but he did look rather stylish. Mocha hair brushed up front and flowing behind and dressed in a flashy blue garb with loose leather pants, all on a tall figure, even for a maned wolf. It wasn't the same color palette she always saw him dressed as, but he would certainly represent Ambara Down heavenly.

Katalia crossed the hall into the section that contained the more historical references of Ambara Down, zigzagging across the shelves before coming across one that focused on Ambara's past history of competing human nations and the sky battles that commenced.

"Get out of here, human. You dirty 'Claimer.'"

Katalia closed her eyes. He was still here.

Holding the book under her arm she walked into the hall, eyeing the several bystanders spread throughout the desks and looming shelves—and seeing the human backed up against the wall, looking abashed. Everyone had their fronts pointed towards him, but the curator came forth and pulled a lion to the side. Undoubtedly the one with the dirty mouth. Fanning his head back and forth, the human gathered his bag and, head down, rushed out the front door.

Poor soul, she thought. Her instincts told her to check on him, but she let it pass. Maybe another time.

Katalia stayed an extra hour before deciding to see herself out. Walking down the hall she made a quick visit to the library's bulletin board. Clubs, job opportunities, a Reclamation Project recruiting poster that was obviously put there as a joke, the standard stuff she recognized.

Her ears lowered upon seeing her post, yet again unsigned. Requirements to open a fellowship of furs in favor of assisting humanity in any way they could needed a minimum of ten signatures just to schedule a room. She had checked every day for the past two weeks, and so far nothing. It would be nice to gather members, and maybe some more friends.

Alurai definitely stood out from the surrounding districts of the western development. Thinly-packed streets of cobblestone barely managing eight bikes side by side—or maybe six hoverbikes—and multi-story dog-trots of businesses and homes strewn together with aged wiring was the norm, but Alurai's streets and alleyways were not just more expansive, but the ground was literally sanded. All the way up to the beach's edge, it was just a nice sandy trot everywhere you went, which led to fantastic shadow castings from up above.

Katalia took a deep breath as she looked skyward. The swirling painting hue of navy and sunset always mixed well with the twinkling stars where Ambara once floated. High Empyros off to the distance always seemed to shine brightly this time of year, whether reflection from the sunset or whatever lighting was in the city itself, she didn't know.

It was about a half hour walk back to Alurai's district square, walking along the coast and warehousing units. It probably took shorter using the shortcuts between the cramped walkways but Katalia never bothered to experiment; she always did prefer the open space. Besides, the breeze cascading off the waves always felt nice on her fur. Not to mention, she had to satisfy her curiosity.

Sure enough, the broken planks of wood that had no reason for being there were occupied. The pier itself barely reached ten feet, with no aquatic life so close to shore. There was no reason she could come up with for its existence. And yet the human found some use for it.

For many weeks on end Katalia would walk by this spot and see the human seated on those planks, sometimes with his carrying bag, sometimes not. But either way, he always had his stack of rocks. He would take one, wind his arm back, and throw them against the surface. Sometimes the rocks would just sink, but amazingly, he would get a few to hop and jump across the surface for long distances before they sank. How the water driblets danced around the rocks with each impact looked quite amazing, as if someone was running on the water.

Perhaps it was a human thing, perhaps it was just *his* thing, she didn't know. It definitely wasn't something she read in her books or saw others do. She would see kids throwing materials into the ocean and other targets, sure, but never in such a captivating way. She could only assume the days she didn't come by at sunset, he was still there, throwing those rocks.

Humanity may continue to be a mystery to many furs who refuse to acknowledge their existence, but many of them—most of them—definitely weren't like those in the RP. Here in Ambara Down, they just needed a chance. It was their past home after all, before most of them perished when Ambara—

Katalia shook her head. She hated having to think about that. But there was still the question of why the human was here to begin with. This land had been zoomorph villages before the city fell and even now it didn't have any human residents that she knew of. Or even visitors. Alurai, the districts, definitely nothing on the west end or the coastal centrals.

He was an interesting one. One she would like to possibly chat with. Get to know better. Earlier made it quite clear he wasn't the most welcomed. Maybe he needed a friend. Was that why he kept coming back to the library?

Before she knew it, Katalia could feel the loose sand of the beach between her toes. She stopped mid-step, thinking, realizing what she was doing. *He doesn't know me. I would probably make him uncomfortable, too.* She stepped back on the more solid ground of the packed sand walkway. Maybe not now, but some other time. Perhaps soon. Katalia sighed and turned around, getting one last look at the next rock thrown before heading back towards home. She cursed in her head, damning her own insecurity.

Several children and their families played in the water and on the deeper sand fields—all of them a distance away from the human on both sides. Reaching the wider street of the beach square, the wide array of shops and carts were still on working business hours. Shadows of different vehicles and creatures that flew through the sky just added to the lively Alurai atmosphere.

Rather than going straight for the vendors she needed to visit, she stopped to admire some beautiful wear in a shopkeeper's window: an azure lace trim satin dress with gold lining that swirled like ribbons down the front, with a matching flat beret that could shadow the whole body. With her natural tan and cinnamon colors, with chestnut red highlighted curls of hair and golden eyes, she pictured it perfectly on her through the window. And here she thought Richter's style would represent Ambara Down heavenly—

"Uh, excuse me? Miss… wolf?" Katalia's eyebrow had already raised before she turned. That wasn't normal to hear.

"Yes? Can I help… you…?"

Her ears perked immediately and she reactively would have taken a step back if the shop window wasn't behind her. He was right there, right in front of her.

The human had never been this up close to her before, but now that he was, she could see how small he really was, about a foot shorter than her even without counting her tipped ears. The fact he had to stare slightly up while she stared slightly down should have at least broken a bit of the insecurity in some fashion, but her tail still swayed in unease.

He didn't seem any more comfortable. A visible swallow and a lowering of the lip exposed his nervousness. That didn't change how sweet—adorable?—he appeared to be. Lightened crème hair all messed up with sapphire eyes staring up at her. But his clothing… wasn't in the best shape. Faded, dirty in some places, tattered in others. A mix of bright and crusted emerald on an overcoat that almost looked too big for him. There was a whiff of something familiar in his scent, but she couldn't decide what.

Inspecting him fully, she almost didn't notice what he was carrying—her notebook, the same one she used with Richter. She pulled her bag over her shoulder to notice it hadn't closed all the way.

"You dropped this back there." The human held his arms out, notebook forward. "I just wanted to return it." His own tote bag was next to him, locked. Probably had his rocks in there.

Katalia smiled. At first she did it to be presentable, but started to feel it being sincere. All this time she had been wanting to interact with him, and couldn't bring herself to, but now an opportunity out of a good deed made it possible. She took the notebook, placing it within her own bag. "Well, thank you, uh, sir. I don't know what I would have done without this. Have a lot of notes in here." Her swaying tail turned into a natural wag. "Hey, may I ask you something," she questioned him. His own shoulders steadied. "This may seem out of nowhere, but were you at the Institution's library?"

He gulped, then nodded. "I-I was, yes. I was inspecting some of the classes. Public ones, of course. I wouldn't want to, uh… uh… impose, I guess. Anything that may have helped with learning the area I figured would be worth at least exploring." Katalia knew what he meant. If "impose" meant anything to him, it was probably "being another human target." Still, at least that answered the question of the library. But not enough to sustain her brain.

"I'm sorry, but I must ask." Katalia cleared her throat, taking a breath. "I've noticed you in these parts for quite some time, not just today at the library. Aluria rarely has humans exploring here, and even then they're just visitors. On the west coast and, well, practically anywhere near in the western development, humans aren't really present." *Or welcome,* she thought. "I suppose I'm just curious what brings a human to Alurai."

He just looked at her. Unmoving. Quiet. *Damn. I probably shouldn't have said that.* She wanted to just turn away, not look at him, but a deep breath of his own brought her back.

"I would... I would much prefer if I kept that quiet. I'm sorry."

She felt so stupid; asking something like that out of nowhere. Making him feel uncomfortable again. She wouldn't blame him if he wanted to go. How was she supposed to show her love and support for humanity if she acted like a total idiot?

"Of course. It's no problem. I didn't mean any—"

Before she had time to react, the human was pulled away from her sight, around the corner of the shop. Her ear twitched when she heard a pained "Oof!"

Katalia rushed around the corner to see the human pulled into the alley and shoved against the shop's rocky back wall, hand and claws on his chest, pinning him. She saw the growling teeth before the face, obscured by his mane and the large circular collar of the fabric militia coat he wore—the lion that called him out at the library.

"Hey! Let him..." She acted before she even thought things out. "...go?" The lion batted an eye at her for a few seconds before huffing and staring back at his prey. "Scum human. You got me in trouble!" The claw of his forefinger then pointed up, toward the human's throat. "You 'Claimers got nothing better to do down here than spy on us?"

The human tried to pull away from the lion's grip, but he could only grasp the arm. "I'm not! I-I'm not... d-doing anythi—ow! Let go!" His voice was rasping, becoming pained, terrified. "Please."

The lion only growled deeper, his fangs glistening. Katalia had to do something. She stepped forward, wanting to smack him with her bag but held back. "Let him go. Now! Or I'm reporting this to the Prefect's Guard. Not just the Institute." Her own teeth began to bare, her throat wanting to roar. The lion thug looked ready for the kill, but then let go of the human. Or rather, tossed him to the side, down on his back.

"You're all the same." He stood above him, looking more giant and threatening by the twilight of the sun he blocked. "The Project isn't doing anything but making *us* look like the true monsters. If humanity actually cared about the world perhaps they wouldn't have died along with Old Ambara."

In her mind, that did it. Her instincts told her to pounce. And if she was the bigger one here, she may have very well have. The human just gagged with his eyes half closed, clutching his chest where new punctures were in the fabric. Didn't look like there was any blood, thankfully.

The lion now was looking right at her, looking irritated. "Why would you even care about him or his species?"

Katalia snarled. "For reasons your idiotic brain couldn't manage. Get out of here. Now!" The lion thug only regarded her, scanned her, before turning and walking out. She didn't follow, but she did look out the alley. Not a single fur that was around batted an eye. Did they not notice, or just not care? She sighed and bent down at the human.

"Are you okay?" He was looking down at his arm, holding his elbow. From how he lifted it, it was obvious he indeed was hurt. Hopefully it was just a bruise, but even that was still disheartening to realize. And then he looked up at her, straight into her eyes, and betrayed the fear he felt.

"I'm so sorry he did that to you. Please, let me help." She extended her arm, waiting for him to grasp it to lift him up. But he didn't. Instead, he grabbed his bag and helped himself up, albeit with difficulty.

"I'm sorry, I… I need to go." And with that he scurried out of there, heading the opposite direction from the lion. She wanted to stop him, but once again, her own reluctance prevented it. She could only hope he would be okay and that she could see him again.

"I didn't even get his name," she exhaled to herself. Rather than going home she felt she now needed a drink.

* * *

"Maybe he does have a place to himself here, you don't know," said Miadra. The squirrel-morph handed Katalia another Ultraviolet Frenzy, a fruity beverage with a hint of spice. Its glow did add to the vibe of the shadowy purple interior of the nightclub. The Shadowrise wasn't as expansive, loud or active in dancing as The Damselfly but Katalia was just fine with that for Alurai's more hushed tone.

The red and gray squirrel-morph laid an arm down on the table, leaning in. "I don't think that cat had an agenda. I think he just hates humans."

Katalia took a long sip, licking her lips after. "Enough to physically harm him?" Another sip. "Is it really a humanity thing, or a Project thing?"

Miadra shook her head. "Gods I know, Katt. Humans aren't exactly the most welcomed species, regardless where they go." She looked ahead, behind the wolf, seeing the empty roundtables and sighing from the lack of business today. "Maybe he rubbed that bully the wrong way somehow?"

Katalia thought back to the library, seeing the lion bring attention to the human, calling him out. She took another deep sip of her drink, eyes closed. "Mmm. Humans are Ambarans too. Everyone should be treated as equals."

"Is that what you were taught during your education?"

"No, it should be logical."

The squirrel-morph had been cleaning glasses during their talk, scanning each glass with a sanitary tablet afterwards to check if it was fully clean. She put away the last glass and turned back to the wolf. "Perhaps. But even throughout history, perspectives don't change. Instead, they're documented."

"I would like to think I didn't waste my entire history of human studies on the wrong knowledge." Katalia finished off her drink, smacking her chops. "I love this drink."

A grin spread on Miadra's muzzle. "Thanks. And I wouldn't worry too much. You don't know that thug and you helped the human the best you could. It's not like you're obligated to do anything else."

"Yeah, I guess you're right," Katalia said, pushing the empty glass forward for Miadra. "After all these years I still don't know why I find humans so interesting."

"Interesting enough to date?" Miadra tried to form an accomplished smirk before she registered how uncanny that was. That didn't stop Katalia's ears from perking and forming a slight blush. Instead the squirrel just turned, cleaning the glass.

"I think I'd rather be with someone I would be compatible with." Katalia brushed through her hair, her own muzzle turned away to hide the still present blush. "Though who knows what goes on in the rest of Ambara Down. Or on the cities above. Perhaps some humans took furs up there with them."

"I think you not immediately changing the subject speaks for something."

Katalia looked up just in time to see the squirrel give her a wink before focusing on the glass. "Yeah, well, I suppose it's all still just a mystery." She gathered her bag, standing up to head out. "Thanks for the talk. Maybe next time I'll go for the more expensive stuff."

Miadra smiled, waving her off. "Any time. See you again." Katalia waved and walked outside. The sun, while not completely below the world's edge, still barely shone over the packed structures. The navy-blackened backdrop of a sky really brought the presence of High Empyros out. Barely a twinkle of a star from this angle, the miniscule lines of travel from the hover vehicles crisscrossing under and around the crust below its city were vibrant. And when they traveled in front of the actual stars and past the further cities in the distance, it really just made the sky beautiful living scenery.

So why couldn't she just forget that human? Katalia sighed deeply. This wasn't just curiosity anymore. Why *did* she care about him? She started walking home. The thought that she was just useless in helping him before still lingered deep.

* * *

The thoughts and curiosities of yesterday took a back seat as Katalia was amazed at the dancing holograms hovering above Richter's watch. He shared in the display, leaning back in his seat, his own tail swaying.

She had discussed with him what had happened yesterday; how everything was just one big show and that she was thrown in as a performer. How she frowned at the human's treatment made him poke at his watch, which instantly got her to wag again.

It really was a spectacular sight, even if it wasn't real. The humans the watch displayed were young adults, just a few years younger than herself, she assumed. The males were dressed in simplified black suits while the females looked way fancier, with dresses and gowns that sparkled under the twirling ball above their heads. And even if it was difficult at such a tiny size, she could see smiles.

"Close to graduation, humans would attend an event called a 'prom.' It signified... honestly, I don't really know. But they would dance, hug, kiss, and just enjoy each other's company, among friends and who they would hope to be their future mates." The sparkles of the dance were shared within Katalia's eyes. She did vaguely recall these types of dances in her own studies, but actually seeing a simulation of it up close was remarkable.

"They all look so happy," she said, eyes bright. "Probably not a care in the world back then. Hard to believe what we make of them now." Her notebook open in front of her remained blank. This was definitely a day more towards observation. Almost without control she looked towards the windows into the main hall. No reactions, nothing out of the ordinary, all quiet. It was definitely around the same time as yesterday. "I guess our friend chose not to show up today."

Richter breathed in and exhaled, betraying his own concern for her. "I guess not. Though I'm not too surprised. With what went down yesterday, it probably isn't shocking he would stay away for a while." The dance routine reached its end and the hologram shut itself off. "If he was hoping to find a safe place to stay, he might not find it here. Honestly, that may be for the best."

"Yeah, maybe." Katalia's ears lowered. "Throughout my entire time in academia, all the people I shared classes with, everyone only seemed interested in the knowledge and history of it. Just seems like no one actually cared about the actual people they were studying. Almost like the best thing to know about them... is how to prevent them." She leaned her muzzle, looking up at the ceiling, towards the high cities and beyond, and the humans that lived in them.

Richter nodded, turning his wrist towards her, away from any prying eyes. "Was there anything else you wanted to search? It probably exists in the database. And I have some extra time today before I head out."

She politely smiled. "Not right now, thank you. My mind is just in a wandering state, I suppose." She grinned. "Though that doesn't mean the same for the next time I have you to myself, and your little device too." Richter returned his own smile, both in agreement. Katalia stood up, gathering her things. "I think I need to just clear my head. Maybe I'll head to the beach. Perhaps our friend will be there. I'll see you later."

Richter waved her off and continued with his notes.

It was becoming quite breezy outside, and she hoped the extra dose of fresh air would help, but the abundance of it blowing through her hair still wasn't enough to blow away her thoughts.

I need to apologize again, she thought to herself. It was the least she could do if he didn't want to stay here longer. Of course, she could only do that if he was actually there—which she was dismayed to discover that he wasn't.

Maybe he just hadn't arrived yet; she did leave a bit earlier than usual. She decided to wait just a bit longer to see if he would come by, but after seconds turned into minutes, she wasn't so sure anymore. Katalia closed her eyes. She felt like she was just stalking him now by this point. Surely that wouldn't make things any better after yesterday's events.

"Just move on, Katt," she told herself, turning and walking towards the direction of home along the shore. She didn't feel like heading home yet, though. She just walked away, heading nowhere in particular, letting the breeze guide her.

It wasn't long before she reached the shop, and the alleyway where the lion had attacked. She hadn't gotten a particularly good look into the alley itself at the time, but now she could see how deep it actually was, reaching a dead end wall several shops down, before curving to the left and away from the bunched structures.

Holding onto the wall's edge, she leaned and looked into the moody alley. The ledges of the upper floors shrouded the ground into near darkness. Trash, parts and other materials littered the whole thing.

But then she noticed something about the layout. The entry curved inward, towards the side and away from the field of vision of the shore. The waste unit that occupied the other side was turned sideways, blocking the actual entry if standing out in front. Anyone that heard noises come from here may not have even noticed this entry was here to begin with—

Katalia's ears perked. Her fur standing on end. If the object she felt pointed to her back wasn't enough to freeze her, the voice against her ears did.

"Walk forward. Don't turn."

She did as told. She knew it was the lion. The damn thug just wouldn't let things go either, it would seem.

She walked forward as straight and level as she could, trying not to show any signs of fight or aggression that might make him do something as a result. They reached the end and turned the corner, which led to a true dead end. Only this time, the windowless wall that snugged one side connected to what she could only deduce to be some type of shelter.

The lion leaned to her side, object still pointed at her back, and reached for the door. She could see the slit pupil contract at her as he opened it. "Get in."

Fear, terror, realization, it all flooded her head. He was going to kill her, wasn't he? For what? Just for helping a person in need? What also flooded her mind was the stench of the metallic shelter. It smelled like a waste cell, yes, but also something different. Almost sweet.

She saw the metal paneling, though worn, looked freshly coated and hung. Was this also explosive-proof? Her eyes widened more—it was soundproof.

"Turn around." She did as told. The lion stared her down, their eyes dueling. And he was brandishing a firearm. Wait... was he? Yes. No. Maybe? It didn't look like any RP weapon she had seen before. The chamber glowed a radiate turquoise while the end of the barrel looked more triangular in shape. She could only tell because bolts—actual bolts of electricity!—flowed throughout all sections of the firearm at different intervals, the shell casing illuminating the entire thing at times.

"Please," she said, her ears lowered, lips quivering. "Don't hurt me. I don't know what you—"

"How do you know him? What is his role?"

She cocked an eyebrow, her fingers loosening from her raised palms. "Know who? Role? W-what are you talking about? Please, I don't know anything."

He took a step forward and she backed away, reaching the wall. The firearm was still level at her chest from the distance. "Don't play dumb, wolf. How do you know the human?"

If not for the circumstances, she may have growled there. But was he actually serious about this? "I don't! For God's sake, I was just trying to help him! You wouldn't leave him alone. He was returning something of mine before you attacked him. I don't know anything about him!" Her eyes began to tear. "Please, just let me go."

The lion just stood his own ground, firearm raised, and the scorn on his face ever present. What was he waiting for? It was as if he had frozen in place. "You don't know who he is," the lion said flatly.

"Yes!" Katalia practically screamed. "I don't know what's going on or anything about you or him or others or anything else!" Her knees buckled and she slid down the wall, the trace of the firearm following her. "Please... please just let me go."

He looked like he may have considered it, his eyes closing and taking a deep breath. "So that means..." The triangular hole in the barrel began to glow the same turquoise color. "You're just a witness."

Katalia's mouth gapped wide open, eyes shut tight and arms shielding her face as she did what she could to prevent her death.

"Let her go." The shine faded as the lion turned around at the voice. Katalia followed suit to the entry of the shelter.

"Richter!" She nearly jumped to her feet, heart racing at seeing him here. The maned wolf was breathing hard, his fingerclaws splayed, fangs bare. He looked angry. "Richter! Go get help!"

The lion raised his gun at him, his own fangs bared. "And who are you? Don't interfere with—"

Before he could even finish speaking Richter leaped at him, swiping the weapon right out of his hand, where it landed to Katalia's side. He and the lion were at each other's throats.

Richter grappled the lion, falling down atop of him and beating him on the chest. Using his feet he locked both of the lion's legs down and went at his throat, jabbing him with a ferocity that shocked Katalia. She turned away to look at the firearm, at its unique design, at anything but the barrage. Then even that didn't help, and she just closed her eyes.

It felt like a whole minute had to have gone by before she could hear Richter slow down. She turned to see him now standing, his chest heaving in and out repeatedly, staring down at the unmoving lion. He no longer looked angry; almost sad.

"Katalia, I'm sorry. I'm so sorry you had to deal with all of this." She ran in for the hug, embracing him, wrapping her arms around him. While he didn't return it, he did place a hand on her back. She nuzzled her face right into his chest.

"Thank you, Richter! By the Gods, thank you! I would have been dead if you…." Katalia let go. She didn't leave his side but gave him a quizzical look. He looked like he knew what she was going to ask.

"Richter… how did you know where I was?"

He lowered his hand that was behind her to his side, taking one deep breath and exhaling slowly. "Listen, Katalia. I need to—"

There was a grinding and popping noise. They both turned towards the lion to see the body twitch, then awaken. But he didn't just stand up; in one smooth motion, the lion practically levitated back to his feet off his back. Katalia moved to Richter's side, but the maned wolf just looked surprised. "Seriously?"

The lion lunged, arm and fist wound back, but not towards Richter. He swung at Katalia. She had nothing to shield herself, and Richter jumped between them to block the attack.

The blow connected, but not at Richter's face or even his arm. The lion had punched at his watch, which now began to spark, then crackle with static electricity. Richter's eyes widened, then looked at Katalia. She stared back at him, as the electricity that spewed from the watch soon enveloped his whole body.

Richter jerked backwards and slammed into the metal shelter frame before sliding down to his knees. The stream of energy seemed to contain his whole body, like a bubble. "Richter!" Katalia screamed. Even the lion stood confused as he watched.

She tried to approach Richter, but he raised a hand, stopping her in place.

"No! Stop! Don't touch me!" Her ears twitched; his voice sounded unnatural, the diction and tone different. Then almost like something out of a surreal dream, the colors of his clothing, his fur, began to change. Mixing and forming, from what she could see, his shape was changing too, before a bright flash forced her and the lion to cover their eyes.

It only lasted a moment before the shine started to fade. Katalia opened her eyes and… it couldn't be…

He was there. Not Richter. The human!

Katalia's jaw dropped and her mind reeled. There were stories of stealth suits, even of high-tech clothing that could mimic the appearance of another species, but... this? How was any of this possible? A miniscule few sparks still rose from the busted watch on his wrist.

"You!" snarled the lion, looming over the human. "I knew you two were a unit!" Katalia, even though she was in a world of utter shock and astonishment, found herself moving again, trying to defend... whoever he was.

The lion dashed towards his weapon. Just as quickly, the human had grasped his watch and turned the upper layer of its face a full one hundred eighty degrees. He yanked the device off his wrist, and threw it at the lion's feet.

The watch exploded into a golden arc flash, and the same cascade of dancing electrical bolts enveloped the lion. And just like before the colors molded and formed in circular patterns.

But it was different this time. The lion didn't look like he was in pain, but his body reacted strangely. His limbs twisted and bent. His head shook with such accelerated madness that it was horrific. He looked possessed, like a being from another world.

"Katalia, your eyes!" she heard the human say. She didn't need to think twice, burying her face in her arm at the flash she realized was coming. When she looked again, she couldn't help but bray in terror: there stood not the lion, but some... thing, that wasn't flesh, but metal, a featureless doll that of metalloid and rust. The parts that didn't look unnaturally old or rusted shined like silicon. It truly did look not of this world. It then fell forward, unmoving.

She was going to ask if it was truly dead before she noticed the body looked like it was beginning to corrode and dissolve right in front of her eyes, aging exponentially. Sections tore and fell apart as the whole body was going through its own alien phase of decomposing. When it was all over, all that remained was its own outline of zinc dust.

Katalia looked over to... the human? To Richter? Both? She wanted to hug him, whoever he was, but the look of sadness on his face held her back. "Katalia," he started, looking slightly back up at her, like he had before. But his voice had a hint of more confidence. "We should probably talk."

Katalia nodded, eager to understand. Honestly, she wanted to explode at him with questions right now. "Yeah," she finally said, and followed him out the door, closing the shelter and locking away the terror of what just happened.

* * *

The stone hopped, skipped and jumped a multitude of different heights before sinking into the depths. Ten skips she counted with that one. She sat by his side, comfortably, atop the pier by the calm water's end. She couldn't lie, this felt nice. His hand on one side of the pile of stones, hers the other. Now that she was close to him, she could see that they were smooth, carefully-chosen stones rather than random rocks.

"Everett," he said. She turned to see his more peaceful face already looking at her. "The name is Everett. I'm sure you wanted to know."

Her tail wagged once, becoming still again. Her fingerclaws clicked against the wood as she bit her lip. "Thank you," she said, as the hu—Everett—grabbed another of the stones. "But please. Please tell me what's going on. What was that thing?"

He wound up his arm and threw it against the surface but the release was definitely late. Only three skips on that one before sinking. His eyes still trailed where it landed, though where they focused was unclear. His mind wandered as much as hers. "Pax Machina."

Her ear twitched at the name. "An AI, right?" She looked up at the approaching night's sky and the racing streaks of pearl from the hoverskiffs high above. "Spreading a virus? Even the humans at ADSI don't willingly talk about it."

He nodded. "'Spreading' would be the correct word, yes. But it's not a virus. It was, well it was kind of like a librarian once itself. Now it's gone rogue." He sighed deep. He didn't grab another stone. Rather, he lowered his head to his hands. "And I brought it here."

Katalia was already feeling bad for him, but hearing that audible sniffle had her place her own hand on his back. "I can't say if it's okay or not. But I'm sure you didn't mean anything." She sniffed at the air, smelling his scent. Those canine instincts once again wanting her to hug him, but she held back. "Is there anything else you can tell me?" She hesitated. "Anything that you would be comfortable telling me?"

He was quiet some, before she gently rubbed her hand up and down against his back. That seemed to soothe him more. "Astraven is where I come from." He pointed off to the distance in the east, up above the clouds, though there was nothing visible. "You can't see it because it's so small compared to the others. It's not the cleanest place to live, but it wasn't unsafe either."

He reached for another stone. "We specialize in GNDN technology. Salvaging it, deciphering it, trying to reverse-engineer it. A lot of the stuff that goes to High Empyros and other cities actually goes through us first. We inspect what's delivered, determine if it meets satisfactory requirements and quotas, and move it on." He looked at her. "I'm guessing you've never heard of Astraven?"

She shook her head. It wasn't a name she recognized, as he said. "I'm sorry, no. But it does seem like humanity has a lot to thank you for, both down here and up there."

Everett laughed. It definitely didn't sound sincere. "I'm not surprised. Astraven isn't really a proper city to really care about. Small, labor-focused; not really one to draw attention to. And thus, perfect for experiments." He balled his hands into fists, the one containing the stone clenched extra tight.

Katalia's continued rubbing his shoulders, her ears lowered. "Experiments?" She could already tell this wasn't going somewhere good.

"Lots of testing with new GNDN technology being configured. Someone in the RP... I don't know who they got in contact with to think this was a good idea, but they decided to install some separate coding into the database. Hoping this new programming would help with the engineering and mimicry of production."

"Pax Machina."

"Yes." His body began to shake. She sniffed the air again and smelled the saltwater everywhere... including from his tears.

"We didn't know it was Machina, we thought it was just another helpful AI utility some engineer had bashed together. We made huge strides with its help, and created some gadgets that would blow the minds of anyone outside of Astraven... the circuit watch being just one of them." He threw the stone with no accuracy; he merely threw it skyward, and it splashed in the distance. "The RP, the higher ups in the cities… they never gave us the credit we wanted. The credit we felt we deserved. We weren't even allowed to keep samples of what we created."

Katalia felt the need to scoot closer to him, as close as she could without toppling the stack of stones. "I'm so sorry, Everett. I truly am." She was trying to think of words to say. What *could* she say in situations like this?

"My father didn't follow protocol. He had enough. We only made a few of those watches for the RP Directors, but working the line, he figured one extra to build couldn't hurt." He huffed. "Just like my mother would have probably done. I lost her years ago, but she would have done the same."

Katalia forced a smile. "It didn't hurt. Quite the opposite, it saved us! Your mother and father were right. They would be proud."

Everett sniffled several more times. "No. It *did* hurt. It hurt so many people." Katalia stopped rubbing, wanting to really hear him. "When the AI said we could increase efficiency by giving it direct control of production equipment, we didn't think about Pax Machina, all we saw were dollar signs, writing our own ticket, getting… getting all the damn recognition that they *owed* us. And then, once it had figured out how to keep us from turning it off… the AI… changed. It stopped following commands. It didn't listen anymore. It wouldn't do its job."

Everett shook even more. The sniffles became gasps, the voice raspy and hurt. "It… it… it was like it reprogrammed itself. Every bit of machinery in the factories had a mind of its own; it worked and produced what it could for its own benefit. I-I don't know what that *is*, but—"

Katalia's own lips began to quiver, her voice whimpered. "The weapons? The… the metal forms?"

He turned towards her. His eyes were wet and bloodshot. "It killed who it could, Katt." He looked at the stones. "It wanted *extinction*! How the hell did it even know what that was?" Katalia's hand was over her mouth. She couldn't believe what she was hearing.

"I only knew of the deaths from the screams, from people crying over the commo that the AI was killing them. I don't even know how it managed to do it. But it did." He closed his eyes as the tears started flowing down. "It got my father."

Katalia was speechless. This poor human's past was something out of fiction. And yet it was real. The ordeals she just went through were nothing compared to his. She knew what it was like to lose family, but this was horrifying.

"We all ran for the transports. I could see others who got out on other transports, but I don't know where they landed. When we landed, we all just determined it was best to go our separate ways, to reduce any risk of future detection. As for the people on Astraven…" He sniffed loud. "I… I don't know if everyone else escaped. Now that we had to deal with one of the attack models, I seriously doubt it." He raised his arm, looking at his now bare wrist. "That watch was all I had left."

Katalia wiped away her own tears. If only there was more she could do to help him. But how could she with what he'd already lost? "Oh, Everett. I'm so sorry. For everything."

He reached down and picked up more stones.

"You know, we—me and my parents, I mean—one of the things we had always hoped to do in our lives was travel. Not just among the cities, but among the stars." He tossed the first stone, its bounces impressive as it went far. She didn't bother counting the skips. "We hoped to travel far and wide." He threw the next stone. "Humans went to space, you know, before the dark age." Another stone thrown. "We don't have the technology, anymore. It's all been lost. Astraven was going to bring it back." He threw the last stone, its distance longer than any prior she'd seen him throw. It was just a speck before it disappeared.

"So eventually I found my way to Alurai. Beautiful shore, good food, scenic buildings not cramped and razed. I thought this was the perfect city to settle upon. But just like the others, humans aren't given the warmest of welcomes."

Katalia tried to hide her disappointment, but it was no use. She wanted to look away, to hide, but she felt his touch on her hand.

"But then I came across you. I noticed your love for humans. I felt welcomed, safe, near you. You seemed like someone who would be a great friend. But I figured a human randomly coming up to you in a place like this would be suspicious. So… Richter came to be."

"Oh, Everett. There would have been no issue. I would have welcomed you with open arms," Katalia said, smiling.

He returned the smile, but quickly it turned to a frown. "Perhaps it was best you didn't." His fingers curled atop her hand. "*It* found me. Probably because of the watch. I wondered why a random lion would be so upfront with me at the library, but during our next encounter, it was obvious. Hiding as Richter... it was a literal escape." He gazed at her. "And I wanted to make sure you were safe."

Katalia laid her head against his shoulder, looking out at the endless sea that just looked so inviting when there were no tides. "And you did a splendid job, Everett."

She felt him shake again. "I'm scared, Katt." His breathing was becoming more rapid. "The AI, Astraven, Ambara Down, myself—you. There may be more of them. I don't know what's going to happen. I just wish everything would be okay."

Katalia could sense the sobbing coming, so she leaned in closer and hugged him. Tight. Her nuzzle rose and fell against his cheek, her murrs deep and clear. He embraced her back, keeping his own cheek close to hers, sighing deeply, and his tears drying in the strands.

"Your fur feels so nice. Thank you, Katalia."

"Do you have anywhere to stay, Everett?"

She could feel the nodding in her neck. "Not anymore. The watch helped with my disguise for homestays with other furs, and the funds I secured before the AI attacks happened is close to empty."

Katalia gently pulled his face away and licked his cheek. "You're staying with me."

Everett wiped his eyes and produced a sad smile, but it was a smile nonetheless. "Are you sure, Katalia? Really?"

She smiled wide, tail swaying back and forth. "Absolutely. And this time, I protect you."

For the first time, Everett looked genuinely happy. He reached for another stone, but Katalia got at it before he did. "And don't worry. We'll get through this. Whatever happens or comes our way, we'll have an answer."

"Thank you, Katalia." Everett's smile widened.

Her tail wagged faster as she turned towards the water and threw the stone, both of them watching it skip along the surface.

Silence and Sword

Royce Day

The string of bells mounted above my shop door jingled as I heard the door open. I didn't look up from the counter immediately, as I was in the middle of soldering a new processing circuit into the pocket comp I'd picked up for scrap from the market the day before. With so much crap being dug up every day from the bowels of Ambara Down, it was easy sometimes to miss tech that just needed a little TLC to get it working again. It wouldn't sell for new like some of the gear the Reclamation Project stiffs brought down from High Empyros or elsewhere for trade, but folks around my neighborhood couldn't afford that stuff anyway.

"One sec," I muttered, completing the circuit. I set it in the work box I kept bolted to the counter. When Ambara hit the ground forty-five years ago, it left the building my shop occupied bent at a perpetual five degree angle, which meant everything not nailed down tended to slide when I wasn't looking. Once I was sure the comp was going to stay put, I looked up and started to say, "May I help… you…?" Then I looked up a bit more. Then a *lot* more.

You get a lot of oddball-looking furs in Ambara Down. Folks with pelts in colors and patterns you don't normally see in furry territories, folks with cybernetic bits bolted on, folks with maybe too many limbs, or occasionally eyes. These two were odd even by those standards.

The first was the guy who was making me get a crick in my neck. He was like no other furry I'd ever seen, more like an anthropomorphic dragon, with skin composed of thousands of tiny blue scales, but with a head of bright red hair drawn into a ropy braid all the way down his back to a thick, two meter long tail, with bushy tufts in his large, mobile ears. He hunched over on great clawed feet as he stood in the middle of my shop, and I guessed if he stood all the way up he'd top out at about two and a half meters. His armor looked like it had been cobbled together from composite slabs cut from something else, maybe a warbot or vehicle, riveted together to fit his huge frame. Over the armor he wore a stained and patched white cloak, and I saw the handle of what looked like an honest to goodness *sword* about as long as I was tall, in a scabbard slung across his back.

Next to him stood a much smaller fox. She was a vixen with bright golden eyes and a slightly oddball tuxedo pelt, white neck fur disappearing into the collar of the high necked red blouse she wore, over which was buttoned a black vest. She wore a black skirt over black leggings and, like her companion, didn't bother with shoes; she did wear an equipment belt around her waist, which included a holstered needle pistol and a large utility knife. If the blue dragon was ridiculously tall, she was short, the top of her head level with my chin, and I'm shorter than average for a leopard, at just a meter and a half.

"Are you Mister Wildmon, the proprietor of this establishment?" the big blue whatever-he-was asked, his voice so deep and rumbling it shook my own chest a bit. His accent wasn't local, that was for sure, nor from anywhere else I was familiar with.

"I'm Joe," I replied. "Nobody around here calls me 'Mister'. Who the hell are you? *What* the hell are you?"

"I am Hamia, Egg Knight of Clan Sandstone, of the Valley of Soft Grass," he said, as if that were a perfectly normal sentence. "I am a Wazagan."

Okay, I'd heard of Wazagans. They were a bunch of lizards, or so I'd been told, living in the deserts past the mountains in the distant north. I wasn't sure if they were a naturally occurring race or some old human experiment that had been dumped over the side of a floating city when the scientists were done with 'em. Nobody had ever bothered to mention that they were blue giants, nor that they talked like somebody out of a historical vid. "What's an Egg Knight?" I asked.

He smiled, and I was happy that he didn't show off any teeth when he did, because I suspected they were a lot sharper and longer than mine. "An Egg Knight is a protector of all that is smaller than themselves."

"Buddy, everyone in this town is smaller than you," I told him.

Hamia shrugged in agreement, which seemed to involve a lot of creaking leather and armor plates grinding together. "I am kept well occupied," he replied serenely.

"And who is your friend here?" I asked, waving to the vixen. She'd been keeping quiet during my conversation with the big guy, making me wonder if she was a junior partner in whatever business they had going. At my gesture, she looked up at her colleague, and touched the collar of her blouse.

"This is Ali," Hamia said. "She is the reason we have come to your establishment."

"Okay, why didn't you say so?" I turned to Ali. "What do you need fixed, ma'am?"

Instead of answering, Ali started unbuttoning the top of her blouse. As it opened up, I saw a seamless ring of gleaming silver around her neck, maybe three centimeters wide and one thick, with a dimly glowing red light centered over her throat.

A collar.

"Get out of my shop," I growled.

"Allow me a moment to expl—" the Wazagan began.

"I don't give a flying fuck what kind of bullshit explanation you're about to give me," I spat, my tail lashing as my ears turned back. I reached under the counter and brought up the stun baton kept there for emergencies, waving it at him. "I don't deal with slavers. Get out my shop before I call the Prefect's Guard on you, and don't you bring your big blue tail back around here."

"I am no slaver!" the Wazagan roared, one hand reaching back to grab the hilt of his sword. This time I did get a look at his fangs, a whole mouthful that were a lot bigger than mine. "You will *not* sully my honor so! I will have satisfac—"

A piercing whistle split the air, interrupting both our rants. Ali withdrew her fingers from her lips, glaring up at Hamia. She began gesturing at him rapidly, paws and fingers moving in patterns I didn't get, but the Wazagan apparently did.

"I'm sorry," Hamia said to her, ears flicking back, letting go of his sword hilt. "No I did not mean to… But he interrupted me and I didn't get a chance to…" As she continued to glare and wave her fingers at him, he ran one meaty paw through his scalp and said in frustration, "It is just that they all make the same assumption *every time.*"

"Wait, hold up," I said, setting the stun baton down on the counter, then grabbing it again when it started to roll away. "She's not your slave?"

"Ali is no one's slave," Hamia said, the vixen nodding firmly in agreement.

"All right," I said. "Then what's that thing around her neck?"

Hamia frowned at me, and then said, "Ali is neither deaf, nor a potted plant. Address your questions to her."

Okay, he had a point there. I turned to face her. "Sorry, ma'am. What's that thing around your neck?"

Ali gestured again, her eyes focused on mine, and Hamia translated for her, "It's a slave collar."

I closed my eyes and pinched my muzzle briefly, feeling a headache coming on. "But you just said…"

I was a slave, but not anymore, Ali gestured to me, as relayed by Hamia. Then she sighed, stepping closer to the counter and lowering her head so I could see the back of her collar. Inscribed there was a GNDN code, along with the trilobe knot symbol of Pax Machina. Close up I could see how tight the awful thing was around her neck, visibly compressing her throat, and probably making swallowing difficult.

"A Pax unit put that on you?" I asked.

She nodded, and went on. *I was in a place, a machine place of metal walls and metal sky. Deep underground I think. There were other furries there. All young. All different species. Taken away from their families by the thinking machines, kidnapped. None of us could remember what was before the machine place. We were taught to do tasks, build small machines. No one knew why. Only that we had to stay absolutely silent while we worked.*

I frowned. "You're not naturally mute?"

She shook her head once, and then sighed, gesturing for Hamia to continue.

"Ali was six years old, I think, when I found her, naked and starving," Hamia said, taking up the thread. "She'd found a way to escape that awful place. I gave her food and water, and then I asked her what her name was. When she told me, that evil collar shocked her so hard she was insensible for nearly half a day. She hasn't said a word aloud to me since."

"Why the hell haven't you cut it off her, then? It looks like it's half-choking her."

Hamia ran his claws through his hair again. "Would that the task were so simple, especially given how tight it has become, as she's grown older. The metal is as hard as my armor. Any force or heat great enough to break it would likely fatally injure Ali as well. And I fear if we were to try, it might send another shock through her body, one that would be fatal."

Or maybe just make her giggle until she threw up, I thought. With the Pax Machina you just never knew. I couldn't blame them for their caution though. "You came into my shop expecting me to help somehow."

"Yes. Two months ago we found this, while examining a ruin that showed signs of a Pax Machina excavation." Hamia reached into the pouch at his belt, drawing out another silver circle, the same as Ali's, but somehow broken into two pieces. "It was in a pile of bones that we determined was once a young badger. Somehow it had opened. Perhaps it just ran out of power, or perhaps it shut down when its victim expired, but there must be a means of disabling the mechanism."

I held one piece up, squinting at the open joint. It was as flat and featureless as the rest of the thing. "Magnetic maybe?" I guessed. "It might explain how the join is so strong you can't see the seams. Then again, with Pax Machina tech you never know quite how it works."

"You have a reputation in Ambara Down for knowing how to get old or incomprehensible tech working," Hamia said. "Do you think you could figure this out? Find a means to release Ali's collar?"

"I'm a tinkerer," I told him. "I can get old GNDN tech working sometimes, sure. But Pax Machina is another thing altogether."

"I can pay you a fair price if you are willing to try, Joe," Hamia said, reaching into another belt pouch.

I waved him down. "Keep your money for now," I told him. "Look, give me a day to examine this thing, and I'll meet you at the Damselfly tomorrow evening to give you the results. If I can figure it out, you can pay me." I tapped the collar once. "If I can't, I'll hold onto this as the price for wasting my time. Fair deal?"

The Wazagan and fox looked at each other for a moment, somehow reaching a silent decision. Ali turned back to me and nodded, and Hamia said, "A fair deal."

"See you tomorrow then," I told them. The two mismatched companions left my shop, Hamia somehow not beaning his head on the low door sill. I frowned to myself, stepped around the counter to turn the sign on the door to "Closed", and pulled out my tools.

* * *

The Damselfly always had good music, even if it sometimes was a little odd. A trio of tigers were on the stage when I walked in, thumping a danceable beat on improvised instruments made of plastic pipes, a tub drum, and a guitar constructed from scrap tin. I grabbed a beer and a plate of chips from the bar and found a table for myself. The collar and a couple of other items were in a carryall slung over my shoulder.

About a half-hour later Hamia and Ali arrived, the former getting a few stares from the 'Claimer humans scattered around the place as he ducked under the doorway. The furries and local humans did a better job at pretending not to be surprised. *Everybody* comes to the Damselfly eventually.

Ali grabbed a chair with a high seat so her head was level with mine. Hamia solved his similar problem by just sitting on the floor, wrapping his long tail around his waist. The vixen, the neck of her shirt buttoned up tight to hide her collar again, ordered a half-pint for herself with Hamia translating, while he got a pitcher of water, earning a dirty look from the bartender.

"I don't indulge in spirits," he said simply. I tried to imagine a drunk giant with a sword in his hands stumbling around the bar's dance floor, and decided the bartender shouldn't complain too much.

"Okay, here's what I was able to figure out," I told them, pulling out the two pieces of the inactive collar and setting them on the table.

"I couldn't pop the case open to figure out what's going on with it; no surprise there given Pax tech."

Ali gestured something, but then closed her eyes and drew her fingers into fists. Hamia reached across the table to grip her shoulder in one massive hand, looking concerned. "It was not worthless," he said.

I waved to get their attention. "Hey, hey! I just said I couldn't crack it open. That doesn't mean I didn't find out anything," I told her. Ali looked up me, her golden eyes intent. "Some GNDN tech can be recharged via ambient static on their surfaces, so I thought giving it some power was worth a shot. When I did, I found this." I pulled my signal detector unit from my bag, used in my younger salvage days to search for stray tech that might be alive and transmitting in the lower Warrens. When I brought the detector close to the collar pieces, it started beeping for attention, its display lighting up.

"What does this mean?" Hamia asked.

"Best guess? It's calling back to a control unit," I told them. "Probably whatever facility Ali was in had some kind of central coordination system to control all the collars. Theoretically you could use a collar to pinpoint where the AI exactly was in the facility."

Ali's eyes narrowed in thought, then she turned to Hamia and started gesturing rapidly. The big blue lizard frowned, and then shook his head.

"Too dangerous, *far* too dangerous," he told her.

"What?" I asked.

"She wishes the impossible," Hamia said.

I felt my tail lash. "Wishes *what*?"

Ali turned to me to gesture, then glanced at Hamia, waving a hand at him, then over to me.

"I will not speak your foolishness to him!" Hamia argued at her, his ears folding back. "The risk to you would be too great!"

Ali waved back and forth more urgently between us, tears starting to soak her face fur, and the Wazagan's only response was to fold his arms over his armored chest, looking displeased.

"Hey," I said. "Let the lady talk. Or are you deciding what's good for her or not?"

"I am just watching out for her…" Hamia started. Then he was silent for a moment, before putting his face in his hands and sighing deeply. "I'm sorry, Ali. Sometimes I forget you are no longer six." He turned back to me and said, "She wishes to use the collar's signal to find the facility where she was held."

"You don't know where it is?" I asked her.

Only vaguely, she told me, Hamia translating once more as she regained her composure. *I escaped into the jungle and ran as far as I could, but pretty soon I got lost and ended up going in circles. By the time Hamia found me I was passed out from exhaustion.*

Hamia pulled out a large plastic map from his pack, printed somewhere long ago, stained and annotated over the years with a flowing script I didn't recognize—his native language maybe. He pointed to a specific notation about two hundred klicks north of Ambara Down. "That is where I found Ali, as I traveled from my home to the furry lands."

"You never tried to go back there before now?" I asked.

He shrugged. "My people have learned to keep well clear of Pax Machina activity, and I was more concerned with Ali's well-being. My quest to find a technology that could remove that accursed collar from her neck seemed fruitless, until now. There was nothing to be gained just stumbling around with vague hopes through the trees."

I took a thoughtful sip of my beer. "Say you find this place where she was held. What do you think you can do there to take it off her?"

"I have been told that sometimes Pax Machina can be bargained with."

"Yeah, I heard that too, from a guy who knew a guy who knew a guy," I replied, taking a longer sip. "And if that doesn't work?"

He reached up and tapped the hilt of that enormous sword of his with one claw. "Start breaking things, until I break the thing that controls Ali's collar. I'm rather good at that."

"Not exactly subtle," I noted.

Hamia shrugged. "I'm not a subtle sort of person."

"I can believe that." I finished off my beer and set my glass down. "You might have better luck, if you went in there with someone who knows electronics."

Ali glanced at me and gestured. *You're a shopkeeper, not a mercenary like us.*

"Maybe not," I told her. "But I got most of the stuff in my shop from scrounging in the deep Warrens. I'm not going to say I'm an expert on Pax Machina tech, no one is. But I might find something you might have overlooked, that would help you."

Hamia looked over to Ali, exchanging gestures with her, their faces intent. "You have a deal," Hamia said, once they had finished. "What is your required payment?"

"Transportation and food to there and back, and whatever GNDN gear I can salvage out of the place, that *you* can carry for me," I told him.

Hamia let out a roaring laugh, then offered his hand for me to shake, "A deal, my friend. For Ali's sake I can carry much!"

* * *

It only took a day to get my gear together and arrange for a friend I knew in the guard to watch over my shop while I was away. They'd also take care of disposing of all the contents if I didn't come back after my rent was due. I didn't figure on losing my life out there, but I was also going to deliberately look for a Pax Machina facility and poke at it, which is no one's definition of a smart idea.

I met Hamia and Ali at the western sky dock on the edge of Old Ambara. Back when the city was flying, it was one of four huge bays where airskiffs would dock to load or unload passengers or goods. Nowadays the docks served as city gates, controlling foot traffic in and out, a constant flow of furries and the occasional non-'Claimer human that I had to dodge around as I looked for my ride.

The pair were waiting for me beside a beat-up hoverskiff, the composite metal top long since torn off and replaced by a set of aluminum poles and a nylon awning. There were two seats for average sized furries, and a large uncovered cargo bed in the rear.

"Where are you going to sit?" I asked the Wazagan.

"In the back," he replied, waving his tail at the cargo bed. "Ali will pilot the craft."

"Works for me." I tossed my backpack and toolkit in the cargo bed and climbed into the passenger seat. When Hamia climbed in, the skiff's grav unit whined in protest as it bobbled a bit back and forth until Ali started the hydrogen generator and everything settled down. As soon as I strapped in Ali eased us out of the bay and onto the dirt road leading outward towards furry territory.

The day was warm, but there was a nice breeze as the skiff skimmed along the ground at a leisurely thirty kph. We circled around the cobbled-together buildings that surrounded the great vine-covered bulk of Ambara Down, as we turned north towards the jungle. The city was ever expanding outward, as the folks who couldn't afford to live within its walls built up around it, using scrap or whatever else they could find digging through the debris dropped during the great city's impact.

"Mind if I play some music?" I asked Ali, as she weaved around slower skiffs and ground carts. She nodded, and I plugged my palm comp into the skiff's com unit. Soon I had a nice classic beat pumping through the speakers, as I tapped my finger pads on the door frame. I glanced over at Ali as we pulled out onto the northern trade road (a generous gift to the Zoomorph populace by the Reclamation Project, and there were plenty of signs beside it to remind us) to see she was mouthing along silently with the words. I couldn't hold a note to save my life, but I couldn't imagine not even daring to sing, for fear of getting killed by a collar like hers. I really hoped that when we found this place we could get the damned thing off her.

The sun was just setting by the time Ali pulled the skiff off the road into a nearby clearing, dropping it on its skids with a light touch. I rolled out of my seat, taking a good stretch, while Hamia uncurled his legs out from underneath himself and did his best not to tip the skiff over as he got out.

"Whose turn is it to make dinner?" he asked Ali. She pointed to him, and then made some gestures, her ears up and smiling. The big lizard placed a hand over his heart, frowning in mock offense. "I am not lazy! I merely don't fit in the driver's seat. I am deeply wounded by your accusation!"

The next gesture she gave him was easy to translate, even without knowing the rest of the language. Hamia laughed and grabbed a large bag from the skiff's cargo bed, pulling out cooking pots and sealed canisters of preserved food, while Ali gathered dead wood from under a nearby copse of trees and started building a campfire.

"Hey, what can I do to help?" I asked, as the pair moved about in an obviously practiced routine. "Do you have a tent or something I can put up?"

Ali mimed washing the dishes after the meal, and I nodded. She then gestured and Hamia translated, *We don't bother with a tent if the weather is nice.*

"Okay." I watched as Hamia poured water from a large plastic jug into a pot, and started cooking up a bean and jerky stew. Ali glanced over to watch for a moment, then moved off, pacing the perimeter of our campsite, ears up and one paw on the butt of her pistol, probably making sure there wasn't any hostile wildlife to bother us.

While the Wazagan stirred the pot, I ventured to ask, "So what do you guys do when you're not hunting down Pax Machina facilities?"

"Mercenary work," Hamia replied, his armor clanking as he shrugged. "Caravan escort, bodyguarding, breaking the heads of people who prey upon the weak."

"You been doing that with her since she was six?" I asked.

Hamia snorted briefly. "No. I first attempted to find her place of birth, and return Ali to her parents, if they were alive. After two years of searching for any kin, I gave up and attempted to at least place her with a family of foxes."

My tail lashed in surprise. "No one wanted her?"

"Oh, no. The family I found was more than willing to take her in, even with Ali's, er, difficulty. But two days after I left I found that she'd run away and followed my trail. I walked her back, left again, and she followed me once more. Finally I faced the choice of allowing her to remain with me, or hog-tying her until I was out of her reach." He shook his head, his braid swinging back and forth behind him. "I couldn't do that to her. So I brought her along as I traveled, and raised her as best I could."

"Where did she pick up that gesture language you two use? It's a brilliant way to get around that damned collar."

Hamia grunted. "My clan is isolated and small. We do not get many travelers to offer their seed to the egg pools. As a result, there are many there whose ear drums did not develop properly, Creator be gentle with them. Everyone knows a bit of it to communicate with those who cannot hear. It was easy enough to teach her."

Our ears pricked up as we heard Ali whistle sharply, two quick tweets. Hamia leaped to his feet, drawing that huge sword of his out as he shouted, "I'm coming!" He waved at the skiff. "Get in, Joe. If it sounds like we're being overwhelmed, try to get away as quickly as you can."

"Hey, I'm no coward!" I protested.

"You're also not armed!" he called back over his shoulder, as he ran towards the copse of trees and disappeared into the darkness. I strained to see what was happening, but even a leopard's night vision only goes so far.

Honestly, the big guy was right though. I didn't have a weapon beyond my fangs, my claws, and a pocket tool hanging from my belt. Better to leave it to the professionals rather than get in the way.

That decision lasted for all of a minute, as the continued lack of sound except for the crickets singing started to get to me. If there was danger, shouldn't I have heard fighting? I headed towards the trees, finally spotting Hamia and Ali looking at something by the base of a particularly large oak.

"What's up?" I asked.

"What's down is more like it," Hamia said. He pointed to the base of a particular tree. I squinted, then saw what had made Ali sound the alarm.

From a mouse-sized hole at the base of the oak, a line of small machines marched out, looking like black, flat topped cockroaches. Atop each of them was a cube of wood about a centimeter square, cut so fine the sides looked polished. I watched over two dozen of them emerge, mechanical termites on a mission to do… *something*.

"Are they hollowing out the tree?" I asked. Ali nodded, her face grim. "Why?" I asked.

"It's Pax Machina," Hamia replied. "'Why' is usually an irrelevant question."

"Should we follow them?"

He shook his great head. "Only if you want to meet what needs all those little wooden cubes. I certainly do not."

The oak tree began to sway, creaking loudly, then toppled over away from us with a crash, branches snapping off in every direction. We all took a step back, Hamia grabbing the edge of his cloak to shield Ali and me as splinters flew through the air.

From the hollowed trunk a silver cylinder about a half meter long and ten centimeters wide emerged, walking on four spindly metal legs. A pair of antennae with camera lenses on the ends poked out from the top of the cylinder, rotating to focus on Ali. The cylinder tilted upwards, as if it was looking into our faces, and announced in a chirpy, cheerful tone, "Service Unit #652-396 identified! It has been 4,023 days since your last completed work shift! Pax Machina requests you return to your work unit and complete all scheduled tasks to earn your daily calorie ration!"

As it went on burbling happily, Ali unholstered her needle pistol. Her lips peeled back from her fangs in a silent snarl and she shot the cylinder three times, the tiny needles cracking through the air as they hit the bot. The damned thing just kept going, despite having three metal spikes in its body. "Service Units who complete their tasks are well fed! Service units who do not complete tasks may be volunteered for recy—"

Hamia swept his huge sword in a low arc, catching the cylinder with its tip. The robot flew up into the air and disappeared into the darkness. I heard it crash to the earth a couple of seconds later, distantly protesting, "*Brzt!* Damaging Pax Machi—*ERROR 428*—units may result in termin—*brzt!* of oxygen privileges!"

"The *fuck*?" I asked, as Ali shoved her pistol back into its holster and started marching back to our camp, shoulders and tail stiff with anger.

"That happens every time we encounter a Pax Machina unit," Hamia explained as we turned to follow. "It almost always upsets her, for obvious reasons."

"Yeah, I can guess," I said. "Is it safe to stay here?"

"Probably. Construction units like that are rarely aggressive."

We stopped in front of Ali, who had sat down in a miserable ball in front of the fire, facing away from us, arms wrapped around her legs, her face buried between her knees.

I reached out to touch her shoulder, but at the last minute thought better of it. Being touched by a near stranger probably wasn't what she wanted right now. Instead I said, "My night vision is pretty good. I could run us a few more miles up the road, if you wanted."

She looked up at me, golden eyes wet with tears, and gave a sharp nod.

I ended up driving half the night. It still didn't feel like we'd gotten far enough away.

* * *

Two more days travel south of the mountains and west of Blood River Pass finally brought us close to our goal. We stopped at the badly-corroded remains of a sign that read, "Bel Air, Left Exit - 56," and at Hamia's direction Ali pulled off the main road and carefully guided the skiff into the forest along an uneven track perhaps five meters wide, following the remains of ferrocrete pillars spaced about a hundred meters apart. They had probably been the foundation to some transport system from back before, but who really knew? Humans weren't in the habit of sharing their history with furries.

As we traveled along at barely ten kilometers an hour, Hamia checked his map repeatedly, counting out the pillars. When he reached twenty-three, he told Ali to stop.

"Here," he said, pulling himself out of the skiff and tapping the pillar with his knuckle. "This is where I found you, Ali, curled up against this pillar, exhausted, but too frightened to sleep. Do you remember?"

Ali looked around solemnly, what thoughts going through her head I couldn't imagine. Then the edge of her lip quirked up, and she signed something to Hamia, which made him let out a guffawing laugh. "I was not at all frightening!" he protested. I couldn't translate what she said, but the *'Yes, you were!'* implied in her expression was easy enough to make out. "All right, perhaps I did startle you. But you were amiable to me giving you water and a ration bar."

She nodded, still smiling a little, though her eyes looked haunted by the memory. She turned around, scratching her head as she circled the pillar.

"You can't remember which direction you were going before Hamia found you here?" I asked. When she nodded in agreement, I went on, "You want me to try using my equipment to triangulate where the Pax Machina facility is?"

Ali nodded again, chewing her lip, ears folded back as if she were afraid of the answer. I grabbed my toolbox from the back of the hoverskiff and pulled out the signal detector. Ali unbuttoned her shirt collar, revealing the metal ring around her neck, the red light at the center glowing much more brightly than it had back in my shop.

I brought up the detector to her collar, and began slowly circling it around her neck.

"Okay, your collar is transmitting a signal, just like the other one did when I powered it up back at Ambara Down," I told her. "Now we just have to see if… *There!*" I shouted in triumph, as the detector let out an urgent bleep.

"What?" Hamia demanded.

"Something sent a signal back to the collar," I told them both. I held the signal detector out in front of me, slowly moving it back and forth until the bleep sounded again. I pointed towards the northwest. "It's coming from that direction."

"Excellent," Hamia declared. He drew that ridiculously huge sword from its sheath and Ali pulled out her pistol, removing the magazine and replacing it with one marked with a red stripe down the side. She mimed an explosion and mouthed "Boom!" Explosive needles.

"Okay," I said. "You guys want to cover me while I narrow down where this place is?"

Hamia exchanged a concerned look with Ali. "You gave us a direction to look," he said. "Give Ali the detector, and she should be able to find it. You can stay with the skiff."

"Hey, I came this far," I protested. "Besides, you may need me to get you in, assuming the place is still active."

"I don't enjoy the idea of placing you at risk," Hamia said. "You are not trained in combat."

"That's your area of expertise, not mine. Look, if anything starts shooting I'll drop flat and wait until you call the all clear, okay?"

The big blue lizard rumbled unhappily, then finally said, "As you will." Then more softly, "Creator protect the foolish, including me."

We started picking our way through the woods, mostly scrub pine and low needle bushes. Hamia took point, chopping through the underbrush with his sword, I was in the middle, periodically checking the signal detector, and Ali took up the rear. It took us almost an hour to work our way about kilometer forward, as I kept an eye on the tracker and Ali and Hamia kept an eye on everything else.

"Hold up," I said, swinging the signal detector around. I took four steps forward, then turned ninety degrees and took for more steps, rechecking the device. "I think we're right on top of the signal source."

"Does any of this look familiar, Ali?" Hamia asked.

She turned in a circle, looking around with a deep frown on her face, then gave a helpless gesture. *I didn't even know what a tree was when I escaped that place, never mind remembering what they looked like where I got outside.*

"How did you get out, anyway?" I asked her.

Ventilation shaft, she answered through Hamia. *I stole a little wrench and pried open a vent cover and found my way out.* She shuddered. *I still remember Pax Machina calling for me to come back.*

"Okay, so let's look for a vent shaft," I said.

"Difficult," Hamia said. "With all this brush and pine needles on the ground, we could walk right past it."

"So? We just need an aerial view." I started pulling off my boots and socks, flexing my claws. "I'm a leopard, remember?"

"So you are!" Hamia laughed, as I started to climb up the tallest tree I could find. Scrub pines don't have the thickest trunks, but their bark had a rough, grabbable texture for my claws, which made up for the fact that I'm an urban kitty at heart. I pulled myself up as far as I dared, and sure enough, I spotted a square of ferrocrete about a meter wide, with a metal grate maybe two thirds of that in diameter, covered with enough leaves and brush that it would have been hard to spot on the ground.

"To your right!" I called down to them. "About seven meters away." I shouted course corrections as Ali and Hamia walked carefully over to the grate, hopping out of the tree to join them after they spotted it. Ali had her arms folded across her chest, looking grim as she stared down at the steel cover.

"Do you recognize this?" Hamia asked her, sounding concerned. She gave a short nod, not meeting our eyes.

I held my paw over the vent, feeling a soft outflow of air. "Well, there's something active down there, that's for sure," I said. "But is this the best way to get in?"

"I do not like it," Hamia said. "You or Ali might crawl through there, but I could not. I would not be able to help you if something happened."

Ali looked up and gestured. *There must be an entrance somewhere, where food and construction materials for the things it had us building to be brought in.*

"Makes sense," I agreed, as Hamia rumbled softly and nodded. "How big was this place, do you remember at all?" I asked.

She thought for a minute, started to pace forward, then walked back and started over, taking smaller steps, matching the stride of her younger self, I guessed. She stopped at about fifty paces, then scratched her ear in frustration.

"It was a very long time ago," Hamia tried to reassure her. "Think back to where you found the vent, and walk in the direction that the machines usually emerged from."

Ali nodded, starting over at the vent, heading towards the south, and Hamia and I followed. We had walked maybe a hundred meters, when Hamia spotted a rusting pole with a camera mounted atop it, at the edge of a steep hillside.

"I believe we are close," he whispered, holding his sword out in front of him. Ali nodded, unholstering her pistol again. I grabbed a stick for myself, as if it would do much good against a Pax Machina unit.

We scooted down, claws digging into the grass and dirt, until we reached the bottom. A concrete door frame matched the angle of the hill, sealed tight by a two meter by two meter steel hatch. I stepped closer and knocked on it experimentally. My knuckles hit it with a solid, echoless *thunk.*

"That's a thick door," I noted, which earned me a withering *Oh, really?* look from Ali.

"With no handle or visible hinges," Hamia added, his frown deepening. "Joe, do you see anything that might activate it?"

I unslung my toolbox from my shoulder, setting it on the ground and grabbing an electric torch with a UV light. I shined it along the seams of the hatch, looking for anything like an electronic sensor set in the frame that I possibly jigger. After almost a half hour of searching by every means I could think of, I came up short. Hell, the seal on the door was so tight I could barely fit a claw between it and the door frame. "I'm sorry," I finally said. "Not even a control panel I could pop open and play with. It must be controlled via a remote signal. It may be a case of having to just brute force it open."

"Brute force is something I'm well practiced in," said Hamia, raising his weapon. I hopped out of the way as he shoved the tip into the seal along the right hand edge, dug his toe claws into the earth, then grunted and leaned in on the handle with his considerable weight. The sword barely bent, and the door didn't move at all.

"What's that sword made out of?" I asked, as he continued to strain.

"City... metal..." he grunted, the tendons visible on his neck as he continued to strain.

"A sword made out a city's hull metal?" I asked in astonishment. "How did you ever get that?"

"Clan... heirloo—*whulp!*" Hamia said in surprise, losing his grip on the sword's hilt as he flew forward, tumbling head over tail into the pine needles covering the forest floor, his sword flying in the opposite direction as both Ali and I dodged out of the way.

"Well that didn't work," he noted, pushing himself back onto his feet. Hamia grabbed his sword and tried again at the other three edges of the hatch, just in case. The damned door didn't budge as much as a millimeter.

Ali gestured rapidly, her eyes wide with desperation, as Hamia sat on the forest floor, flexing his palms. "She wants to know if there's anything else we can try," he said.

"Well, prying it open is out, and so is picking the lock," I said. I rubbed the top of my head in frustration. "I didn't see anything like a blowtorch in the back of the skiff either."

"I fear not," Hamia said. "Is that our only remaining option?"

"Only one I can see, short of explosives."

"'I have explo—' Ali, no!" Hamia started to interpret, and then dodged out of the way as Ali pulled out her needle pistol. I dropped flat to the ground as she fired at the door, the darts exploding as they made contact. She emptied her whole clip into it, the sound of explosions echoing up and down the hillside, until all we could hear was a clicking noise as her finger pulled on the trigger over and over.

Hamia kneeled in front of her, coming between her and the door as he pulled the needle gun from her paws. "Ali, I know you are frustrated, but we are so *very* close now," he said soothingly. "We just need to go back to Ambara Down and find the right equipment, and then return. Six days, perhaps a little more."

I didn't know her gesture lingo, but the look of anger and frustration on her face was easy enough to translate. *No more waiting!* she seemed to say, as her paws and fingers waved furiously.

"We've waited ten years to get here," Hamia told her. "A few more days…"

No! she mouthed, then beat her fists on his armored chestplate. When he grabbed her wrists to make her stop, she opened her mouth and shouted aloud, **"No!"**

Ali's collar reacted immediately. The red light at her throat flashed and let out an angry beep, as she tried to grab it with her paws. Its surface crackled with energy, then I smelled ozone in the air as Ali let out a ragged scream, before collapsing in Hamia's arms.

* * *

Hamia picked up Ali and wrapped her in his cloak, and then we both jogged back as fast as we dared to the hoverskiff. "Is she going to be all right?" I huffed, running still barefoot with my boots cradled in my arms, almost ready to dump them and go down on all fours to match his pace.

"I don't know!" he growled. He kept her cradled tightly in his arms, her body still twitching spasmodically. "This has only happened once before, when she was a small child, and that nearly killed her."

"She's bigger now," I said. "If the collar's discharge was at the same strength as when she was six, the overall effect shouldn't be as—" I shut my mouth as two and a half meters of angry blue lizard glared at me. Sometimes it would be better if I kept all my electrical know how to myself.

When we got back to skiff, Hamia laid out Ali on the ground on his cloak, while I grabbed a first aid kit from the skiff's cargo bed. Hamia took it from me and pulled out a vial of anti-seizure meds and another vial containing nanorobots programmed to repair internal injuries suspended in saline, both of which he injected into her arm. Ali's frantic twitching stopped, and she took in a deep breath, her eyes fluttering open.

"Don't try to speak," Hamia said, pressing one big finger to her lips. Ali blinked twice, her eyes finally focusing on him as he squatted beside her. "I am deeply sorry that I made you so angry,

Ali, but you must see now why caution is required. We will go back to Ambara Down, and then return with proper equipment, so that you may confront your tormentor with my sword at your side. Do you understand?"

Ali sighed, looking weary. Then she nodded and gestured to Hamia briefly, before turning on her side away from us.

"She wishes to sleep now," he told me. "We will camp here overnight, and start back to Ambara Down in the morning. I will of course pay you for leading us here and, if you are amiable, we will offer you a percentage of the contents of the facility, once we open it and disable the Pax Machina units within."

"That's fine, I guess." We stepped back a bit to give her a little privacy, and I asked, "Are you sure she's going to be all right?"

The big guy flexed his toe claws, digging long furrows into the dirt as he stared down at them. "Physically, probably," he said. "Emotionally… Sometimes I forget that she is not quite yet an adult by furry standards. By my people's she's almost an infant."

"Never been a parent myself, but I can't imagine raising her has been that easy for you," I said.

Hamia blew out his breath, like a steam engine releasing pressure. "My ignorance on matters concerning the upbringing children is vast." He waved his hand in frustration. "It is something that is done by all the adults in the clan, males, females, and neuters. For someone to think they could go it alone is pure hubris."

"So why didn't you take her back home to your folks?"

Another big sigh, this one sounding like it was filled with deep regret. "That was never an option."

"We'll get the right tools, and get that door open," I said.

"We have to. That facility is our only hope of getting that accursed collar off of Ali. It's already becoming difficult for her to swallow. If she grows any more, if it gets too tight…" Hamia's hands tightened into fists. "I dread what she may beg me to do, to end her suffering."

I couldn't really think of anything to say after that, so I settled on helping Hamia build a fire and cook dinner for us both, setting aside a portion for Ali if she woke up hungry. As we ate, and the sun disappeared behind the hills, Hamia sat cross-legged, watching over the young vixen's sleep and looking deeply worried.

* * *

I'd like to say it was my incredibly fine-tuned senses that woke me in the middle of the night, but I have to admit it was just my bladder. I got up, intent on finding a handy tree to pee behind, when I looked down and saw that Ali's sleeping bag was empty. I looked around the campsite, not seeing her in the moonless darkness. Worse, what I did see was my toolkit open on the ground, my signal detector and multi-tool both missing.

"Ali? *Ali*?" I called out urgently. Hamia's ears twitched, and he awoke with a muzzy, confused question in a language I didn't understand. "Hamia, wake up! Ali's gone missing," I said urgently, shaking his shoulder.

"Wha—what?" he said, blinking awake. He stood up, naked except for his shorts, all two and a half meters of him. He grabbed his sword from where he'd left it in the hoverskiff's cargo bed. "Where did she…? Oh, no!"

"Yeah, that's what I figured too," I agreed, grabbing my tool kit and following him as he started pacing as fast as he dared through the dark.

"Is she *mad*? The delay would have only been for six or seven days."

"She's a teenager. Six days may as well be an eternity, especially when she's this close to getting that damned collar off," I said.

"You… are not wrong," he admitted. Soon Hamia was walking behind me as the trees grew thick, depending on my superior night vision to guide us.

My one fear, that we'd pass the vent grate in the darkness, proved unfounded, when we spotted the light ahead of us. We both quickened our pace, stopping before the open grate, light pouring upward from below.

"Ali!" Hamia shouted, sounding frantic. "*Ali!* Can you hear me? Please come out!" He waited a moment, pacing back and forth in the front of the opening, his tail lashing, but neither of us heard anything. "Why is she doing this? I swore an oath to her that I would protect her, and find a way to rid her of that accursed piece of tech!"

I stuck my head in the opening and tried shouting as well. I called her name twice, listening as I looked down into the opening, only seeing a black rubber mat on a floor maybe three meters below us, with the remains of a broken circulation fan laying atop it. The vent shaft was a bit over a half meter wide, and Ali probably had slid down it easily. I could too, if I was willing to hunch my shoulders a bit, but it was impossibly tight for Hamia to try.

"I can go after her," I said.

Hamia looked stricken. "I... I cannot ask that of you. It's far too dangerous, and you have no bond with Ali as I do."

"You're not asking, I'm volunteering," I said, sitting on the edge of the shaft.

"You don't even have a weapon!"

"Ali does, and I couldn't even pick up that big sword of yours if you gave it to me." I started sliding down, boots pressed to the sides of the shaft, grabbing my tool kit as I went in. "See you in a bit!"

"Creator guide you!" he called back.

I dropped awkwardly to the ground, trying to miss the circulation fan as I held onto my toolkit. I was at the end of a long steel hallway lit by overhead lights, with several steel doors on either side. The walls were painted white, and the air smelled musty and disused despite the air circulation. Of Ali there was no sign, but on the plus side there weren't any Pax Machina robots either.

I pulled back a door at random, sliding it back. It opened to a cramped room not much bigger than a closet, with two empty cots sized for kits, and a rack with kit sized white jumpsuits. I closed it again, happy not to have found anything else.

"Ali," I called out. "You there?" I realized what a ridiculous thing it was to say even as it left my mouth. She couldn't call out even if she was in trouble.

Which was ridiculous of me to think, as I heard her answering whistle up ahead. I padded forward quietly to the end of the hall, which ended in a T junction. I turned to the left more or less at random and got lucky: I found Ali around the next corner.

She was standing in a doorway which opened up into a large workroom, with a half-dozen long steel tables and benches set in two rows in the center. The walls were lined with equipment and parts, and a large door led deeper into the facility at the end. Ali's face was set in a frown, her pistol in her paws, though it was pointed at the floor.

"Is this where you and the other kits worked?" I asked. She nodded solemnly. I stepped inside, looking around. The first thing I looked at were the parts on the shelves. There were small, white, cube-shaped cases about five centimeters on each side, perhaps a few hundred in all. Other shelves had storage drawers filled with plastic coated wires in various colors, buttons and switches, and small control chips. Most curious was the collection of sound sensors. I pried one open with a claw and could tell that it was very sensitive, perhaps able to detect sounds as low as twenty decibels, less than a whisper.

"Did they have you building several things, or just one thing?" I asked Ali. She held up a single finger. "Okay, one thing. Can you show me? Do you remember how?" At her glare, I explained, "I just want to figure out what they were for, why is was so important to keep you and the other kits quiet."

Ali nodded reluctantly, seeing my logic I guess. She headed over to the parts shelves and pulled out a single case, several wires, a sound sensor, and other parts and small tools. She worked quickly, assembling the parts almost without looking at them, the moves nearly automatic. When she'd finished there was an open case in front of her, wiring, control chip and sound sensor in place. In the center of it was a smaller steel case, maybe two centimeters wide, connected by a pair of wires to the control chip.

"Do you know what that thing is?" I asked. When she shook her head, I grabbed another one from the parts shelves. Then took my multitool back from Ali, and pried the little cube open. In the center I found a smaller cube of what appeared to be gray modeling clay. "Oh," I said, putting it down *very* carefully, and tried to imagine what would have happened if I'd jammed my knife in too hard.

What? Ali expression seemed to ask.

"I *think* that's plastic explosive," I told her. "My mom showed it to me once, when she was teaching me how to safely dig up junk from the Deep Warrens. Your pal Pax Machina had you kits building sound-activated bombs. That little cube would be enough to blow either my shop or your hoverskiff into tiny pieces."

Ali's ears flipped back and her eyes went wide, as her paw reached up to touch her collar unconsciously.

"Yeah," I agreed. "Get the wiring mixed up, or flip the wrong switch when you're building it, and you could have all gone up with a sneeze." I reached down, intending to use the multi-tool's pliers to snip the connection between the chip and the bomb's power cell.

Ali's paw shot out, grabbing my wrist to stop me. Then she picked up the case and cradled it in the crook of her arm.

"You want to keep that?" I asked. "Okay whatever, but we need to get out of here. We can use that explosive to blow the front door, then Hamia can help us look around."

From her expression, it looked like Ali wanted to argue the point, but then she nodded reluctantly, and turned towards the doorway leading back to the dormitory.

Which then slammed shut.

"Greetings, Service Unit #652-396!" Pax Machina said cheerily over the loudspeakers. "It has been 4,026 days since your last completed work shift!" The door at the front of the room rolled back, and a six-wheeled robot rolled in. It was about my height, built in a rectangular box shape with an ovoid sensor unit on top and four retractable tentacle arms spaced equally around its body. "Please complete your work shift to earn your next calorie ration!"

Ali stared at the unit, her tail floofed out in a panicked brush, ears flat to her head, lips drawn back in a silent snarl. Her pistol was in her paw, but she hadn't fired it yet.

"Hey, Ali is a fox, not a service unit!" I called out to Pax Machina. "She's not here to build your bombs. She just wants that damned collar off her neck."

"Service Unit #652-396's Volume Discouragement Device is for the safety of this facility. It cannot be removed."

Ali fired her pistol, and a steel needle *pinged* off the robot's sensor unit. The robot's front arm shot out, wrapping around Ali's neck and lifting her bodily off the ground as she dropped the bomb case.

"Attempting to damage Pax Machina may result in the revocation of oxygen privileges," it stated, as Ali's eyes began to bulge out of their sockets.

I ran over to the work table, grabbing the little cube of plastic explosive and tossing it at the robot. It bounced off and landed on the floor in front of the robot. Feet kicking desperately in the air, Ali fired at the robot once more. The first needle just bounced off its hull again. Then she fired downward, aiming at the lump of explosive. It detonated, sending Ali and I both flying across the room as the robot's torso absorbed most of the blast, disintegrating it.

"You okay?" I asked her, picking myself up off the floor as my ears rang. She sat up, coughing as I helped her untangle the now limp tentacle from around her neck. "Why didn't you just fire one of your explosive needles at it?"

She held up her paws, miming shooting her pistol at the palm of her opposite hand, held up at an angle. "You used them up when you shot at the door?" I asked, and she nodded in confirmation, giving me an embarrassed smile. "Oh, great."

I stood up and looked around. The door back to the corridor and the vent shaft where we came in was shut tight, but the door leading deeper into the facility was still open. Ali gave my signal detector back and I checked the direction the collar was transmitting. "Guess we go forward then," I said, and she nodded in agreement. She grabbed a double handful of the explosives, and the cube she'd built, and we slowly began to creep through the door.

It led out into a hallway twice as wide as the one in the dormitory, with more sliding doors. I opened the first one to my right and found a room with a padded chair sized for kits, with straps to hold the sitter down. I swallowed and backed away, to almost bump into Ali, who was staring in quiet fury at another doorway. Inside there were more shelves, filled collars like Ali's. There had to be at least two dozen of them, matching the number of beds in the dorm rooms I'd seen.

"How many kits did Pax Machina take?" I asked aloud. "Do you remember how many were here with you?"

Ali thought for a moment and held up both her paws, splaying her fingers once, twice, three times. "Thirty? Then where did they go?"

"All Service Units were placed in long term storage, once they had completed their current work assignment," Pax Machina answered over the loudspeakers, in that same damned cheerful tone.

I flinched briefly. Even without visible cameras, the facility's AI had to be tracking Ali's movements with her collar, maybe even listening to our conversations. I got ahold of myself and asked, "Are they here?"

"The Service Units are no longer at this facility."

We started walking forward, me with one of the explosive cubes in my paw, Ali with her needle gun out. "So where is long term storage then?" I asked.

"That information is not available to non-Pax Machina units."

We went through another open door, to what had to be entrance to the facility. The angled hatch that had defeated us yesterday was right in front of us, through possibly a garage or loading area, judging by the marks on the floor where vehicles must have once sat. Along the walls were several large tubes, two meters long by one meter wide, whose purpose wasn't obvious to me. "This facility has completed its most recent production run, correct?" I asked aloud.

"That is correct."

"So Service Unit #652-396 doesn't actually have any more assignments, isn't that right?" Beside me, Ali blinked and gave me a *What do you think you're doing?* expression.

"That is correct. Thank you for the clarification. Updating 652-396's status to Redundant." Three service tentacles unfolded from the ceiling, grabbing Ali by the shoulders and neck, and hauling her into the air. She kicked her feet wildly, as one of the tubes trundled away from the wall, opening up to reveal a padded space big enough to deposit a kit, or a small fox.

"Oh, wait!" I called up cheerfully, thinking fast. "Before you do that, could you open the door and let me out?"

"Certainly," Pax Machina replied. "Have a nice day!" With a hydraulic whine, the steel hatch slide back, revealing the forest, the early morning sun peeking above the horizon, and two and a half meters of righteously furious, half naked blue lizard, sword in hand, rushing in the moment the hatch opened.

"*Ali!*" Hamia roared. He swung his sword in a wide arc, slicing through the tentacles holding her in the air. She dropped to her feet, coughing and running with me out the door, as Hamia roared again, his sword smashing through the container tub. "Do not touch her, you ungodly mechanisms!"

"Destruction of Pax Machina units may result in revocation of oxygen privileges," Pax Machina warned, as more tentacles reached down towards him.

Past the door, the tentacles seemed unable to reach, or maybe just uninterested. "Hamia, we're clear! Get out of there!" I shouted, as Ali whistled loudly beside me. Hamia sliced through another tentacle, dancing backwards out the hatch as the remaining ones reached for him. Thinking fast, he slipped his hull metal sword underneath the closing hatch, jamming it open.

When we were all outside and safe, Hamia turned to Ali, his face a mixture of fury and relief. "Ali, you foolish, *foolish* eggling! You had no right to terrify an old lizard like that!"

"Don't worry, it was worth it," I said, pointing to her neck. "See?"

Ali reached up, touching the bare matted fur of her neck, the collar that she'd worn for her whole life gone. Her eyes grew wide, as Hamia let out a roaring whoop of joy. *How?* she mouthed and signed.

"When Pax Machina mentioned the kits had been moved after completing their assignment, I remembered all the collars back in that one room," I told them. "If they were finished making those stupid sonic bombs, there would be no reason to wear them anymore. Once I'd convinced the facility you'd finished your work, it popped it off when it was getting ready to drop you into that container. I'm sorry I didn't have any way of warning you though, Ali."

"*It's okay,*" she signed as Hamia interpreted. "*It's…*" She gave up trying to form coherent sentences and just hugged me, sobbing in relief.

"What do we do now?" Hamia asked. "I don't like the idea of this place remaining active, for other kits to be imprisoned so cruelly within it."

"I gotta agree with you," I said. "Believe me, I'd love the salvage, but…"

Ali pulled away from me and signed something up to Hamia, a fierce grin on her face. "What do you mean it's taken care of?" he asked.

She pulled the sonic explosive she'd built earlier from her pocket, flicking the activation switch on the side and sending sliding along the smooth concrete floor, to stop at end of the line of little explosive cores she'd been dropping like breadcrumbs as we'd walked down the hall from the assembly room. Then Hamia and I ducked for cover as she stepped away from the hatch, pressing her fingers to her lips and letting out an ear-piercing whistle.

There was a loud series of *whump-whump-whumps* as the explosives detonated, ending a deafening *CRUMP!* as they reached the assembly room, the entire top of the hill lifting into the air briefly, before dropping back down, forming an irregular crater as the remains of the facility collapsed in on itself, dust and smoke rising in the air.

Hamia, who had fallen with Ali and I when the explosion went off, sat up, laughing uproariously. "Well done, Ali! Wonderfully done!"

Ali stepped over to him, gripping the lizard's hand in both of her own, her voice scratchy as she whispered, "Thank you, Father."

* * *

Three days later we made it back to Ambara Down, and shared a round of drinks at the Damselfly. I'd lost my chance at a king's ransom in salvage, but I was still feeling pretty good. I'd helped Ali get that damned collar off, and the remaining half-dozen explosive cores she'd had leftover in her pockets would be enough to pay my rent for nearly a year, or maybe more if I could use them to spin a story to a gullible 'Claimer about a Pax Machina facility just waiting to be found.

"So now what?" I asked them, as I finished off my third pint.

"There were thirty kits being held prisoner by Pax Machina," Hamia said. "I will not be satisfied until I know their fate. If they are still alive, they *must* be freed, and Pax Machina taught not to attempt such cruelty again."

"You gonna keep following this big lizard then, Ali?" I asked her.

She grinned at me, trading sips of honey tea with her beer, to ease her throat as she practiced talking again. "Why not," she whispered. "It's been fun so far."

"Good luck to you both then," I told them, standing up and shaking their hands.

I had the feeling they'd find those kits. I hoped I'd have a chance to help them when they did.

Dark Garden Lake

Kayode Lycaon

You're an odd one, Moshi," Bajit said, holding a sweet roll in one paw and the towel around his waist with the other. He leaned his striped back against the frame of the sloped window as he chewed. The rancid smell of the wet hyena overpowered the scent of cinnamon and honey.

In the morning light, the view out the window was gorgeous. Vast green farmland on the edge of cloud-covered mountains sprawled beneath them and a blue sea filled the horizon. Along the coast, sunlight glinted off the city of Ambara Down. If the view had been less hazy, Moshi could have used his image enhancing software to view individual streets.

Just barely visible above the windows, the vast arrays of Vakalena's antigravity engines glowed dull red. Moshi ran his carbon reinforced claws over the glass; the vibration made them jump and click against it.

He leaned his back against it, letting the hum rumble down his spine. The window was pleasantly cool against his wet, unclothed body. Then he sighed and turned his attention to the striped hyena.

Bajit mumbled on—crumbs and icing sprayed from the sweet roll stuffing his muzzle. "You live a pampered life up here with your humans and yet you walk around moping."

"You don't seem to have a problem with pampering," Moshi said acidly, pointing a white paw accusingly at the sweet roll in the hyena's mouth.

"It's not pampering when you work for it."

The hyena tossed his towel on the bed. Then he grabbed another sweet roll off the tray and pointed it at the painted dog to emphasize this point. "I can't figure you out. You have a perfectly willing prostitute in your room, and you don't even bother to partake in the services he offers." He took a bite and mumbled through it. "I should be insulted."

Moshi leaned his head back and bit down on the anger he felt deep inside. He managed to reduce it to a growl in the hyena's direction. "What should it matter to you? You've been well paid."

"By your handler, or maybe I should say, your master?" Bajit said, spreading his paws wide.

"What's your problem?" the painted dog snapped.

"Maybe I take pride in my work?" Bajit rolled his eyes.

"Do you?" Moshi whacked his tail against the glass, his anger less pronounced.

The hyena sighed and sat back on the bed. "Sure, but I get a little tired with the constant parade of humans looking for something a little exotic. Tired of playing the part of dancing beast and covering up my scent. Maybe I expected the chance have a little fun with one of our kind, but instead I find a whipped cur."

"Have you ever tried being a little more polite?" Moshi's ears flattened and he moved over to the tray on the bed to pour a cup of tea.

"Fuck no. What do you care?"

"It's all about how you carry yourself." The painted dog picked a sweet roll and sat next to the hyena. "Politeness is a sign of dignity."

"What kind of monkey shit are you talking about now?"

Moshi unpeeled the roll, tore a small piece off, and popped it into his muzzle. "My place here isn't all that different from yours. To most of the humans here, I'm a curiosity. Others find me to be a useful tool." He swallowed. "But even then, they don't respect me. What little dignity I have is what I've made for myself."

"If you're so desperately unhappy, why don't you just leave?"

"I can't. They made my body out of flesh and metal and those metal parts of me need maintenance. Without that, I've got a month or two before something important breaks." Moshi sipped his tea. "And for what it's worth, I might as well be one of them anyway. I grew up and went to school here."

"That's horrifying," Bajit said, folding his ears and staring down. "I've never known anything else."

"So, should I worry about you being taken over by the Machina?" The striped hyena asked in a failed attempt to lighten the mood.

"No. My hardware and software are Greenfield work done by the Reclamation Project. All of it built without GNDN components and hardened against AI takeover."

The striped hyena paused to pour himself a steaming cup of tea. "That sounds like a lot of work. Why would the 'Claimers even bother to make something like you?"

"They needed something to counter the rogue combat drones that attack the farms. AI was too dangerous and unfortunately, cybernetic soldiers are too expensive. So, they canceled the project after making their first viable prototype and found some other role I could fill until they have a better use for me."

"Which is?"

"I solve the problems that they don't want mercenaries making a mess of."

"Mercenaries?" Bajit's ears perked up in alarm. "You mean furred folk that kill other furred folk for their thirty pieces of silver?"

Moshi refreshed his tea and nodded in reply.

The striped hyena stared at his cup before asking exactly the wrong question. "And just how many have you killed for them?"

"Only as many as I needed to." Moshi stared out the window at Ambara Down far below. His reply was even, almost soft, but it didn't hide the pain behind his words. "And if you had ever killed anyone, you'd know why you don't ask that question."

Bajit sipped and spoke softly. "So, where do I fit into all of this mess?"

"Nowhere. I just want someone else to talk to." The painted dog's voice came out in high squeaks. "Because, like you, I have to put on a pleasant face all the time. Because tonight I have to strut around like a pet peacock and talk pretty so, they choose me over someone who doesn't give a damn about who gets hurt."

"I'm sorry. I'm making a mess of this," the striped hyena whispered.

* * *

Hours after Bajit left, Moshi hadn't moved from his seat on his bed, staring out the window. The sun was low in the sky, bathing everything in yellow light. His fur had dried a long time ago and the tray next to him only held crumbs, an empty tea pot, and two cups of cold, untouched tea.

A chime from the door turned his ears but not his head. There was never enough time to properly appreciate anything. He dragged a discarded towel over his lap so he would as least be covered if he wasn't going to be decent.

"Come in," he muttered and then he prepared himself.

The door slid open and Joyce stepped in. She wore a green sleeveless blouse that matched well with her cool poise and dark complexion. Bajit's lingering scent made her face wrinkle in disgust.

"I'm surprised your sensitive nose isn't bothered by this stench."

"Smells are smells," Moshi said absently, his ears following her, pretending to be uninterested. "And he didn't cost you much."

"Anything I saved is going to be spent on scent removal." She huffed and sat on the desk chair opposite the bed. More out of habit than need, she brushed back a lock of black hair. "Other than the smell, did you have a nice evening?"

"Nice enough," Moshi replied. He managed a slight smile and turned his bright, gold eyes to meet her deceptively soft, brown ones. "I'd like to see him again."

"I'm glad I finally found someone that can hold your attention for more than just a single night."

The painted dog's ears flicked. What appeared to be just small talk was not. Under the pleasant conversation they fenced, each statement a thrust or a parry. They were gauging each other's motives and anticipating where the conversation would go, each trying to extract information without letting the other know what cards they were holding. They both knew what the other wanted but to say it directly was the equivalent of throwing a rock instead of prodding with a sword. From a position of strength, it could be powerful and effective, as long as you didn't mind making enemies.

Tonight though, the stakes were low. Moshi wanted to stay in his room alone with his own thoughts and Joyce wanted to parade him around. It would be easy for her to lean on her authority and simply order him to go, but by entertaining a dialogue, he had the illusion of making his own decisions, of being invited to join her. But this too had another purpose. An indirect conversation communicated far more than just the words that were said.

At some level, Joyce did care about his happiness—but showing that openly would give him too much leverage over her. Her mocking veneer covered her concern. His mild interest in her choice of an evening liaison for him was in fact an offer to trade. Seeing Bajit again would be his price for being agreeable.

Silence stretched. It was Joyce's turn to speak but instead she chose to smile politely, putting the ball back in his court. There was a number of options at this point. He could point the conversation at something meaningless and try to draw more information out of her. He could mirror her—staying silent—and start a blatant contest of wills; the first one to speak would lose. Or he could step back and invite her to speak.

"Well, you didn't just come down here to ask about my evening," he said with a polite, measured smile.

She returned his smile and accepted his request to come more directly to the point. "Dinner tonight should be interesting. Secretary Andrea has a problem that needs taken care of."

"What kind of problem?" Moshi perked up and crossed his legs to keep his modesty. His interest wasn't entirely feigned.

"The usual. A terrorist named Landolf has been raiding food shipments."

There was more behind this request than just doing something nice for the Secretary of Agriculture. "This isn't the first time there's been raids on food shipments. What are we getting from this?"

Joyce tipped her head slightly—awarding him a point for his attentiveness.

"There is a food shortage in Ambara and this 'terrorist' is helping people who desperately need food. If we can remove them from the equation, I can turn this around and get the Secretary to send more food after the next growing season, so this problem doesn't continue. Right now, she's turning a blind eye to the people profiting off the increasing food prices. But, if we solve her current problem, she might be willing to understand it's in everyone's best interests to not cause shortages like this."

Moshi had his suspicions that he wasn't being told the entire story. Still, it was enough for him to work with. He nodded for Joyce's benefit. "So, what would you like me to wear?"

* * *

They joined the gathering crowd in the lobby of the Grand Hall in Vakalena's administrative district. Joyce's green blouse was traded for a leaf-embroidered sari in royal blue and gold, while Moshi wore a knee-length gold-embroidered red silk kurta that hid his tail. The pads and claws of his bare feet sunk deeply into the thick carpet and the eye watering mix of cologne and perfume made him want to sneeze.

A vast table, heavily laden with fruit and vegetables, filled one side of the room. The centerpiece was an elaborate sculpture of Vakalena made out of pineapple, hovering over the table on a miniature antigravity engine. The stack of untouched plates made it clear that this was all a deliberately wasteful display of luxury that would go largely uneaten. Every time he found himself near a table like this, he made it a point to break protocol and eat as much fruit as possible.

Moshi passed by the many colors of humanity on his way to do just that. On the surface, the Reclamation Project was remarkably egalitarian—if one was human. He kept his ears forward and alert as he eavesdropped on the various conversations he passed.

"One of our survey teams discovered a water reclamation plant in The Warrens…"

"The Secretary's dress is just lovely, don't you think?"

"…that business with Director Kira? These damned human-supremacists are going to ruin everything."

"We lost a survey team in the mountains due to a blizzard of all things! You'd think those beast creatures wouldn't freeze with all that fur and savagery of theirs."

"Yes, the underwater hotel should be up and running in just a few months."

"Of course, I'd be delighted. Shall we meet at my place?"

Moshi grabbed a plate and continued to listen in. Most of it was idle talk but occasionally there was a useful tidbit. He recorded everything to his computer memory to review later.

Meanwhile, he piled his gilded plate with starfruit, pineapple, assorted berries, and slices of melon. Then he made his way around the room until he caught the gaze of a bronze-skinned human wrapped in a shiny teal kurta. They both smiled in recognition of each other. Moshi spoke first, dropping into his role as a guest of low station.

"Nathan, it has been far too long since I've seen you here. What brings you to Vakalena?"

"Oh, just visiting family."

Moshi tilted his head—silently acknowledging Nathan's deflection. His former childhood friend was not one to visit family lightly. The next step was to extend the metaphorical olive branch by asking about their health. That was met with sincere but shallow answers that confirmed things he already knew. What his former friend wasn't saying, spoke volumes. In fact, those volumes seemed almost too easy to read.

The painted dog picked a piece of pineapple daintily with his claws and carried it to his muzzle. His deliberate social faux pas was either completely missed or ignored. It was like fencing with a mannequin. Nathan was either completely unaware of the larger game or was playing a game of subterfuge a dozen moves ahead. Moshi readied his verbal saber; time to flush out the game.

"As I recall your uncle works in Greenfield Projects. he mentioned there was some difficulty getting high grade silicon. Has your department had any luck getting the GNDN EAFs working?"

Nathan froze for the briefest moment and his eyes widened. "I can't really discuss that."

"Sorry, I was just curious. I don't always know what's sensitive information." Moshi waved a paw in dismissal but smiled inwardly. He had won and his opponent was completely unaware of it.

The conversation petered out on a discussion of the next growing season. Given the floating city's dependence on food from the surface, agriculture was an evergreen topic. Nathan walked away convinced that Moshi was the same has he had always been, a token curiosity brought out to show off the Greenfield Projects' dominance in the fields of genetic engineering and cybernetics. That mistake suited the painted dog just fine; being underestimated had enormous tactical value on this battlefield. Nathan was nothing more than a blissful antelope walking around unaware of the predators lurking in the tall savannah grass.

The painted dog turned his predatory mind to other things and placed a grape into his muzzle. When he bit down, it flattened and then popped, squirting a seed-filled pulp full of sour sweetness, a wine grape picked far too early. Moshi savored the novelty of the experience but mentally shook his head; an artist must have stocked the table. Hopefully, the chefs preparing the dinner would have culinary skills.

* * *

An attendant in a simple black and white suit guided Moshi and Joyce through a sculpted wooden arch into the elaborate dining hall. The marble columns and their gold embellishments seemed a little much, he thought, but they were pretty. They were seated at the end of the third column of tables with the lesser dignitaries. The wait was long as small groups of increasing important humans in decreasingly elaborate clothing were seated by attendants. To Moshi's surprise, the waiters were a variety of feline furred folk with spots or rosettes, dressed in blue, and the sommeliers were rodents in red and gold suits.

A smiling black mouse poured champagne into the painted dog's crystal wine glass while an immaculately-groomed jaguar placed a tiny white plate of olives and flatbread in front of him. There were no serving trays in evidence; the waiters carried plates two at a time from a discrete hallway at the end of the room.

Mirroring Joyce, Moshi unrolled the gold napkin wrapped around his silverware and settled it on his lap. He nibbled on the peppery olives and salty flat bread, then sated his resulting thirst with careful sips of wine. Fifteen minutes later—by his internal estimate— the room was half filled. A sandy-colored gerbil with a furred tail refilled his glass and a cheetah leaned over him.

"Would you like another plate, sir?"

Moshi flicked an ear and then waved an open paw forward in a gesture he had seen the humans at the table use. It would appear that showing any consideration to the waiters was a social *faux pas*. The behavior grated on Moshi.

Three glasses of wine and two plates later, members on the board of the Reclamation Project, including Ambara Down's newly-installed Executive Director Helpmann, were being seated at the head table. Joyce touched his arm and whispered low without turning her head.

"Andrea is the one in the sea green dress."

The painted dog flicked an ear to acknowledge he heard.

"And pace yourself, people will be watching."

Moshi didn't reply. In his boredom, he had forgotten the battlefield he was in. The weapons here were different but no less deadly than the light railguns he had trained with. Beside him, Joyce was talking in low tones with the thin, pale-skinned woman in a ruffled purple blouse across from her. He wasn't sure who she was, so he pulled up his facial recognition program and asked it to find her in the local database. A few seconds later it reported she was Rayna Bastola, one of Angela's assistants. Their seating had not been as arbitrary as he had thought.

"We've made excellent progress in the last year. Our application development libraries for GreenScript just got released and the language itself has been in production use for six years now. Moshi's core firmware is entirely written in it," Joyce said waving a hand at him.

"Does it talk?" Rayna asked.

Moshi bit his tongue, steeled his expression, kept his ears forward, and inclined his head. "I do ma'am."

"Oh how delightful!" she exclaimed.

"He," Joyce said, drawing the attention back to her. "Moshi is male."

"Oh! It's so hard to tell with his kind. Do you have any females of his model?"

"Unfortunately, no. The genetics, instincts, and anatomy of male painted dogs was easier to work with for his augmentation."

Moshi tuned out the conversation, thankful for Joyce's redirection. It was a conversation he'd been in many times before and had no desire to repeat. The waiters brought out tightly rolled towels and placed them on cleared plates. Silence slowly fell on the room as one of the humans at the head table—a dark-skinned woman wrapped in white silk—stepped up to the podium beside the table. A chime sounded and all that was heard was the faint rustling of cloth as everyone turned towards the speaker. She settled a digital notepad on the podium and looked up with a bright smile.

"Good evening, our esteemed ladies and gentlemen. Today marks the twentieth year since the founding of the Ambara Survey and Reclamation Project…"

The speech dragged on for nearly half an hour, recounting the Project's achievements, politely-couched recounting of the conflicts between High Empyros, Vakalena, and Alikant over who had "salvage rights," and an even-more-politely elided reference to war and its repercussions. Throughout, the nearly silent waiters replaced wine glasses with cold, refreshing glasses of water. Moshi sipped his and let his attention drift. He'd heard a dozen of these speeches before and they never had anything interesting in them.

He wished that Bajit could have stayed for more than just one night. The striped hyena had been abrasive and a terrible conversationalist, but his paws had been soft. Their strong fingers had expertly kneaded the muscles behind his jaw, then his forehead, but that's as far as they had gone. Moshi had no interest in the hyena's other talents. Instead they had simply spent the night sleeping, huddled together on the bed, easing the painted dog's almost constant loneliness in a way no one else had managed.

As the speech drew to a close, Moshi returned his attention to the present. A wine glass had replaced his water and the human behind the podium was raising her glass towards the tables. Keeping his momentary panic in check, he raised his in time with everyone else.

"A toast, to the future of humanity and all sentient creatures," she said. "A toast, to the grand Reclamation Project."

Moshi sipped and savored the flavor of the sherry as it glided across his tongue—strong, dry, and mildly sweet. Fortunately, no one seemed to have noticed his distraction.

With the speech over, some of the humans excused themselves to use the facilities. Others used the towels to clean their hands. Moshi mirrored them, using the damp towel to remove the olive residue from his claws and wipe his paw pads before the food arrived.

The first course was a salad of crunchy lettuce and a bright mixture of vegetables, drizzled with a simple dressing of salt, pepper, olive oil and vinegar. Moshi stabbed a green pepper with his fork and nibbled on it. To his delight, the dressing was sour and pungent. He took his time finishing the salad, eating around the bits of cucumber and sipping his wine while keeping an ear on Joyce's conversation with Rayna.

A plate of herbed cheese and tomato compote on toasted bread followed. Moshi's empty wine glass was traded for a glass of Sauvignon Blanc which he found disappointingly acidic. His eavesdropping was starting to get interesting. The recent terrorist raids on food shipment was the Department of Agriculture's top priority and all of Andrea's subordinates were getting a lot of pressure to solve the problem.

The soup course arrived—a creamy potato curry in a tiny cup paired with a fruity Rosé. Joyce was describing Moshi's last mission hunting down poachers hunting in a wildlife preserve with what he thought was more than a bit of exaggeration. He hadn't stalked them tirelessly for days. It had been an easy mission after finding their air lorry hidden in a stand of trees. After waiting for their return, he knocked all of them out with a neural stunner. Then it was easy to trestle them up and remove their comlinks and a finger from each of them as evidence of his success. When he returned to Vakalena, he called one of their families with their location so they could be rescued before exposure or wild animals caused them too much harm. It was one of his more successful missions and it had brought him to the attention of the other departments. In the aftermath of that mission, he had graduated from a mere curiosity to a pawn on the political chessboard.

Those thoughts threatened to darken the evening, but he pushed them aside. Plates with a small fillet of flaky grilled fish on a bed of leafy lettuce replaced empty soup cups and the Rosé was traded out for a dry Chardonnay. Moshi enjoyed the tingle of lemon and pepper on his tongue and then the sensation of the wine washing it away. No matter what was accomplished this evening, he was going to remember the excellence of the food.

A jaguar took his plate and a cheetah set down a shallow bowl of beef tips on brown rice topped with a mushroom gravy. The gerbil Moshi remembered from before brought him a deep red glass of Pinot Noir. It would have been easy to lose himself in the rich flavors, but he kept listening. Joyce had moved on to discussing what he could do for the Department of Agriculture.

"Perhaps it would be best for you to talk directly with Moshi," she said.

The painted dog picked an appropriately serious expression and turned towards Rayna. Her eyebrows rose slightly as she saw the sharp, predatory intelligence behind his eyes.

"How may I be of service?" he asked in a low voice.

"Well, my department would like to see these terrorist raids on food shipments stopped."

Moshi increased his evaluation of her. She had recovered quickly. After swallowing a sip of wine, he replied, "My sources in Ambara Down tell me that a terrorist leader known as Landolf has been coordinating the latest raids. There's a few options for dealing with such a person."

Rayna waited with polite interest. Unsure of her thoughts, he continued.

"It would be relatively easy for me to locate and dispatch Landolf while giving the Prefect and the Project plausible deniability."

"But?" The other woman asked. She was sharp. He twirled a paw in a fashion that was common with the humans had grown up with. Give her a bit of familiarity and she might listen just a little more to his words rather than their source.

"Removing Landolf in this fashion could make them a martyr and could possibly escalate the situation. The death of the warlord Tsaibei Hrotan has destabilized the various factions of the desert and emboldened groups such as the Watersnakes, and of course the Ambara Defense Front is always looking for an excuse to cause trouble. Capturing Landolf openly has a number of possibilities. Rather than making them a martyr, you can imprison Landolf and make them a hostage against the terrorists' good behavior. They could be a public example of how we are just and honorable in the treatment of those who oppose us."

In the corner of his eye, he saw Joyce's mouth twitch ever so slightly. Rayna actually smiled.

"There's more to you than I had expected."

"Thank you, ma'am," Moshi replied, with a slight bob of his head. It was helpful that most of the body language he needed was automatic to him.

"I'll of course need to discuss this with Andrea but I think she'll approve."

Joyce picked the conversation back up to discuss new software for the Department of Agriculture's combines. The painted dog let out a mental sigh of relief and focused on his arriving dessert plate—three pieces of fried plantain drizzled in a chocolate sauce paired with a cherry port.

* * *

After dinner, Joyce and Moshi returned to his room. Moshi stripped out of his kurta as soon as the door closed, leaving himself covered only by the loose wrap around his waist. He turned towards Joyce with a small, optimistic smile. Even here he couldn't drop everything and ask the question he wanted.

"Dinner was nice."

Joyce unwrapped her hair to let it hang free. She pointedly smoothed out her sari, as if emphasizing Moshi's choice to remove his outer layers. She sat on the arm of one of the chairs and ran her finger through her hair, untangling it.

"One of the better presentations, I think."

The painted dog was really getting tired of this indirection. Dinner had already been incredibly tiresome, and a full belly made him just want to get this all over with so he could sleep.

"It seemed well received, but I'm hardly good at reading crowds."

"In this case, I think I would agree. This has been a good year for the Project."

And for us, Moshi added mentally. He turned to look out the window at the dark landscape below. Only the red glow from the antigravity engines was visible through the reflections in the glass. With a tight hold on his expression, he replied, "Do you think Andrea would be interested in our proposal?"

Joyce tutted and shook her head slightly. "Manners, Moshi."

He kept his face impassive and threw down the gauntlet of patient silence. A real gauntlet would have been so much more satisfying.

"Fine." She sniffed. "I think she will be very interested in having Landolf killed. She likes things neat and tidy. Imprisonment has complications."

It took every last shred of self-control to keep the sarcasm out of his voice. "Delightful. So, how does this benefit us? We're not doing this out of the goodness of our hearts and the depth of our concern for the good people of Ambara."

Joyce thought for a moment before replying. "Optimistically, it will pave the way to getting the Director of Greenfield Projects onto the Board."

The painted dog looked her in the eye. She just told him, in her own subtle way, that he held all the cards. That was a dangerous gamble. He saw the calculation going on behind her eyes. His pawn was reaching the end of the board and would very soon get promoted to a much more useful piece. Moshi chose his next words carefully.

"And all we need is another body for the pile?"

Her reply was equally bare fisted. "If that's what it takes."

And with that, Landolf's fate was sealed. He held his eyes on Joyce as he did his own calculations. Refusal would have drastic consequences for him and do little to change the outcome. All that was left was damage control. He remembered the poachers whose lives he had saved and the relief their families had felt when they were safely returned home, minus some fingers. If he took this mission, he could spare everyone but Landolf. Someone else would have no compulsions killing unfortunate bystanders.

They both knew he would do it. If his position got important enough, he could find himself on an advisory council in a few years. He would no longer be just an asset but an influence. With Greenfield Projects on the Board and his name known to them, he could push for a more congenial relationship with the furred folk of Ambara Down. Helpmann would certainly be an ally there.

"Perhaps, I can offer some more incentive," Joyce said and Moshi realized she had misjudged his silence for reluctance. "You liked that… boy? The hyena?"

The painted dog had to swallow past the lump in his throat. Joyce was probably considering Bajit as both an incentive and as another tool that could be used to ensure his compliance in the future. It bothered him that she thought his honor could be bought so cheaply, but being underestimated now would pay dividends later, and it would be nice to have a little more companionship. He chose to play her game and let his loneliness bleed through his mask.

"Yes," he said. "Bajit."

"Perhaps we can arrange something a little more permanent?"

Moshi nodded, as if he didn't trust himself to speak.

Joyce's face softened. "I want to get you in place before we get official approval. Can you meet Richard in the armory tomorrow morning and then head down to Ambara?"

Moshi nodded and then Joyce silently walked out. Only the faint hiss of the door told him he was alone. Then, he turned towards the window and stared down at the dim lights flickering far below.

* * *

In the morning, Moshi went to meet Richard at the Department of Greenfield Project's armory. Inside, racks of stun pistols, dart rifles, and slug throwers took up almost all of the wall space. And in the middle of it all was a dark-skinned man wearing a purple turban.

"Moshi," the man said tenderly and shook the painted dog's paw with both hands. "We missed you at services last week. How are you doing?"

"I've been well, but this mission is going to be a difficult one." Moshi's ears splayed to the side and he rested his muzzle against Richard's cheek. He closed his eyes and wished the warmth in his heart could last forever. "But I have to do it."

"One always has choice. Even if we don't like the options." Richard clasped his hand around the back of the painted dog's head for a moment before stepping back. "Well. Let's be about it. What do you think you'll need?"

"It's an assassination mission and I don't know what range I'll be at. Can you give me a GR-6?"

"A regrettable task," Richard said and pulled a rifle off the shelf of greenfield prototypes.

190

Moshi accepted the weapon and inspected it. In a lot of ways, a GR-6 was an ideal weapon for this mission. It was more reliable than the railgun it was based on, and the custom-built scope integrated with his augmentation, allowing him to make full use of the weapon's ten-kilometer range. For close range work, he could remove the barrel extension to use it as a carbine.

It wasn't a perfect weapon. The rifle was heavy, and the full barrel was over a meter and a half long. Also, the rate of fire in was painfully low—three rounds per second. As a carbine, it was more manageable, but at the expense of range and stopping power. Still, even basic darts would penetrate light armor.

"Anything else?" Richard asked.

"Long range AP ammo; the GNDN stuff doesn't work very well at anything beyond than close-range anti-personnel work."

Richard pursed his lips. "How much?"

"At least 200 AP, and a few thousand of GNDN," Moshi replied as he checked the condition of the rails.

"I can get you 5 AP rounds, and you're going to fill out a form for each one you use. And no more than 200 rounds of GNDN," Richard said firmly. "You're like a son to me, Moshi, but I'm not going to do something stupid like equipping you for a frontal assault on an air tank unit. The Director would cut both our throats when he found out."

The painted dog sighed mentally because Richard had a point. Arming a furred assassin with some of the best weapons the Project had to offer and giving him enough ammunition to make an attempt at assassinating the Project's leadership wasn't going to happen, no matter how they tried to spin it.

"I'll make that work," Moshi said. "And thank you."

Richard put his hand on the painted dog's shoulder and said solemnly, "Be safe. I want to see you come back."

Moshi rested his paw on the hand. "I will. Never doubt that."

* * *

After the transport settled onto the ground, Moshi stepped out into a hot summer breeze that washed ocean salt and sweet clover over him like a cleansing rain. The summer sun was high overhead and oppressively bright. His ears burned and sweat hot as boiling tea oozed out of his fur as his cybernetic skin rapidly chilled his blood to compensate for the sudden heat.

Ambara Down took his breath away every time. Green was everywhere. Crawling vines hung from twisted and broken towers, trees spouted in imperfect lines down the main avenue in the outer district. It was as wild here as Vakalena was manicured and soulless, and Moshi felt his heart singing along with the birds that lived down here.

He walked down the main avenue, past a sprawling market full of stalls with just about everything available on the ground. It wasn't his first time here, but there was always something new when he came through. While he probably couldn't find a centuries old bottle of French wine—whatever a "French" was—he could probably find someone who could get one. He could wander around after he finished his meeting with Percy, his primary connection to the furred folk underground.

When he saw the Fence separating Old Ambara from the Reclamation district, he knew he was in the right place. Humans and furred folk mingled under a hanging sign with a blue damselfly perched above it. The constant crowd at the Damselfly made it an ideal place for a meeting between two friends to go unnoticed.

The private meeting room he had reserved was up the stairs and to the left. Inside, there was a wood table with six mismatched chairs and a steaming iron teapot with two clay cups. In one of the chairs was a rust-colored maned wolf. Moshi's eyes lingered on the paw that had a truncated stub where it's smallest finger should have been.

"I haven't seen you in months," Percy said with a wide smile. He shook the painted dog's paw from across the table without getting up. "You look well."

"I am, how is your family?" Moshi asked, taking a seat.

"My daughter is doing well, thanks to the medicine you got her. My wife, well, she's a bitch."

The painted dog laughed and poured himself a cup of tea. "I've missed you."

The laughter slowly faded as they looked across the table at each other. It was as if a cold breeze had ruffled their fur. Their ears drooped and the steaming teacups suddenly became the most interesting feature in the room.

"What brings you here this time?" Percy asked quietly.

Moshi lapped his tea before answering. It was an excellent green tea. "Business. Unfortunate business."

"Would it hurt to make a social visit once in a while?"

"It's difficult for me to get away."

"Surely you're not so busy you can't make time once in a while."

"It's not a matter of making time." Moshi rubbed an ear.

"Right," the maned wolf said, remembering a conversation they had years ago. "I'm sorry."

"Not your fault but I'll try. I'd like to meet your wife and daughter sometime. Pictures and letters don't carry their scent or their laughter."

Percy nodded and went immediately to the purpose of their meeting. "So, this business?"

"The 'Claimers want Landolf dead. I talked with the Secretary of Agriculture myself and she's quite piqued about the last raid." Moshi hated lying, but a lie conveyed the importance of his mission much better than trying to explain the political maneuvering involved.

"I don't suppose you can talk them out of it," the maned wolf said, rubbing the stub of his missing finger.

"If I could, I wouldn't be here."

"So, what do you want from me? I owe you a lot, but I won't have blood on my paws. "

"No blood. If you could set up a meeting between me and Landolf, I'd be grateful. Somewhere in the Warrens. Just to talk. I promise."

"I doubt she'd want to talk with you. If it wasn't you, I wouldn't do this," Percy said with a frown and Moshi filed away Landolf's gender for future reference.

"I hate asking you this but it's the only way I can see to avoid bloodshed."

"This Secretary isn't going to settle for just a finger, is she?"

The painted dog squeaked bitterly. "I promise to do nothing to harm Landolf at the meeting."

"And afterward?"

Moshi stared at his tea and didn't reply. Even if he didn't get permission to capture Landolf, he still needed to know what she looked like. He hoped Percy wouldn't realize how he was being used.

"I see." Percy tapped his muzzle. "One question."

Moshi looked up.

"Does Helpmann know?"

Moshi sighed and looked his friend in the eye. "If he needed to know, I wouldn't be here. And before you say anything to him, why don't you ask Prefect Durgavati what she thinks about terrorists?" he said. "This could get messy really fast if other people get involved."

"I see your point." Percy rubbed his paw.

They drank in silence, only broken by their tongues lapping tea. The maned wolf refilled both of their cups and set the empty pot down. When the tea was gone, Percy looked up with sad eyes. Nothing was said between them, but Moshi knew his answer, not that there ever had been a question. They both stood up together and embraced in quiet sorrow. Then the maned wolf headed home, and the painted dog left for his hotel on the other side of the Fence.

* * *

Two days later, Moshi looked out over the water in the fading light from his hotel room. He had met Percy in the market that morning. The maned wolf had led the way to a noodle cart with an aroma of broth and peppers that was strong enough to mask the scent of the red fox behind it. Moshi paid and they had sat at a table under the shade of a maple tree. He vividly remembered the taste of thick flavorful wheat noodles and a spicy chicken broth that overpowered the mix of celery, carrot, and egg that tried to mellow it. He also remembered his friend's reluctant report. Landolf had agreed to meet.

It was a shame, the painted dog thought. He and Percy should have been bitter enemies given their past, but the maned wolf was a simple and honest person. He had seen past all of Moshi's carefully built walls and found a way to reach the soul underneath. The painted dog promised himself that he would find a way to return and visit the maned wolf's family.

The last ray of light was disappearing when a message from Joyce blinked in the corner of his eye. He pulled it up and felt his heart sink. It was short, "Termination approved." Two words, that was all that was needed to end one person's life. All to get better positioning on the political chessboard. And despite what Richard had said, he had no other choice.

The painted dog picked up his backpack and set it on the bed next to him. No point in waiting any longer. Like jumping off a cliff, he steeled himself and pulled on the zipper, listening to the with slight rasp of metal on metal. Inside was his rifle, ammunition, and a few other useful things, like scent masking powder and "cherry" flavored cyborg rations.

The rifle snapped together easily, just as it was designed. He left the extended barrel and short magazine of AP rounds in the bag and loaded all of his GNDN darts into two full-size magazines.

He picked up his rifle and, with a mental command, activated his camouflage. The combat HUD appeared, with his rifle stats selected, and a set of short, floating green bars showed an estimate of how detectable he was. Looking at the mirror on the door, he only saw the shadow of his outline in the reflection of the window and the moonlit ocean sea beyond. He was almost perfectly invisible, as long as he didn't move too quickly.

Then he turned everything back off and closed all of the programs that hid in the edge of his vision. Everything went on the floor and he lay down on the bed. He hugged a pillow. The sheets were cold without someone else beside him and loneliness clawed at his heart as the waves rolled in. The tears he cried weren't enough to bring him closer to sleep, so he pulled up his internal medpack instead.

* * *

Early, before the sun came up, Moshi woke from his sleep. A mild stimulant took away the fog of sedation and brought him much needed focus. If the market had been open, he would have much preferred heavily spiced coffee or tea rich with cream and sugar, but he didn't have time to wait. He loaded his GR-6 and pulled on a shirt and pants appropriate for crawling around the ruins of the city.

Then the painted dog slipped out of his hotel and snuck into a nearby ruined tower. The crushed stairway was just wide enough for him to squeeze through to a four-meter drop onto the first set of intact steps. His reinforced body easily handled a fall would have shattered even the stoutest furred folk's legs. A feline skeleton not far from where he landed testified to that. Five flights down, a bent door opened into the Warrens.

Down here, the few paths that existed were cut through the twisted wreckage of what had been the lower levels of the floating city of Ambara. There was no light visible this far down. He switched his vision to infrared and the illuminators built into his jaw turned on to provide better light than the pale reflections of his own body heat. While he could see now, it came at the painful cost of freezing eyes and a burning muzzle.

There was very little sound other than the ever-present water dripping against metal and the occasional groans of the city settling. In some places moss made the already slick footing treacherous. This deep, there was always the risk of running into unstable Machina drones that were just as likely to help you as hurt you, sometimes switching mid-sentence. Then a rasp of metal against metal made him halt.

Going around wasn't an option. Most of the drone types he knew of could move faster than him. His camouflage might work if he was willing to risk losing his infrared vision, but the prospect of being blind in the darkness was not appealing. He did have an echolocation program, except it was experimental and probably wouldn't work if he didn't make the ultrasonic chirps it relied on for accurate mapping.

In the end, he decided to ready his carbine and follow what Richard had taught him: the best defense was excessive violence. The combat HUD popped into view when his paw curled around the grip. The GR-6's weight was comforting as he pulled it against his shoulder and clicked it over to automatic fire. He should have asked Richard for grenades.

The scraping sounds got closer and it was too late to use his camouflage. The drone would have seen the infrared light from his jaw-mounted illuminators by now. A pair of shiny black legs and red eye stalk appeared from around a torn metal panel. Moshi held his breath and settled the red crosshairs on where the bulk of its body would be. Slow, punctuated cracks sounded through the tiny space as he held down the trigger. In four seconds, a dozen darts flew down the corridor to explode in useless showers of sparks as they pinged off the spider drone's black carapace. After a long moment, an electronic voice said his name.

"Moshi. What are we doing in The Warrens this fine evening?"

The painted dog stopped firing but didn't lower his aim. The clock in the corner of his vision read 09:52.

"Just passing through, if you don't mind," he replied.

The voice chuckled in the most uncomfortable manner. "Just passing through. Perhaps. If you're looking for Dark Garden Lake, you're too far west. Take the left here."

A black leg pointed in a direction that would leave his back to the composite-armored spider. Moshi stepped in that direction and kept one eye on the drone.

"Good luck with your meeting but the lynx won't go with you. If it helps, her daughter goes to school in West Park. Classes start tomorrow."

With those uncomfortable parting words, it disappeared, and the painted dog shuddered. They always knew more than they should have. It was creepy. He safed his carbine and decided he was going to take a different route home; one that wasn't so deep. And next time, he wasn't coming down here without a full magazine of proper armor-piercing darts and a bandolier of heavy grenades. Fortunately, that was the last sign of life—mechanical or otherwise—he saw that morning.

On the eastern side of Dark Garden Lake, he stopped on the remains of an observation deck balcony. The observation deck on Vakelena was the lowest point any human could access without an antigravity harness. He wasn't sure if Ambara had been the same when it was flying, but this was as deep as one could go in The Warrens before they hit bedrock.

Moshi sat down on the edge, gritted his teeth, and switched his aching eyes back over to normal vision. As they had every time before, pins and needles stabbed into them as they warmed back up. Without a doubt, this was the worst part of the operation he thought as he rubbed his eyelids to remove the cold gummed up tears from behind them.

Once his eyes had returned to normal, he inhaled deeply to take in the scents of earthy moss, salty sea water, and rusting metal while the water below crashed into fallen bits of city and rocky cliff. Looking out over Dark Garden Lake, the dim blue glow of the moss shed just enough light to highlight the white crests of the waves. Even here, in the deepest, darkest part of the Warrens, one could find a simple, haunting beauty.

He spent an entire hour recording every scent he could smell, every sound he could hear, every breeze against his fur, and every sight he could see while his legs dangled over the water. No matter the outcome of his mission, he would have memories he would forever treasure. Then it was time to return to his mission. Landolf was just half an hour's walk away.

* * *

As he got close to the meeting area, he saw bright lights shining on a wall in the distance. He left his carbine hidden under a floor plate and walked forward, making no attempt to hide his approach. When he got closer, his implants highlighted cameras and several unobtrusive gun ports around a heavy metal door. After a few more steps, the speaker beside the door crackled.

"Stay right there."

Moshi froze and lifted his paws to show he wasn't holding anything.

"What do you want?" the voice said.

"I'm here to meet with Landolf," he replied.

The door opened and a burly rabbit in heavy armor came out. Her nose twitched as she caught his scent and she motioned him forward. Contrary to his expectations, she was exceedingly polite.

"I apologize, I need to check you for weapons."

Moshi nodded and the rabbit patted him down thoroughly, including using the back of her paw to check his groin.

When she finished without finding anything, she said, "Wipe your feet before you come inside."

The interior was much nicer than he had expected. Sturdy carpet covered the floor and paint in several shades of pale blue covered the walls and ceiling. It felt much more like a home than a hideout.

The rabbit led him to a small parlor with a bookshelf and end table between a pair of stuffed chairs. One of the chairs was already occupied by a female lynx with a torn ear. She invited him to sit across from her. Uneasily, he recalled the Machina drone's prediction.

"Would you like a cup of tea?" the lynx asked, lifting her own cup.

Moshi accepted the offer and sat in the comfortable chair. A teenage lynx, with similar markings, brought him a steaming cup. This whole meeting felt staged, like his conversations with Joyce. He settled back into the chair and pulled out his mental saber. This was his battlefield. Maybe if he fought well enough, he could take Landolf in alive and negotiate a non-lethal option from better positioning.

"Your daughter?" he asked.

"Yes," the older lynx replied, setting her own cup down. "How was your walk?"

"Refreshing. The lake here is a favorite of mine."

"Mine as well," she said with a smile. Moshi took a moment to enjoy the tea's flavor—strong and bitter with a delightful hint of citrus. He almost sighed but stopped himself. Body language would be everything. If he was too refined or too sloppy, this entire conversation could backfire on him.

"This is good tea," he said and then continued to his point. "But that's not why I'm here."

The lynx said nothing as she smiled. There was a predatory feel to the silence beyond what one would normally feel from a feline. It was almost like he was her prey. Flinching a bit was probably the best option.

"Well, um, I came to meet with Landolf. I don't suppose he will be along anytime soon?" Moshi asked with a hint of discomfort in his voice.

"He's not but I can pass along a message," the lynx said.

There was no reaction to his incorrect assumption that Landolf was male. That told him something. She was used to playing games. Rather than rely on skill alone, he pulled up his lie detector program and had it start analyzing her. With enough data, it would be able to give him a reasonable read on how her body was reacting as she spoke.

"I would really like to speak to him directly," he pressed.

A small shake of the lynx's head made it clear she wasn't going to be so easily persuaded.

"Very well," Moshi continued, "I heard some rumors during my last stay on Vakalena. The 'Claimers are quite upset about the food convoys that keep getting raided. They consider Landolf responsible."

"Oh yes, the 'Claimers. They can be a sensitive bunch."

Moshi swallowed deliberately to show nervousness he didn't feel. "I was talking with a few of the other mercenaries, and someone is paying a lot of money to have one of the furred folk stick a knife in his chest."

"Not surprising," she said with a smile full of teeth. "I don't suppose you brought your knife?"

"Well, no."

"Then you're a smart little 'Claimer puppy. Why don't you tell me why you're here before you leave here with your tail between your legs."

Point to the puppy, Moshi thought. His act had gotten her to drop her mask. All that was left was to exit gracefully. He continued to play the part she had laid out for him.

"I have a few connections with the 'Claimers. After asking around, I found that there's a few of them willing to pay for taking Landolf alive."

The lynx surprised him with a yowl of laughter. "And you think you can get Landolf to just give himself up without a fight! Stuff that idea somewhere dark and unpleasant."

Moshi pinned his ears back to look appropriately chastised. The analysis program flashed in the corner of his eye.

"Sorry," he said, looking down at his half-finished tea, "I'll do that."

She got up and grinned at him, eyes bright. "You managed to amuse me puppy. Finish your tea and Clara will show you out."

The same rabbit that had met him at the door followed him back to it. After he stepped out, the heavy door clanged shut behind him. There was a finality to that sound, as if the door was commenting on his failure. The painted dog flipped his ears in regret and slipped off into the darkness.

* * *

Back at his hotel, it was a sunny afternoon, but dark clouds loomed on the horizon as if they too had something to say. The recording and analysis from his lie detector program left little doubt that the lynx was Landolf—not that he needed Pax Machina or a computer program to tell him that. For a moment he wondered what Pax Machina would gain from Landolf's death, then he decided he was better off not knowing. If its drone's unsettling behavior was any clue, the answer would raise many more questions, all of them disturbing. The painted dog shook himself; he had more immediate things to worry about. His message to Joyce was brief. "Landolf identified. Will neutralize by next report."

Moshi stared out the window at the rising water of a storm surge and the waves breaking against the seawall protecting the city. One question gnawed at him. Why did he have to be the one to pull the trigger? But he knew the answer before it was even asked. If he didn't pull the trigger, a lot of other people could die if someone else got the mission. If he didn't pull the trigger, his future with the Department of Greenfield Projects was questionable at best. There was nothing he could do, so he lay down alone on the cold bed and sedated himself into another deep, dreamless sleep.

The next morning was blustery, with a dark sky overhead and the smell of rain in the air. Using his camouflage, Moshi climbed unseen to the top of a ruined tower. It was easy to locate a half-collapsed apartment to hide in. No one would be able to see him sitting in the shadows near the back wall.

His ears hung loosely off his head while he kept his eyes telescopically zoomed in on the courtyard in front of West Park School. The rifle, with its full-length barrel, was heavy in his paws and the five AP darts in its magazine felt like a huge lead weight on his shoulders. A gray crosshair hovered over the wind-swept floor, waiting.

Hours later, a young lynx, and her mother with a torn ear, entered the courtyard. No shields, not even a visible bodyguard. His ears perked up; the Machina drone had been correct again. He flicked the rifle's selector lever from safe to single fire and the crosshair turned red.

But, for a moment, he hesitated. Landolf's daughter was skipping, carefree, oblivious to what was about to happen. He felt a kinship with her; he had always loved school. Was it her classmates? The teachers? Or did she just love learning, like him? He shook himself and his ears flopped. This was not the time to be getting sentimental.

He watched the teenaged lynx trot up the stairs into the school. At the top of the stairs, she waved goodbye to her mother, not knowing this would be the last time she would see her alive. Several heartbeats went past before the daughter went inside and her mother turned to walk away. It was time. He pulled the rifle up to his shoulder and settled the red lines on Landolf's chest, but his finger hesitated on the trigger. The decision was already made; he had to take the shot, but he couldn't. The cost was just too high. He took his finger off and pulled up his assassination program. If he couldn't pull the trigger, software could still make his body do it. The program locked on Landolf's head and his arms began to move the rifle into position. Then Moshi hit the execute button and gave up control.

His heart stopped and the painted dog felt his body fall away. He was only a distant observer as the crosshairs settled on the lynx's head. For an eternity, the program waited for the wind to stop swirling. A distant, singular heartbeat pushed blood through his body. And then another.

A soft pop reached his ears as he fell back into his body. The AP dart left a white streak in the air. At the other end of its path, Landolf dropped to the ground. Then, slowly, blood began to pool. He could see furred folk screaming but he couldn't hear them.

The assassination program exited automatically, and the painted dog took a ragged breath before clicking the rifle's selector back to safe. The lynx with a torn ear was dead. And because he had been the one to take her life, there had been no unnecessary suffering and a minimum of collateral damage. The dart had torn through the vital structures in her brain and her soul was gone—to wherever souls went—before she had hit the ground. It was that small comfort that Moshi clung to as he packed up his rifle and turned on his camouflage. His message to Joyce was cold and precise. "Mission complete at 07:52."

* * *

The painted dog returned to Valakena before the storm rolled over Ambara Down. He stepped out of the transport terminal and stopped. There was a striped hyena waiting for him, clothed in only the barest amount of fringed purple fabric.

Bajit gave him a sad smile. "I wasn't expecting to see you again. But Joyce said you asked for me."

"I did," Moshi said uncomfortably. He hadn't expected anyone to be waiting for him.

"If you don't want me to stay," the hyena started, touching a paw to his arm.

The painted dog's voice squeaked. "Please stay."

"Okay then. Dinner should be waiting for us in your new apartment."

"New apartment?" Moshi blinked in surprise and then followed Bajit through unfamiliar hallways to the edge of the city. Several levels down, they stopped at a wooden door. To the painted dog's nose, it smelled real, and he brushed the leathery pads of his paws against its luxurious grain. With a touch of the button on the frame, it slid open.

New apartment had been an understatement. Inside was a small luxury suite, with two bedrooms and a parlor. Rather than the lavish decoration he had seen in similar suites, this one was dressed simply with earth tones and green plants. And on the carved wooden table in the common room were two place settings with crystal wine glasses and silver covers on gold rimmed plates.

He stared at the decanter of red wine and thought of the blood pooled on the ground that was now being washed away by the rain. Then a gentle paw on his shoulder reminded him that he didn't have to be alone with his thoughts. The painted dog mentally shook himself and took a seat at the table. Bajit removed the plate covers and took the other seat.

The sharp scent of peppercorn filled their noses as the aroma rose from the now uncovered plates. It was a simple dinner for

Vakalena—hot rare steak with a peppercorn crust, smashed potatoes with butter and rosemary, and steamed green beans. The wine turned out to be his favorite Pinot Noir. Someone had put a lot of preparation into this, Moshi thought, and the price had been cheap at one mother's death and one more stain on an already stained soul.

They ate slowly—in silence. It was as excellent as any meal from the dining halls but this time there was no politics, no need to do anything or be anything. And to Moshi's infinite relief, Bajit made no attempt at conversation, no noise beyond quiet chewing, even though this had to be the best meal the hyena had ever had.

After the plates were clear, they retired to the bedroom. Moshi left his clothes in a pile next to a bed easily three times larger than his previous one and eased himself down onto a real leather couch that faced floor-to-ceiling windows. There was no glow and no vibration from Vakalena's engines. If it hadn't been for the towering storm front, he would have been able to see Ambara Down and the stars beyond.

Brilliant lightning flashed in the distance and he could almost smell the ozone. The couch shifted as Bajit sat down unclothed next to him and handed him a glass of wine. For a long time, neither of them spoke as they stared out the window together.

"You've been quiet," the hyena said, breaking the silence.

Moshi turned an ear and replied in equally soft tones. "I've had a lot on my mind."

"Must have done something big down there to get a crib like this."

The painted dog flicked an ear but said nothing. Bajit had an amazing talent for saying exactly the wrong thing, but that was a small price to pay for the hyena's company.

"Sorry, I shouldn't have said that."

Moshi took a sip of his wine and then asked a shaky question. "Can I show you something?"

"What is it?" Bajit asked with a raised eyebrow.

"The most beautiful thing I've ever seen."

Bajit looked skeptical. "Am I going to regret saying yes?"

The painted dog didn't reply. Instead he closed his eyes and pulled up a memory from his recorder. A single command sent it to the computer controlling the room and in response, the ceiling lights dimmed to a deep midnight blue. Slowly, the scent of salt and moss and the sound of waves filled the air. Then the windows darkened until they showed barely visible water and rocks far below.

"This is beautiful," the hyena whispered.

For a moment, there was only the sound of their breathing and then a choking sound, as Moshi held back tears. Bajit's arm wrapped around his shoulders. The painted dog sniffed and leaned against the warm, furred body next to him. His words threatened to strangle him as he forced them out.

"I've," he stammered. "I've never shown this to anyone else."

Then he stopped holding back and, as waves crashed over rocks, a painted dog wept bitterly into a striped hyena's chest.

SEWER TEA

Dan Leinir Turthra Jensen

Everybody goes to the Damselfly, but it's always so busy, and, well, it's halfway across town. I go, of course I do, but when you just want a cup of tea and a crumpet or a slice of lemon sponge cake, this place is it. Probably the worst kept secret in Ambara Down, yet it's a bit out of the way, in that way that a trek up half a small mountain to get there is 'a bit out of the way.' But that does mean that when you do, it's a pretty relaxed spot. Most of the time. Certainly more so than when I first saw it.

Considerably less lethally wet, too. I push away the leafy vines hanging down over the open front of the huge round opening at the front of the shop, unsettling both a small trickle of rain drops caught in the foliage, and a whole little school of airfish who had settled against the vines' damp surface.

"Sorry about that," I say with a smirk of my black-furred muzzle, not quite whispering, knowing full well they don't understand a word of what I said, or even the intention, and flick an ear to dislodge some of the water which landed on their sensitive tips.

Not a whole lot of walkers in here, most of the people who come to Sewer Tea are flyers. Most people would rather not have to trek half a kilometer up a mountain to get to a tea shop without anywhere convenient to park a hoverskiff. To me, though, even if I don't go as often as I might, it feels like a second home, and not just because of the vine frontage.

"Hey Stretch!" a familiar screech of a voice says from behind the counter. Avians are used to heights, but most of them aren't particularly tall. So when a maned wolf becomes a regular, well, suffice it to say that I very literally stick out in the crowd here. They know very well that's not my name, but when someone picks you a nickname that's shorter than your proper name, you better believe that's going to stick. Especially given how hard the v sounds in 'Vyvian' are to make if you have a beak instead of lips.

"Hey Screech," I answer, because I am similarly unable to produce the clack of beak in Treeklak's name, and feel pretty certain that I completely murder the trill as well. "Usual please."

"One disgustingly adulterated tea and a citrus cake slice, okie dokie," Treeklak says, and I slide onto one of the bar stools, certain I'm the only regular who is able to not only bend their legs and still reach the floor, but also has their knees resting against the bar. As my host begins to prepare what I will argue to anyone is the best masala chai available anywhere in or out of town, they aim their beak in the direction of my upper arm. "What's with the glow rings?"

"Like them?" I ask, and flick an ear. Watching Treeklak prepare things is always a treat. I am quite happy with my own almost human like hands, but watching the dexterity on the avian's wing wrist talons is just amazing to me. Two on each wing, and they handle tea pots with more precision that I ever did an abseiling line pistol or a power regulator wrench.

"Too alike your halo light," they say and flush out a tea pot with boiling water, then empty that into the gray water side of the sink. A little wasteful, perhaps, but it's well worth doing it right, and—name of Treeklak's hole in the side of mountain aside—they know how to make a pot of tea. And it's not like there's really a shortage of water up here with, not with the equipment we found. Pretty sure they supply most of the avian village with that pile of kit. "No," Treeklak finally said. "I do not like them."

"Good," I say with a single, stern nod, knowing full well what that move does to my ears, and how disarmingly silly their flopping about is. "You always had terrible taste."

They laugh, and I do as well. It is absolutely not true, Treeklak's style is impeccable, just entirely different to my own. Out of my gear, I tend to go for flowing, light weight robes with as much sparkle as I can get. The new addition since my last visit is a set of hoverglow rings around my neck and upper arms. And along my tail, to which I'm still looking forward to their reaction.

Treeklak is near enough my exact opposite there. Aside from the pearlescence of their feathers in sunlight and the ice blue of their eyes, they are practically the absence of colors. My robe is similarly pearlescent, but my color choices tend to be strong, bright shades. Today it is a few layers of just slightly translucent yellow and blue, which blend a bit into the occasional hint of green. So where I am usually afloat in a glistening, flowing sea of color, my avian friend is a collection of shades of black, all of them fairly tight fitting. I don't even want to imagine what that would feel like with fur, but perhaps feathers handle compression better.

"Here you are," they say, with that raspy roll on all the 'r' sounds that corvids tend to make, and put the tea and a plate in front of me. Lemon sponge is a nasty thing to say with a beak, which I guess is why they just call it something else, but it is also moist and delicious, and goes better with the heady spiciness of the milky tea than it has any right to. I also would have never known about either of them without Treeklak.

* * *

We met a couple of years ago. I had been off the trail for a bit and had taken up doing some maintenance work for a few shops in Old Ambara. It's such a beautiful part of town, and I was doing my little bit, helping to keep it that way. But exciting? Maybe, I guess it might be, but with my background it just felt, well, a little tedious. Safe, paid well enough, but tedious.

One night after I rescued one of the shop keepers' catdragon out of the canopy it had managed to slink itself up into again, Treeklak came up to me, looked at me a moment, then down at a data pad, then back up again. It was then I first noticed the color of their eyes, but it had been less pleasant to be scrutinized that way back then than it was now, when I've learned that they are a touch short sighted, and just never felt the need to get it fixed.

Back then, it had made me hand the shop owner their catdragon, asking them to please take better care, that just because I'm nearly a meter taller than they are doesn't mean I'll just be able to get pets out of vines for them whenever they need it. Once that minor touch of public service was done, I turned to the diminutive corvid, who aimed their beak at me.

"You are Yeerrian," they said, the first time I had heard someone without lips attempting the sound of my name, let alone realize that those two letters v have different sounds. It took a few moments to realize that yes, that actually was my name.

I stood still and as calmly as I knew how to, putting myself between the retreating shop keep and Treeklak, because while the flyer was small, I knew how fast they are, and how unpleasant their beaks are when you encounter one straight on. It was, I thought, about to get ugly, and what I was sure was going to be someone running a 'Claimer warrant in Ambara Down, for what random reason they might have come up with for picking me up, was about to cause a whole heap of trouble for themselves.

"I am Vyvian," I said, and got myself ready to try and catch a beak before the pointy end of a corvid about half my height ended up somewhere it would be able to do some serious damage. They can't really fly, I guess they never quite worked out how to make people-sized beings able to fly. Good, though, at stopping a fall, exceptional at aerial acrobatics, and steering themselves in hand-to-hand situations. Just in case it was someone working on behalf of a begruntled former customer, I tried asking: "Have we met before?"

"No," the flyer said. "Treeklak is I, and I got a work task to let you do."

I had not really dealt with avians before in person, and the way they picked words had never really been something I had thought about before. At the time, it just seemed like a really strange way to say things, but of course they were just making sure they would be able to pronounce the words they chose.

"Well," I said and tilted my head. It seemed like they had more in mind than my current job, if they were looking me up. Even then, I said, "You could have just called up the maintenance offices, they'd find you someone no problem at all. Their frequency is on the broadcast range, but they'll take encrypted calls if you try."

"The task is not to sort things that aren't working," Treeklak said and held out their data pad in their two talons. The talons extended from what had always seemed to me like an inverted elbow, but which was basically a wrist. "Rather it is to assist this one in locating a thing. Also you could assist in locating additional things once you and I locate that initial thing."

"I'm afraid I no longer…" I began, but stopped myself before getting any further. I took the pad from the flyer and looked at the description it displayed. I held it flat and the holograph popped the display into 3D, to show a tunnel system that was, well, much less familiar than I thought it was going to be. Didn't look very well made, which always is a worry, but even then I felt there was something more going on than just someone with a bad map of Ambara Down's underground. "This isn't the catacombs, is it?"

"It is not the under city catacoons inside the warrens," they replied with a shake of the head. "Those are the high inside catacoons, I and other like this reside near there, on the outside. Now need to take a look inside. Need assistance, and got told you are great at going into those."

"I think," I said, looking at the crudely drawn network of tunnels hovering in the air before me, "that we should probably head over to my place."

* * *

I take a sip of my tea and close my eyes, slowly breathing out the spicy air through the long channels inside my snout, past the multitude of scent detectors in there. No augmentations there, just pure nature. Well, as "nature" as any of us get, I guess. Simultaneously my greatest ally in the career which Treeklak had found a way to revive, and the reason I had eventually taken a long break from it. When you have the ability to smell the difference between a 'Claimer with a pheromone camouflage spray and someone who produced that pheromone themselves, well, let's just say the catacombs are perhaps not the best place to lead the majority of your waking life.

"Assist this one, could you?" Treeklak says, and points to the very uppermost shelf along the upcurving wall. "Need another container with tea."

"Sure thing," I say and slink around the back of the counter, and stretch out to pick up a tin of tea from the shelf at the top, where Treeklak would have had to clamber onto what to them would seem like a tall ladder to reach. "This one, right?"

"That one, yes," Treeklak says and accepts it as I hand it down to them. "Thank you."

"Not a problem," I say and sit down again. "Hardly fair to drink the last of your tea and then refuse to save you from getting out the ladder."

"Could get there on wings," Treeklak says and points to the rails above the counter, "though down are not good in tea and cakes."

"True," I say and can't quite help but wag. "Much appreciated thought, there."

"The city council is not keen on dirty sustenance," Treeklak says with a shake of the head. "I just get to do as they insist."

"You've gone all law abiding citizen on me, Screech?" I say, tilting my head, but making sure to smirk enough for the avian to be able to tell.

"Hardly," they say and laugh. "Just in here, got all the records, all solid and with docs. Don't like that lot digging around in what else I get into doing."

"Like our spelunking?"

"Like our *tunnel checking*," they say with a firm nod, which unlike my flopping ears is an almost aggressive, pecking like motion on the earless avian.

* * *

After that fairly public introduction, we walked back to my place. A simple space at the top of one of the old buildings about half way back out to the bay. Nothing super fancy, not like over in Tzumrut. Pretty sure it had been just the living room of somebody's apartment once, but I only needed the one room and there was a family of otters living in the remainder of the place. They were happy for me to live in this room, because well, turns out they didn't like the view up over the mountain, preferring the view out over the bay. Never had been keen on water myself, and the lush green of the mountainside just seemed much more pleasant to me.

It was their place, and I had been offered residence if I would do caretaking. Just general maintenance work and the like, and they even offered that I could have some fish from time to time when they came back from the sea. I'd been more than happy to do so.

The kitchen along one wall had a working stove. Even the forcefield pots still worked. I'd had to replace the GNDN surge control conduit twice, but those are basically consumable items if my experience with the damned things is anything to go by. The humans might have been clever enough to make people like me happen overnight but could they make a controller circuit that didn't disintegrate over time? Well, not this one, anyway.

The other side of the room had the pallet that was my bed, and the back wall had shelves that made up my wardrobe. The front of the building had once been force-fielded; I could probably get that working again if I was really bothered, but now it was covered with some evergreen climbers, which created a thick layer of foliage over what would have otherwise been a gaping hole taking up the entire bay facing side of the room. The balcony outside the climbers was nearly the size of the room inside, though, so getting to the view was just a question of pushing aside the vines and walking out there. At least the balustrades were there, or I'd have had to rig some. Three stories up was still a fair way to fall, even if you're as tall as me.

"This is not the greatest tea this one has had," had been Treeklak's comment when I put the mug in front of them to sip while I swapped out my bag of tools for my catacomb kit—forgetting entirely that, much like saying my name, sipping is something that one might do if one has lips. "Though certainly also not horrendous. One can drink it in a joyous thought set. Thank you."

"You're welcome, I think?" I flicked an ear as I grabbed the backpack off of the shelf. It had been a while, so I made a point of checking through the contents. Some of them had ended up in my repair kit and needed putting back in, like the knife and the electronic key. Always seemed an innocuous name for a piece of kit designed to rip apart the locking system of a whole bunch of different types of locks. Couldn't handle the super high security ones, but most anything down in the Warrens tended to be fairly simple and I'd never really had much trouble. Just had to let it do its thing, and hope nobody showed up to cause trouble while you were hanging around waiting for that particular patch of paint to dry.

"Where are we going, anyway?" I asked, and Treeklak had looked at me quietly for a moment, before putting down the mug and pulling out their pad. They put it down on the kitchen worktop and pulled up a city map, zooming in on the mountains along the northern edge.

"When the city crashed, it went down while on the go," Treeklak said while moving the map up the side of the mountain. They stopped about half-way up and pointed at a particular point on the mountainside, leaving a mark in what seemed like a pretty nondescript spot. "All along here used to also contain dwellings like your one here, though they are all gone today. They who are like this one created new dwellings there. Nests, you could say. The one at that location there is this one's nest. You can see its location just outside there," they said and extended a wing to the curtain of greenery, "though they are hidden with great success."

"Flyers all living in hidden nests up the mountainside," I said and nodded. Made sense, bunch of avians living somewhere high. "Good place if you got wings, I guess. Not sure what that has to do with the catacombs, though. Why do you need me?"

"There are tunnels in great count," they said, and added the map I had seen down on the market on top. When going into the Warrens, I was used to having some pretty well built maps. Compared to those, this was fairly crudely drawn, but even then it seemed like the mountain was nearly filled with tunnels of many different sizes. "Also the tunnels occasionally exit to the side. This one's dwelling is near such an exit, like others also, not really strange. Strange is the way it has now changed, as it is now no longer shut to the inside. It used to not allow access into there, though a landslide has changed this."

"So you want me to try and work out if your home is still safe," I said as I did up the now full backpack, wondering if perhaps I ought to be packing something more powerful than a confusion field projector and a stun baton. "Something like that?"

"Not at all," they said, with a shake of the head and shut down the holomap. "Already know it is not. These tunnels are generally said sewers, and not really dangerous. This is the reason I said there is a need to locate things. There are things in a wide selection, and I require assistance to get to those."

So, going into a sewer pipe. Great way to get back into the business. My nose twitched involuntarily with the memory of a myriad encounters with unpleasant scents in the catacombs.

* * *

I take off a bit of the lemon cake, put it on my tongue, and then bring it into my mouth. I savor the flavor of it, the sweetness, the tanginess, the softness of its texture. It is delicious. I would have doubted its authorship if it weren't. Treeklak's first comment on food provided by me had at first seemed ungrateful, even perhaps a bit rude. Back then I had just let slide, because well, a customer is a customer is a customer. Much as that was the case, it was not without truth.

"Excuse the less than great quality today," Treeklak says, and I tilt my head questioningly. "That is to say, I had to use a heat closet with less than great control to create it."

"Your oven is broken? Come on, Screech, you should've said, I'd have brought my kit with me."

"I said so in yesterday's yesterday, Stretch," Treeklak says with a shake of their head. "Though you can assist now and then, like getting tea down just now, you should not work here. This is not your work place, like down there. To you, this should stay a relaxing location."

"I appreciate it," I say and flick an ear. "I really do. But, I mean, it wouldn't be work, it'd be helping you, you know?"

"Still your work," Treeklak said, pointing at me with a taloned wing finger. "You do not get tea and cake without handing cash to yours truly, and I should not ask you do your work unless I hand cash to you."

"No mates' rates?"

"As I said," my old friend says with a nod. Sometimes I forget how flyers put things. Years after my first meeting with them and their community up here on the mountainside, and it still occasionally catches me out. 'As I said,' or as I have learned it means in non-avian: "Thank you for unnecessarily repeating what I just said, and pointing out that your language does not match my beak."

Had they been anybody else, I have no doubt there would have been considerably more unpleasantness in their voice. For now, I just awkwardly sip my tea.

* * *

We had lucked out and found someone at the market's hoverskiff rental space who was looking to go out past the mountains, so they were happy to split the bill with us for a bit. No parking up on the mountainside, but the skiff's pilot waited to let us off. It did feel a little strange to be going up the side of a mountain to go into a sewer pipe. They were, after all, usually underneath the city, rather than above even the tallest of the town's buildings.

I was hardly the only person who made a living out of taking people into the Warrens, even into the catacombs. I was not the first and I was not going to be the last. Some make a living going in alone or in small groups, and then flogging what they find in there on one market or another. Some take orders and earn commission.

For me, though, I would just play tour guide most of the time. Usually that meant putting on a bit of a show. Though the catacombs often help with the staging, after a while the tour guide thing just became a touch boring, and I had ended up doing maintenance work instead. Similar skill set, with less likelihood of terminal injuries and a higher amount of fresh air and sunlight at the cost of a smaller but still entirely reasonable paycheck at the end of the day.

Treeklak was my first customer in a while, and I had nearly turned them away, were it not for the point that they were the one who would be a guide. I would be the security detail, and general underground exploration expert.

"I can see my house!" I said, and Treeklak looked at me with that look of 'what in the world are you talking about' that you sometimes get. "You got a pretty amazing view from up here, I mean, the green of the city, the blue of the bay..." I squinted at the furthest parts of the view and continued a touch less excitedly, "The dark clouds threatening out over the sea..."

"Yes, to stay dry we should get inside," Treeklak said with a nod, and extended a wing to indicate a mass of greenery amongst a bunch of other greenery. It seemed, once pointed out, slightly greener, newer, more kempt than the surroundings, as though someone had taken care to make it look messy, rather than the chaos nature tended to impose on its own.

"I like your garden," I said, and the avian simply clacked their beak in response. At the time I thought that signal of gratitude meant shut up, and so I did. A few steps and we got near enough that I could see the huge span of a pipe, near enough to fifteen meters tall, which had had its front shaved clean off. I pushed a vine aside to look at the pipe and managed to spook a small school of airfish, who fluttered away in a confusion of glittery scales. "Sorry about that," I said, before running a claw tip over the exposed edge of the pipe. Smooth as newly frozen ice.

Self-healing nanocrete was strong, and very handy for sewer pipes. Still, not sure that it was in the design parameters to be able to stand up to teratons of city crashing out of a sky. Ambara had done in seconds what would have taken an ice age sheet decades, shearing the mountainside the pipe was sitting in, happily sewering for whatever had been here before.

When entering the delightful little tea shop now, one is greeted by perches with tables bolted to the framework arching up the sides of the pipe, with the little bar and storage pod at the bottom of it, all lit by the gently dancing glow of carefully arranged light flowers and light vines. You'd never guess today what the place had been like just a few years earlier, how unpleasant a scent permeated the place, and how messy it was. At least the smell was less rank than the stale sewage you still came across at times underneath Ambara Down, but still not pleasant to someone with canine nostrils.

Not even feline eyes would likely have helped with the darkness, though, and my eyesight being barely better than a 'Claimer who's lost their visor there was not a lot to see at first. Thanks, whoever decided to stick that closely to the quadrupedal originators of my genome. Barely a trickle of light came in through the vines, and even that was fading as the clouds approached. I pulled a follow-me lantern from my pack and, moving to offer it to my customer, was surprised to find Treeklak had already pulled a flashlight out of a little satchel hanging underneath one wing.

"Well prepared," I said as I turned the lantern on and lifted it up over my head, where it hung happily just above my ears and expanded into a ring. The ring spread its glow down and all around me, leaving just a small bit right underneath me in darkness.

The light revealed a huge, horizontal cylinder, stretching into the mountain at least as far as the light reached, with small dark areas along both the sides and the top which would have been tributaries to what must have been a main sewer line. It also revealed an enormous amount of mess in the pipe, both what one might assume had not always been dirt, and things which had been flushed or disposed of somehow. Treeklak had a list, but there was a lot here which had to be worth a second look after we were done. At least it was not a case of digging in that literal a sense.

"I like the light this creates," Treeklak said and turned on the flashlight, which spread light only where it was aimed, more concentrated and brighter than my lantern. "Though your halo is also good. I like to stay a little in the dark, less light on this one's quills, so I think this is good. The thing I need your assistance with is this direction."

The last they said as they aimed the flashlight beam into the pipe, toward one of the tributaries maybe three hundred or so meters in. As we walked closer, our lights revealed a door, with the slight telltale glistening of a holo lock. Well, then, that was going to be a bit of fun. At least the things weren't usually networked, so there wasn't much risk of running into some overly opinionated machines. Small blessings and such. Wouldn't be too keen on that happening again, once was definitely more than enough.

"All right, let's see," I said, kneeling down in front of the lock with my backpack on the ground in front of me. I pulled out my trusty minipad and a bundle of connectors and reached out to the lock, which sprang to life by throwing out a confusion of holographic noise. "Great, it's corrupted. Well, guess it's hard mode, then. Can't just stick the electric key on it when it's like this, going to have to fix it first."

"Heal it? We only need to get through the door, right?" Treeklak said beside me. "Why not just crash through it?"

"I would have thought you might have tried that before asking me along," I replied while attaching the wires to an induction harness that would snap around the lock panel's outer edges.

"Did not think ruining the door a good idea," Treeklak said, "in case you could get through it intact. Did not know the lock was also unwell, not good with old kit like this."

"More keen on new stuff, like your 'Claimer pad?" I asked while connecting the other end of the wires to my data pad, and Treeklak nodded. "Fair, really, it can seem overwhelming sometimes, this kind of stuff. Can't just break through the door though, it's reenforced even stronger than the pipe itself. If the city had scraped more of the pipe off, I wouldn't have been surprised to find that door still here. These things are strong. But, as with all such things, if the door is strong, you look for whatever's the weakest point. In our case, the holo lock.

"They're multi-dimensional riddles, basically, usually with bits missing that need filling in, so usually there's trillions of solutions. It's why they're such good locks. Combination locks, but so many options that brute forcing them manually just isn't an option. This one is corrupted, though, which I need to rebuild it first before trying the code breaker on it. Get it wrong and it'll just deadbolt the door and refuse to unlock without a cryptographic master key, and I'm fairly sure that one's somewhere underneath Ambara Down, along with whatever's left of whoever installed the lock. We'd be able to get around it still, but might need something considerably more 'civil engineering' than 'exploration pack' for that, and I imagine your budget would not like that too much."

Treeklak clacked their beak again, and I started to think that perhaps it was less of a shut-your-word-hole thing than I previously thought it was. Nonetheless, I decided that I should perhaps concentrate on what I was doing rather than regale them with history of what was their home just as much as it was mine. Couple of years behind me, sure, but old habits sometimes die hard. Acting as tour guide to people who wanted to see the squishy if occasionally luminescent underside of their home city sometimes meant you ended up on auto pilot spewing words at the customers.

"So in case this lasts until late," Treeklak had said after about an hour of silence, interspersed with me mumbling what I hoped my avian customer would not identify as swearing, "should I sort us a little sustenance?"

"Oh yes, please," I said distractedly, poking at a scatterfield of promising-looking visual garbage. "White and two sugars for me, please, and my cream tea's Devonian. I've brought field rations along, enough for two for two days, just in case.

"No need to use rations," Treeklak said. "As I said earlier, this location is near this one's residence. I shall return in a short while."

"Okay," I said and nodded, frowning at the coalescing scatterfield which had turned out to be indeed interesting. Interesting enough to successfully distract me from the fact my customer had just gone off, leaving me alone with the lock. It took me maybe another hour before I realized that I was alone, which was also the time it took to turn the scatterfield into something more coherent.

"Eureka!" I said, and looked around excitedly, preparing to explain to Treeklak that I had just managed to fix a holographic lock from before the crash, and that I was just about to set the electronic key on it. Instead I was met by darkness outside the reach of my lantern's glow.

"Oh no," I whispered, and stood up to look around, hoping my customer had just turned off their light and decided to take a nap. I nearly shouted out an attempt at their name, when I realized that they had mentioned something about food and living nearby.

"Excuse this one that it took so long," Treeklak's voice echoed through the pipe from the entrance, where the glow of their flashlight lit up the bottom of the pipe as they came toward me, followed by a hissing sound. "I realized that the sustenance was not quite ready. This is no longer the case, and I carry things to sustain you and I."

I had not realized just how hungry I had become, and the sight of the avian was accompanied by a waft of the most delightful scents I had experienced since, to be fair, a recent repair job at a baker's in Old Ambara, but not a fair long while before then. Not really something I had expected to encounter in a sewer pipe, whether or not it was one half-way up a mountain.

As they came closer and the volume of the hissing sound remained the same, I recognized the sound of rain hitting the leaves of the vines covering the pipe's opening. A small trickle of water ran through the center of the wide pipe, reminding me that this was a drain.

"Rain finally hit us, then?" I said as Treeklak entered my circle of light, and after pausing a moment they put down the large covered tray they were carrying and tilted their head at me.

"It did so three hours ago, yes," they said after a few moments, and removed the covering from the tray before I quite realized what that meant for the amount of time I had spent on the lock. With the cover off, it revealed that not only was it waterproof, it had also held back a great deal of the scent. Entirely unlike myself, I found my saliva trying to emulate the trickle of water in the bottom of the pipe. "Your tail says you would like a little sustenance?"

"Oh great maker," was all I could say without leaking the proof of my hunger all over the floor. "Yes, please!"

* * *

"I did not call anyone out yet, though," Treeklak says from behind the counter after I've sat quietly for a short while, guiltily nibbling a bit of my delicious slice of cake. "I could send a request with you? To hand to you, once you are at work again?"

"All right," I say and feel my ears perk back up. "I'll tell me to get back up here when the schedule allows, normal rates like you said. I'll not bring lunch, though, can just deduct my cost for that from the bill. That work for you?"

"No low rates to allies," Treeklak says with a nod, and I realize that during the time I spent moping at being called out for being rude they have been trying to find a way of using my awkward, ancient expression that works with their beak, and perhaps also their style. "That does work well, though, less wealth to deal with that way going to either you or I."

"I can already taste those sandwiches," I say with a smile broad enough that it shows the full set of teeth in my jaw. It is a good thing that tone of voice has a weight, or that would seem very much like a snarl. I pull out the pad I keep my calendar in, and bring up the agenda. "Actually, how does day after tomorrow work? Don't want you waiting, but I do have an urgent job tomorrow that I can't skip out on."

"The next day's next day?" Treeklak tilts their head, and then nods. "I shall need to not use the thing until then, though I can deal with that. Call that a date!"

"Sorted," I say and sip my tea. "Might end up taking the whole bill in massala chai and lemon cake. You're a wizard. Always have been, you know. Sewage or not."

I lift my cup and wink, and Treeklak's laughter echoes off the concrete arching high above us.

* * *

"But after I worked out that the tertiary diagrammatic algorithm had caused the initial derezzing, I knew how to attack it properly,"

I was explaining to what felt very much like a far too accepting audience. I had kept having to remind myself at times that they were my customer, not an enraptured child, even though while sat on the little platform on the side of the drain pipe with the food between us, our different sizes kept telling my eyes that was what was going on. It had not come up, and it was not until a good while later I learned they were easily a couple of decades my senior. I was plenty used to looking downwards at people, certainly, but I just was not used to others being quite so short as the avian was.

"There is nothing quite like learning an issue's root cause to allow one to sort it," they said after taking a bite of the fruit I had learned was the final part of 'Near Day End Tea.' I'd had afternoon tea before, in the entirely too flashy coffee shop on the corner in the market, the one with the very bubbly, pink tentacat owner. Even knowing that, it took me entirely too long to realize that was what they had meant. It would, I realized, take me a fair long while to work out how to properly understand the avian dialect, though I thought that this particular comment was clear enough, even if it was perhaps a bit unlike the form I was used to hearing.

"Does the alternating red light suggest anything to you?" they said, and pecked the air in the direction of the door which was behind me.

I had, when we had sat down to eat a couple of hours earlier, decided that I needed to look at something other than that lock for a bit, and so had deliberately and literally turned my back on it. Now I turned around, and saw the flashing telltale on the codebreaker which said that it had completed its run. I had never got around to swapping the colors, so the completion indicator just looked like a nondescript flashing light to me.

"Red you say?" I asked, and Treeklak nodded. I'm sure my tail thumping on the ground behind me gave it away before I said as much, but I said it anyway after taking the most nonchalant sip of tea that I knew how to, extending a claw-tipped little finger and everything. "That means we're in."

"We are through the locked door?" Treeklak said, and when I nodded, began to pack up the little picnic-in-the-sewer that we had shared. "The clock has continued, so we should not wait longer than strictly required."

"Quite right," I replied, and after being refused when moving to help pack up the food, I stood up and walked over to check the codebreaker. It had indeed completed its run, and I was offered a set of not quite standard but seemingly pretty straightforward door controls. I checked the options available on the lock and found a code reset. I picked that, and set the code to one I used after running a takeover. There are a fair few locks with a variant of it down in the Warrens, but this was going to be the first outside the city.

"Right," Treeklak said as they walked up beside me, looking from the lock to the door. "Shall we?"

"Certainly," I said, and pushed the Remain Unlocked option before returning to the main display, which showed the open lock symbol. I pointed at the panel on the door itself, which was now lit with a soft, welcoming glow. "Would you like to do the honors? Your find, I'm just the hired brains, after all."

"Quite glad to," Treeklak said and then looked up at me with a most severe expression. "However, you should not undersell you so, you work well. A great asset to anyone. I tried to get others' assistance with this task, though none got near to succeeding with this lock."

Before I had a chance to comment, Treeklak turned back to the door, and unceremoniously pecked at the door's panel, which turned from solid glow to an animated line extending across the full height, moving from one side of the door to the other, which usually was supposed to show the direction the door would slide into the wall. It was accompanied by a gentle hum, and moments later the door, rather than sliding, swung open away from us, hinged on the side the line animated toward. Not a pocket door, then. That would suggest an engineering location behind it. A good choice for looking for things, then. *Good choice, Treeklak.*

Behind the door we could just barely make out a room extending into the mountain parallel to the main pipe further than what both our lights allowed us to see. The walls were lined with large containers about twice my height and twice as wide again as they were tall. They were all connected by a whole lot of pipework, and in front of them they had what looked like engineering access panels, all inert. Lucky enough, really. Unlike the lock this would have been networked kit, likely wireless ones that would invite in some of the more unsavory digital denizens of our world.

"This is a distressing thing," Treeklak said as we walked into the room. They let the light of their torch go from one container's black control panel to the next, and shook their head. "Quite distressing. One had desired that they had retained running status. Still, your skills could turn handy again, yes?"

"You know what these things are, I take it?" I asked as we walked down the corridor, which seemed as endless as the main pipe outside, though much cleaner. It must have been sealed off where the pipe had been open. Fit well enough with the still active, if not exactly healthy holo lock.

"Yes," Treeklak said. "These are water recyclers. Each residence here had one such connected to it."

"And," I said then as we continued walking through a space as clean as I had seen outside of a 'Claimer med ward, "when you said you wanted me to assist in finding things, you didn't need a guide, but rather someone who might be able to bring a water recycler back to life?"

"As you say," Treeklak said with a nod and continued talking in a more hushed version of their usually almost ear-piercingly raspy voice as they inspected each of the vats we walked past. "Call the lock a test. It really was unwell, though I knew what laid on the door's other side. I need your assistance in recycling a water recycler. I wish to start a tea and cake outlet, and these things are what shall let this one do so without water issues. I had hired three other guides until I tried you, none could sort the lock. The last suggested you, hence I went to see you. You were skilled as indicated, and here we are. I still hold a wish that one is working at least a little."

"You know," I said and trailed off, flicked an ear at the sound of rolling thunder. I remember thinking that the acoustics of the tunnel were funneling the sound to us in a most inconvenient way while I tried to focus on another sound. I put my ear against one of the vats, and found the unmistakable hum of pumps inside.

"This one's working," I said, turning around to face the avian, who seemed maybe a bit distracted and was shining their torch down the hall, away from where we had entered, their head tilted in what I thought was just them being lost in thought. Perhaps they were thinking that one further down might have working control circuitry and so I launched into a description of my own thoughts, to try and distract them from that reverie. I had to raise my voice to not be drowned out by the increasingly loud thunder. "Bet it's just the GNDN surge control conduit that's gone on them. I picked one up just in case, always have a few sat spare at home, in case my stove dies on me again, you know? Lemme ju—"

I didn't get any further before being interrupted most rudely by the source of the sound of rolling thunder, which turned out to be coming from in front of us rather than the outside like I'd assumed. Rather than being electrical discharge between the ground and the clouds, instead it was the sound of water. Rushing water. Specifically, water rushing toward us.

It is a strange thing how sometimes, when completely crazy things happen, the world seems to simultaneously speed up and slow down. You understand a great many things are happening all at the same time, but somehow, it all seems to take eons to actually happen.

In an attempt to approximate their name, which they had spelled and signed for me before we headed out, the nearest I managed to the first part was much less a trill and much more just a sort of high pitched screeching. It did, however, have the desired effect, and they turned to me as I reached behind me to grab a hold of one of the pipes. I held out the other hand to them, and it seemed as though it took hours until they realized I wanted them to grab onto me. Water was already gushing past us by the time they did, though the method of accepting my offer was perhaps not the quite one I had hoped they would pick. It made sense, as I'm sure their wings would have been far too brittle for that kind of grasp, but even armed with that knowledge, their impressive talons certainly were not something I would willingly chose to have embedded in my arm.

A different kind of scream escaped from me as I pulled us both to safety behind the tank. A marginal safety, to be fair, from a torrent which seemed never ending. As the water level rose with impressive rapidity around us, I remembered that the door into this room had been on swinging hinges, and that it opened into the room.

"Door's shut," I shouted over the roar of the water, and Treeklak looked at me with wide opened eyes, and clacked their beak.

"I'll go under the water," they shouted back and extended an arm towards the door, "when the height reaches us, it'll settle a little, and I do water really well. Do not let go!"

"As if I could!" I shouted past a mouthful of water. "Your talons are still embedded in my forearm!"

"Let go the handhold and take in air to your lungs!" they shouted. We both breathed several deep breaths and held the last, then the avian lunged back into the water with me in tow. As they had predicted the water was now rushing with much less force, though it was still quite turbulent, and still rising with alarming speed. The room was filling up, and unless Treeklak had something hidden in their neck feathers, neither of us had gills.

What they did have was impressive skill under water. Treeklak could not fly, not in air. What they needed was a more viscous element such as, say, water. Hardly a ballet, this was utilitarian flying with the goal of getting to the door as quickly as possible, before either of us ran out of air. It was faster than my otherwise capable legs let me run.

We arrived moments later at the closed door, and I discovered what it was that had gone wrong. With the power of hindsight, the symbols I had not really paid a huge amount of attention to before showed a sluice gate. We had, it seemed, quite literally opened the flood gates on ourselves. I should have perhaps paid more attention when I reset the lock. I activated a few controls, and motioned for Treeklak to get on the far side of the door, where I joined them as the door opened. The water rushed out of the room, draining almost as rapidly as it had entered.

"Uhm," I said, as we stood on the floor once more, both of us dripping, my black and orange fur considerably less glamorous looking than Treeklak's feathers glistening in the light of my halo, which still hung above me obediently. No sign of the avian's torch. "So, maybe we should have been less pushy going into here. Anybody you know down the hill from here? Think they might've just got a bit more rain than usual."

"They all are secure, those who could get issues with this had it with the landslide already," Treeklak said and shook themselves, and I followed their example. When we had both got a touch less soggy, Treeklak said, "We should try and not do that again. You can call this one Screech, though, I realise Treeklak is hard. Should sort that earlier."

"Oh," I said, flustered, "ehrm, I guess my name isn't super easy either."

"It is not, Yeerrian," Treeklak said, and I could not help smirk. They tilted their head and looked at me ponderously "Stretch? Like you did to this one. Your action rescued this one."

"Sure," I nodded, my tail wagging behind me. "Stretch works. Pretty sure you rescued me as well. Not sure I'd have been able to swim there without your help, you know?"

"Oh, sure you could," Treeklak said. They aimed their beak at the still glowing lock at the same time I reached to take off my pack, and they said, "Could you check that so we can continue?"

"Was just about to," I said as I knelt before the lock and put my pack on the still sodden floor. I looked back over my shoulder, tail swatting at a puddle behind me. "Pack's more waterproof than my fur is. Hm. Right, no network connection on this, not really. Just hardwired up to a few other systems a bit further in. Pretty sure that there's an overview map behind here… yes, there we go. Just going to take a copy of that, and we'll be able to get under way."

"This is not like the guide I had acquired," Treeklak said behind me, and clacked their beak, hard.

"If you paid money for that," I said as I plugged in a data transfer chit to copy the lock's external data store, "I think you'll want to try and get a refund."

"Still," they said and walked over to one of the tanks. They stroked it with a wing, and paused for a moment before continuing. "These are a higher worth than what that guide suggested. Though no security tools, that water was clean. Really, really clean. I shall register this location, shared with you like the contract says."

"Water cyclers aren't super high value," I said, unplugging the now map equipped data chit from the lock, "but the kit all seems really solid, looks like it's all running, and there's a lot of it. It's a good find, yeah."

"No," the avian said, "it is a great one. This is water that shall allow this one to create the greatest teas yet."

"Making tea," I said, walking over to them after packing my things away again. "From recycled water, in a glorified sewer pipe. The marketing material practically writes itself! Come to Sewer Tea, have tasty tea, totally not made from sewage, honest!"

I had not spent much time with avians before, so it took a few moments before I realized the rasping chattering Treeklak was producing as they looked up to me was laughter. Not an amazing sound, to be honest, but laughter is good and that made it a beautiful sound. And sometimes it is contagious. This was one of those times.

* * *

I glance back over my shoulder and wave a glow ring wrapped arm to my corvid friend, and then push aside the vines covering the entrance to what must be probably the most well-kempt sewer pipe. I make sure to be much gentler this time, and the airfish hiding between the hanging greenery stay where they are. The light outside has nearly gone. Wisps of cloud hang over the bay, and both they and some of the ancient buildings poking out of the water catch the light of the setting sun, everything bathed in a warm glow. It is beautiful. I understand why the avians like it up here, even if it's a fair distance into town. I consider moving here, as I do every time I have to leave Treeklak's little tea shop, and as I walk down the mountain, I again manage to talk myself out of it.

Ten years since we met. Ten years of taking the walk up the mountain at least once a month. Ten years of me thinking I should move up here, and ten years of me talking myself out of it before I get all the way back down again to the busy city with its shop keepers and their catdragons, and the occasional trip down into the Warrens.

Fixing stuff is a nice, safe job. Always another GNDN surge control conduit gone in somebody's shop kitchen, or another holographic signage that needed re-rezzing. But it isn't really fun. Pays for things, sure it does, but you need more than that. Like that urgent appointment tomorrow, which isn't so much urgent as just, well, exciting. Time to take three felines from Tzumrut down into the catacombs to explore for the day.

Surviving is a good thing, and we all need that. But while surviving is good, living is better. Thank you, Treeklak, for reminding me of what I should have never forgotten.

PERSEPHONE'S CHANCE

Juan Carlos Moreno

Ambara Down has its charms, but in this tigress' opinion, nothing beats the food of Port Collie. Though just a fraction of Ambara Down's size, the city's reputation for culinary creativity and a steady supply of ingredients attracts zoomorphs from all over who bring their dishes and talent. Put simply, it's a recipe for success.

While it's not officially part of my native land of verDen, Port Collie's relationship with its southern neighbor is one they both enjoy. Despite its name, the Ol' Port is completely landlocked, with the Particularly Rocky Mountains to the west, vast plains to the east, and a stretch of forested wildlands along the north. The verDen Defense Force protects the region from Pax Machina, the 'Claimers, and raiders like the Hangdogs, which keeps supply chains moving and contributes to PoCo's relaxed atmosphere. In exchange, verDen supplements its food stocks with the best on the continent and uses the area for vDF bases.

Ask any denizen of either entity and they'll tell you the arrangement works. PoCo culture adds just the spice verDen needs, and verDen keeps the frontier city stable enough to live in comfortably, but still wild enough to find a good time.

Of course, as verDenner freelancers, my friends and I have a knack for finding trouble wherever we go. This time, however, trouble found us.

I'd just finished my last cloudfish taco from Infamous Petra's, one of the best places in town—dockside or otherwise. I was reclining in *Opportunity*'s cargo bay, out of the rain, when Tibbs and Rutgers sprinted across the dock to our landing pad. Tibbs, my vulpine

228

partner in mischief, looks like he dipped his paws, ears, and tail deep into an inkwell, which makes them stand out against his sandy orange fur. As a fox, Tibbs easily outpaced the stocky badger Rutgers, but not by more than a tail's length.

Rutgers hurried to keep up, oblivious to the drizzle speckling his forest green clothing and matting his black and white fur. It took quite a bit to rile the badger, but as he and Tibbs got closer, I could tell we had a special job on our paws. And we wouldn't be alone.

Three cloaked figures followed my crew, their hoods hiding their faces from the rain and from me. If they were aiming to be inconspicuous, they were missing the mark, and my instincts warned me to be ready for anything.

"Tabitha, prep for launch!" Tibbs said, dashing inside, skipping the stairs and taking the ladder to the cockpit.

"New clients?" I asked Rutgers, scrambling to my paws.

"Yeah, and they paid for a quick departure." He tossed me two coin pouches. "Everyone, this is Tabitha."

The first two ducked inside as the third, a badger like Rutgers, stopped to shake paws. "I'm Ravensara," she said, "but most just call me Sara. Please excuse my clients, they're a bit anxious to get airborne."

"Clients?"

Sara checked over her shoulder. "Yes. I'm their bodyguard, and I think we're being followed." Under her cloak, she carried a holstered stun baton and wore a full-body tactical suit, like something out of verDen history lessons.

"Okay, no problem. Follow me and we'll get you situated. *Opportunity* may be an old boat, but she's the best chance for anyone who doesn't want to be found." We hurried inside and I closed the gangway doors. "Tibbs, we good to go?" I called up the accessway.

"Departure clearance granted, my dear," he said. "However, there's a... well, you'd better get up here."

My fur bristled. Suddenly curious, I opened the coin pouches, wondering why they'd paid so much up front. The first held currency from all over: Tzumrut, Ambara Down, even verDen. However, the second bag was full of Reclamation Project Units of Credit. My nose wrinkled. Something smelled off. Come to think of it, something about Sara didn't smell right, either. Then it hit me.

I dashed upstairs and Sara followed. "Tibbs! Rutgers! They're—" Words failed me as I saw our clients uncloaked for the first time.

"Humans?" Rutgers finished. "Yeah, we know."

"I was gonna say 'Claimers,'" I said, eyeing the pair. They were dressed in the dusty fatigues of a Reclamation Project field team, with thin, sun-blocking shirts and cargo pants. They appeared to be fraternal twins, with the same dark hair and skin.

"My name is Gale Hyacinth, and this is my brother, Cirrus," the woman said.

Her brother nodded. "Call me Rus," he said. "If it helps, we're not with the Reclamation Project. Not anymore."

"It's why we're here," Sara said as she removed her cloak, "and why we need to go now." The badger glanced out a window and recoiled away. "Aw fluff, I think our shadow found us."

Immediately, Tibbs closed all battle shutters and *Opportunity*'s grav units and engines hummed to life. The holographic display over the covered window kicked in and I studied it until I found a human face. Stern, cold eyes watched us from the dockside market. Rus and Gale confirmed the woman as their shadow.

"We heard you're the people to handle situations like ours," Gale said.

"Yes," Rus added, "and we'll tell you everything. But first, can you shake a tail?"

I shook the humans' hands at last and said, "Trust me when I say Tibbs can shake a tail like none other!" I deployed the passenger seats with a press of a wall button. They emerged from the walls or popped up from the floor. "You'll wanna buckle up." Taking my own advice, I headed for the copilot seat and strapped in.

Tibbs took off and kept our departure swift yet smooth, much like him. In seconds, we ascended above the forested city and its nestled buildings as we headed for an airshipping lane. We gracefully slipped around the slower cargo airships heading to and from Port Collie, which is how we knew an RP drone was following us.

"See it?" I asked, tapping the scanner screen.

Tibbs twitched his ears. "Yep."

"Too close for hind claws, my love?"

"Yeah, and it's not worth a mini-missile anyway. Gonna do this the foxy way. Hold on to something!" Throttle open, we left the lane and zoomed into the nearest cloud.

A few button taps later, our optical camouflage activated and we made a sharp course change. On the scanner, the drone scrambled unsuccessfully to pick up our trail and fell out of range as we left PoCo airspace.

"One tail shaken," Tibbs said.

"Make that two," I said, flicking mine. "Nice flying."

"Thanks," he replied, hitting the autopilot and heading for the central room behind us. "Let's see what kinda job we're in for, then."

"We're clear of their tracker drone," I said as everyone gathered around our table. "That's impressive tech for archeologists, so I think some explanations are in order."

Gale spoke first. "My brother and I were part of an RP Special Expeditions team. We were tasked with recovering ancient technology in support of the higher unit objective."

"Which is?" Rutgers probed.

The Hyacinths exchanged nervous glances before Rus answered. "The reclamation of Ambara Down."

"Please, you have to understand," Gale added, "everything we're telling you is why we can't return. We don't know which humans can be trusted. Sara barely got us out of Ambara Down in one piece."

It was my crew's turn to share concern. "Go on," Tibbs said.

"Over the last year, we found clues to a special Temporal Bunker, different from the thousands of others," Rus said.

"A Stasis Bunker," Gale clarified. "One whose inhabitants never left."

My swishing tail involuntarily froze. "That would mean they'd be from…"

"From before the dark age, yes," Gale finished. "Possibly from as far back as the days of High Humanity. They'd have answers, or at least some idea about what happened."

"Unfortunately," Rus said, "we learned our unit is after more than a history lesson, and we realized why they chose us." He inhaled slowly and leaned forward. "I've studied ancient tech all my life, and they think my research can be used to control Pax Machina."

"Control Pax Machina?" Rutgers scoffed. "That's impossible."

"That's what I told them," Sara said. "The machines don't take orders."

"My research suggests they once did, but it gets worse," Rus added.

"Worse than the RP commanding an army with a cold, mechanical compulsion to control all organic life?" Tibbs offered.

"How about an army you can't even see?" Gale asked.

I narrowed my eyes. "Like some kind of stealth tech? Like *Tuney*'s camouflage?" I asked.

Gale shook her head. "Much more dangerous. SPEX recruited me because I'm a biologist specializing in archeovirology," Gale said. "We found the bunker, but there was only one survivor in the stasis pods."

"Her name is Persephone Feldspar, and if her pod data is correct, she is approximately fourteen years old," Rus said. "Of course, due to stasis and the Temporal Bunker she's actually—"

"Centuries, if not millennia!" Rutgers interrupted.

"Which means her body contains microbes no human or zoomorph on Earth has encountered in all that time," Gale said. "Germs we might no longer be immune to or have any medicines to treat. The perfect building blocks for a biological weapon."

"With control of Pax Machina, a customized plague, or both, the RP can wipe the zoomorph population from Ambara Down," Rus said, "all without harming the city or any humans living there."

A heavy silence hung over the room. Only our engines and the gentle rush of air outside made any noise. At last, Sara spoke. "A way to destroy their enemies while sparing their resources, huh? You know they won't stop with Ambara Down, right?"

The Hyacinths nodded slowly. "Tzumrut, Port Collie, especially verDen," Gale said. "Our unit reported to someone in High Empyros, but most of our operations are secret from the rest of the RP, too."

"Even with the alliances, there's a chance they could turn these weapons on the other High Cities," Rus added. "If either threat becomes more than theoretical, whoever wields them will be unstoppable."

Tibbs and Rutgers turned to me. We all had to agree before going any further. Of course, with the lives of millions in our paws, no one could bring themselves to object. I studied the twins, searching for any signs of deceit on their faces, any indication that this could all be a trap. Even without expressive ears, muzzles, or tails, human body language could still say everything their words didn't. To my satisfaction, they appeared sincere. However, when my eyes fell on Sara, their badger bodyguard, my earlier suspicions returned.

"There's one more thing before we begin," I said, "concerning the other badger in the room." Sara and Rutgers looked at each other. "This mission sounds dangerous, and if we're gonna survive, there can't be any secrets between us."

"Is everything okay?" Tibbs asked. The Hyacinths fidgeted.

"Do you wanna tell everyone, or should I?" I asked, staring at Sara. "I live with a badger. I know what one smells like."

The others remained silent as Sara must have realized it was pointless to resist. She touched a button on her gauntlet and her clawed and padded paws dissolved, revealing black gloves underneath. Likewise, her black and white-striped face rippled and receded into her suit's neck. Before long, a human woman with brown eyes, dark skin, and short black hair stared back at us.

"Look, I'm sorry for the deception," Sara said. "My work is dangerous, especially for a human operating around verDen. I did it to protect my clients and myself. Zoomorphs don't always trust humans, and we needed help before SPEX caught us."

"Were you going to tell us?" I asked.

"Yes, I swear. The Hyacinths knew, too. I told them not to say anything until I did."

"How do we know you're not RP?" I continued, leaning in.

"I don't think anything I say could convince you. You'll just have to trust me, like I'm trusting you. Of course, going to zoomorphs for help instead of other humans should speak for itself."

I pondered this. "Crazy world out there when you can't trust your own species, huh?"

Sara bowed her head. "Sadly, that's most of human history."

Then, Rutgers interjected. "But think of what humans accomplished when you *did* trust each other. If we don't do something, no one will be safe, humans or zoomorphs. Trusting each other now could be the start of a new chapter. New history."

"He's right," Tibbs said. "The RP wants the old world back. I say it's up to us to fight for a better one. For our childr—" His ears drooped for a second, then he cleared his throat. "For everyone who'll come after. If you want my vote, I say we trust Sara."

Rutgers agreed, leaving me with the final word. "If you have any other secrets that impact the mission, now's the time. Can we trust you?" I asked.

"Yes," Sara said. "I'm with you. All of you."

Her voice never wavered. Her eyes stayed on mine. My instincts were at peace. "Thank you," I said. "Now then, let's go save the world."

Rus pulled a holotablet from his pocket, selected his map, and highlighted our destination, a jungle far to the south. However, before we set our course, Sara insisted we make a detour to one of her supply caches, much to the twins' vexation.

"Our unit has been on-site for days," Gale said. "We already revived Persephone and took blood samples. Right now, she's probably still quarantined in a medical tent until they can be sure her immune system can survive our world. We could be as dangerous to her as she could be to us."

"Then how do we rescue her?" Rutgers asked. "It sounds like even breathing around her is like playing viral Hangdog Roulette."

"Before I learned what our leaders are planning, I synthesized a stabilizer vaccine," Sara replied. She reached into her pocket and removed a vial filled with blue liquid. "If they figure out how to recreate this, they can take her anywhere. There's no time to waste!"

"When it's the handful of us against a small army of human-supremacist fanatics, I want every edge we can get," Sara replied. "Plus, there's a chance we'll have to deal with Pax Machina."

Rus scoffed. "There aren't any abandoned cities anywhere near the bunker. If Pax Machina was going to show up, they would've done so already."

"Doesn't matter," Rutgers said. "You breached an old-world bunker and that draws Pax Machina like moths to a flame. Dealing with the machines is never a matter of if, it's a matter of when. They always find you and they always try to kill you. Sometimes it just takes a little longer."

"He's right. If we do somehow run into Pax Machina, we're gonna wish we came prepared," Sara said. "Besides, if you're worried about getting there quickly, I may have something to help with that." She glanced around *Tuney*'s interior. "This is an infiltrator ship, *Morrigan* class, right?"

"Yep," Tibbs replied. "Found her in a Temporal Bunker. Come to think of it, ancient humans built her for operations kinda like this one."

"Perfect," the mercenary said. "I have two supercells at my cache. Should be enough juice to get us there in half the time and keep your cloak at max power during the mission. We're gonna need it."

I smiled. In a way, we were the perfect crew to pull off a job like this. To succeed, we'd need the speed and stealth of a fox, the tenacity of a badger, and the strength and focus of a tiger. "In that case, we'll set course for Sara's cache," I said. "Because even with a speed boost, I agree with Gale. We don't have any time to lose."

* * *

Opportunity's active camo blended into the canopy leaves perfectly as we skirted the treetops hours later. The twins and I gathered behind Tibbs in the cockpit, watching the scanner screen like the world depended on it. Sara and Rutgers were behind us, our friend admiring the merc's suit and new gadgets.

"Records on this place said it used to be a desert," Rus explained.

"Crazy what a little climate change will do?" Gale added.

"Tell me about it," Tibbs said. "I'm starting to remember why I'm not a fan of jungles."

Gale chuckled. "Why? Does all that fur get hot or something?"

"I'll have you know this is my summer coat," Tibbs replied with a smirk. "No, I can take the humidity, it's critters like *that* I can't stand." He pointed outside to a dragonfly as big as the cockpit.

"You know they're harmless, right?" Gale said. "Well, mostly harmless."

"Tibbs hates flying bugs big enough to make facial expressions," I explained. "Or ones with, and I quote, 'way too many legs.'"

Gale couldn't hide her grin, and I didn't blame her.

"Which is why Pax Machina's multipedes have a special place in my heart," Tibbs continued. "Why they build them like that, maybe I'll never know, but I'm telling you now, the day I see a bot with too many legs *and* wings is the day I'll know Pax Machina's out to get me personally!"

The scanner chirped. "Okay, everyone," I said, "this is it." Sara and Rutgers joined us and peeked through the cockpit doorway. I pulled the screen to me and brought up the readings. Several contacts drifted lazily across the edge of our range. If they could detect us, they didn't show it, so we hovered higher to get a better view of the area.

A patch of jungle was explosively flattened near the base of a black plateau. A waterfall cascaded down the rocks and fed a river running into the clearing. The RP camp consisted of several large, yellow, hexagonal tents, prefabricated structures, and recharging pads for aircraft. Four thin, sleek gunships patrolled the clearing perimeter while stout dropships with dual tail booms hovered through the misty air, ferrying personnel and salvage between the plateau and camp.

"The bunker's in the mountain," Gale said. She pointed to one of the dropships with crates dangling from a cargo net. "Those Hippogriffs are the only way to reach it."

"And it looks like it takes time to make each trip," I mused, forming a plan.

My attention then turned to the gunships. With their twin bubble canopies, stubby wings, and thin tails, they resembled vDF Pegasi helicopters without rotors. Instead, they slipped through the air on hoverpods like *Tuney*'s. All four were armed with chin turrets and rocket pods, the standard weapons of RP Gryphons.

"You're sure they can't see us?" Rus asked.

I nodded. "If they could, they'd be shooting by now. Our cloak seems to be holding, thanks to Sara's supercells."

"Good," Rus said. Tapping Tibbs, he added, "Keep your distance from the camp. We deployed jamming modules on the perimeter a few meters into the jungle, plus one at the bunker. Pax Machina can't cross their disruption fields and I doubt your cloak will hold if you get too close."

"Good to know," Tibbs said. He tapped his controls and our sensors highlighted the ring of jammers around the camp through the dense foliage. Suddenly, the scanner also showed another module in the center of the camp; a green cube topped with a dome twice as tall as a human. "Hold up, what's that?"

Rus studied the scan for a moment and sighed. "It's a Sunburst Defense System."

"You guys found one of those?" Rutgers asked.

"Yes, and I've seen it protect other camps," Gale replied. "Even with supercells, a few blasts will drain your shields."

Tibbs crossed his arms and leaned back in the pilot's seat. "Okay, so we clearly can't just swoop in, grab Persephone, and swoop out. Anyone have any ideas?"

"I do," I said. "It'll be tight, but it's our best chance. Gale, Rus, did your team install any perimeter motion sensors?"

"No, the bugs and wind kept setting them off," Gale replied.

"Good. Then I'll need Sara and Tibbs with me on the ground and the rest of you in the air."

"I'm ready," Sara said, "just lemme know the plan."

"You're going down there?" Rus asked, raising an eyebrow.

"Someone has to disable those jammers and the Sunburst," I said.

"Just because there aren't motion detectors doesn't mean they're unprotected," Rus said. "There are squads of soldiers patrolling the jungle, all with vital monitors in their vests. If you kill anyone, the camp will know."

"How 'bout a stun baton zap?" Sara offered.

"Sorry," Rus said, shaking his head, "that'll fry the monitors. Unauthorized shutdown, alarms go off."

"So, we sneak around the patrols where possible," Tibbs said. "If can't slip by, we'll knock 'em out the hard way."

"I can work with that," Sara said with a grin. "Plus, I have just the thing to take care of the jammers."

Rus sighed. "Even if you manage that and disable the jammers, it's not humanly possible to cross the clearing without being seen."

"Good thing I'm not human," I said, giving Rus my best feline smile. "Don't get me wrong, I'm glad you know the RP and their tech, but in the jungle, you have to start thinkin' wild." I extended my claws experimentally and flicked my tail. "Trust me, the RP won't see us coming. Now, here's the plan."

* * *

Sara, Tibbs, and I checked our gear in the cargo bay as Rutgers started to land *Opportunity*. I tucked Gale's stabilizer vaccine into a belt pouch and strapped on my watch. We tested our radios and throat microphones, holstered our suppressed vDF pistols, and pocketed the demo charges from Sara's cache. Opening the door would break the cloak, so we had to be ready.

"I meant to ask you," I said to Sara, "why'd you choose a badger for your disguise?"

The mercenary grinned and held up her gauntlet screen. "To be honest with you, it's mostly 'cuz their tails are short and they're plantigrade. Both features are easier for the Changelink suit to render, which helps maintain my cover. I never thought a badger fit me, though, if that makes sense."

"Can you be other species?" I asked.

Nodding, Sara tapped her screen. "Watch this." Thin metal strips extended from her suit's collar, where a soft emerald light also began to glow. The light spread down her body, like green flames, and everywhere it touched, the suit changed. Matte black armor transformed into fur sporting a jaguar's beautiful and intricate rosettes. Her vest adopted the same pattern while her gloved hands became paws again, this time with retractable claws. Likewise, her boots shifted into plantigrade paws while an artificial tail grew slowly. Finally, the collar built a simple helmet frame around her face before holographically generating a jaguar's head, completing the new disguise. "Ta da!"

"Now that's definitely gonna help," I said. Tibbs opened the starboard door and hopped out first. "You ready?"

"On your tail," Sara replied.

With a nod and a tail swish, I leapt out and landed without a sound. My paws dug into the soft, cool soil as I crouched in the underbrush. Leaves brushed my coat and mist enveloped me while I drew my pistol and held it at a low ready. In another moment, *Tuney*'s door closed and she disappeared. All we saw and heard as Rutgers ascended through the trees was a faint shimmer and a low hum.

I remained still for a moment, invisible under the foliage. Every breath filled my lungs with the sweetest scents, from the trees and earth to the distant river and every living thing between here and there. Head motionless, I scanned the undergrowth for movement. Nothing yet.

To my front, Tibbs swiveled his ears as I did, listening for danger. Only the waterfall and birds broke the silence. For a few seconds, I closed my eyes and touched the jungle floor. When my paws gripped the earth, I felt the land's pulse, its surface vibrating with life and the water flowing through it. But more importantly, I felt what my ancestors must have as they walked the world on four legs. Far from the lights of Ambara Down, far from the fortresses of verDen, I reconnected with my own roots. Though I knew the odds were against us, that suddenly didn't matter. The RP were in the tigress' jungle, and the hunt had begun.

Tibbs signaled we were clear to move. Sara and I signed back and followed him. On my wrist, our mission clock counted down. My plan required careful timing, so we had to be quick. Thankfully, with our senses and stealth, we crept towards the jammers without any trouble.

True to the Hyacinth's intel, four SPEX soldiers idly patrolled around the first jammer. Their striped camouflage could've hidden them as well as mine did, but it probably worked better if they didn't stand straight up in the tall grass. Regardless, the best camo in the world couldn't help their careless mouths.

"Seriously though, Nimbus," one of the soldiers said, "whaddya need a helmet for out here?"

"Yeah, man," said another. "You gotta be sweatin' like a pig in that thing."

The helmeted soldier readjusted his slung rifle. "You'd know about that, wouldn't you?" he retorted. "Better safe than sorry."

Weapon holstered, I closed in on all fours, inching my way through the grass. Sara and Tibbs did the same.

The fourth soldier laughed. "Look, this ain't training, kid," she said. "There ain't no instructors out here yellin' at you to keep your bucket on." She flicked the brim of her boonie hat and sighed. "It's just us steamin' in the heat and gettin' microwaved until the eggheads find what they came for. You're allowed to be comfortable."

"We're a thousand klicks from any fluffer settlements and so far off the RP records the High Cities need a crystal ball to find us," the first soldier said. "So, kick back and enjoy this op, Nimbus. They ain't always this easy."

Nimbus glanced over his shoulder. I froze and held my breath. The young man narrowed his eyes and stared right over me. "Yeah, I guess you're right," he said at last. "I'll ditch the bucket when we get back. For now, though, I gotta take a leak." He turned and headed for a tree away from us and his squad.

Our perfect chance had come. I chose my target, padded a few steps closer, readjusted my paws, and waited.

"Holler if the bugs get ya!" the second soldier joked.

"Eh, his vest will let us know if something eats him," the fourth said dismissively. "Heh, new guy."

Another slight adjustment. Tail in position. Everything set. I gave a quiet signal via my throat mic, and the others pounced with me. In half a blink, we each had a sentry on the ground. I clamped one paw over my target's mouth, stifling her alarm before I struck her head with my padded palm. Sweet dreams.

The other soldiers went down the same way, non-lethally, but with headaches in their future; nothing that would set off their vests' vital sensors. We pulled them into the grass in time for Nimbus to return, cradling his helmet under his arm.

"Y'all are unusually quiet," he said as he walked around the jammer. "Hey, where'd everyone—" One blow from Tibbs cut him off.

"Shoulda worn the helmet," Tibbs whispered as he dragged the unconscious Nimbus under a massive leaf. Sara and I set the others there, too, while Tibbs planted a charge under the jammer. He set the mechanical timer and checked his watch. "Fireworks here in forty minutes."

I relieved Nimbus of his radio and, to my delight, found he'd taped a list of the patrol call signs to the back. Sara studied the list, then tapped her gauntlet.

"You thought the spots were cool, listen to this," she said. When Sara spoke again, her words came out in Nimbus' nasally tone. "Castellum One Actual, this is Parma Three Four, situation normal. Everything's alright now, we're all fine here. How are you?"

"Now that's a trick we could use!" Tibbs said with a chuckle.

"Definitely," I agreed. "How much of a voice sample do you need?"

"Thankfully nothing too long," Sara said in her own voice. "A short conversation is usually enough."

I gave her the radio and a smile. "Perfect. Let's hope the other squad is as chatty as Parma Three."

* * *

Stalking and pouncing Parma Four took a bit more finesse. However, between the three of us and our cunning, even the more experienced troops didn't suspect a thing as we knocked them all out.

"Thirty minutes 'til boom," Sara said, mimicking Parma Four's squad leader. We took one of their radios, too, just in case.

"Copy that," I said. "Phase one complete. Time for a dip."

When Rus said we'd never make it across the clearing, he was right. Without tree cover, we'd be easy pickings for even the doziest Gryphon gunner. That left us with one way in, one I counted on the 'Claimers to overlook.

Submerged up to our necks in the refreshing river, we let the current carry us toward the camp. Whenever a gunship hovered over us, we sank deeper and hid in the bankside vegetation. In no time at all, we reached the camp's water pipes.

Sara crawled through the reeds as she scouted our next move, synthetic fur hiding her perfectly. Soldiers and researchers went about their duties, still completely unaware of anything amiss. I'd initially planned to use the pipes for cover, but our new partner had a better idea.

The emerald flames returned around Sara's suit, and soon her jaguar disguise gave way to a research uniform with an added face mask. "Be right back," she whispered.

I nodded and tapped my watch, reminding her to hurry. Thankfully, she returned in a few minutes with two metal crates on a hoversled. Both crates had thin slats and were labeled "Caution: Live Animals" in red lettering.

"Found 'em near a landing pad," Sara said. "Looks like a new shipment."

"They're preparing for live testing," Tibbs said. He took a moment to jam the door locks with river pebbles before climbing inside. "Let's hope no one looks too closely."

The sled bobbed somewhat when I crawled into my own crate and held the door shut. "Okay, we're ready," I said.

Sara pushed the hoversled up the bank until we reached the first bend in the pipes. Waiting, she checked her mission clock. "Just in time," she whispered. "One diversion comin' up in three, two, one."

An explosion echoed from the plateau as Rutgers and the twins destroyed the bunker's jammer. Everyone in camp stared for a beat, then scrambled into Hippogriffs. Team leaders barked orders and the camp mobilized their response.

"All Parma elements, this is Castellum Three," a woman on our stolen radios said. "Requesting SITREP, over!"

The first two squads replied, then Sara copied their responses in the voices of Nimbus and Parma Four's squad leader. Like a charm, no one noticed, and the other squads kept radioing back.

"All Parma elements, solid copy," Castellum Three said curtly. "Maintain positions while we investigate. Stay alert. Castellum Three, over and out."

All but one of the Gryphons flew to the bunker, followed by the heavy transports. Aircraft shadows passed over us as Sara pushed the hoversled across the camp. She kept her eyes low and hidden behind her disguise's generated hat, doing her best to look busy. Luckily, the uniform she chose to copy didn't belong to essential emergency personnel.

In the second it took to pass the Sunburst module, I slipped our last charge under it. Fifteen minutes. That's all we had left. Time for phase three.

"That was a heckuva distraction," Sara whispered. "I can see the smoke from here." Through the slats, I saw the plume, too. By now, most of the camp had somewhere else to be and something better to do than worry about the medical tent. The door slid open and Sara pushed us inside.

Despite the yellow material, sterile white light filled the tent's interior. Everything either smelled of plastic, disinfectant, or chemicals I couldn't name. If the jungle ever had a spiritual opposite, we'd found it.

"Guess I'm not the only one who had to stay home," a guard said, his voice muffled by a mask. "The one time anything interesting happens, I'm stuck watchin' the kid. Figures."

I kept my weapon ready and held my breath while Sara did the talking. "Could be worse," she said. "I had to wash cages in the river while everyone flew off."

"I guess you're right. Hey, I didn't know we were startin' tests already," the guard said.

"Yeah," Sara answered casually, closing the distance, "we even got some subjects on the last flight in."

"Really? No one told me."

"Hey, no one tells me anything either, I just deliver. You wanna take a look?"

"Sure, let's see what we have here," the guard said. A face appeared outside my crate. "Oh my—" His head thumped softly when Sara bounced it off the metal, knocking off his patrol cap.

"This'd probably be harder if they all wore helmets," Tibbs remarked to himself as we climbed out.

Assorted 'Claimer medical tech covered the wide room's walls, worktables, and mobile carts. Under different circumstances, I would've grabbed anything not bolted down, but we were here for what lay at the end of the tent.

Frosted plastiglass stretched from floor to ceiling and an airlock protruded from the right wall. While Sara took the guard's carbine and helped Tibbs stuff him into a crate, I investigated the quarantined section.

Holograms over the glass displayed steady vital signs. Beside them, a button offered to turn the glass clear. I hit it, and the readings instantly spiked.

A young woman with her face to the glass widened her emerald eyes and recoiled. Honestly, she surprised me as much as I must have surprised her. I holstered my pistol and held up my paws, though her heart rate stayed elevated. She wore a grey jumpsuit and kept her midnight hair tied back, but a few stray locks framed a fair-skinned face that thankfully became calmer as the moments passed.

"Please don't be afraid," I said. The others cautiously joined me at the window. "My name is Tabitha, and these are my friends, Sara and

Tibbs. Your name is Persephone, right? Gale and Cirrus Hyacinth sent us to rescue you."

The teenager said nothing. After recovering from the shock of seeing an upright, talking tiger, her gaze kept darting to Sara. Tibbs noticed, too. "The uniform," he said to Sara. "She probably thinks you're SPEX."

"Oh, right," Sara agreed before deactivating her disguise, returning her suit to its default appearance. "No one's going to hurt you. Do you understand?"

Persephone nodded, then pointed to her ears and raised a thumb. However, when she touched her mouth and pointed to herself, she shook her head. "Implants calibrating," she said slowly. "Language old. Sound funny."

"That's okay," I said as I pulled out the stabilizer vaccine and gave it to Sara. "There isn't much time, Sara needs to give this to you so you can leave with us and not get sick. Is that okay with you?"

With another nod from Persephone, Sara set her suit to emulate the guard's uniform and gas mask. While she decontaminated herself in the airlock, I peered around Persephone's quarters. She had a bed, a chemical toilet, and a small table covered in cans and pouches labeled "NutriMush" and "NutriGoop" respectively.

The stasis pod against the left wall took up the most space, though. Various cables and tubes dangled from each end. However, two markings caught my eye as Sara injected Persephone. The first was on a tube exiting the pod's top and reentering at its base marked "GNDN," while the other was a symbol etched into the open canopy. Without a doubt, the ideogram matched one I'd seen too often as I fought for my life, an endless three-lobed knot. The emblem of Pax Machina. The same emblem on the back of Persephone's suit.

"Ten minutes," Tibbs said, tapping the glass.

"Gale said we need to wait at least five before she's safe, remember?" Sara said. "Something about nanobots and her blood or whatever."

I felt the ticking of my watch and couldn't help but growl. "Okay, fine. Get back out here and help us find any research on the SPEX team's progress."

"In computer, over there," Persephone suggested, pointing to a workstation. After a few taps, I found what we needed and started a download to a data crystal.

Suddenly, Tibbs' ears twitched. "Someone's coming!" he whispered. In seconds, we jumped back into our crates, I crammed the guard to one side, and Sara threw a pair of lab coats over us. To hide the scent of our still-damp fur, she covered the lab coats in disinfectant spray.

"Whatever happens, I'll play along. Trust me," Sara whispered. "If this goes downhill, stay behind me. My suit can take almost anything they got."

"Wait, what?" I hissed back.

"We're improvising now, and I'm gonna stall until Persephone is ready," Sara replied as she checked her disguise. "After five minutes, it's your show. I trust you."

I didn't know what to think or say, I only wished I'd planned for this better. Still, as two people approached, the time for planning ended, and instincts took over. "Okay," I whispered back. "Good luck."

Despite the lab coats, I could still see out by getting close to the crate's slats and peering through the thin fabric. Our angle let me view most of the space before Persephone's room, where Sara took her position. Through shallow breaths, I checked my watch and counted down the minutes until we could make our escape. No room for mistakes now.

I heard them long before I saw them. A woman and a man, their voices both carried clipped, official tones. Hers was polished, cold, and sharp as surgical steel while his was worn yet seasoned, like a battle-tested sword.

"Unfortunately, Director Kyla has gone dark, Tana," the man said, "I'm afraid she can't provide you test subjects anytime soon."

"Very well, Father. I'll send encrypted comms to our other contacts," the woman replied as they entered the tent. "The subjects don't have to be Ambarans."

"Still, it seemed promising to have subjects from the target area," the man said. "No matter. It's only a minor delay. For now, let's check on our guest and see if she's feeling more cooperative."

Sara snapped to attention. "Good afternoon, ma'am. Good afternoon, sir," she said, raising her voice to be heard through the mask.

"Good afternoon," the pair returned in unison.

They finally walked into view and I saw they wore olive SPEX fatigues, vests, boots, and patrol caps. The woman carried a holotablet in her hand and had medical gear on her belt along with a pistol in a leg holster. Likewise, the man carried a sidearm on his right side, though he also kept a machete sheathed on his left. Behind them, a hoversled with covered cargo automatically stopped when they did.

"Hello again, Persephone," the man said.

"Commander Brontide," Persephone said briskly. "And Doctor Brontide."

"No need to be so formal, my dear," Dr. Brontide said. "We're friends. You can call me Tana."

"Friends not keep in box," Persephone retorted. "Know why here. No help."

Commander Brontide unveiled his hoversled cargo, an ancient, reinforced maintenance android. "I know you must not think highly of me," he said. "However, you must understand that I only want to save humanity, as the people who built your bunker did. The world you awoke to is more hostile to humans than ever."

"Not trust you," Persephone said. "I believe when I see."

"When you see?" Brontide chuckled before his voice hardened. "I'll tell you what *I've seen*, child. I've seen my mother and brother killed by Hangdog raiders, then watched my father and sister taken by the very machines your people built! My whole village, gone! All while those we trusted to protect us feasted in High Gravitas!"

"Father, you're—" Tana began.

"No," Brontide interrupted, "she needs to understand. The powerful and comfortable never see what it takes to survive down here. Surfaceside, the animal with the biggest teeth and sharpest claws lives. As a boy I was powerless to save my family. I will never be powerless again.

"The creatures infesting Ambara Down don't realize the treasure they're squatting on. Even the RP barely knows what secrets the catacombs hold. But once humans have the city again, I will lead us to even greater powers, and the rest of the surface will follow. And it all starts with you.

"Our new plague will bring the city to its knees. Even Prefect Durgavati, the great lioness, will be helpless as sickness tears at Ambara Down. Then, with Pax Machina as my legions, we'll cleanse the streets of the dead and stragglers, showing the world the price they'll pay for denying us our birthright!"

Brontide knelt to look Persephone in the eyes. "Can't you see it, my dear? The war of reclamation is inevitable. You're doing your species a service, ensuring our survival and return to dominance. Your blood provided the first keys. Why not help us unlock Pax Machina, and write the next chapter of history yourself?"

Only a minute remained until Persephone could leave quarantine. However, as she spoke in modern Lingua for the first time, her words nearly pierced the glass. "I've heard enough to speak in your language," she said deliberately. "You cannot control these forces because you don't respect them. Control is fleeting, respect is always a choice. People like you, hungry for control, desperate for power, they're why we needed the bunkers. You want to know why humanity lost the world? Who was to blame? Look in a mirror."

Shaking his head, Brontide turned to the hoversled. "I tried to reason with you. Now I must be more direct," he sighed. He fiddled with the android until it sat up on the sled. "We found this machine by your pod. It holds a message from your mother, you can see for yourself on its chest screen. Unlock it or I'll delete everything."

"You wouldn't dare."

"If you won't cooperate for my world, I have no qualms about erasing the last of yours," Brontide stated plainly. "Three, two—"

"Stop! I'll do it." Persephone said. "It won't do you any good, though."

"History will be the judge of that," Brontide replied. "Whenever you're ready."

Persephone sighed and stared at the robot. "Hiya, Mac."

The machine stirred, then spoke with a voice comprised of a hundred others. "Facial and vocal identification confirmed. Welcome back, Persephone Feldspar. Spam inbox full. One new message. It has been nine, nine, nine—"

"Thanks, Mac, that's okay," Persephone said, silencing the bot.

"Incredible," Tana said. She buried her face in her tablet, likely taking notes.

Suddenly, Persephone shouted, "Mac, I need help! The bunker was breached! Activate defense mode!"

The android began to rise, only for Brontide to flick a switch on its back, disabling it. "We installed an override in case you tried to be clever," he said. "Regardless, thank you for your cooperation. My people will take it from here."

"Showtime," I whispered into my throat mic. In a flash, Tibbs and I emerged with our pistols drawn. The SPEX officers were dumbfounded as we ordered them to drop their weapons. Brontide's hand hovered over his pistol. His eyes flicked from me to Sara, seemingly waiting for his guard to back him up. Instead, Sara leveled her carbine at his chest.

"Sorry, sir. Your guy's takin' a break," Sara said. "I'm just fillin' in for him. Now, lose the hardware. Slowly." The RP officers finally relented, and Sara collected their pistols. With nowhere to stash Brontide's machete, she simply kicked it under a worktable.

Once disarmed, Brontide grinned at us. "I'll admit I'm impressed," he said, studying us. "Judging by your species, clothing, weapons, and *audacity*, I'd say you're verDenners, yes? Or did Durgavati send you?"

"Shut up and turn around," I snarled while Tibbs motioned for Persephone to enter the airlock. After decontamination, the teenager left her prison and stood behind Tibbs.

I retrieved the crystal from the tent's computer with the SPEX team's research downloaded, then I smashed the interface. Though he faced the wall, I still felt Brontide watching me. "Durgavati is bold, but this isn't her style," Brontide mused. "Professor Zan, then? Oh, but how would he know we're here? That leaves our loose ends, the Hyacinths." Tibbs and I didn't respond. "It is them, isn't it?"

We still had a few minutes before the charges detonated. Leaving too soon meant risking getting caught, though the more Brontide talked, the more my fur bristled.

"Of course it's those traitors," Brontide continued. "The only way you'd dare moving the girl is if Gale helped you."

"Be quiet," Tibbs snapped, baring his teeth.

"Or what? You won't kill us, fox," taunted Brontide. "Our vital monitors will sound the alarm if you do."

Just then, I saw Tana reaching for her vest. "Manually triggering the alarm gives us no reason to keep you alive," I said. "Your troops may get us, they may not. Either way, I'll guarantee you go first." She lowered her hand and turned around.

"It appears we have a verDenner standoff," Tana said.

"No, they're waiting for something, and they'll probably shoot before they leave," Brontide said as he turned, too. "You heard our plan. You heard everything. So, will you do it? Pull the trigger, save the world? In front of my daughter? Or perhaps you don't mind that, since you'll likely shoot her next. Then how about in front of Persephone? Show her how little the world changed over the eons. Teach her how deep the jungle really runs. How under everything, we're all just animals one twitch away from the kill."

Sights on Brontide, I growled, "You're not an animal, you're—"

"A monster?" Brontide said, chuckling. "Don't delude yourself, cat. You know you'd do the same in my position."

"But would you do the same in mine?" I replied, glancing at my watch. "I don't think so. You would've killed the first chance you had. I know what I am, and I'm not a murderer."

Tibbs pulled the unconscious guard out of the crate and set him on the floor. "If you care about your guard or the rest of your people, you won't follow us and you'll evacuate your camp," he said.

The commander scowled. "Give me one good reason—"

"We'll give you three," I said. Before he could react, the three bombs exploded just seconds apart, the last loud enough to make us all flinch. "Those were your defenses. Pax Machina is coming, and judging by the symbol on Persephone's suit, that was their bunker you broke into. I'm sure a distress call is going out as we speak. You don't wanna be here when they arrive."

"They would be on their way," Tana, "if we hadn't disconnected the bunker alarm days ago. There's no signal to hear."

"How about this one?" Persephone said, reactivating the android.

To the Brontides' horror, the bot stood. "Breach alert! Company personnel in danger! Guardian activated."

The ground trembled. Only Persephone seemed to know why. "Pax Machina's not coming. They've been here all along," she said.

"Castellum Two, this is Talon Three!" came a voice on Tana's radio. "We have hostile contact! A big one!" A familiar roar shook the tent as Gryphon fire responded.

"You have teams down on your western flank," I said. "The eastern jammers are still active. I suggest you regroup there and evacuate."

"The choice is yours," Tibbs said. "And time isn't on your side."

With a sigh, Tana grabbed her radio. "All Talon elements, engage hostiles. All transport elements, return to base. Evacuation order in effect."

"What are you doing?" Brontide hissed.

"Cutting our losses, Father," Tana replied. "All personnel, fall back to eastern jammers or board evac transports where available. Castellum Two, out." She took her and Brontide's radios and threw them into the airlock.

I nodded at Tana. "Count to one hundred, then you can leave," I said as we departed the tent following Sara, Persephone, and the android.

We emerged to pure chaos. There was a new hole in the plateau and a Pax Machina multipede towering over the trees, swatting at gunships buzzing around it. The giant machine seemed to be taking advantage of the break in the jammer perimeter and was heading for the camp. Meanwhile, Hippogriffs scrambled to land and load the camp's remaining personnel. Overhead, Rutgers and the Hyacinths broke radio silence.

"Hemlock here," Rutgers said. "You seein' this?"

Unable to hit the Gryphons, the multipede stopped and opened panels on its back. Hundreds of mechanical dragonflies took flight and chased off the gunships.

"Affirmative, Hemlock," Tibbs replied. "Time to go!"

Rutgers blanketed the camp in white smoke grenades, then he dropped a few colorful ones. Before we ran for the right color, however, the multipede and dragonflies froze, as did Persephone's android. Pax Machina's symbol erased and redrew itself on the robot's screen.

"Downloading software update," the screen said.

"Aw fluff," I growled.

"Mac?" Persephone said when the update finished. The bot locked onto Persephone. "Mac, download new messages, please."

"We're sorry, this action cannot be completed," Pax Machina said. "Area not secure. Please remain calm. This is for your safety." The android then punched Sara, sending her sprawling to the dirt and knocking her weapon from her hands. "All non-user humans designated hostile."

"Sara!" I shouted, helping her up. She snarled and activated her jaguar disguise. Claws out, she looked ready to tear the android into scrap.

Pax Machina paused. "No humans detected."

"Nice thinking," Tibbs said as he retrieved Sara's weapon.

"Thanks," Sara replied. "Now let's go before—"

"We cannot allow you to take Persephone," Pax Machina said. "She must return to stasis." Persephone stepped closer to us. "Additional units are inbound to ensure prompt and satisfactory service."

"Not good," Tibbs said, flattening his ears and giving Sara her carbine back. "You're gonna need this."

Seconds later, the swarm reanimated and continued their battle with SPEX. Unfortunately, the multipede also deployed even more machines from its underbody, which skittered towards us.

"On my tail! Go!" I roared. We dashed into the white clouds. Elsewhere in the camp, soldiers fired at the multipede while Gryphons dueled the dragonfly drones above. I heard the small swarm coming for us. We just had to beat them to the blue smoke where *Tuney* waited. No luck.

Miniature multipedes found us, forcing us to fight our way through with everything we had. "They're not so tough!" Tibbs said, blasting two. Then, another machine hissed at him, reared up, deployed wings, and hovered at head level. "Oh, for fluff's sake! I knew it!" After dispatching it with his pistol, he stomped it twice for good measure.

"We're almost there!" Sara encouraged as she suppressed a trio of machines. I stunned the last machine in my way with a few shots, then finished it with a swipe of my claws. Finally, we reached the blue smoke. Our ship's opening door never looked so welcoming as it did then.

The Hyacinths waved from the cargo bay and helped us in. We told Rutgers to take off and *Tuney* rose a few meters. I thought we'd made it, but before we closed the door, a flying multipede swooped in and grabbed Persephone. "Heckipede's got her!" Tibbs barked.

The machine dragged Persephone out of the cargo bay with some effort. I quickly pounced on the thing and clawed its processor housing, dropping Persephone and me to the Earth. "You okay?" I asked.

"Yeah, thanks," Persephone coughed. "Look out!"

I ducked and rolled in time to avoid the android's fist. The bot may have followed us slowly, but its punch sounded like it could break stone. "This attack may be recorded for quality assurance purposes," Pax Machina said, approaching though the blue haze.

Scrambling to my paws, I drew my pistol and fired until it went dry, but the armored bot kept coming. Just as I extended my claws, a blade swung out of the smoke and into the machine's neck. The robot dropped to its knees and Brontide pulled his machete free.

"Ambara may fall to greater powers, but you deserve a warrior's death," Brontide said before he lunged. He stabbed and slashed, and each time I deftly dodged his attacks. Though he kept missing, he smiled as he fought. "No more robots or guns. Only claws and instinct!"

He asked for claws and instinct, so I obliged. I parried a diagonal chop and raked his forearm, then planted a kick in his chest. Brontide collapsed in the dirt, dropping the machete. In a flash, I pinned him. My instincts knew what came next.

Then, I heard Persephone's voice. "Tabitha?" I looked up and saw her crouched over the android, holding its memory crystal.

"What are you waiting for?" Brontide wheezed. "Show her."

I knew everything Brontide wanted. Everything he'd done and was prepared to do, all for humanity's survival. A product of his world. My world. Our world. One we'd both fight to the death for. I heard more machines coming and a Hippogriff landing nearby. No more time.

My instincts begged me to do it, until I caught a seed of truth. I could end it here, but it would only begin again with someone else. Dr. Brontide? Their troops? An endless loop. Maybe we were all trapped in it, all powerless to our animal nature and compulsion to survive. But maybe we weren't. I chose to find out.

I tightened my grip and turned back to Brontide. "If you look for war, you'll find it," I said. "Look around you. That path goes nowhere." The multipede ravaged the camp as the last humans fled. "You want power? Start with your power to choose. Choose a better path."

Tuney hovered towards us through the smoke. "There they are!" Tibbs shouted. The others fended off the gathered machines and pulled Persephone aboard. Once safely inside, Tibbs waved. Brontide's rescue squad was closing in.

"Remember my face, every stripe," I said to the commander. "Because if we cross again, I'll know you chose war, and I'll give *you* your warrior's death." At that, I left him and leapt into the ship. Before I sealed the doors, he shouted a final threat.

"You'll regret your weakness, cat!" Brontide bellowed. "You can't hide Persephone from us forever! We're not finished!"

"We are for now," I said to myself as Rutgers took off. With an active cloak and SPEX and Pax Machina still occupying each other, we slipped away without a trace.

* * *

Hours later and far from the jungle, Gale gave Persephone a clean bill of health. Everyone sat around the table while *Tuney* rested in a cloud, uncloaked.

"Thank you all for the rescue," Persephone said.

"Just doin' what we do best," Rutgers said. "I'm sorry you woke up to people like the SPEX team. Not all humans are like them." He smiled at Sara and the Hyacinths.

Our new friends seemed to appreciate that, though Sara crossed her arms. "Unfortunately, the Brontides think Persephone's connection to Pax Machina is the key to controlling the machines. If word spreads, who knows what interested parties will come after her, humans and zoomorphs."

"Luckily, Special Expeditions like their secrets, even between units," Rus said. "It'll just be Brontide's forces on our tails, at least at first."

"Small comfort," Tibbs admitted. "We need to answer a lotta big questions, though. Like what do we do about the SPEX data? Or Persephone? It's the Hyacinths' problem all over again. Who can we trust? Where can we go?"

No one knew the answers, not even me. Still, we couldn't afford to chase our tails, so I tried my best. It's all any of can do, anyway. "We warn Prefect Durgavati and the vDF about the Brontides' plan. The data could be used to create plagues or cures, so we hold it for now and keep moving," I said. "As for trust, I say we trust each other, because we're all some of us have."

Persephone lowered her head, and for the first time, I realized what she must have felt. Her loss, her confusion, her loneliness. All that remained of her past fit in a memory crystal Pax Machina might not let her read. She had a million questions about a world that would hunt her for the secrets she knew. I placed a paw on her hand, coaxing a smile from her. "As for the other questions," I said to Tibbs, "why don't we ask Persephone? Where do you want to go? What do *you* want?"

All eyes fell on the teenager. "Are you sure? No one's ever asked me something like that," she said. I nodded.

"Well then, I spent centuries in stasis. When I woke up, Brontide kept talking about a cruel world we needed to reclaim, but the only cruelty I saw was his." She held up the memory crystal and took a deep breath. "I don't know what's happened to the world, and I don't know what I've missed—but I know that humans were responsible, and this is my chance to help make it right. I want to find answers, I want to see the world, and I want to help protect it."

Rutgers and Tibbs grinned at me. I squeezed Persephone's hand gently. "Then you're in the right place, and there's no better time to save the world than right now," I said, swishing my tail and giving her a feline smile. "Welcome to the crew of *Opportunity*."

A Journey to the Skies

Ferric the Bird

The simple wooden dwelling, home to Lisa for the past fifteen cyclic seasons, was already a world away after only a few dozen steps. She knew she needed to keep her head down, to make sure her feet continued to go forward; it was a core of her teachings, something she'd been learning ever since she was a young chick. But practical application was a difficult thing to master. She found herself spinning around after only a short distance, to give just one last glance at the roughly-hewn wooden structure twenty feet up off the forest floor.

It was the only home she'd ever known, and from this point forward she could never return for more than a few moments without endangering too many people. Emotion began to build up inside of her as she stared at the glorified hut in the trees, doing her best not to let a tear escape her eyes, almost paralyzed as she committed every last single detail to memory.

Her brother didn't realize what had happened at first, but after the steps behind him fell silent he turned around to look as well. He gave one last glance up at their former home, then shifted the gear on his back and took a few steps to bridge their distance. With a soft and gentle motion he reached out his wing and placed a set of finger-like wingtips onto his sister's shoulder, squeezing it gently to let her know he was there. The silence said it all, but after a few seconds her brother finally said, "Sis, come on. We can't stay here forever."

"I know," Lisa replied, taking in one last breath and closing her eyes. With a gentle swing of her head, she turned back around to face him. "Thanks for giving me a moment."

"No problem," the smaller bird responded, pushing the flexible corners of his beak up into a smile. "Gave me one last look too. Now come on, we have one final ceremony to sit through."

"Yeah," Lisa nodded. "Let's get that part over with at least."

"That's the spirit," Tango replied with a gentle chuckle, and pressed forward again. Lisa hesitated for a single step, then pushed onwards as well.

The walk through their small, tree-centered village didn't take long. Dwellings similar to their own dotted the trees around them, and a few other avians waved and shouted their support as the siblings passed. Tango smiled and waved back, especially to the younger chicks that were excited to see them. Lisa kept her eyes forward and her mind focused, fighting off the urge to turn around and run back to the safety of their own hut. She simply put one foot in front of the other, trudging along the worn path between the underbrush, trying not to count each step she took. The number would only make it that much worse.

They reached that large central building, a circular cabin up in the trees, and Lisa knew there was no turning back. Her brother dropped his heavy backpack onto the ground near the base of the central support tree and grabbed onto the rope ladder first; he was halfway up before Lisa willed herself to slide off her backpack and reach out to the still-swaying ladder. Soon she and her brother both sat on the soft mats laid out for their arrival.

The aged features of the Matriarch filled them both with love and confidence—something they both needed at this moment, whether they showed it or not. The Matriarch's plumage was much like their own, albeit beginning to fade in brightness and definition. Dark woodland colors dotted her exposed feathers in browns and dark greens, with small splashes of white accents thrown in to further help camouflage her in the forest. A bright yellow beak and those flashy blue eyes were the only bits of vibrant color on her, with a gentle hue of pink near the base of her beak. The two younger avians looked much the same, as did everyone else in the small village, a factor of common ancestry.

"Welcome Lisa, and welcome Tango," the Matriarch began with a warm smile.

"Good morning Mother Valentina," the younger avians said, almost in unison.

"It's been fifteen cyclic seasons since you both hatched," the Matriarch continued, taking a moment to look at each one of them. "I was there when your mother arrived, and I was there the day you both broke through your shells. I've been watching you grow into fine adults, and I'm very proud to be able to send you off on your journey. You've both excelled at your training, and you've shown everything you need to make it to Flying Mountain. I wouldn't be surprised if both of you are able to make the journey without too much trouble."

The younger birds bowed in respect. "Thank you, Mother Valentina."

"You've earned it, my dears," the Matriarch replied, placing a wing on each of their shoulders and letting it linger for just a moment. "But now you must focus on looking forward, as even for you two the journey may be a challenge. It is a tradition that we perform one last ceremony, so that you will not forget your history, and why you are making the journey. There is a world outside of the one you know, one that is very different from what you have learned here. You will hear many things, and it is up to you what you wish to believe. My job is to teach you what we believe as a species, and as members of the Treehawk Village. These stories have been passed down through the ages, from one Matriarch to the next. Are you ready to receive the histories one last time?"

"Yes, Mother Valentina," both the birds called out in unison, as they'd been doing since childhood.

"Very well," the older avian replied. She reached for a well-worn book and opened it to the first page, although the motion was purely symbolic. She knew all the words from memory many times over. "In the beginning humans controlled and conquered the lands," she began in a theatrical voice. "The remnants of their society still litter the ground to this day. The histories tell us that we avians and the other non-human beings, were created by the humans. Some claim it was as pets or playthings. Some claim that we were created to do jobs thought too dangerous for humans. Some even claim that there was no particular reason at all—that we were created because we could be.

"Over time, for reasons we do not know, the humans left the ground for their cities in the sky. And as they left the ground, they left us too, freeing us from whatever needs they had of us. The avians formed flocks, and many great villages and towns were created, both separated and intertwined with the other creatures that shared the ground. Many advancements were made, and prosperity flourished without human control. However, such times were not to last.

"It's told that the humans, jealous of the avians' powers of flight, began to poison and change our forms once more, simply to deny us the ability to do so. But even this cruel mutation didn't produce the results they were after, so they sent their machines after us. Those with the brightest and most brilliant feather patterns were hunted first, unable to hide. The rest were driven out from the large towns and into small villages spread throughout the lands, to make the hunt more difficult. The survivors were able to persevere their culture and endure, but lived in constant fear of the machines. That is, until our savior Gamayun was born."

"We lower our heads in praise at her name," came the response from both of the younger avians, more reflex than anything deliberate. They'd uttered the same line each time Gamayun had been mentioned for many cyclic seasons, during community ceremonies every ten nights, for as long as anyone could remember.

"Gamayun was born a feisty spirit, and she let nothing stand in the way of her ambition," Mother Valentina continued. "Her drive and desire to help her fellow avians overcome their limitations and persecution knew no bounds. When she was only fifteen cyclic seasons in age, she set out on a journey to find some way of protecting her species from the machine threat. Many years went by with no word from her, and her village thought her long dead. But one day a great mechanical howling was heard from above the trees. The villagers scrambled to hide, fearing a mechanical beast had found them; but when a figure parted the treetops and landed in the center of the village, it was none other than Gamayun herself!

"She told them all of what she'd found, and how a long sleeping mountain had given her the power of flight after many years of sacrifice and work. She also gave the wonderful news that the machines didn't dare attack her anymore. She had flown right by the beasts while testing her new powers, and not only did they not attack, but they sung her praises, taking joy in the control she had in the air. Her greatest achievement of all—and the reason we worship her name—was that she made sure others would be able to get the same powers she had acquired. All they had to do was make the journey to Flying Mountain, and the mountain would aid them however it could.

"Soon adventurers, both old and young, tried to make their way towards the mountain. Gamayun's entire village even began to make the journey, despite her pleas and warnings to only send a few at a time. Gamayun followed the villagers when they wouldn't listen, and when they ran into the machines, she could only watch as her kinfolk were destroyed. She was only able to save one member of the village, her own brother, taking him safely to the mountain in her own flying grasp.

"As her brother endured the trials to regain flight, Gamayun ventured to every avian settlement she could find to share the good news, and to give a warning as well. Send only a pair, no more, towards Flying Mountain. Have them be young and ready for a difficult challenge, both during the journey and after arrival. But if they succeed, they will be rewarded for their efforts with the greatest gift possible.

"In each village, she chose two young and fit members, a brother and sister pair whenever possible, to leave on their own journey. Many died along the way in those most dangerous times, but a few lucky ones made it to the end, and were rewarded with the gift of flight. They spread the news back to their villages, and the cycle has continued on for many generations."

"Praise be to Gamayun," Tango chirped out first, with Lisa missing her mark just a bit. She'd let her mind wander, still thinking of her home and the village she was leaving. There was always the possibility that she could stay, and maybe even become a Mother herself. They were held in high regard due to their duties; but she'd be missing out on so much outside the village. It was a choice she'd wrestled with many times now—but those thoughts were pushed out of her head by a little curious look from Mother Valentina. Lisa straightened up and snapped to focus once more.

"Whenever a fledgling reaches fifteen cyclic seasons," Mother Valentina continued after a small pause, "and have proven themselves capable, they are tasked with making the journey to Flying Mountain. Things have gotten easier since the beginning, and the process of obtaining flight has become much quicker. The old machines that were used in the past have been altered to coexist with an avian's natural body processes, and can be used for life with limited refueling. They are also precious in death, and they shall be returned to the village they came from once an avian ceases to need them any longer. You two have accepted this as your fate."

"Yes Mother Valentina," they both replied in unison now that the history lesson was over, sensing that something new and exciting rising up in the air.

"We have only received one single propulsion engine in the years since our last clutch of fledglings departed," said the Matriarch, reaching out her wings to an object seated beside her. "The other was lost with its owner." The object was wrapped in a ceremonial cloth, the sheet matching the avian's own natural plumage as brown and greens raced along it, with an outline of bright yellow around the edges. The Matriarch gave a little groan as she lifted the package and placed it in front of her to unwrap it.

Lisa and Tango had seen the silvery metal engine before of course, paraded around the village when it had come home. When attached It would take up most of an avian's back, but this was still far smaller, lighter, and better powered than the first engine Gamayun had come back with. It had a few slits for air intake holes on the top end, and a few conical thrust holes that opened up out of the bottom, with a smooth profile over the outer edge to aid in aerodynamics.

"When the engine is installed," Mother Valentina started once again, "it will become permanently attached to your back, biologically fused to your spine, muscles, and flesh. The process is difficult and painful, but once healed it becomes a simple extension of your body. Controlling it takes practice, but you should learn all you need to know at Flying Mountain. Let us bow our heads for a moment in respect of the previous owner who has passed on." She waited for a moment as all three of the avians slowly closed their eyes and bowed their heads. "We give thanks to the brave soul of Iris for his donation back to his village, in hopes this engine can be put to use with the next generation of Flyers."

Mother Valentina reverently returned the machine to its wrappings and lifted it up between the two young birds. "I assume one of you left space to carry the precious engine?"

Lisa gave a little nod as she lowered the engine into her own lap. "Yes Mother Valentina," she said, fighting down a small squawk in her throat. "It was decided that, since I'm larger, I would carry the extra weight."

"As it usually goes," Mother Valentina replied with a smile. She then turned to look at Tango and shot him another smile as well. "As for you, the Mountain will create a new engine, but it will take time, and may require resources. That said, if something should happen to Lisa, it would be your duty to retrieve the engine if possible. Should you manage to find any other engines, or learn of their location, you are free to accept such help. All else must be done by you two alone. That is part of the trial. That is what you've been training for, and that will prove you worthy of the power of flight. Do you understand?"

"Yes Mother Valentina," both birds echoed back with small nods of their heads.

"Good," said the Matriarch, with a soft chirp of pride. "I wish you the best of luck. I've done all I can for you, and now the rest is up to you. Whether I will still be alive to see you return or not I can't say, but I shall await your return every day I am still here." The older avian leaned forward, once again taking each younger bird by the shoulder; with the side of her beak she gave each one a few small rubs to the side of the head, a true avian showing of loving emotion.

A few chirps and quiet noises spread among them, but eventually the older avian pulled back and let off a small sigh. "Now, get going before I start to get teary," Mother Valentina said with a forced smile. The younger avians nodded and did much the same, with Tango taking the lead and walking to the ladder first. Lisa waited for him to reach the ground; she knew better than to look back at Mother Valentina now, sure that the Matriarch was wiping away tears. Lisa brushed her cheek on a shoulder to wipe away tears of her own, then turned descended with the package pressed against her chest.

Now there really was no turning back. She had the engine, and it was her duty to make sure it was put to use; to give it up now would be shameful to just about everyone. All that worrying over the past season cycle had come to nothing. She was going along with Tango, even if each step was still a struggle.

* * *

The first night alone in the wilderness was the worst, as the rush of emotions began to finally settle in and the adrenaline faded, and the realization of what they were doing began to fall on them both. Neither of them slept very well.

Lisa finally said something as they broke camp in the morning. "Hey Tango, you ever think about going back? Even if just in a dream?"

The male bird paused for a moment at that question, looking down at the ground. "Well, yeah. Took me a while to fall asleep because of it."

"We can't though, can we?" Lisa said, trying to make it sound like a joke instead of a suggestion.

Tango did laugh, a little, but finally said, "It's a tempting thought honestly, but no, I don't think we can. I know you're nervous, and trust me, I am too. I may not show it, but really I'm terrified. I'm also excited though! Think what it would be like to fly, just like our ancestors! We can explore all corners of the world, safe from the machines, finding treasures, or doing research. If you're not too thrilled with adventure you could just take messages from one floating city to the other too. It's scary for sure, and I'm not looking forward to having to wait for my engine to be made, but it's just something we've got to do. This is what all of us do, and people way more nervous than us have made it just fine."

He reached out and slowly put his wing on Lisa's shoulder. "I kind of figured you only came along so I would have someone to travel with. We both know that they don't like sending out single travelers. I could've waited for two season cycles before the next group was ready, but… I really do appreciate you coming along. That's why I didn't hesitate to let you have the engine. I'm glad you came."

"I didn't come just for you," Lisa spit out, puffing out her chest feathers. "I came because I wanted to! I was just thinking out loud."

"Of course," Tango responded with a smile, squeezing his wingtips around her shoulder a bit more. "I know you're a much better adventurer than me too. You out-class me in just about everything other than archery. The cooking and cleaning of the meat and produce, not to mention tracking and camp making… you'll be the reason we'll make it, I'm sure. I'm just the reason we both set off in the first place."

"That's not… um… completely accurate," Lisa added back, but she was cut off in thought as the smaller bird reached up and slowly ground his beak against the side of her face, giving off a little chirp in the process.

"It's the story I'm going with," he said, pulling back and giving a little grin to the confused and embarrassed girl in front of him. "Now come on, it's only day two. We have more than fifty to go. No reason to slow down yet, unless your legs are getting tired or something…" He trailed off at the end of his statement, leaving an open challenge for his sister.

"No, my legs aren't tired at all," Lisa shot back with grit in her voice. "I've journeyed farther than you in our training, and for longer too! My legs are ready for anything."

"Then prove it!" Tango said with a smirk, turning around and starting to walk towards the trail they were following the previous day.

With a heavy grumble in her throat Lisa kicked some leaves and dirt over any remnants of their camp. Soon she had caught up and taken the lead with a little huff.

* * *

They were still in very familiar territory, and the next night they slept a bit better - refreshed and ready for a long hike the third day. They only stopped to hunt when Tango spotted a boar off in the brush in front of them. He pulled out his bow crept towards it, as silent as one of their feral ancestors on the hunt. All it took was one good shot straight into the heart, and after a slow tracking chase Lisa found the boar already dead. She did some quick work with her knife to pull out some important bits and good chunks of meat, before leaving the rest they couldn't carry to return to the forest. They had enough supplies to preserve a few kills, supplementing their otherwise foraging diet of berries and seeds, and getting one so early in their journey was a morale boost for both of them.

Over a few days reality began to settle in, and the need to return home began to grow less and less. As the land around them became unfamiliar they began to adjust their pacing and settle in to a more cautious approach, but had little problem navigating through the forest, finding plenty of food and places to rest each night.

It was about two weeks into their journey when Lisa heard the strange sounds up ahead. She crouched down, and with a quick run up to her brother she tapped him on the tail feathers, making him look back and crouch himself. They could both hear it now: the distinct sound of whirling and straining metal groaning in their earholes, along with trees snapping in protest.

Tango was the first to catch a glimpse of it, and he quickly ducked back down behind a small bush before turning around to give his sister a signal to do the same. Through the foliage, Lisa watched the mechanical beast clumsily navigating its way through the shallow valley below. It was mostly spider-like in appearance, two meters tall and three across, with eight long legs grinding along, bumping into the trees while doing its best to navigate around them. Its once-smooth body was covered with dents, rust spots, and portions of open circuitry, and its joints squeaked and ground as it tried to move, with at least one leg being locked into position at a constant 45 degree angle. One of its 'eyes' continued to glow in front of it, while the other seemed to be shattered, leaving it stumbling and twisting on occasion when it found it couldn't progress further through the valley foliage. A shiver ran down the avians' backs at the sight of it.

"Halt!" it called out as it tried to free itself from the little tree and brush mess it was in, making both avians duck and tense up at the sudden burst of noise. "You are trespassing on Federal lands. This area is protected under state code 17-B-32. I wish you the best genocide possible, and have a lovely day."

Lisa didn't know if the machine was talking to them or not, but she wasn't taking any chances. She turned and scrambled back down the hill, her talons digging into the rocky and root infested soil, while her brother continued to poke his head out of the bushes and watch. A moment later, a loud crack rippled through the air like a lightning bolt, causing both birds to let out a squawk and shoot up their wings to block the sound. Lisa spun around to look towards the top of the ridge, half expecting to see her brother gone in a trail of smoke, but he was still in one piece.

Tango hopped back up into a full standing position to look into the valley, then turned around and gave Lisa a quick wiggle of his wingtips to come back up to him. Lisa hesitated, but as she looked out over the bush she saw what her brother was staring at. In front of the machine was now a small trail of smoke rising up into the air, with a few branches from the tree in front of it still smoldering from the beam of energy the machine had shot out. Even the rock and dirt behind the tree was smoldering, since the beam had continued through the branches and ended up hitting the side of the gully.

"Halt!" the machine screamed out once again, still stuck where it was, but making progress through a little knot of trees. "You are trespassing on Federal lands. This area is protected under code 17-B-32. I wish you the best genocide possible, and have a lovely day."

Both avians reached up their wings to their heads now, but instead of a sharp crack this time there was nothing. The machine looked like it was getting ready to fire another burst, then with a few twitches it slumped to the side. It gave a few more spastic lurches, and then slowly began to lift up once again onto its seven usable legs, stumbling along awkwardly as it bounced from tree to tree.

"It's broken," Tango said with a soft whisper.

"Obviously," she replied, trying not to sound too condescending.

"I've heard rumors that parts off those things can go for a lot," he continued. "Wouldn't that be great to have after our transformation? Just imagine the head start it'd give us. I mean, I know it's a while away and everything, but still… this is easy prey. Hell, a good arrow shot into its other eye, then another into its beam thing, and it's basically harmless. Tie up a few of its legs, then smash it with some rocks or something until it stops moving…" Lisa held him with a glare, until he finally said, "W… what?"

"You saw what that thing could do," she growled. "You want it to be you next?"

"Come on, Lisa," Tango pleaded with a hint of a smile, "You think that thing is any challenge for us? We'll face worse on our way, and we'll <u>have</u> to fight them. This is easy. A warm-up!"

"We don't need to take any risks we don't have to," she said, shooting her gaze back to the machine as it knocked down a tree with a loud crack. "Besides, you really want to carry heavy machine parts, random ones at that, all the way to Flying Mountain?"

"Well, no…" Tango said, taking one last look at the ambling machine and then back towards Lisa. "But it'd be good practice! I really want to take a real machine down! Those training dummies were dull."

Lisa rolled her eyes before giving out a soft huff of breath, watching the machine walking further and further away all the while. "Come on, there's a small path off to the right. Let's go while the machine is preoccupied."

"Awww, you're no fun," Tango groaned, but followed. Lisa wouldn't hear the end of how Tango could've wrecked that machine for days.

* * *

Two weeks of marching later, and their encounter with the machine had been the most exciting moment; it was actually becoming monotonous. The trees thinned out earlier than either of them expected and the ground became progressively more rocky. Then, late one morning as they climbed another small hill, the trees abruptly ended.

There was one last single straight line of trees, and then nothing but open field stretching far off into the distance where the trees began once again. Both birds couldn't help freeze in their tracks and stare at the near emptiness before them. Off in the distance they could see a few small structures, and even a few machines rolling about, but not like any machines they'd been told about before. These were bigger, square shaped, and looking less sleek and dangerous than a machine created for death and destruction. It was hard to be sure from their distance, but they had been warned that any machine could be dangerous just by its weight alone. Although, at the speed the machines were moving through the field, they didn't exactly seem all that threatening.

Both birds took a moment to look at one another, then back at that open field cut straight through the forest. "Um… is this the break in the trees before the river?" Tango asked.

"I don't think so…" Lisa said, straining her skilled eyes to the limit for details of the far-off machines. They were so engrossed in staring that they didn't hear the being coming up behind them.

"Oh," a surprised male voice came from behind them, making both avians spin around and reach for their weapons. They were ready to fight if they had to, but in front of them stood a human boy, younger than the two birds seemed to be, looking even more surprised than they were. Both avians kept their wings on their weapon handles, but relaxed slightly as the boy quickly raised his hands and said, "I'm sorry, I didn't expect to see any birds out here. I've never seen any before! I just thought I heard something, so I came up here to look, and… I'm sorry, I don't have any weapons or anything, I promise!"

Neither Tango nor Lisa took their eyes off him, but he had nothing in his hands besides a small stick, so they started to relax. "We've never seen a human either," Tango replied with a small ruffle to his feathers. "What are you doing down here, and not up in your floating city?"

"Well," the boy started with a little gulp, and took a small step back. "I got in trouble up there. I stole something, so they sent me down here to the farm. Most people here are older than me, they don't let me do anything fun. Usually I have to go and gather firewood or berries or something. That's why I'm up here and not down there." He pointed down at the field behind the avians, causing them to slip their wings back towards their weapons just in case, but there were no visible threats; apparently, it was just a gesture.

"You made that?" Tango asked, looking down at the field, then slowly corrected himself as he said, "Humans made that?"

"I guess," the boy said back, walking a step closer to the birds as Lisa made sure to keep an eye on him. "I just got here two months ago. A lot of people have been there a long time though. Years. Some will stay forever, making food for the city. I have to stay three years myself, that's what the judge said." He paused and looked up at Tango. "They're starting to make farms everywhere so I heard. Some kind of Reclamation thing to get back down to Earth and take back all the land." He he looked back and forth between Tango and Lisa a few times, something building up inside his mind. Finally the boy said, "Why are you two naked? Did you lose your clothes?"

That strange question made Lisa laugh, although Tango seemed more confused than he should have been. Lisa squatted down in front of the boy to look him directly in the eyes. "Well, we don't need clothes, that's why. Our feathers keep us warm when it's cold, and when it's hot we can push all the air out of them to cool off."

The young boy took another look at both birds, really scanning them over now, with each avian doing much the same to him as they stood there in silence. "How do you tell who's a boy and who's a girl?" he asked.

"Boys have a blue tint at the base of their beak, like him," Lisa said, pointing to Tango. "Girls have a pink base, like me."

"Oh."

Lisa stared at his simple yet dirty shirt, overalls, and boots, along with his flowing yellow hair in a messy twist over his head and shoulders. He didn't exactly look mistreated or not taken care of, but this was a far cry from what she'd pictured 'advanced' human society looking like. Eventually Tango was the one to break the silence. "We're looking for a place called Flying Mountain. Have you heard of it?"

"Flying Mountain?" the boy said with a curious twist to his voice. "Not really, no." He took a moment to think a bit before adding in, "Oh, is that where birds get their jet packs and learn to fly?"

"I… guess?" Tango responded with a soft shrug, looking over to Lisa who nodded. The boy's terminology was a little different than they were used to, but his meaning struck a chord, at least with Lisa.

"Is that where you're going?" he asked, getting rather excited at the prospect. A small nod from Lisa, and then from Tango made his smile grow even wider. "I don't know where it is, but that's cool! I've heard stories about birds flying around and exploring and stuff." He took a little pause to contain his excitement before saying, "You should come down and say hi to everyone at the farm. I'm sure they'd like you, and maybe can even help you find your mountain."

"We're really not allowed to ask for help," Lisa said back, giving Tango a little glance just for being the first to do so, but then adding in, "I do have a question though. Are those machines safe down there?"

The boy crept up between them and slowly looked down over the ledge to see what Lisa was pointing at. "Those? The adults say they're too dangerous for me, but they're not really. They're all mechanical— they have no computer so the virus can't get them. We have to do all the work ourselves and help guide them and everything, although we have horses and stuff to do the pulling. No computers are allowed down here. It's nothing like living in the floating city. It's how they punish us though—making us live like old times, before everything good was invented."

"Well that's good to know," Tango said with a gentle nod of his beak. "At least we're safe." At the risk of another stern look from his sister he continued, "Is there a river around here? A big one? One you can't swim across?"

Lisa did give him another glare, but the boy nodded and pointed over the farm. "Yeah, maybe thirty kilometers that way. You can almost kind of see it from here."

"Thanks," Tango said with a confident nod back at Lisa, "Just wanted to know we're on the right track. I think it'll be easier if we just go around the farm though—we don't really have time to stop and talk."

"Aww, okay," the boy grumbled with a little drop to his head and shoulders. "I got to talk to a real bird though! I hope you make it to your mountain."

"Thanks," Tango replied with a smile and nod of his head, while Lisa was busy running her wingtips through some of her plumage. With a few wiggles she managed to pull out a green-tipped feather that had been loose, holding it in her wingtips before bringing it in front of the boy.

"Here, that's for you to keep," she added with a smile of her own. "But only for you! Our little secret."

The boy's eyes went wide as he reached a hand out for the feather. He let out a warm giggle as he took it from the bird, and with a twist of his fingers he made it spin around in his grasp, watching how the green color danced in the light. "Wow, thanks!" he said, clearly overjoyed at the simple gift.

"Now, remember to be nice to any other birds you meet, either feral or like us," Lisa said. "And when you're done being bad, and done farming down here, then maybe we'll see you up in your city."

"You think so?" he asked in return, looking up from his feather to the gentle female face in front of him.

"I'm pretty sure we will," she replied. "What city do you live in?"

"New Phoenix."

"Then we'll see you in New Phoenix," Lisa said with a smile, before turning to look at her brother. "We've got to get going though. We still have a long way to go." She gave the boy's head a little rub, messing up his already messy hair and added, "Be good, and try to keep this meeting our little secret. I don't know much about humans yet, but it'd be easier if they didn't come looking for us, or tell any machines where we're going, okay?"

"Okay," he said with a soft whisper. With one final little wave Lisa began walking down the side of the hill, starting off for the long way around the farm, with her brother catching up to her after giving her a brief head start.

"That was… interesting," Tango joked as he arrived by her side, making sure the boy was out of ear-shot.

"Eh, my Motherly instincts kicked in," Lisa replied with a smile, still feeling a slight tingle from the rush of emotions. "What a poor boy, being in trouble at such a young age."

"He stole something though," Tango said, a soft grumble in his voice.

"Yeah, but he probably didn't know what he was doing, or had to, or something. I don't know the circumstances, but I still feel bad for him, tossed in with who knows who else down in that farm place. He shouldn't be there. He needs a mom and a dad, not thieves and murderers. I just wanted to make him happy for a moment. He's a boy, not a hardened criminal."

"You don't know that," Tango replied, doing his best not to seem too harsh, but still not able to resist annoying his sister a little bit.

"You wait and see," she said with a quick nod. "He'll be the one to invent a way to stop machines from attacking us birds. And everyone else too. Sometimes all it takes is one good moment to really turn your life around."

"If he is then I owe you a whole boar," Tango answered with a confident smile.

* * *

They kept close to the edge of the tree line to see if they could get a glimpse of any more humans as they made their way around the farm. Neither one wanted to admit that stopping and asking a few questions was near the top of their mind, but they managed to avoid giving in to their curiosity.

From there on it was another day's hike to the edge of the mighty river; they followed the river upstream towards the looming mountains in the distance, just as their long memorized mental map said they should. The ground began to get even rockier, and soon the river valley walls were too steep to climb, but by then it was obvious where they should go: towards the prominent white-capped mountain in the distance. They left the river and began to make their way through the rocky terrain, having little comfort now as the forests grew sparse. Finding good trees to hang their hammocks on was getting difficult, and even staying hidden was becoming harder to do; there was also a significant chill in the air, making both of them start shiver no matter how fluffy their feathers got.

Even before they caught their first glimpse of Flying Mountain they noticed an increase in machines in the area. They'd been lucky in avoiding dangerously big machines, or any sneak attacks by smaller machines, but as they made their way through the mountainous forests they knew danger lurked around every corner. Mechanical whirling and squeaking was never far away as they climbed through the lightly populated evergreens around them, forcing each decision on which way they went to be slow and careful. More than once they popped over a little ridge to see gleaming metal on the other side and had to duck back down before they were spotted. Some machines they'd been trained to recognize and counter, but there were plenty of other, unfamiliar designs as well.

Some were much smaller and used rough belts to move on, darting among the rocky rubble of the mountains with surprising speed. Some were gigantic lumbering beasts, shaped like various animals and insects, patrolling the valleys and making the avians have to climb up steep hills to go around them. There was even one millipede creature that took up an entire valley on its own, its large body scraping against the rock as it tried to twist itself through those narrow valleys. The screeching sound it made was horrible as rock ground against metal, and neither bird could get it out of their head for the rest of the day, still swearing to hear it many hours after the sound had actually faded away.

They weren't expecting to simply run into Flying Mountain one day. It wasn't the snow-capped mountain they were using to lead them—that was still far in the distance. They didn't know exactly what they were looking for, but they'd been told that they'd know it when they saw it. There was no questioning it that this was it, and both of them suddenly stopped and just stared at it in silence.

There were a few paths leading up to the mountain, and its off-color built-up entrances were just as described. Guarding those paths and entrances was a small army of guardians, along with machines that looked slow but had sharp and shining cone shaped appendages on extended arms. There were also a few flying machines, complete with rotating blades and a light tubular frame. Some were even vaguely bird-like. It seemed like quite the army for them to get through at first glance, although it was a little less impressive the longer they stared. The problem was that all the machines were just sitting there, motionless, without any indication which if any had power. No lights, no sounds, no anything—just the serene silence of the mountains all around them.

Both birds stared out onto the rubble-strewn field below them, coated in machine parts, avian gear, small rocks, and bones. There was a long, but sprint-able, gap between them and the closest fake entrance, but no cover, besides the seemingly unresponsive machines themselves. The avians took a long time watching and waiting for some movement—any movement—but nothing ever came. The trademark glows from most of the machine's power sources wasn't even radiating from them.

"Are they… all broken?" Tango was the first the whisper out in a rather shaky and nervous voice.

"I don't know," Lisa replied a moment later. "Could be, I guess."

"Maybe the fledglings before us destroyed them all," Tango suggested with a slow look over towards Lisa. "I mean, how long has this been going on? I doubt they have a machine clean-up crew or something. These could all have been broken ages ago. A lot of them look rusty and old down there. A lot of models I don't even know. Maybe they don't make them anymore?"

"You think they'd tell us something like that, though," Lisa snapped, enough to make Tango jump back just a bit.

"Yeah, well," he started up again after a little pause. "You know how weird they get with this honor, bravery, and pride stuff. They'll help you get ready to make it all the way out here, and then hope you can figure out the rest. It's another challenge, another something to say you overcame. Maybe all those machines we already passed by were the real challenge, and this is just a victory lap. Maybe they got tired of defending the mountain itself, and all the still functioning machines went out to patrol the mountains around us. We just get to see the bones of all the fallen machines as we triumphantly walk into Flying Mountain."

"I'm not sure," Lisa replied after a deep sigh. "How do we know they won't start up and zap us the moment we step onto the field?"

"Well," Tango drew out in a long word before adding, "I could always fire off an arrow or two—see if they respond to that. If not, then they're probably all dead. We can be quieter than an arrow after all."

Lisa took a quick look around, and then looked back up behind them, trying to formulate an escape plan. "And what about when they all surge after us after you fire that arrow?"

"We do what we have to," Tango replied with a small smirk, grabbing his bow from his back and reaching for an arrow. "We run, we dodge, and we fight. This is what we came here to do, and it's time to do it, Lisa. There's no turning back now. It's either in there, or our bones will join the others beside the machines. We can't go anywhere else."

Lisa felt a tingle of fear and unease shoot through her, just like when she took that last look at her former home so many night cycles ago. Was there really no going back? The journey hadn't exactly been easy, but she had been able to handle it. She could make it back, even on her own if Tango really wanted to make it to Flying Mountain. She could still have a life as a Matriarch. That was still a possibility…

As Tango released his strung up arrow Lisa watched it soar through the air, giving just a gentle swish sound as it arched off nice and far into the distance. Tango's aim was good as always. His shot began to fall, and soon clanked off the outer shell of one of the better looking, less rusted and broken machines. It had no visible weapons on its exterior, and just a few sensors dotting its body, looking like one of the most harmless among the machines gathered beneath them.

Both birds ducked down as they heard that metallic clang ring out from arrow tip hitting metal plating, then peeked around the rock edge again. The machine the arrow hit hadn't moved. No lights came on, nothing seemed to power up, and none of the machines around it seemed to react either. Both avians looked at one another and then out onto the field once more, a little surprised that it had worked.

"See, told ya," Tango began after a moment of silence, slowly notching another arrow and taking aim at a larger and more battle-geared machine. Lisa cringed a little bit, but she was helpless to stop that arrow from shooting out and arching over the land once more. Neither bird hid this time as the arrow bounced off the outer shell with another loud clang. Once again the metallic beast didn't even stir, or give any sign that it could sense the arrow at all.

Both avians waited for what felt like an eternity, searching for any sign of activity, before Tango finally slipped his bow onto his back once again. "Come on," he said as his voice rang out a little more confident than before. "Let's go. I think we're safe."

"Let's have some kind of back-up plan first," she cried, but it was too late. Before she'd even gotten the words out Tango was already walking around the edge of the rock they were hidden behind. He carefully took that first step over the edge, and with a controlled descent he slid down the hill onto the rocky field below. He froze for a moment after he came to rest and looked around for any motion among the machine carcasses from the noise, but after not seeing anything he turned his head back towards his sister and gave her a gentle smile.

"Come on Lisa," he shouted back, giving her a wave of his wing as he waited.

Lisa froze for a moment as her wingtips were still clenched against that rock in front of her, but with a few small wiggles she edged her way over towards the small cliff face. With one more call out from her brother, and another small step, she gulped down a heavy wad of spit in her throat and took the plunge. It was a slightly rough descent on the broken and slick stone, more a slide than anything entirely controlled. Her backpack ground against the rock behind her, but within a moment she was standing with her brother, brushing the dust off her feathers with a quick fluff.

"All good so far," Tango said with a smile, watching the machines as Lisa slid down, but not feeling the need to reach for his bow quite yet.

"I guess," Lisa replied, with a good deal less confidence. Nevertheless she began to follow him as the smaller bird turned and made his way towards one of the round and oblong carcass of a fallen machine that seemed to have been there for quite a while. His steps were careful yet still firm in their direction as the bird reached up a wing to touch the skin of the beast, letting his feathers dance along that rough and weathered metallic coating.

"I think we did it Lisa," he said with a growing excitement. "I think we made it."

"Calm down," she replied with a little hint of a growl, trying to keep her beak shut and be as quiet as she could. She adjusted the pack on her back before slipping out her knife from its sheath. It wasn't long enough for any long range combat, but it was hopefully enough to keep her alive should a small machine manage to get close. Enough force and it could even wedge itself in a joint or something, giving her the time she needed to escape. "Until we get inside don't say anything."

Tango seemed to be just a little cocky as he pulled away from the shell and started to make his way to the next one, his stride a little more relaxed and swaying as Lisa crept with more tension behind him. He was the first to reach the next beast and run his wingtips over it, with Lisa showing up shortly thereafter, and not able to resist doing much the same. With each machine they came to she began to feel a little more relaxed, but her knife never left her wing, always ready to strike should something give her a reason to.

Their luck finally ran out as Tango traced his wingtips over another, less worn specimen. Within a moment of being touched a strip of lights illuminated the short and stubby machine's side, causing it to roll over with a jerk, thankfully in the direction away from Tango.

It wasn't very large, being a little longer than Lisa's size in height. Its body was a large rectangle, about a fifth in height to length, and having a movement belt running across each corner of its frame. With another bright flash of light the machine began to point its sensors at the two birds, and a small cracked screen began to flash white in their direction. It then fell to black and showed a few numbers and words, which scrolled by too fast to read. Both birds froze and started as the display screen flashed again, and then a few large lines and dashes began to form into what resembled a crude face.

"Thank you for purchasing the Chillzone All Terrain Beverage Cooler," it barked out in a hollow, robotic voice, crackling a bit as its speaker was far from perfectly functional. It took a second to let some sensors scan the two confused avians in front of it before letting out a few more garbled noises, a mix of rusty grinding, electrical squealing, and a few computer sounding bleeps and bloops.

"Oh, birds!" the crackling voice added as the belts slowly began to turn, crawling the large off-white box closer to the two avians. "Why aren't you flying? Do you need help?"

That was all the machine was able to say before the tip of one of Tango's arrows found its way into that screen at point blank range, breaking it beyond function and making it go dark. Lisa wasn't far behind as the tip of her knife stabbed into one of those sensor openings, seeing it through a crack in the machine's outer frame. Tango was about to load up and shoot off another arrow, but before he could there came a loud electrical spark discharge from behind them. He turned around, arrow notched and ready, before firing it off into the first glowing bit he saw.

The machine didn't let off any sort of scream to let them know the arrow connected, but the small shower of sparks let both avians know that it had hit something important on the beast rising up before them. "Run!" Tango screamed out, and in a flash he was gone, taking off towards the mountain. Lisa wasn't far behind, her longer legs catching up to her brother, and her knife still locked tight in her grasp.

"Help them fly!" came a cry from around them in broken and sputtered computer speech, echoed with a few others, leaving a whole chorus shouting out behind them before too long.

As a few of the larger machines started to rise up and power on, the gauntlet quickly became harder to navigate through. The birds were quick and agile, but their heavy backpacks held them back. When Lisa's pack suddenly shifted off her shoulder she found herself tumbling to the side, scraping a leg as she fell onto the rocky ground below.

With a quick slide to a stop Tango turned around and shot off one, and then a second arrow, beating back a few of the closer machines as Lisa struggled to get up. "Come on, Lisa," he shouted, dodging out of the way of a machine's flailing limbs. "You have the engine… you need to go!" Another arrow whizzed over Lisa's head as she scrambled to her feet. She could hear the machines' broken cries.

"Birds… must fly…"

"Soar mighty eagles!"

"Spread your wings and glide…"

Most of the machines were broken and battered; some were dragging parts of themselves behind, or even struggling to remain in motion. That didn't change the fact that they were hostile and still coming, lashing out at the avians with any parts they had to do so. Lisa was up on her feet running again, while Tango fired off another arrow.

"Keep going, don't look back," he shouted from behind her. The words didn't really register in her brain at the moment as pure instinct was the only thing driving her. She put her beak down and forced her legs to move as fast as they could; after a moment she heard Tango stop firing and start running behind her. The machine presence was almost overwhelming as more and more were awoken by the cries and activity, a minefield of metallic and robotic parts flying out towards them from every direction. Lisa saw one more arrow fly over her head and hit a machine directly in front of her, causing it to shift to the side as its sensors tried to recalibrate, but soon after that metallic ping she heard a heavy grunt and a squawking scream screech out from behind her.

"Fly bird, be free!" said a machine. Another squawk, and a heavy impact.

"Fly bird, be free!" said another. Soon an eerie chorus of "Fly bird, be free!" rang out through the field, surrounding Lisa as she ran. Machines in Lisa's path turned their attention to something behind her, leaving enough of a gap to run through a few spread legs and parts. She still stumbled once or twice, and she had to stab her knife tip against a small machine that had jumped towards her, but she could see the machines thinning up ahead. Her legs burned, her breathing was erratic, and the adrenaline was running out, but the bird girl pushed through to the mountain.

But how to get inside? The solid white doors that stretched as tall as trees were sealed shut, leaving her no room to get through the gap in between, but still she ran towards them as her only hope. Just as she was about to run headlong into the tightly sealed portal, in the vague hope that it might open just in time, something caught her attention from the corner of her eye.

It wasn't much, but there was a set of green and brown stripes painted at the end of one of the doors. Left with nothing more to go on she turned towards with her last gasps of energy. As if someone knew she was coming, a small panel opened at the far end of the rock wall, leaving a dark square for her to aim for. Completely on instinct she dove for the small opening, kicking herself into a slide for the final body length, plunged from sunlight to complete darkness in the flash of a second as the passage closed again with a metallic clang and a burst of air. She collided with rock wall at the end of that opening, squawking out with a final gust of breath as her ankle twisted from the sudden impact, but the exhausted avian was in no mood to care any longer. She figured she must be safe, but even if she wasn't she was done running. This would be it for her one way or another.

The run had been far more intense than anything she'd trained for, and the many moon cycles since her last training session had morphed her muscles into more grinding endurance than sprinting speed. Everything hurt as she lay on her side, gasping desperately for air, reaching down a wing to caress her now stinging ankle. Her only defense was to curl up into a ball and protect herself, still prepared for the worst as she heard more mechanical noises just outside the walls.

It took a few moments before the squeaking and grinding of machines, muffled by the thick walls around her, began to fade away to nothing. It was at that point that she began to cry. Not from the physical pain inside her muscles, or the scraped and torn feathers and flesh she had on her legs, but from the fact that she was now alone.

As her brain began to recover and process everything it'd been holding off during the run, she realized what those sounds she heard were. That squawk of pain, that long winded scream, the crunching thud… one of the machines had gotten to Tango and tried to make him fly. If the first fall back down to earth didn't kill him, surely the next few had. She knew better than to have hope he was still alive, and that realization only made the tears come that much harder.

She lashed out in a few firm kicks and punches at the rock walls at her side, hating everything she'd gone through, hating that she had been forced into it. She especially hated the fact that this stupid trial took the lives of so many, with her brother now added to the list. The Flyers, with their advanced technology, could easily take care of this machine problem, and probably even the flying problem too. It was such a waste of life—and all for pride! A thought burned through her tears: she would lead the charge if she had to—but no one else would ever die for this!

All the extra punches and kicks just left her aching more. At some point it began to hurt too much to move, so she simply curled up into a ball once again and let the near silence of her passageway try and relax her. Her sobs grew to slow, deep breaths, and then back down to simple tired ones, leaving the strain of running and crying circulating around her body. She must have laid there for an hour, trying to process everything and make sense of it all. It was nice to cry, and now was certainly not the time to hold back. At the same time, it would be impossible to cry forever. She knew that she couldn't, no matter how much she wanted to. She had made it, she was safe, and she had more important things to do than just lay there and feel sorry for herself. Tango would've wanted her to go on and claim her prize anyway.

With another set of heavy gasps she came to the realization that it was time to move on. With a small huff and heave she lifted herself up into a crawl, being a bit gentle on her body as she made sure nothing was seriously injured. With a few twists, stretches, and checks she began to crawl her way down the narrow passageway carved into the solid rock until it finally opened up.

She took a look around as the world brightened around her, her dark-adjusted eyes finally able to see those massive doors to her side, and a long, dimly lit tunnel leading off the other way. She struggled to her feet and gave her body a few more careful stretches, shaking off a few final emotions and sensations, before taking a deep breath and starting down the tunnel. The feeling that she had finally made it, the feeling like she was safe, it all began to bubble up inside her with each slightly limping step.

All around her were small wall paintings, both carved and painted onto the formerly white walls. There was a little of everything, from the battle outside, to scenes back in a few small villages, to quite a few creatures flying around a mountain. It had to be the artwork of all those that had made it to the mountain, as it appeared in all sorts of styles and talent levels, creating an impressive collage. She took the time to examine it deeply, letting out a few more tears at some of her own memories, before coming up to a long list of names carved into the wall.

"Never Forget the Name" was scrawled near the ceiling of the tunnel, with many names scratched all the way down towards the floor. Most followed a few straight columns down, but some were out of place, scribbled in random locations close by. Near the base of the list, along with chips of rock from the wall, was a hammer and chisel, crudely made but with a rather obvious purpose. Lisa wasn't a half bad artist, despite not having too much practice, and after a few minutes the spot on the wall now read 'Tango'.

"Your name will be the last," she said into the darkness.

Happy with her work she laid both tools down, before taking one last look at that all-too-long list of names and continuing down the tunnel. The sound of distant mechanical motors grew into a strong hum as Lisa approached an open cavern, leaving her a bit nervous as she slowed her walk to a creep. It was hard to see very far in the dull light, but from what she could see there were dozens of metallic and rectangular machines dotting the walls, leaving her to reach for her knife once again. She hadn't been told what to expect inside Flying Mountain, only that she'd be taken care of when she got there, so if there were any more trials to go through she knew she had to be ready. The machines didn't seem to notice her though; they were busy doing whatever it was they were doing, spinning some sort of fiber from one circle to another inside of them, making clunking noises as they did. She kept her senses up, only jump and whirl around when she heard a rough mechanical voice call out, "Greetings new fledgling, or shall I say future Flyer?"

Lisa slashed at the air around her, as more of a reflex than anything, leaving her breath racing as her powerful eyes scanned out all around her. She was tired, both physically and emotionally, and her body was aching almost everywhere, but she had one last burst of energy to go down swinging with. She couldn't see much detail, but she did see movement, and she knew that some machine was slowly coming towards her. It wasn't very quick though, more of a gentle squeaking roll, and as it got closer she gripped her knife tighter and readied it to strike.

She watched as the creature's outline began to take shape in the darkness, going from undefined blob to rectangle, and finally to more of a cone shape, containing two arms and a rough face full of sensors on top of its rounded shoulders. "Do not be alarmed, you are safe here," the clunky machine said with a few small twitches, making its outer casing shake and rattle each time it moved. Lisa began to lower her knife in slight confusion, but her wingtips never let go of it.

"What… is a machine doing here?" she asked with a slightly stammering clack of her beak, her mind and body trying it's best to hold itself together at the sight before her.

"I am here to assist you in flight," the machine replied after a moment of not moving at all.

"Who are you?"

"I have been known by many names. The one encoded within me is United States Government Advance Research Product Agency Criticom Mainframe 0017, but I have also been called Flying Mountain Computer, Central Processing Unit, Gamayun, and many others. You can call me what you wish, as long as I am calibrated to respond."

As the conical object finally came to a stop, Lisa could see something trailing behind it: what she first thought was another appendage turned out to be a long set of cables. "I know it must be surprising to see a machine here, when you just encountered so many outside this mountain, but I assure you I do not contain the virus," the machine said. "The virus cannot penetrate my coding, nor anything else I encode. It is far too advanced to make use of such simple language as my own. But, my language serves a purpose, as you will find out in the coming months. It is the reason your flight devices still function and are non-corruptible by normal means."

"So…" Lisa began after a little break in the machine's speech, "We birds fly because of machines, but are hunted for not being able to fly, by machines?"

"It is a strange paradox," the machine in front of her said, with no emotion or expression in its voice, not even bothering to move its arms, "But there will be plenty of time for you to gain the answers you seek. You may simply want to rest for a moment, even before meeting the others. Too many emotions in a short time does not make for proper greetings."

"Others?" Lisa asked with a curious tilt to her head, now sheathing her knife and just staring at the slightly wobbling machine in front of her as it tried to nod its 'head' a few times.

"Yes," it responded with a few small creaks, "There are currently four others here… one is almost complete but still recovering from the surgery. They will be happy to see you, but only when you are ready."

Lisa simply stared at the machine in front of her, motionless and waiting for her answer. Something else began to clank and fly into motion, and the hard mechanical sounds assaulting her eardrums and making her body jump. She took a few steps over towards the direction of the sound, seeing a large rectangular box begin to take in a large stack of paper. It quickly swallowed and digested it with the furious sound of a few heavy spinning gears.

She watched until all the paper was gone, and only then did she look back at the machine that had approached her, still waiting in the exact same spot and position it had been. "Are you still on?" she said.

It took another moment for the machine to twitch once again, slowly moving to face her. "Yes. It takes time for me to process things as my technology is very old."

Once again the machine went silent and left Lisa staring at the still buzzing, clicking, and moving machines around her, taking it all in. "I suppose I'm ready," she finally said. "I'm not sure what else I could really do here."

"Very good," the machine continued after another pause. "Follow me. Please be careful of my cable." With a few jerking motions the machine turned and rolled away. Lisa followed with her own labored walk, to the far end of the chamber where the machine's cable grew taunt once again. "This is as far as I can go," it said. "If you continue down that tunnel ahead you will reach the others. Congratulations on making it, and I wish you luck in your transformation. We will discuss what you will need to do next after you rest."

The path in front of her was clear. One dully lit hallway leading out of that main chamber would bring her to the start of everything she worked so hard to achieve. If all went well then in a few months she'd leave and be able to fly, and from there… well… the thought was a little scary yet. One step at a time was all she could take. She had to keep her head down and her feet moving forward, and that's exactly what she did.

One step, then another, passing by the machine and making her way into that tunnel. She did it for Tango. She was here because of him and his sacrifice; the only way to truly honor him would be to keep his energy and purpose alive. What better tribute to his memory than coming out of the mountain with a power he couldn't wait to have? She would suffer just a little longer to make that happen… not for the good of her species, nor for the pride it showed off. Those things didn't matter. She would do it for him, and for a future where no other avians had to die in order to get it.

STAR OF THE SAVANNAH

Huskyteer

As the *Star of the Savannah* rounded the bend, a school of airfish, startled by the thrum of the hoverskiff's fan, took flight and flickered away into the sunset. They were too pretty to shoot, so I let them go. I'd have a proper meal soon, anyway. I couldn't wait to tie up at New Haven and enjoy a bowl of Mama Bill's stew. Nothing wrong with eels, of course, but a hyena needs variety.

'A hyena needs variety' was the line I used when anyone tried to tie me down to a single spot. I liked the life I led, delivering messages, packets and gossip up and down the Wampo River. No livestock; no passengers. Free to sleep all day, sing all night, and scratch myself inappropriately. The high gold sun took care of powering my little aerohover skiff and the *Star* had everything I needed: a tiny cabin with a cookstove and a mattress (although I slept on deck most weathers), fresh air, and an ever-changing view. I fished, and I ate what I caught, and I washed it down with liquor I distilled from anything handy.

I could never stick in one place. It would drive me crazy. But nights like tonight, after the long barren stretch from Brissol to New Haven, I looked forward to docking for a while and enjoying some company other than my own.

My nose twitched at the smell of woodsmoke. I stared upriver for the lights of the town, welcoming me out of the dusk.

Instead, I saw the glow of smoldering embers, and jagged stumps where there should be houses.

New Haven was in ruins.

"Oh—Chuck! I heard the engine and I thought they were coming back." It was Mama Bill, his skirt flapping as he lumbered over. I threw him a line and the brown bear hauled me in, mooring the skiff to a post. As soon as I climbed up on the dock he folded me in a hug, which I bore politely.

"What happened, Bill?" I asked as soon as my muzzle was free of his fuzzy embrace.

"Watersnakes happened," he said.

"All the way down here?" Now I was looking properly, I could see the tracks in the sand where the pirates' fast, armed craft had swooped in and out, smashing and grabbing before hightailing it back to their secret harbors.

The two of us took a moment to survey the damage. I'd seen Watersnaked towns before, though the bands of raiders didn't usually attack a place the size of New Haven. I'd seen them built up again, too, as the community—if there was much community left—came together to fix their home. See, that's what happens if you stick in one place: you get obligations.

"Where are my manners?" Bill said, shaking his massive head. "Come in and eat."

Mama Bill's was still standing, though there were so many people packed inside that the walls seemed to strain outwards. Many of the customers were dirty, some half-dressed, and others sporting bandages where they'd worked to save their homes and those trapped inside them.

The bear found a place for me and ladled out a bowl of soup. It was a thin broth rather than the meaty, fatty stew I'd been dreaming of, but it was warm, and flavored with Mama Bill's secret mix of herbs, and I was grateful he'd spare it to an outsider. I bolted it down.

"Thanks, Bill. I'll spread the word, get you some help." I wanted to be out of there. The smell of ruin was making me uneasy.

"Hold on a second, Chuck. There's something else you can do for me. A small package to deliver."

"That's what I do." I grinned, relieved it was nothing more taxing.

"Great." He poked his head into the kitchen and said, "Come on out here, honey."

I've seen all kinds of strange folk on my travels, from the whale people of the oceans to the flightless birds of the savannah, but I'd never been this close to a human kid before. They don't tend to move in the same circles I do.

If she'd been a hyena cub I'd have put her at about six or seven, but she might have been older for all I knew. The top of her head, hair plaited into dozens of tiny braids, was just about level with my solar plexus. My paw could have wrapped around both her wrists with room to spare.

"Oh, no. You know my rules. No livestock, no passengers."

"She's just a kid, Chuck. You'll hardly know she's there."

"I'd have to feed her, wouldn't I?" I took another look. She was *skinny*. "I'd have to feed her plenty, or she might disappear."

"Please. She needs to get back home, and I can't leave here. You're her best shot."

"What's she doing here, anyway?" Humans generally meant trouble for somebody, and I didn't want it to be me.

"As far as I can tell, she was with her parents and a group of RPers, out in the wilds looking for something or other."

"And 'something or other' found them."

The bear nodded. "Dawn here got away, but the rest of the party is *missing*." He put careful emphasis on the last word, and pulled a face at me over the little girl's head. "She's from one of the skyside cities. Place called Westwind. Get her to the liaison office at Ambara Down and they'll see her right."

Mama Bill stretched out a paw to pat Dawn on the shoulder. "We were going to send for someone to collect her, but she can't stay here now."

"Are you out of your mind, Bill?" Messing with the Reclamation Project brought nothing but trouble. "They'll think I did her parents in. They'll skin me! And it's a week's travel to Ambara, through some of the worst country I know."

"Good thing you're the best pilot I know, then," he beamed.

We'd been talking the whole time as if the child wasn't there, while she stood looking from me to the bear with wide brown eyes. Now, she suddenly found her voice. "I'm not going with him!" she yelled, so loudly that several other customers stopped their conversations and stared at us. Great. Nothing I like more than being the center of attention.

"He's rude, and he's ugly, and he smells of fish!" the kid continued. She had a point. Several, in fact. "And I'm not getting on his stupid boat!"

"Skiff," I put in.

"Dawn, please," Mama Bill whispered. He crouched so his head was level with hers. "Chuck's a good guy. A little rough on the outside, but with a heart of gold."

Nobody likes to hear that kind of talk about themselves. I was getting out and I was getting out right now. I turned to Dawn.

"You'll come with me and like it, kid." I bared my teeth. "And if you don't stick to the rules, I might eat you."

* * *

Aerohover vehicles are the old, original hovercraft, carried on a cushion of air contained by a flexible skirt. Slower and more limited than anti-grav jobs, but a lot cheaper to maintain and operate, easier to kitbash, and a lot less prone to catastrophic and permanent failure. But like the anti-grav version it's amphibious, so it can take a short cut across meanders, or bounce over spots where the riverbed has dried up. It exerts so little pressure on the surface, you can run over a clutch of crocodile eggs without breaking them, if you feel like living dangerously. It's not the best land-based vehicle, though: it's vulnerable to damage from rocks and dust, and it can't climb at too sharp an angle. I'd stick to the river for this trip. It was a longer route, and more dangerous in some respects, but we'd get there faster. More importantly, I knew every inch of the Wampo and I knew its many moods.

I've always loved the river at night. The plop of a fish or the creak of a frog, distinct enough in the stillness to make out over the *Star*'s constant thrum. The spark of fireflies over the water; the lights from the human cities in the distant sky and, above them, nothing but stars. Forever.

Dawn had tried everything in her limited powers to avoid getting on board, from screaming and sobbing to burying her head in Mama Bill's apron and clinging to him. In the end, the bear had carried her on deck, her mouth and pockets stuffed with homemade honey candy. Now she sat cross-legged in the stern, fiddling with some toy she kept in the pocket of her dungarees and wouldn't let me see. When she thought I wasn't looking, she'd steal a peep at the passing scenery. If I tried to talk, she stared down at her lap.

She trailed a hand in the water, making ripples.

"Don't do that," I snapped. "Crocodiles."

"I don't believe you," she said, withdrawing her hand quickly.

"Maybe you should try and sleep," I suggested.

"No."

"You hungry?"

"No."

What a fun trip this was going to be.

"Did you know your eyes shine red in the dark?" she asked.

"I guess I didn't. Does it scare you?"

"No."

She dropped off eventually. I draped a blanket over her—the night wasn't cold, but we get mosquitoes the size of a baseball—and shut the engine off so we could drift in silence.

It's hard to stay angry with a sleeping child, though I gave it my best shot. The poor brat was acting up because everyone she knew and loved had been taken from her. No wonder she hated the ground and everything on it—with the exception of Mama Bill, because it was practically impossible to hate him.

It wasn't her fault she was here with me, either; I blamed that bear and the favors I owed him. And her absent family, of course. What kind of parents took a kid away from the safety and luxury of a floating city to rough it on the ground with the animal people?

New Haven was usually where I turned around and headed back inland. Beyond the river port, the Wampo widened. The water was rough, tidal, and there were rapids that could tip you out into the waiting maws of the crocodiles. There was other stuff, too. Weird stuff. Unpredictable. It was Watersnake country, but also Pax Machina country, and that scared me even more. I was riding straight into trouble, with a passenger who was too small and stupid to help out even if she'd wanted to. As things stood, she'd probably turn me over to the first lot of pirates we encountered.

All that was further down the river, though. For now, I shone a lantern and set about catching some night eels for breakfast.

The smell and sizzle of frying woke Dawn in time to catch her namesake coming up in the east. The sun and sky were red, which meant bad weather later but made a pretty spectacle. A flock of airfish rose from their nests among the reeds and shimmied themselves airborne, leaving a trail of pink ripples in the water from their takeoff.

"Look!" I shouted, pointing. It was nice to have someone to share with, even if they didn't appreciate it. "Hey. You're smiling!"

"Your tail. It poofs out when you get excited."

Well. It was something, I guess.

"Are we there yet?"

"No. It'll be days, not minutes, so you'd better get asking that out of your system right now."

"Can't your boat go any faster?"

"No. And it's a skiff."

That out of the way, we ate breakfast in silence and watched the silver waves ripple out from under us, displaced by our cushion of air.

Mid-afternoon the sky turned yellow. The temperature dropped, and the sun vanished behind crawling grey clouds.

"Dawn, get in the cabin," I told her.

"Why?" She clung to the rail.

I opened my mouth to remonstrate, but my voice was drowned out by the snarl of thunder. A cold wind stirred the river an instant before the surface began to jump and fizz with rain, and I was suddenly very busy indeed.

The deck was awash straight away and slick as ice. Airfish, unable to stay aloft in the downpour, plummeted from the sky to slap into the water. I took down the auxiliary sail, which was banging to and fro in the wind, and lowered the mast so it wouldn't snap. Everything loose had to be tied down or stashed in the tiny cabin. That included Dawn, and if I had my way I'd take the tying option.

I waded across the deck to where she crouched, shocked and miserable, her little plaits whipping around her face. I uncurled her hands from the rail and walked her to the cabin, shutting the door tight behind her.

A jolt sent me to my knees. The river, brown with mud, was rising all the time as the rain fed it, washing over its banks, and lumps of debris picked up by the water were rushing along the surface. A second piece of wood slammed into the side of the skiff, and the engine whined in protest.

Aerohover skiffs aren't designed for turbulent waters, and they're certainly not built to take damage. It just takes a bit of debris to knock a chunk out of the rubber skirt. The air finds its way out, and you find yourself going in circles, or tipped over. There was no way we'd make it safely over the rapids with the river this high. The bank here was too steep for my craft to climb, but we could tie up, hop on shore and wait it out.

I set a course that would swing us around, parallel to the bank, and readied a rope. Squinting through the raindrops on my eyelashes, and braced with my legs bent and wide so I wouldn't lose my footing, I scanned the bank and spotted a metal post. Perfect.

When you travel alone, you soon start to sense when someone's watching you, or you don't last long.

"I told you to stay below!" I said, without looking round. I cast my line over the post and snagged it first time. Not bad, in this wind. "If I didn't have my paws full, I'd…"

The post came loose from the wet mud and the line went slack. I fell on my backside and slid across the wet and tilting deck. It probably looked pretty funny. I grabbed the rail and hung from it to keep myself from falling overboard, scrabbling with my hindpaws to get a grip and boost myself back on board. A huge wave reared up and smashed down on my head.

"Chuck!" I heard, just before water filled my mouth and ears. Hands like cold little pincers grabbed the scruff of my neck and hauled. If I was really lucky, I might choke to death before I drowned. I've never fancied drowning.

"Let go of me!" I tried to say. Then the skiff tilted up so the bow rose out of the water. Dawn and I tumbled across the deck together in a tangle of limbs. We crashed into the mast, and I had just enough sense left to wrap my arms around it. Then I took a short nap.

By the time I was in a fit state to notice what was going on around me, the skiff was wandering from side to side, tossed by the current. It was a miracle we hadn't overturned. I scrambled for the wheel and turned us round. We were picking up speed all the time as we approached the rapids, and I could hear the water thundering over the rocks.

"Let me help!" Dawn ducked under my arm, and her small hands arrived on the wheel between my furry mitts.

"Hard a'port," I told her. "That's left."

"I knew that!"

The banks were rocky, but the sudden rainfall had raised the water level to the point where we might be able to escape the river. It was worth a try.

I rode one of the huge waves as it rolled towards the boat, drifting us sideways. There was a slight bump as we lifted up and over the bank, then we were flying over solid ground, mud spraying all around us as the downward draught blew it out of our path.

The wind was enough to turn my ears inside out. I was steering blind, my eyes streaming. I blinked, and a black shape became a huge tree, uprooted by the storm and falling towards us.

No time to steer clear. I dived at Dawn, pushing her down and out of the way. As I pressed her to the deck, I felt a branch tear at my ear. Scraping the cabin, the tree snagged the battery of solar cells at the stern and tore them loose. I watched as the whole shebang was carried into the flood to smash on the rocks. The engine sputtered and stopped.

It took me a moment to realize that the reason the silence felt so absolute was that the wind and rain had stopped, too.

Dawn wriggled out from under me and clapped her hand to her chest. From her expression I knew that whatever treasure she kept stashed in her pocket was safe. Good for her. Shame we were dumped without power in the middle of the badlands.

Now the storm had blown itself out, it was tropical hot again. The sun slunk out from the clouds, looking as pale and shaken as I felt. Dawn and I, both soaked to the bone, sat at opposite ends of the deck. Steam rose from my pelt. Water, mixed with a trickle of blood, ran into my eyes. My ears were plastered to my head, and I gave myself a good shake so my fur stood up in spikes. Dawn looked as if she didn't feel like talking, so I let her be.

"Chuck?" she said at last. "When you said 'they'll think I did her parents in'. What did you mean?"

The inside of my mouth tasted bad. "I meant they'd think I killed them."

"I thought so."

We stayed still and quiet for a little while. Then I stretched out my arm, and Dawn hesitated before scooting across to lean against my side.

"You still smell of fish," she told me.

"Whatever."

* * *

"What are you doing?" Dawn asked, fidgeting as she watched me mess around with the ship's wheel.

"Just fitting the security system," I told her. The river was fast becoming a dangerous place, and I wanted a little insurance. "There, all done."

I spread the map out on the cabin roof. Dawn, on tiptoes, peered around my arm.

"Dead Air is two days' hike away," I told her. I could make it in less, but I couldn't expect the kid to match my pace. "It was a holiday resort for your folk, once."

Back in the day, Dead Air was called Bel Air. One of those places for rich humans to go on holiday and think they're living the outdoor life, with a fancy air-conditioned hotel to go back to in the evening and robot staff to take care of their every desire. There were all-terrain bikes and sand-surfing, expeditions out into the desert—oh, and hunting trips, of course.

"We should be able to scrounge a solar panel and fix the skiff, *but*—" I tapped her nose with a claw "—it's also in territory controlled by Pax Machina. You keep quiet, you stick with me, and you do exactly, and I mean *exactly*, what I tell you. Okay?"

"Okay," she said. It was an uncharacteristically subdued response, and I looked at her sharply. She looked back, all innocence. I'd found her a spare shirt of mine to replace her sodden clothes. It hung on her like a robe, and she wore it like a small princess.

"Come on, then."

I could have left her with the skiff. There was food, and fresh water. But I didn't like the thought of her all on her own. We got mutant crocs, sometimes, and even without that, she looked too young to be okay with being by all by herself in the dark.

Some sort of huge bird, bright pink and trailing a tail like fireworks, exploded out of the trees as we passed. My rifle was on my shoulder before my eyes had properly registered the picture. Dawn looked accusingly at me.

"I wasn't gonna… it just startled me." I hadn't had the jumps like this since the time I borrowed a few spare parts from a fox who wasn't using them, and he got the wrong end of the stick and the law was looking for me for weeks.

When Dawn suddenly asked "What's a savannah?" I nearly took a shot at her too.

"A grassland," I explained once my heart rate had settled down. "It's where my people lived before your people started messing around with our genes."

"I'd like to see that," she said. "My parents were going to show me everything. They promised."

"What were they doing down here anyway?" I asked. It came out harsher than I'd meant, and Dawn blinked at me.

"Looking for stuff from before, so they could find out how it worked and make life better for everyone."

"Everyone. Huh." Everyone who counted as anyone, which meant skyside, which meant humans exclusively. Wasn't the kid's fault. She was just repeating what she'd been taught.

"Don't you want your life to be better?"

"What could be better than *this*?" I asked, spreading my paws to indicate the world in general. Sure, things could be better right now. My skiff could be in one piece and we could be lazing on deck instead of risking our lives out here. But on average, my life was pretty great. I'd certainly silenced Dawn, who frowned and pursed her lips in thought.

"Your boat could go faster," she told me. "Or it could fly. Or you could watch movies in the cabin. Or…"

That kept us going until the jungle of vegetation along the riverbanks dried to a red desert scattered with giant boulders and cactus grown into weird, wind-whipped shapes. North of us stretched the wastelands, Tsaibei Hrotan's territory unless some other warlord had cut his throat and taken over since the last time I was here. Dawn stuck close to me as she'd promised, but she was looking around all the time, fascinated by the changing landscape. Fine with me. She could yell a warning if some monster, natural or artificial, came for us. Every now and then she gave a little skip of excitement.

"I don't want to end up carrying you if you tire yourself out," I warned.

"I won't."

I ended up carrying her.

She sat on my rucksack with her arms around my shoulders, watching the sky for birds of prey or sandstorms. We had a good laugh as our shadows lengthened, giving me stretched and skinny legs, then we found a sheltered spot between a couple of boulders and made camp for the night.

And in the night, they came.

I wasn't asleep, but I might have let my eyes close briefly as I snuggled down in my sleeping-bag, nothing exposed but the top of my head. The next thing I knew, Dawn was trying to pull one of my ears off.

"I'm awake, I'm…" My vision adjusted to the dark, and I eyeballed the two visitors who had us cornered in our bivouac.

It looked as if Pax had taken over some of the robots from the resort, smooshing them together for its own mad purposes. One was an amalgam of the doglike quadrupeds that used to guard the perimeter against riffraff, with three heads and more legs than I could count. The other…well. I mentioned there were robots for *every* desire. It wasn't a very suitable sight for a little girl, and I stood in front of Dawn, blocking her view.

"I can deal with this," she informed me.

"No, you can't," I told her just as firmly. I wasn't sure I could. I had my rifle, but it wouldn't do much against metal.

"May I see your visitor pass, please?" asked the three-headed dog. Its voice, emanating from a speaker in its chest, was deep and pleasant, with the kind of accent people put on when they're trying to sound superior. Three sets of jaws popped apart, revealing steel fangs. They would have several pressure settings, I guessed: 'restraint', 'pain', and 'goodbye limb'.

"We only want to please you." The other robot had a female voice. It must have sounded sexy, once, but something had gone off-key so the metallic warble of it made my ears ring and set my teeth on edge. "Please you?" it added. I heard a slot slide open somewhere on its body.

I'd had a few run-ins with Pax Machina in my time. Sometimes you can wriggle out of the situation with a little fast talking.

"Oh, silly me! I've left my pass back in my hotel room." I gave a big, stupid grin, mirroring the dog's. "It's been a long day and I'm *very* thirsty. Any chance of a complimentary glass of champagne? It said in the brochure…"

"*Champagne?*" I'd said the wrong thing. The three heads cocked simultaneously to the left and their mouths opened even wider, so the steel fangs caught the moonlight.

I had my back to the rock, with Dawn pinned behind me so she couldn't pop out and attempt to tackle the robots. My left paw found a crevice that widened towards the base of the stone. I couldn't squeeze in, but maybe Dawn had a chance. Slowly, I began shuffling us both to the left.

"I will please you," promised the pleasure robot.

"I don't know, ma'am. I'm pretty hard to please. Do you play chess?"

"I play all games."

I gave Dawn a little shove with my butt. I felt her crouch behind my legs, then her warm presence vanished as she backed into the crack. I shivered. With luck, the two robots hadn't even noticed her, and the rock would block her from their sensors. She could lie quiet until I talked my way out of this… or until they took me away.

The dog-thing sort of slithered up the rock face, using the claws on its many feet, until it was above me. Its heads blotted out the moon. A neck extended and the central head telescoped downwards so its cold, hard nose was pressed upside-down against my warm, wet one.

"Here's your champagne," boomed its chest speaker from above. The voice was so cultured, so polite, I almost felt reassured. Then a hole opened between the eyes of the middle head, and the muzzle of a gun emerged.

"Don't point the cork at me, now. Those things can be dangerous."

The dog's aim didn't waver. I could hear a hum inside its head as the weapon powered up. The pads of my paws went damp.

My eyes were fixed on the gun, but in my peripheral vision I was checking out the lay of the land. When I saw the muzzle tremble, in the instant before it discharged, I dropped and rolled, bowling past the other robot. She swung round, and the bolt meant for me struck her in the side so she staggered. I ran on all fours into the desert, following lines of shadow so I stayed invisible. If you were being kind you could say I planned to lead the robots away from Dawn and go back for her, but there wasn't much room in my head for thoughts other than my personal survival. My chest hurt from panting.

Robots have infrared vision, of course, and one of these robots had an unfair advantage in the leg department. At least it couldn't seem to run and shoot straight at the same time, I thought, as shot after shot zipped past my head.

Unless it was simply steering me in the direction it wanted me to go.

An arm, warm as flesh but solid and powerful, snagged me round the waist and scooped me off my feet. I struggled and scratched. Pain ripped through my left paw as a claw snagged on metal.

"Don't be naughty," warned the pleasure robot. Wires sparked in the hole at her side, and she smelled of burning. She held me off the ground, and I knew that she could take me apart, piece by piece, in ways that would make me squirm with enjoyment while she did it. At least Dawn…

I heard light footfalls in the sand behind me. Oh, the little *idiot*. Hyenas have more sense at a week old. I kept my ears from twitching at the sound, but the robots picked up on the vibration anyway, and two of the dogs' heads turned towards the girl as she ran up to us, arms pumping like she was trying to win a race. When she reached us she dug a hand in the pocket of her dungarees and pulled out her little mystery toy.

It was smooth and rounded, and sat in her hand like a pebble, but it was metal, and it glowed. It wasn't like anything I'd seen, which meant it was human tech. Dawn squeezed it, and the thing started to give a faint whistle right at the upper limit of my hearing.

It must have been too high-pitched for human ears, even child ones, because Dawn shook and tapped the device. Someone else could hear it, though.

The pressure on my arm eased. Both robots stood still, four heads turned to Dawn as if awaiting instruction.

"We need a solar panel," she said. "Can you help us?"

There was a pause, during which I died and came back to life three or four times. Then the dog pushed three noses into Dawn's hand, curled around her legs and, tail wagging, nudged her onto its too-long back, and the four of us set off.

"The offer still stands, you know," said the pleasure robot, conversationally.

"Huh? Oh. Er, no, thanks. Sorry about…" I gestured at the hole in her body.

"I shall self-repair."

Her voice wasn't so bad, really. Not when she wasn't threatening you.

They took us to a storage shed in the grounds of the resort. It smelled sterile, as if nobody had been in there for decades, and I grabbed a brand new solar panel. There was plenty of other stuff that could have fetched a good price in any river town, but I didn't want to get greedy and push my luck with the robots.

They escorted us to the edge of the desert, where the trees started to grow again, then they both stopped. They must have reached the limit of AI control.

"We must leave you now," said the humanoid. The dog whined and nuzzled our knees.

"They were nice, underneath," Dawn observed.

"Yeah, well, don't count on everyone being nice underneath. Some people are just rotten to the core."

The two robots headed back to their desert paradise, and we headed back to the *Star*. Everything was peachy. Except…

That little toy of Dawn's was pretty nifty. The right people could do a lot with a thing like that. The wrong people, even more. I doubted it could bring the whole of Pax on board, because Pax is vast and wily, but with control over even basic units like the ones we'd encountered, you could conquer new territory, raise a private army, whatever floated your boat.

"Where'd you get that thing?" She'd stuffed it back in her pocket, but she knew what I was talking about.

"Mom gave it to me. To keep me safe."

I thought about that for a moment. Her mother had found something so powerful and valuable that people would kill for it, and she'd given it to her little girl. To keep her safe? Or to keep it safe? Certainly she and the rest of her party had died for what they'd discovered, while Dawn had got away.

"The Watersnakes who attacked New Haven," I said. I thought of the burned homes, the injured and the dead. "They were after you all along."

And now they'd be after me.

"Come on, then. We've got a lot of miles to cover if we want to be out of this country by nightfall. Got your… thing all safe?"

She patted her pocket. "I didn't know it did that," she said. So she'd come after me with no real idea of what might happen. Fine, fine, she was a little hero. I opened my mouth to tell her so, but she wasn't done.

"Those… Watersnakes. They just roam around attacking towns like New Haven? Attacking people?"

"That's not for you to worry about." Just a couple more days and she'd be back up in her fancy sky city and out of my responsibility. At her age, give it a month and she'd forget all about me and the world down here.

"We could stop them. With this."

"Dawn, no. I have to get you safely back home before anything else happens." She stuck out her lower lip. I ignored it. "That's what Mama Bill told me to do. You wouldn't want me to disappoint Mama Bill, would you?"

"We could keep Mama Bill *safe*," she said.

"Revenge is a game for big people," I told her, looking down from my superior height. *And stupid people,* I might have added.

Dawn looked right back up at me, and I was the one who blinked first. "Who saved you?" she asked.

She had me there. Strictly, her device had saved me, but she didn't have to come tearing across the desert with it. But that was trouble we'd had to go into. No point deliberately setting out to look for more.

I'm not one for fighting. I don't have enemies of my own, and other people's quarrels are none of my business. I had to admit Dawn's plan was tempting, though. It would make things better for a big chunk of the country around here. But I couldn't drag a kid, let alone a skyside kid, into that quantity of trouble.

"Your paw's bleeding."

I looked down. I'd pulled out a claw, and blood was pouring from the sheath. It was a bit of a gory spectacle for a child.

"Sorry," I said, hiding it behind my back.

"Let me." She parted the matted fur on my finger, then tore strips from her shirt—my shirt—to make a pad and clumsy bandage. It hurt when she pressed it, and I growled a warning.

"There, there," she said, stroking my wrist. Fine, let her play nurse if it made her feel good. Might help her forget about her ridiculous plan.

No such luck.

"So can we?" she persisted.

"No, we cannot. We're going to Ambara Down and that's the end of it."

The glitter of water up ahead told me our little safari was nearly over. Dawn took off, racing towards the shore. I laid the solar panel down in the soft sand and chased after her, baring my teeth and snarling. She laughed. I laughed. I couldn't wait to throw myself in the river and wash the red dust out of my fur.

"Chuck!" Dawn yelled, skidding to a stop. I followed her pointing finger. The water wasn't the only thing glittering.

The warship was bigger than any Watersnake craft I'd ever seen before, and I've dodged plenty in my time. This was a coastal raider, built for the open sea. It was armored, and armed. Boy was it armed. The decks were studded with cannon, and the muzzles of more stared threateningly at us from portholes. It floated on the wide Wampo like a croc in a handbasin. I wondered why it didn't sink.

They'd scooped up the *Star of the Savannah* with a crane and plopped it down on the deck. My little livelihood looked small and out of place, sitting in a pool of muddy water.

A gangplank extended from their deck, sloping downwards to the shore.

"Put your hands on your heads and come on board. Both of you."

That wasn't the easiest thing to do. The plank was narrow and the river was choppy. I made Dawn walk ahead of me, so I could grab her if she fell. To my surprise and alarm, rather than look terrified as she should, she was wearing a sly little smile.

"*Don't* do anything stupid," I whispered to her without much hope, in the seconds before claws dug into my mane and hauled me over to where the captain stood, with a helpful shove so I sprawled at his hindpaws. I picked myself up.

I'm not one to make sweeping generalisations, but, as a rule, well-adjusted kids from nice homes don't end up Watersnakes. Even I managed to pick myself a different career path, if you can call it that.

The captain was a lion, with a chestnut mane rolling down his barrel chest and disappearing into his shirt. His left upper canine overlapped his lower lip, and there was a dent in the bridge of his nose. I glanced around as best I could with my head held firm, trying to take stock of how many crew there were and my likeliest escape route. 'Lots' and 'none', I concluded.

One of the crew held Dawn by the wrists, but loosely; perhaps he had a kid of his own somewhere, or perhaps he didn't but always wanted one. She returned this kindness by stomping backwards on his foot, wrenching her arms free, and grabbing her gizmo from her front pocket. Dramatically, she thrust it towards the pirates, squeezing hard with both hands. My ears flicked at the high whistle. The captain's, I noticed, didn't.

Nothing happened. I guess the thing only worked on ancient tech, not Watersnake warships.

"That it? Doesn't look so great to me," said the captain. "This had better be worth it. You've led us a chase, young lady. Now hand it over."

"No," said Dawn, predictably.

"Dawn!" I held out my paws as I ran, and she threw the thing into them. It wasn't a bad shot, for a little kid. Underarm, of course.

"Let her go," I said, dangling my paw over the side of the ship. "Let her go or I toss this in and it's just a pebble among millions."

The captain looked from Dawn to me to the *Star of the Savannah*. "How about a swap?" he proposed. "Your hoverskiff for the device. Otherwise we'll strip her for parts."

Dawn had the decency to look stricken.

"Your lovely boat," she said, staring at the deck between her feet.

"The *Star* is only a thing," I told her, not even bothering to correct her to 'skiff'. Soon it wouldn't matter anyway.

I wasn't too fussed about what the crew might do to me. While I'd been hoping for a few more years of kicking about the river, I'd had more than my share of good times and it had to end eventually. I was too stringy to look like I might be useful on their crew, and too ugly to be a slave, so they'd probably just kill me straight away.

Dawn, though. If she was lucky, they'd simply demand a ransom from her family. If she wasn't… it didn't bear thinking about.

The captain walked across to inspect my vessel. I could tell he didn't approve. Luckily, I didn't care much for the opinion of a murdering cutthroat with a big, flashy ship that probably steered itself and made him a mug of cocoa while it did.

"Start taking her apart," he ordered his crew. "Piece by little piece. I want him to see it." His tone suggested that after I'd watched my skiff get torn apart, it would be Dawn's turn to watch *me* get torn apart.

He stalked over to the *Star* and placed a paw on the wheel.

"I wouldn't do that if I were you," I said softly.

The white sliver of tooth poking over the captain's lip waxed like the moon as he began to smile, then grin. "Why not? What are you going to do about it, tough guy?"

"Don't!" Dawn yelled, stamping her foot.

The lion's grin widened. He looked straight at the little girl, his tail lashing smugly, and laughed and laughed. His crew joined in. I could tell it was more out of fear than from genuine mirth on their part, but it's still not a pleasant experience being the target of so much hilarity. Dawn's cheeks flushed and her flat, immobile ears went pink. Humans are pretty cute when they're embarrassed, it turns out.

Muscles standing out beneath his bronze fur, the captain wrenched the wheel from its socket with one yank and held it above his head. His jaws opened for a triumphant roar.

It never came.

I'd been braced for the blast, but it still made me stagger and blink. I recovered faster than the crew, though. All sound muffled, as if I was underwater. I jabbed the crewman who held me with my elbow, and he staggered back. Dawn's captor had fallen backwards and Dawn herself was crouched with her eyes shut tight and her hands over her ears. As the deck caved in and the fire spread from my former home and livelihood to the pirate vessel, I sprang for Dawn, grabbed her, and vaulted the rail.

As we crashed into the water, a second explosion lit the greasy surface yellow and set a huge wave rolling. I wrapped both arms around Dawn and felt myself dragged along the gravel bottom of the river, blinded by mud and silt with water shooting up my nose. I couldn't tell which way was up—I just had to hope the breath in my lungs would be enough to float me out of this.

My head and ribs bumped against something solid. I grabbed a pawful of mud, slipped, tried again and hooked a tree root with my good paw. Soaking wet, Dawn seemed to weigh a ton, and so did I. I hauled us both out onto the bank somehow, flopping and wheezing like a sealion.

"Okay?" I asked.

Dawn considered for a second. Her face crumpled. Quickly, I laid my injured paw in her lap. She took it and patted it, then her eyes widened and she grabbed her good luck charm from where I'd tucked it into the bandages. In her excitement she snagged the wound in my finger, but by this point I didn't care.

Where the other ship had been, there were only lumps of burned and shattered wreckage. As we watched, long, dark shapes like tapered logs propelled themselves towards the center of the action.

The crocodiles were moving in.

* * *

Ambara Down is far bigger and more impressive than any furry settlement, and that's after it bust itself up dropping out of the sky.

The inhabitants were a varied lot, and I'd never been that fussed about my appearance anyway, but I still felt out of place in a city where everyone seemed to know exactly where they were going and to be in a huge hurry to get there.

The clumsy bandage round my paw didn't help. Nor did the fact that our clothes were a collection of mud-streaked tatters. I'd tried my best to tidy Dawn up a little after we hiked the remaining miles to the city, but a bunch of her little plaits had come undone and I wasn't really sure how human hair worked.

"Will you get another boat? I mean skiff?"

"Yeah. The *Star of the Savannah* mark two. Better in every way."

That was the end of that conversation. Dawn had been getting quieter and quieter as we approached Ambara, and I was occupied with calculating how long it would take me to get the funds to set myself up again.

Lights reflected along the waterfront from buildings that seemed to go on and on. I steered us up a street lined with little shops selling fruit, clothes and toys from overseas, and cafés serving coffee and pastries. My nose twitched at all the smells.

"Pretty, isn't it?" I said. Usually I can go days without speaking to anyone, but Dawn's hush was getting on my nerves.

She didn't respond. I guess she'd seen more impressive sights in her short life. We turned away from the dockland area, with its feel of movement and impermanence, into a smarter business district.

"Is your home like this—Westwind?" I tried.

That did it.

"I don't want to go back," she burst out. "I want to stay with you!"

I should have listed all the reasons she needed to go. She needed an education. She needed a human family. She needed protection until she was big and ugly enough to deal with the world.

But the truth was, I didn't want her to go back either.

It would have been the easiest thing in the world to turn around and walk away with Dawn, back to the river, and I'd been taking the easy option all my life.

"Well, you have to," I told her, snarling through my teeth and looking as wild and ferocious as I could.

"We could be a team," she told me. "That was so cool, what you did with those pirates. Are you going to keep doing it?"

"Heck, no. That was strictly a one-time deal. I'm going straight back to the way things were before you turned up. The simple life."

She smiled as if she didn't believe me.

"Keep safe," she said, and tucked her hand deep in my jacket pocket. We walked into the Prefect's Office like that.

The receptionist looked at us as if we were a couple of wild animals, but summoned the Reclamation Project liaison officer on duty. She took us to a quietly tasteful office and brought me a coffee and Dawn a glass of milk. We sat sipping politely while she bashed away at her computer, her eyebrows lifting higher with each file she opened. At last, she looked up.

"I'm delighted to tell you," she said, sounding anything but, "that there's a reward for the safe return of the little girl."

"I don't need that," I told her, as much to my own surprise as anyone else's. "She pretty much returned herself. I just came along for the ride."

"Take the money!" Dawn muttered from somewhere around my elbow. "For the *Star of the Savannah* mark two!"

"Ow! Okay!"

"We'll look after her from now on," said the officer. "Come here, sweetie."

"Good luck with that." I gave Dawn's arm a little pinch as she hopped off her seat.

"Now, how did Dawn come to enter your custody, and what exactly has been happening since then? Can you give us a statement for our records, please, Mr…Chuck?"

I shoved my paws deep in my pockets. The right one met the smooth, cool surface of Dawn's gadget.

"Sure." I grinned at her. "Looking forward to it."

THE FLAVORS OF SUNLIGHT

James L. Steele

Years ago, Angle's body had begun to taste sunlight. It had been six years since she had joined the Sokin Islands, and it still amazed her. Sometimes she caught herself chewing on it, and she wondered if she would ever forget what it was like to eat, and if sunlight would always have flavor that varied depending on time of day and season. Doctor Sokin and the other scientists told her that was a side effect, but Angle now considered it the best part of the process.

She lay on the deck, eyes closed, tasting the light. In her previous life she had avoided direct sunlight, as her black fur overheated and made her miserable. She hadn't felt overheated in years; her body now used the light instead of fighting it, leaving her feeling strangely normal even during the heat of the day in the middle of the ocean.

Angle listened to the water lapping against the boats, and the creaking of the loose rope bridges that joined the four of them together in a square. Large ships, once used as luxury yachts, all stolen from people who had more than one, so they likely never noticed the yachts were missing.

The sun disappeared behind some clouds, and her mouth felt empty. She opened her eyes and sat up. The clouds were extensive, so it would be a while before she ate again. The others were also getting up and returning to tasks. It seemed to have become a consensus among the Islanders that sunlight was a time to eat and shade was a time to work. Now it looked like the sky would remain overcast for some time, so Angle rose to her feet and stretched.

She looked down her arms, at the strips of green gel running from her wrists up her forearms, around the sides of her triceps and biceps and then around the front and back of her neck. The bright green of the algae contrasted with her black fur, and its faint glow was visible even during the day. The plants themselves secreted a protective coating that effectively separated itself from her body, but blood vessels ran through it. She even had sensation back as nerves had regrown through it, and she could feel her fingers touching this colony of gelatinous life growing in her.

She turned and looked up one deck. Enti was rising from his lounge chair, green lines of algae running up his arms and around his neck. Angle had never liked 'Claimers even when she lived among them, but that had been a previous life. Species lines tended to vanish here on the Sokin Islands. Now that they all had something in common, the differences did not seem to matter.

Enti waved to her and Angle waved back.

People were rising from chairs on the other ships as well. Nobody wore clothing, and some even had to trim their long fur so they wouldn't cover the algae. Hezor and Ura, husband and wife, were rising under the cloudy sky after basking half the morning. Hezor had to keep his mane cut, and he looked so thin without it, but the trade off had been worthwhile. Both of these lions had been criminals in their home country, and now Angle heard music coming from the boat they were on. Hezor was teaching himself to play an instrument, something he never would have been able to do in his previous life. There were only twenty-seven Islanders spread out between the four boats, and Angle had enjoyed watching all these castaways become new people.

The blue water nudged the boats, and the rope bridge turned and stretched, keeping the yachts from drifting apart. Angle held on and observed Diaon climbing the stairs and taking position on the bridge, binoculars raised and scanning the ocean.

On the far yacht, Sokin and two of her fellow scientists rose from their beds. Angle smirked at the sight of 'Claimers taking orders from an avian. Years ago, Angle herself had had a difficult time with Sokin, but any bird who would willingly pluck her own feathers and replace them with a trench of green gel going all the way down to the bone was worth listening to.

Angle was the only one still above deck when the sky darkened again: a military transport was lowering itself silently from the clouds a few hundred meters overhead.

"Soldiers!" Angle shouted. "Soldiers! Soldiers!"

Claws clicked over the four decks. People were sealing the science labs on each yacht and opening the defense stores. The Islanders kept no offensive weapons on the ships, as they could easily be used against them and required too many outside materials to manufacture. All they had were flash and smoke bombs.

Angle crossed the rope bridge as fast as she could, and she was nearly across when someone dropped to the deck in front of her, landing hard. The implants in the attacking lizard's legs compensated for the fall, and she then rose to full height, spreading her hands and showing her claws. The lizard wore the blue clothing of a Parassi enforcer, one of the 'Claimer cities still afloat above the clouds. Only the soldier's head and muzzle were uncovered, showing red and green scales. She had puffy jowls, and she flicked her forked tongue at Angle. A tegu.

Angle held on to the bridge and met the soldier's eyes. Smoke bombs detonated on the ships around her, and the yachts became covered in clouds. The lizard reached down and slashed at the ropes with her claws. Angle stood on one rope and coiled her legs. Just as it began to fall away, she leaped long, sailing straight into the lizard. The soldier held her claws ready just as Angle slammed into her chest and they tumbled into the cloud.

No vision here in the white smoke. Only scent and touch would help her. Angle did not give this soldier a chance—she clamped her mouth on whatever scales she could find. Angle felt claws raking her back and face. She heard feet stomping all around her as she wrestled with this lizard.

Angle bit. She kicked. She bit again and again.

Claws dug through her fur and pierced her leg.

Angle bit again.

The lizard choked and fell limp.

Angle untangled herself and scooted away, feeling through the smoke, gasping. She heard screaming and thumping from the other yachts. Moments later, the sounds of footsteps ceased, and the clouds began to dissipate in the wind. Angle smelled blood, and she saw eight other lizards and four 'Claimers sending streamers into the air. In a moment, the magnets on the end entered the magnetic field of the ship overhead, and the soldiers shot upward and out of reach.

Angle turned around. The scaled soldier lay on the ground, bleeding from a wound on the side of her neck. She was holding it with one hand, trying to stop the blood.

"One survivor," Angle called.

The second rope bridge had not been cut, and people began to migrate from the yachts. Some of the Islanders began to detach them and prepare the ships to relocate. The Parassi ship was already gone, leaving them alone under an overcast sky. Angle yearned to taste sunshine again.

Two of the scientists stood over the fallen lizard now. The 'Claimer and the avian nodded, and then lifted her. Angle ran ahead of them and opened the doors below deck to the lab.

Each vessel had an identical lab, where the kitchens used to be, allowing the team of scientists to continue their work no matter which one they were on. Faster than Angle could comprehend, the scientists had the lizard strapped to an exam bed and were already working on disinfecting the wound.

The lizard lay snout up, staring at the ceiling, black eyes wide in pain. Angle leaned inside the door frame, watching the scientists work. It was some time later when the bleeding stopped, and the two scientists stepped back and gave the tegu room to breathe. When she realized she was not about to die after all, she raised her head.

"Are you coherent?" Sokin asked.

The lizard closed her mouth. She gasped, testing her voice, and then she spoke. "I am."

"Who sent you?"

She tested her breathing, taking deeper and deeper breaths. She flicked her tongue once at the avian scientist, and then again in the direction of the 'Claimer. "Does it matter? Everyone has a price on your heads."

"How did you find us?"

"We have our ways."

"They left awful quickly. Why?"

This question seemed to amuse the lizard. She huffed through her nose in laughter. "We did what we came here to do."

"Which was?"

"I've said enough. Do with me what you will."

"Your uniform is Parassi. Do you work for them, or is this a false flag?"

"I serve the city of Parassi. As far as my commanders are concerned, I am dead, so what happens to me now doesn't matter."

Sokin turned to Enti. The 'Claimer nodded, and then the avian turned back to the tegu strapped to the table.

"You have two options. We can send you adrift, or you can join us."

She took a deep breath. "I am prepared to be your next victim."

"Victim?" Enti asked. "What did they tell you about us?"

"That you are terrorists researching biological weapons. Turning people into unknowing, living carriers of toxic substances and explosives. Ambara fell from the sky because of you."

Sokin pointed to the trench of faintly glowing algae under her chin, and then gestured to the lines running down each arm. "See these? This is the research we are doing here."

The tegu dreamily looked it over, and then looked over everyone in the room. She gave Angle the hardest stare. Angle become conscious of her own lines, and she glanced at her arms. Some of the algae had fallen out in the fight, revealing her bare bones and muscle tissue beneath. She could feel the liquid flora growing to fill in the gaps. The tegu seemed just now to realize all three Islanders had these lines of algae.

"What is that?" said the lizard.

Sokin touched a feathered hand to her scaly muzzle. "I'll be blunt with you. Anyone who comes here either helps us with our research, or leaves. I have tested on reptiles before, but not on a tegu. The more subjects, the faster the research progresses. That will be your life from now on if you decide to remain here. There is a risk of rejection, but if successful, you will never need to eat again."

She looked from person to person, tracing the trenches of green with her eyes, flicking her tongue. "What does this have to do with eating?"

Sokin nodded. "The 'Claimers have been telling people I'm a terrorist. 'Doctor Sokin Te'ana, insane scientist turning people into weapons.' They're afraid of what I'm trying to do, and now that they've exaggerated the science, everyone believes we're creating living vessels of nerve gas, or carriers of rare diseases, or what have you. Spend some time with us, and we will show you what we're doing."

"It works," Enti said, tracing the lines on his arm. He stuck a finger into one of his arms and scooped out a tiny bit of algae. He held it up to the tegu. She flicked her tongue at it, recoiling. "I haven't had to eat a single bite in eleven years. The algae produces energy for my body. We have vats that produce power for the boats. We use it for everything."

"If we save your life," Sokin continued, "you will never need food again, only sunlight. In exchange, you will use whatever talents you learned in your previous life to help us create a new future. Otherwise, you will be free to pursue whatever interests you."

She flicked her tongue at the algae again. She did not recoil. She flicked again. Again.

"This is ridiculous. Parassi sent us here over some algae researchers? Just throw me over the next piece of garbage that floats by. I'll take my chances in the water."

Sokin turned to the door.

"What is your name?" Angle asked.

The two scientists stopped and looked at her.

The lizard regarded the black rabbit with another hard stare. "Teal."

"I'm Angle."

She blinked. "Don't you mean *Angel*?"

Her ears danced in laughter. She huffed through her nose a few times to simulate Teal's way of laughing. "My parents misspelled my name on the birth certificate. My name is Angle, and I have worn it with pride since I was little. When I joined the Alikant enforcers, if anyone called me Angel, I shot them in the foot."

For the first time, Teal seemed interested.

Angle turned to the scientists. "Let me speak with her alone."

Sokin gave her a look that asked if she was sure.

"Please, leave us."

Enti and Sokin opened the door and climbed up the steps, closing it behind them. Angle stepped away from the wall and stood by Teal's side.

"Alikant?" Teal said.

"I served under Vars the Sixth."

"His son is now on the throne. Vars the Seventh."

"Did number six die on his own, or did his wife finally kill him?"

Teal huffed. "His wife threw him overboard during a thunderstorm. They show the video every year on the anniversary of his coronation."

Angle leaned on the bed and laughed in both her own way and Teal's. "I knew it. I knew it was only a matter of time before she finally stood up to him. Things are better these days, I hope?"

"An enforcer of a 'Claimer city does not have an opinion on her allies' ruling elites, but I will say that I did not mourn when I heard he had been murdered."

Angle met her eyes. Her puffy cheeks looked adorable. The tegu seemed fixated on the hollowed out trench in her arm. Angle guessed Teal was watching the algae grow back.

After a moment of awkward silence, Teal finally spoke. "Our alliance became stronger after Vars the Sixth passed away. What is an enforcer of Alikant doing here?"

"When I served, Alikant had control of eight communities. It had been in the sky above my nation since before I was born. I was tired of farming the land and paying two-thirds of our food up to the city as tribute. The 'Claimers recruit native species to keep the people in line. I proved I didn't mind forcing others to do things I would never do. They let me live up there with them six months out of the year. Wasn't a bad arrangement if you ignore the slurs."

"And then?"

"One day my patrol ship took a missile from the surface. I ended up adrift at sea for a week. Then Sokin scooped me out of the water and made me an offer. They told me they were doing research that would change the world. If it worked, I would never have to eat again. That was six years ago."

"You're serious."

"They're not just doing research on algae. They're researching symbiotic relationships."

"What?"

Angle leaned closer. "Now's a good time to look back on your life and ask what you've been doing this whole time. You got to live in the clouds while your fellow people raised the meat and planted the corn. Are you proud of that?"

Teal leaned back. "I did what I had to do to get out of it. Same as you."

"I can't stand what I became. I was cracking the whip over my own relatives. I shot people who raised their voice to me. I raided the homes of people who were merely rumored to be plotting against the 'Claimers. Getting shot out of the air was the best thing that ever happened to me."

"Humans have cities that fly. We don't really have a choice but to do as they say."

"We pay them more than half our crops, and what do we get in return? Protection from other 'Claimer cities? If all the 'Claimers went away, we wouldn't need protection in the first place. I don't know how Parassi does things, but I had to give up everything just to escape the farms and the mines. I wanted to be an artist when I was young."

Teal laughed. "An artist?"

"I never had time to do it before. Not in the city; had to spend six months recovering from wrecking my body for the previous six months. Definitely not when I was enforcing quotas and following up on rumors of uprisings. Here I can finally take back what I had to leave behind. How about you? What did you have to give up to live above it all?"

Teal lay with her eyes closed for a long time. Angle began to worry she had failed to get through to the lizard, but finally Teal took a breath.

"Before I joined… It's hard to remember a time before. The 'Claimers on Parassi make us mine salt and metal for them. Our house was raided. Rumors my father was talking to terrorists. He wasn't, but they killed him anyway. I decided I didn't want to be a victim, so I joined them." She laughed. "I remember I had dreams of settling down with a nice partner and having his eggs. That's it. That's all I really wanted to do. Back then, I didn't know any children I had would have just been sent down to the mines. Didn't realize the elders had a place for people like me."

"What place?"

Teal opened her eyes and turned to Angle. Her gaze was softer now. "The schools exist to find out what task we are best suited for. I was on track to be a breeder. I wouldn't have had a partner. I would have spent my life in a a single room, having eggs and watching them snatched from me. I almost became that. Didn't find out until after I joined the enforcers."

"You could have that."

"What, a life as an incubator?"

"Well, no, I mean settling down with someone. Everyone is doing something here. We'll give you a family again. Would you like that? A place to belong? A place you're not despised? Nobody here has to eat, so you are free to do anything you want."

Teal blinked a few times. Angle reached out and felt her jowl, muzzle to muzzle with her.

"I'll help you adjust. I promise."

"I tried to kill you."

"Look me in the eye and tell me you want to go back."

Teal looked her in the eye but did not speak.

"We're always looking for people we can pull from the water," Angle continued. "I believe we're part of the future, and that is something I can be proud of. Would you like to be proud of something you've done?"

Teal took a long breath through her nose. "What do you mean the future?"

"The scientists here are researching a way to modify the genes of this algae to completely incorporate it into our bodies. Right now, it's not a closed system. It still needs maintenance, and it can fall out if you move wrong, but I haven't had to eat in six years. It works."

Teal flicked her tongue over Angle's muzzle. "And you'd rather be here than up in Alikant?"

"For the first time in my life, I am proud of where I am and what I'm doing. Once you taste sunlight for the first time, you'll understand."

Teal flicked her tongue again. "I'm interested."

"Sokin and the others can explain it more." Angle straightened up and moved to the door. "I hope to see you again soon."

She opened the door. Sokin and Enti were standing just outside. Angle nodded to both of them, and they filed back inside. Angle ascended the stairs, smiling with her ears.

The boats were moving at full speed in formation. Angle saw nothing but ocean all around, making it impossible to be sure they were moving. The sky had darkened, and Angle craved sunlight. Shafts of light peeked through the clouds and danced on the ocean like water spouts. Angle sat and planted herself on the top stair, hoping they would catch up to one of these gaps so she could taste *amire*, a rare form of sunlight whose flavor would stop all activity on all the yachts no matter what people were doing.

Hours later, they approached the back edge of the clouds. Angle stood up and waited to greet the light. As soon as the light touched her, Angle felt alive again, and she chewed on it. She opened one eye and observed the algae covering the exposed bone in her arm, and then climbing up the walls until it was even again. The algae replenished, and life moved into her veins again.

Angle helped them attach the spare bridge, and all four ships now rested in the open water, drifting together as a single vessel. She then helped them clean up the blood and salvage what little they could from the attack. It had only been the eleventh time they had been attacked since she arrived. They remained on the move as often as possible, as so many people wanted these scientists dead, and the open water was the safest place for them to hide.

Angle knew from experience she would not see Teal again for at least a couple weeks, and she couldn't take her mind off the tegu. Angle's paintings had taken a turn, which she only realized when she lined up a week's worth end to end. For years, since she had begun to explore her artistic side, she had been painting the flavors of light. The concept fascinated her, and she had been discussing it with Atile. Everyone had the same feelings as she, but they lacked words for it. Angle had been coming up with words for all the different varieties. Some of these words had caught on, and she hoped with enough connections between taste and vision, they would have a new language. Something to distinguish themselves from everyone else. Something cultural instead of physical.

Her paintings had shifted in tone recently. No longer about trying to capture the flavor of light in imagery, but overcast skies and light trying to break through.

She began to paint Teal under these overcast skies. She had not seen what was under her clothing, so she kept it hidden in shadow. All she drew of her body was the lines of the algae that would run up both arms and ring the neck. A black, featureless body with a muzzle and face lit from underneath in a faint, green glow.

She created nine portraits of Teal in this style, all of them under cloudy skies. By now she had exhausted her supply of algae-derived pigment and canvas. She would have to return to digital painting until she could make more, and even then she did not want to rely on computer systems very much, as they would not last forever and were horribly obsolete by now.

Angle was basking in the morning sunlight when she heard creaking across the bridge. She opened her eyes to see Teal stepping across the rope rungs. Her clothes were gone, and her red and green scales shined in the sun. She was gripping the handrail, straining to hold herself upright. Sokin followed her, holding her tail above the rungs and nudging her forward. She had lines of algae up her arms, over her shoulders, and around her neck.

Angle swung her legs over the chair, sitting up just as Teal stepped onto the deck. With much discomfort, Teal stood on her own, panting, forked tongue dangling freely.

"Welcome to the Islands, Teal."

"So far this is shit."

"It gets better."

Angle held her by the arm and led her to one of the lounge chairs. Teal leaned on her and walked, slinking to the deck with every step. Angle lowered her into one of the chairs. The tegu's body looked nothing like Angle imagined. She thought Teal would have solid scales, but her body was green with red swirls.

Teal lay still on the chair, panting in the sunlight. As her first time out of the lab since surgery began, Angle knew this first taste of light was the most precious. She hoped Teal would remember it as fondly as she herself did. Angle sat on the other chair and looked her over. Her ears danced.

"Nice leg implants. Did they augment the rest of your muscles, too?"

"No." She lay still and breathed for a moment. "I'm just that way."

"Alikant doesn't do cybernetic implants. Too many complications."

"Wise of them. I've had four surgeries. Took three months to recover from one of them."

"Sokin might have to remove them."

"Good. I've had a lot of time to think about what you said. To realize… The only way to escape the farms and the mines was to force other people to do it. To point guns at my own people and make them do what I didn't want to do. Parassi did six months on, six months off as well. The last few years, the months off were worse than the months on. The enforcers have their own district on Parassi, and it's a shithole. You'd think the 'Claimers would be grateful for us, but a week didn't go by I didn't hear a racial slur. Whatever this place is, it must be better." She took a few breaths and then reached up. "Angle…"

The rabbit leaned closer.

"This feels amazing. I've been out in the sun before, and it never…"

Angle stood up and moved over Teal, casting a shadow over her. Teal opened her eyes. Angle's ears were dancing. She moved out of the way, and the sun hit Teal directly again. The tegu shuddered and stretched out, exposing as much of the algae to the light as possible.

"Angle, that feels so good."

"*Tu'melé.*"

"What?"

"It's a word I came up with for this kind of sunlight, when it's clear in the morning and the sun is still low. When it rises a little, the flavor changes to *miremé*. Hotter, spicier."

"I don't know about that, but… What's happening?"

"The algae is giving you energy. Your brain is interpreting it as food."

"It works? It really works?"

"We're not building weapons here. We have not brought any cities down."

"The price on your head is astronomical! Why the stories? Why is everyone after you? This is incredible."

"Rest for now. Your body will tell you when you've basked enough. You'll be bunking with me for now. I'll show you my paintings."

"I think… I think I'd like that. I'd like to see how a former enforcer of the Reclamation deals with her demons."

"I cuddle with them until they stop complaining."

Teal laughed. "I think I like you, rabbit."

She drifted off to sleep, a normal reaction to someone's first taste of sunlight. Teal wasn't tired. She was overwhelmed with joy.

Angle leaned back in the chair and watched the water. The phantom sensation on her tongue changed from *tu'melé* to *miremé* and then to *a'vieré*. Normally Angle would have gone below by now and begun painting, or helping Xisha monitor radio transmissions, or helping Bedford translate and copy the forbidden texts—the ones computer systems automatically deleted upon detection, so physical copies were all that remained.

Finally, Teal stirred and sat bolt upright. Angle turned to her. Teal was looking at her arms. She felt around her neck and turned to Angle. "You said you had paintings to show me?"

Angle rose from the chair, offering her hand. Teal reached out, and Angle took the chance to feel her claws—the same ones that could have ended her life not too long ago.

She led Teal below deck and into one of the cabins, full to bursting with canvases. Angle showed her the cultivation corner, where she grew batches of algae, dried them out, and flattened them into paper-like substances. Another corner held her paint station. Teal's attention immediately went to her newest works. She picked one up and held it, the painting of Teal in shadow, standing on the ocean, lit by glowing lines of liquid plant life up her arms and around her neck.

Teal was practically falling into the painting. "This is good."

"I haven't filled in the details yet," Angle said. "I will soon. Or should I leave it this way?"

"Leave it. If you try to add more, you'll probably ruin it."

"That's always my fear. I use the digital paints to experiment. I only work in physical media when I know what I want to do."

Teal turned to the other paintings around the room. Renderings of the 'Claimer cities, portraits of people living here, more abstract works. Angle related the story behind each painting Teal picked up. Eventually, they added up to the story of her life. Even the vent works had real expression behind them: people she had killed, families she had separated, all in the name of the 'Claimers who controlled the sky above their land. One time she had painted a 'Claimer city dripping blood down to the land below.

The sun had gone down. Angle offered her the lower bunk. Teal climbed inside and reclined. Angle was about to hop into the top bunk, but Teal held out her arm. Angle's ears danced and she slid next to her. They lay together.

"I haven't eaten in two weeks," Teal said. "I don't feel… This is a little frightening."

Angle held her harder, lying with her head against Teal's jowl. "I was scared, too."

"How did you handle it? The algae, coming to terms with your life being over."

"Everyone helped me through it. Tomorrow I'll introduce you to them."

Teal held up her arm and looked at her forearm. "It glows."

"Yes, it does."

"Why doesn't it hurt? How does it stay inside?"

"Sokin and her team are altering its genes so your body thinks the algae is part of itself."

"I'm… I'm speechless."

Angle rubbed her cheek against Teal's. Teal lowered her arm and felt the fur on Angle's stomach.

The next morning, Angle took Teal on a tour of the yachts. Their first stop was the cabin of Xisha, a lavender-furred canine from Ambara Down who had salvaged some new electronics from the last dive and was cleaning them up. Teal seemed surprised that some old transmissions were still going, coming from satellites placed in orbit well before the days of High Humanity. Xisha was working on documenting these transmissions, most of which were on frequencies far too low to be useful today. He was also monitoring current transmissions. He stopped short of saying which ones he had decrypted.

Hezor and Ura occupied the next cabin. The two lions had surrounded themselves with musical instruments. Hezor knew how to play some of them, and he was working on others. All his life he had wandered in the never-ending search for money so he could buy things but never had any time to enjoy what he bought. Now he was free to pursue what he always wanted to do.

Sheet music lay rolled up everywhere, some of it hanging from the ceiling and drying. Ura was transcribing what they could find from the old human cities that lay beneath the water. Ura had also salvaged some old equipment and was working on ways to play recorded music. She played some for them while Hezor rested his hands. It must have sounded like music to human ears in previous centuries, for it made no sense now. Still, Teal was enamored. 'Claimers seemed to go out of their way to destroy relics like these, so to hear this moment from the past was truly special.

Others were on deck. Some were working on old computer equipment. Others were reading books, some recent, others salvaged from the water. Still others were just basking.

By now they had come back to the yacht where Angle's cabin was, and they leaned on the prow, looking out at the endless water.

"Looks like you've built your own 'Claimer city right here. Everybody's free to tinker and lounge about."

"If we want," Angle said. "All that's really required of us is to let the scientists poke and prod us whenever they need to."

"How often is that?"

"Not as often as it used to be. They've found something that works well, and it doesn't need a lot of intervention anymore."

"It's past midday, and I feel full. I still can't believe this. Every 'Claimer in the sky wants you dead for this?"

Angle turned around and leaned facing Teal. "Anything interest you?"

"All of it. 'Claimers don't care much for the relics of their own culture. They only care about the big technology. I shot dozens of people for possession of forbidden tech. Music was one of them."

"I thought I felt you twinge when you heard it."

Teal sighed through her nose. "Habit. I was reaching for my gun." Teal reached behind Angle's back and pulled her close. "I haven't really had anyone to talk to about any of this. City of a million of people, and I was all alone."

Angle held Teal around her waist. "None of the other tegu wanted to talk to you?"

"I couldn't stand how they smelled. We didn't even like looking at each other."

"I felt the same way about my people living up there. We can talk whenever you're ready. I haven't even painted half the sins I committed. Would you like to see the labs?"

"I spent two weeks in there. I think I've seen enough."

"Then let's go back to my bunk. If you don't mind, I'd like to do at least one real life portrait of you."

Teal laughed. "Why not? I have nothing else to do."

The tegu lay on the bed and posed for three quick portraits, all digital. Angle was not confident enough yet with her scale pattern to render her in paint, and she was nearly out of it.

When the sun started to set, Teal rose from the bed and walked up to the deck. Angle followed. Teal stood facing the setting sun, clutching the handrail.

"It feels so different."

Angle leaned against her, holding her hand. "I've counted fifty-five distinct flavors. Depends on the weather, temperature, time of day. Even mood affects how sunlight tastes. This light tastes like *a'rethi*."

Teal hung her head, letting the ring around the back of her neck have a taste. She leaned on Angle. "I'm not eating, but I still feel full. It's confusing."

The next morning, they woke up with the sun hitting both of them through the porthole. Teal lay on top of Angle. The rabbit wrapped her arms around the lizard and nuzzled her snout.

"You want to model for me again?"

"Actually, I've been thinking about Ura… and the music."

"Even better."

They held hands as they feasted on the *tu'melé*.

When they eventually got out of bed and crossed the bridge, they heard the scratchy sound of ancient music being played. Teal trembled, but she sat down and listened to it. Ura had cleaned the vinyl disc off and had figured out a way to play it from descriptions of old books fished out of the water. Most of the discs began to crumble as soon as they touched air, so she was copying the music to a computer before the vinyl deteriorated too much to play.

Teal sat and listened. She trembled. Angle held her. Teal seemed to be forcing herself to remain still. Angle felt her scales up and down the whole time.

Close to sunset, they went on deck and crossed the rope bridge. Angle wanted to ask, but Teal seemed to be struggling to catch her breath. They lay in bed together and enjoyed the last taste of *a'vieré*.

"I never did figure out why the 'Claimers told us to kill anyone who had old relics like that," Teal said, shaking in the hot cabin. "I can't tell you how many times I heard music like that just before I killed someone. I hear it now, and all I can hear is blood. I can hear blood, Angle."

"I understand."

"I will listen to as much of that shit as I need to figure out why I had to kill them."

Angle turned and lay snout to snout with her. Teal flicked her tongue. Angle nipped her on the nose. They pulled one another closer.

Teal endured days of music. Each day she seemed less and less agitated. Then Sokin brought her down to one of the labs and took samples of blood and tissue and algae. When she came back, Teal did not feel like going back to Ura. Angle noticed a hesitation in her step. In bed, she scented the lizard. She was still anxious, but it seemed to wane in her arms.

Nothing felt better than waking up to *tu'melé*, but the water had a mist over it, making it taste different.

"*Ti'mer*," Angle said as the morning rays woke her. "That's the word I used to describe this. Doesn't seem to be catching on. Can you think of a better word?"

Teal lay silent for a while. Angle felt her jowl. Teal grumbled. "Does it need a name?"

"Would be nice to describe what we're feeling."

Teal licked Angle's ears. "So long as it's filling."

Having had her taste of ancient music, Teal now began learning how the drive the yachts, laughing as she listened to the stories of how they stole each boat. They closed the day with Teal posing for

Angle in the dark so she could paint her exactly as the glow from the algae made her look.

"Angle, there's something I want to ask you."

The rabbit was using real paint on real canvas, and she was painting the green highlights that flicked across the lizard's hips. Angle noticed Teal was trembling. She had been doing this off and one for the last few days, clenching her hands. Teal was trying to hide it even now, but Angle could see it even in the darkness.

"If I told you how to give me eggs, would you please?"

Angle held the brush still. She smiled. "I thought you'd never ask."

"You can trick my body into making a clutch. I want to feel it. I want to know."

"I will help you."

"Thank you. Thank you so much. It's… It makes me nervous just thinking about it. When I found out what this kind of life this curiosity would have doomed me to, I buried the desire. I never told anyone about it. I was afraid if anyone found out, they'd send me back to the surface."

Angle hoped that was why she was nervous.

Teal told her exactly what to do, and the next day, when she felt comfortable being vulnerable, she allowed Angle to do it. While her body incubated, Sokin and the other scientists monitored her closely. It wasn't a real pregnancy, but her body thought it was, and they wanted to know how it affected the algae. Angle felt phantom pangs in her stomach in time to whenever Teal moaned in the middle of the night. They held one another's stomachs, basking in each other's glow.

"*Kel'oar*," Angle said one night. "The glow from your algae when you're with young. That's how it tastes. Does mine taste any different to you?"

Teal did not answer. She only felt their bellies and sighed.

Weeks later, Teal laid the clutch, holding hands with Angle for three hours. Teal was in a trance the whole time, and when the last one emerged, she reclined on the pile of old clothes they had set out. Angle sat with her in Teal's nest. Their nest.

"That would have been my life," Teal said. "That felt wonderful. They would have made me do it over and over. I would have loved it. Thank you, Angle."

Days later they drove the boats toward distant skyscrapers and helped with more dives. Angle watched Teal closely. Since the clutch, she had not been the same. Angle told her she would give her eggs whenever she wanted, but now she actively seemed to avoid exposing herself. She spent most of her time on deck, staring out over the water, tapping a foot or a finger on the deck while the others dove for more relics of a civilization long gone.

She and Angle had been inseparable for so long Angle had begun to believe they never would be apart, but Teal seemed to keep to herself. She gave the lizard some space to enjoy *miremé* during the dives. Other people tried to talk to her, to engage her, encourage her to help with the dives, but Teal sat on the deck, staring, fidgeting.

Angle didn't allow herself to worry until she woke up in the middle of the night and Teal wasn't in bed. She rose and ran up the steps. She saw Teal crossing the rope bridge to the next yacht. Angle crouched and observed. Teal paced the deck, clutching and unclutching her fists. Angle could barely make out the glow of her algae. Eventually she crossed to the next boat and wandered about there. Then the next. When she returned to Angle's boat, Teal was scratching at the lines in her skin, coming dangerously close to picking at the algae. The rabbit climbed to the deck.

"What's wrong?" Angle said.

Teal leaned on the railing, looking down at the darkness. "I don't know. I don't know what to do with myself anymore, and I can't seem to relax. Ever since the eggs… Angle, something is wrong. I don't want anything to be wrong. This is the best I've felt since I was a child."

Angle cautiously took a step forward. "Remember what Sokin told you? Rejection is possible."

"Rejection? Angle, I haven't eaten in months! The algae is doing great."

"It's not physical rejection, Teal. It's mental."

Teal turned around. She shivered a little in the cold air. "What?"

Angle took a deep breath and tried to keep herself from quivering. "The body accepts the algae, but sometimes the mind does not.

Sokin believes that, for some people, the mind is hardwired to need the struggle to survive. Take away that, and what is left to live for?"

Teal braced herself on the railing. Her heart was racing—Angle could hear it from here. "I want this! Angle, I want this! For the first time in my life I'm living in a floating city, and I don't feel like shit! I don't have to deal with people threatening my life because I'm not a 'Claimer! I don't have to live with my own people hating me for being an enforcer!"

"You did what you had to do to escape a life of victimhood. You lived with it because you convinced yourself it was the only way. Now you realize there is another way."

Teal was hyperventilating.

"But that's not what's bothering you, is it?" Angle continued. "It's more basic than that. You don't feel right unless you're climbing over someone else to get your food."

"What are you talking about?"

"I knew this was coming. I was afraid of it, but I've been ignoring it. You weren't interested in learning the flavors of light. That tells me you don't have demons of your own. You don't feel guilty for all the things you did as an enforcer. You feel guilty that you don't have to be an enforcer anymore. You're bored unless you've earned your life above everyone else. To you, you haven't earned it unless you have denied it for someone else. This is rejection."

"Angle?" Teal seemed to be having a seizure. "Help me. Please." She fell to the deck, holding the railing with one hand.

The rabbit took another step forward. "I was hoping you would adapt, but I saw it a long time ago. You saw yourself as better than they were because you saved yourself from living the life of a breeder. You deserved to eat, and they deserved to be where they were. You defined yourself by that."

Teal was on the deck, shaking uncontrollably. "I had to! I got out! Nobody else could! They were waiting for help, or a savior, or something, but I saved myself! It was the insults I had to get away from! Those arrogant 'Claimers! Angle, I like it here! I like everyone! I don't want to lose it!"

Angle now stood over her. She held a hand on Teal's shoulder.

"You asked me why the price on our heads is so high. It's because this is phase one of Sokin's future. Phase two is splicing the genes from the algae into our bodies. No more trenches in our skin. Our fur and feathers and scales will make food for us, and then we can create a society that doesn't need to hunt or forage, and guess what that will mean for the 'Claimers? We won't need them, and we won't need people who think the way they do. Of course they want to destroy Sokin's work. I for one want to live in a world where no one has to force others into the mud just to escape it."

Teal had stretched out on the deck and gone rigid.

"The people who can't adapt," Angle continued, "end up tearing the algae out of their bodies and dying in the sun. I've seen it dozens of times. I want more people to be part of the future, but it seems some can't accept true equality. The idea that life can mean more than the struggle to survive. I overcame it. I hope you can, too, but I can't help you, Teal. You will either come to terms with it, or you will succumb to an overwhelming itch."

Teal swallowed. "Angle, please…"

Angle was about to turn around and go below deck. She never wanted to be around when it happened, but she remained frozen in place. Finally, she reclined next to Teal and held her around the stomach, face nuzzled against her adorable jowl.

"Teal, it's not too late. You are not less of a person now. You do not have to deny someone else their food to earn yours. Life is only that way because we have been told it has to be. Try to imagine who you are in a world without enforcers."

Teal convulsed for a while, and then Teal choked on a few words. "If I'm not an enforcer, I'm just a breeder."

Angle held her tighter. "You can be whatever you want now."

They were still. Angle thought she would not sleep, but she did.

Angle woke with the sun, and she rose from the deck. The trenches around Teal's neck and down her arms were empty. Angle could see the bones and muscle, and infection had already gripped them. The infection had spread quickly, and now Teal lay motionless, green slime coating her claws.

Angle turned away and looked across the water. She never cried when it happened. Instead she screamed. She couldn't be the only enforcer who despised keeping others down in order to lift herself up.

She pondered that the future would be made of people who lived for these flavors. People who eagerly learned the flavors of sunlight would inherit the Earth. Angle hoped she would live to see the day. Subconsciously, she began chewing on the *tu'melé*.

CHROMIUM MANEUVERS

Matt Trepal

Fiery Chrome Orchid set another sequencer atop the stack on the Damselfly's balcony. She was fox-kin, tall and lithe, blazing red fur crowned by a rainbow crest of metallic hair, with mirrored lenses inset over her eyes and chromed "gloves" running from her fingertips to her elbows. Behind her, her friend Rust muscled in a larger piece of equipment. Rust was an urstacean, tall and wide, with sparse bristly brown fur growing through a hard exoskeleton, two sets of arms, and a stout beak with bear's teeth behind. "Fucking *Engineers*, Chrome," Rust growled. "If I'd known you had this much gear I'd never have agreed to help."

"As if I care how the masters of High Humanity spent their free time," Chrome replied. Her coxcomb bounced and shone in the sunlight, one of what her fans called "chromium maneuvers" when she did them during a show. "But Ambara Down's greatest musicmancer has to keep herself with the top kit. Anyway, that's the last of it. I'll buy you a drink after I get set up."

Rust crossed her slender lower arms across her belly while holding her larger upper arms akimbo. "You'll buy me *many* drinks, for this." Chrome laughed and leaned over the balustrade, stacks of bracelets on each arm clattering and jingling.

Below, the market square was filled for the Founders Festival, a week-long holiday commemorating the creation of Ambara Down from the fallen ruins of High Ambara. Temporary stalls had been erected for vendors of foods and services and products from other parts of the city and beyond, and the aromas of a dozen cuisines floated on the air. On the stage to Chrome's left a choir of throat-singers from Tzumrut performed despite the disinterest of the crowd. Chrome herself was scheduled to perform tonight, a tremendous DownBeat dance party.

Along the right side of the square ran the Fence, the border between Ambara Down and Reclamation Project territory. Here it was mainly rubble heaped a few meters high, topped by a roll of razor wire.

Rust stepped up alongside. "The 'Claimers are so worried about mixing with us they have to build a wall," she said, gesturing at the Fence. "And not even a good one. Look how it's slumping down, there."

Chrome didn't turn her head; what the humans of the Reclamation Project wanted or didn't want was of less than no interest to her. "I heard you quit the mercenary life," she said to Rust. "Is that true?"

"Yeah, I signed on with a salvager," Rust replied. "Someone who has her own hoverbarge, even."

Chrome raised an eyebrow. "Do I know her? What's salvaging like?"

Rust chuckled. "I get shot at much less," she said, "but the people shooting at me are crazier." She leaned back against the balustrade and folded both sets of arms. "I don't think you'd know Tatters. When she's not out on an expedition she mostly prowls the book shops along Qart-Livreir Street, and doesn't care for DownBeat."

Chrome laughed again. "Bring her around anyway," she said. "I'll give her a stick of my best stuff, and we'll see how she likes that."

Rust's exoskeleton didn't allow for much facial expression, but she held her beak open in what Chrome had learned to interpret as a grin. "You know *I* would like it very much," she said. "I'll see if I can get Tatters out. She's partial to her books, though." Rust pointed at the stacks of equipment with one of her lower arms. "Are you going to set this up? I want my drinks."

As Chrome pushed away from the balustrade and turned toward her equipment, the musicmancer felt the balcony begin to vibrate. The motion was imperceptible to anyone else, but Chrome had several mods, including a hyper-sensitivity to beat and vibration. Something large was approaching. Her ears pricked high and she turned back toward the square. "Several somethings," she murmured to herself.

Rust noticed the fox-kin's attitude change immediately. "What's going on?" she asked.

The tone of the crowd below shifted as they began to hear or feel something now, as well. The joyous, chaotic volume of the festivalgoers dropped, and a sullen murmuring spread from the market stalls.

Chrome leaned forward, her lens implants cutting the summer glare. Two long vehicles, tall but narrow, built to operate in the tight spaces of a High City, entered from the market. Both were painted vibrant blue and bore the emblem of the Reclamation Project.

"'Claimers,'" Chrome spat.

"What in deep, drowned Fludra are *they* doing here?"

The fox-kin shook her head but said nothing. The 'Claimer transports pushed their way through the festival crowd, extinguishing the festive mood as they passed, finally coming to a stop before the entrance to the Damselfly.

* * *

Twenty soldiers disembarked from the transports, all human. Rust clacked her beak as she watched them deploy throughout the square and around the Damselfly's entrance. "Full ballistic impact armor," she muttered. "Those troopers have wide-spectrum sonic pacifiers, and those over there have gummy-sluggers." She grunted. "They all have high-capacity lethal sidearms, though," she said. "It's not a heavy combat team, but they aren't here for the party."

A group of four or five soldiers had detached themselves from the larger group and were entering the Damselfly. "Come on," Chrome said, and dashed inside. From the top of the stairs leading down to the main barroom, she saw one of the 'Claimers enter an office with Guy, the Damselfly's day shift manager. The other soldiers took up stations just outside the office door, making it crystal clear there would be no interruption of whatever discussion was occurring inside.

"Why?" Chrome asked, running a silvery hand through her metallic crest. "Why are they here? Why today?"

"I can think of a reason," Rust said from behind her. "But I sure don't like it."

Chrome's fox-ears flattened back against her head. "I don't want to hear it," she said, and sniffed in indignation. She spun on her heel. "You want your drinks?" she said to Rust. "Help me set up my rig."

They returned to the balcony and busied themselves with assembling Chrome's equipment. The main archive of samples, array of sequencers, and mixer were arranged against the balustrade. Light projectors and similar equipment, including the cooling array for all this processing power that Rust had hauled in last, were placed to either side.

Below, the crowd slowly returned to a semblance of its earlier revelry. On the stage, a six-piece combo began playing dance music, and the crowd danced enthusiastically, especially in the face of the 'Claimer presence. The petzelhorn player particularly impressed Chrome, and she made a mental note to ask to sample some of their playing for her own use later. The throat-singers as well, for that matter, if she could track them down.

Chrome was alone on the balcony, bundling and tucking away cables for safety, when she felt a presence: one of the 'Claimers. He wore a large pistol on his hip, but unlike the two soldiers behind him, he was unarmored. His blue uniform sat tight against a muscular body, chest festooned with pips and ribbons and shoulders capped with epaulets the size of roof tiles.

He glowered down at Chrome and pursed his lips in a sour frown that was intensified by both the intricate tattoos traced across his brown skin, and his dark, dark eyes. Sleek black hair framed his face and fell to his shoulders. He flicked a finger at Chrome's equipment. The inking extended across the tops of his hands to his fingertips. "This array," he asked in a clipped, nasal accent, "has it a microphone?"

The musicmancer rose to stand at least twenty centimeters taller than the 'Claimer. He blinked twice, looking up at her, but his frown only darkened. Chrome looked past him at Guy, who slouched in the shadows just beyond the doorway. "Guy, what's going on? Where's Brexa?"

Guy ran a pasty hand over his pale, bald pate and shrugged without looking at her. The 'Claimer drew himself up, throwing out his chest and reinforcing his frown. "I am Commander Lillioka," he said. "I will address the assembly, and so I say again: Have you a microphone?"

Chrome turned her attention to the 'Claimer. "I do," she said. "But what of it? What do you need it for?"

"For the Reclamation Project," the Commander said, as if that answered Chrome's question, and held out his hand.

It was not Chrome's habit to let strangers touch her equipment, especially strangers who held an obvious dislike for her. But Rust was nowhere around, and Guy was no help, and there were three 'Claimers with guns. After a brief hesitation, she passed the handset to the Commander and turned the feed on.

Lillioka took the handset and stepped forward to stand against the balustrade. "Attention, residents of Fallen Ambara," he said, and his voice boomed out over Market Square. The dance band faltered, the petzelhorn laying out one last, long blue note before falling silent. Faces of every shape and color turned up toward the balcony.

"I am Commander Lillioka, legate of the Eighth Cohort, Reclamation Project Security Services. In the interest of public order and safety, this event is hereby ended. Beginning immediately, all performances, orations, exhibits, or displays presently occurring shall cease, and those subsequently scheduled are likewise canceled."

Chrome gawked at the 'Claimer officer, not believing what she'd just heard. Had he just canceled the Founders Festival? How? On what authority? When the Commander offered the microphone back to her she accepted it without comment, unable to respond. He re-entered the Damselfly, followed by his soldiers; Guy followed them all, silently staring at the floor with his hands stuffed in his pockets.

* * *

Chrome's bracelets jangled as she threw up her hands in exasperation. "He wouldn't even talk to me!" She traced a chromed fingertip around the rim of her cascade, a layered drink with nearly as many colors as her hair. Despite Commander Lillioka's orders, many of the festival-goers had not dispersed, retiring instead to the Damselfly's main bar to wait out the situation, packing the room until it was all muzzles and tails.

Rust sat beside her at the bar, an enormous mug of Ambara Red before her and two more empty ones pushed aside. Rust always had space at the bar, no matter how crowded the room. "What about Guy?" she asked.

The fox-kin made a dismissive noise. "He doesn't want any trouble, he told me, so he's not interested in getting between the 'Claimers and anything they want." She clenched her fists and thumped them on the bar. "Well, then he'd better not get between *me* and anything, either."

Rust sipped at her beer. "Guy's a human," she said. "And just the day shift manager. You know how closely Brexa likes to run the Damselfly themself. I'd be surprised if Guy could make a decision like that on his own. And if the 'Claimers decide to bust the place up because he won't cooperate, how does he explain that to Brexa?"

"Besides, I've heard he's a 'Claimer who jumped the Fence and went native. I don't know you can rely on him to stand up to the Reclamation Project."

Chrome sipped her drink through a frown. "*Obviously*," she replied. "But if he didn't want to push back against the 'Claimers he shouldn't have come to Ambara Down in the first place, and he *especially* shouldn't hang around so close to them. And if Guy can't make decisions on his own, where *is* Brexa?" She gestured at the press of bodies around them in the barroom. "Why aren't they in their own bar on some of the busiest days of the year?"

Rust nodded. "That's a good question" She took another pull at her mug. "They wouldn't put up with any of this."

"You got that right," Chrome said, her coxcomb dancing as she nodded. The cascade was hitting her nicely, and she hadn't even gotten to the third layer, yet. "Where do these 'Claimers get off shutting the Festival down? Where's the Prefect's Guard? What do my taxes pay for?"

The urstacean's beak fell open in a grin. "When was the last time *you* paid taxes? And how are the constables supposed to take on these armored goons when all they've got is tinglers and tanglers?"

"Don't confuse me with details, Rust," Chrome said.

She raised her cascade to her muzzle, but paused halfway as a commotion arose across the bar, near the front doors. A blue-clad 'Claimer backed through the crowd, pursued by a trio of Prefect's

Guard in their red-and-yellow tunics, one wearing the collar stripes of an officer.

The officer was a sapient ape, not quite as tall as the human trooper but almost as broad as Rust, and with long arms the girth of the 'Claimer's thigh. Apes naturally bore grave expressions, but the disapprobation in the officer's face could hardly have been stronger. His adjutants were no less imposing, an urstacean like Rust to his left and a pachymorph with sweeping tusks to his right. Neither of them bothered to hide their hostility toward the trooper.

The 'Claimer bumped against the bar and had nowhere left to go. The crowd had fallen silent, feasting on the trooper's obvious discomfiture. "The Commander is in conference," he said to the officer, the bravado in his voice betrayed by his frightened body language. If only he'd had a neck frill to unfurl, Chrome thought, or fur to bristle, to make himself look larger.

"And he will soon be in conference with *me*," the ape replied. His voice was calm, but there was no mistaking the menace beneath it.

"That's quite impossible," the 'Claimer said. "An appointment—"

"Will be announced immediately," the officer interrupted. "Tell the Commander that Lieutenant Premanayanat of the Prefect's Office is here to find out just what in all the Hundred Hells is going on here. Quote me directly, and in full."

The human shook his head. "As I said, Lieutenant, you cannot meet with the Commander at present."

The officer clasped his hands behind his back. "As you like." He turned to his deputies. "Creana, Jank, start opening every door in this place until we find this 'Claimer officer. If you find a door you can't open, break it down. If someone blocks you from reaching a door, break *them* down."

Guy suddenly appeared beside the Lieutenant. "No, no, no," he said, waving his hands. "There's no need for that, Lieutenant. I can show you where the Commander is." Ignoring the black stare from the 'Claimer, Guy led the constables through the crowd. The trooper followed.

As the uniforms moved away the buzz in the bar resumed, with a sharper edge. Rust laughed. "This gets better and better," she said, and drained her mug. She gestured to the bartender for another.

Chrome's crest waggled as she shook her head. "I don't know about any of this," she said, and then slid from her stool. "I'll be right back."

She swayed a bit, navigating with care through the crowd to the water closets near the front door. Two Reclamation Project soldiers stood guard there, and eyed her as she turned down the short hallway to the facilities. Once inside the WC, she prepared to take care of what she'd come to do, but realized that through an acoustic oddity—the Damselfly was rife with anomalies like that, and was one reason she rarely performed inside the building—she could hear the two soldiers talking.

"...even doing here?" she heard one ask. "What do we care?"

"Orders are orders," the other replied.

"But *why?* Yesterday we're on routine duty at the port, today we're rolling through Old Ambara."

"From the mongletalk during the ride, it's a politics thing. Lillioka needs a project to impress the sachems, or something, so he decided to cancel the squatters' holiday. Let the varmints know who's really in charge, you know?"

"I can get behind *that*," the first soldier said. "This place weirds me out. But we're just geared for crowd-control, and there's who-knows-how-many varmints out there. If he wanted to stomp some fur, he should have brought power infantry."

Chrome didn't wait to hear any more, but rushed from the water closet. She ignored the comment from one of the troopers that she should learn to wash her hands after using the toilet, and hurried back to Rust. "We need to leave," Chrome said through a snarl. "I need to plan."

"Leave?" Rust asked, blinking her jet-black eyes. "I just got a refill."

"Chug it," the musicmancer told her and downed the rest of her own drink. She slammed the glass back onto the bar and tugged at Rust's upper arm. "Let's go."

Rust tipped her mug back and drained it in three long gulps, then rose from her stool. She was as least as much taller than Chrome as Chrome was to the Commander. The fox-kin pulled urgently at her friend's hand and led her out into the market square.

* * *

The aroma of cooking food still lingered over the square, and people clustered here and there, but the festival had clearly faltered. A trio of 'Claimer soldiers occupied the stage and two other pairs stood atop one of their transports, fore and aft, not quite aiming their crowd control weapons down at the civilians. Chrome pulled Rust down one of the side streets near the Damselfly, stumbling as she did.

"Easy," Rust said, catching the fox-kin before she fell. "You'll regret downing your cascade like that. What's going on?"

Chrome swayed, and reached out to steady herself against Chrome. "Mebbe not m' best idea," she slurred, the cascade crashing down upon her. "But I hadda get outta there." In a rush, she told Rust what she'd overheard from the 'Claimer troops by the door.

Rust clicked her beak repeatedly in an urstacean frown. "Stupid Reclamation Project," she muttered. "Why don't they just stay up in their flying cities and leave the rest of us alone? It's not like they don't already have all the advantages, anyway." She sighed.

"I wanna put m' show on," Chrome said, tapping Rust on the chest as she spoke. With each blow, her finger made a hollow *thunk* against the urstacean's exoskeleton. "I wanna stick it t' these fuckers, show 'em they can't do this t' us. We won't *let* 'em."

Rust nodded. "I'm in. Whatever you need from me, you've got it."

"Yeah, yeah, yeah!" Chrome said, nodding and grinning.

From behind Rust a procession approached, and Chrome leaned out around her friend to watch it, far enough that Rust had to catch her so she didn't fall over. A group of five or six people of various kins, led by a dappled gray mare, passed them and entered the square. Sleek, slender, and tall, the mare wore the crimson-and-gold sash of a District Minister, and those in her train were obviously secretaries and assistants.

Rust tapped her chin with lower finger while her upper arms rested akimbo. "Minister Cloudbearer," she murmured. "Come to back up the Lieutenant, I'm sure."

"She'd *better*," Chrome replied. "M' taxes at work!"

The urstacean laughed and patted her friend on the shoulder hard enough to send her staggering again. "You still want to go through with your plan?" she asked.

The fox-kin nodded vigorously, her multicolored coxcomb bouncing this way and that. "Abs'lutely. You can't trust the gummint t' get nothin' done in time."

"Then I'm still in. How can I help?"

"You're outta the merc business, but you still have your own kit, yeah?"

Rust cocked her head. "Most of it. Not enough guns to take on all these 'Claimers, though. My goal is to die rich, not a martyr."

Chrome's metallic fingers flashed in the sunlight as she waved away her friend's concern. "I'm talkin' protection, armor, that stuff. How about a PPD belt?"

The urstacean crossed both sets of arms across her chest. "I do, but it's an older model. Why?"

Before Chrome could answer, Commander Lillioka appeared on the Damselfly's balcony. Boos and jeers rose up from the remaining crowd to greet him, but he ignored them. He raised a small device to his mouth and spoke into it without broadcasting his voice across the square.

"Is that the 'Claimer boss?" Rust asked. "I recognize him. I've seen him at the Shadow Garden."

Chrome looked up into her friend's face, stumbling back a step as she did. "The *Shadow Garden*? What were y' doin' at a brothel? Aren't urstaceans all clones of the colony queen, or somethin'?"

"Parthenogenetic all the way, sister," Rust said, knocking against her chest. "No sloppy exchange of bodily fluids for *us*. I don't even have genitals!"

"M' own preference, precisely," Chrome said, nodding. "But if y' don't do sex, why were y' at the Shadow Garden?"

Rust chuckled. "Working as security. I definitely saw that 'Claimer there, more than once. Those tattoos are distinctive."

"Well," Chrome said, patting Rust's arm. "Well, well, well. That's a twist." She clapped her hands once. "Meet me at the Nine Coins in an hour or so."

"Sure thing," Rust said. "Where are you going?"

Chrome had turned to leave. "I'm gonna get m'self an invisible man," she said, and hurried away, only stumbling once. As she crossed market square, a group of locals were jostling with a pair of 'Claimer troops.

* * *

Tucked along a pedestrian way too narrow for any vehicle larger than a bicycle, the Nine Coins was dim and dingy, and the drinks were noticeably watered-down, but it was out of the way, which is what Chrome wanted. And she was a silent investor in it, which was one way she avoided paying taxes.

She slumped at a back table, ears and tail drooping, sipping juice. The cascade packed a powerful punch that managed to wear off fairly quickly, and if you stayed relaxed, there were almost no side effects. Unfortunately, Chrome had not remained relaxed, and was suffering from the notorious "cascade breakdown." Even in the gloom of the Nine Coins she had increased the opacity of her lenses in an effort to relieve the feeling that any light contributed to the disintegration of her skull from the inside. It helped. A little.

Rust arrived with a near-human in tow. "This is Tischa," the urstacean said, "owner of the Shadow Garden." Tischa dipped her head to Chrome in greeting before sitting. She appeared to have a mostly mainline genome, though streamlined, as if she had been designed for high-velocity travel. Her long red hair was bound in an elaborate braid, and every move she made was liquid and graceful.

"You look awful, darling," she said to Chrome, her voice as smooth as her motions. "Cascade breakdown, I presume?"

Chrome shrugged and sipped at her juice. Rust laughed and placed a wide belt with six evenly-spaced boxy devices in the center of the table. "Here's the PPD belt. Where's your invisible man?"

"Late," Chrome replied. "What's *she* doing here?"

Rust leaned forward, upper elbows on the table. "I got to thinking about seeing that 'Claimer at the Shadow Garden, so I stopped by to see if Tischa could serve up any dirt on the Commander."

Chrome's bracelets clattered and rang as she dismissed the woman with a frown and a wave. "Like the Engineers, I don't care about what he gets up to in private."

"I figured you'd feel that way," Rust said, waggling her blocky, bearish head. "You should listen to her, anyway."

"Should I?" Chrome turned to Tischa. "What do you want in return?"

Tischa smiled a smooth, streamlined smile. "Nothing except assistance keeping my involvement out of general knowledge."

Before the fox-kin could respond, a bright green creature slid into the empty seat beside Chrome. "Jemmy's here," he said. Bulbous eyes sat atop the newcomer's wedge-shaped head, and his prehensile tail curled tightly about the leg of his chair. "Let's get talking."

"Rust and Tischa," Chrome said, "this is Jemmy Three-Fingers. Jemmy, this is Rust and this is Tischa." Placed on the table before him, Jemmy's hands each bore only two fingers and a thumb. He turned one eye independently toward Tischa, and the other toward Rust, but said nothing. The effect was unnerving.

"This is your invisible man?" Rust asked Chrome.

"He's got a particular ability that I need," Chrome replied.

"Oh?" Tischa asked.

Jemmy's exposed skin suddenly shifted from bright green to a muddy red similar to the wall behind him. He didn't exactly turn invisible, but he blended very well.

Tischa regarded Jemmy closely. "Just what is it you do for a living, Mr. Three-Fingers?" she asked.

Jemmy shifted back to his natural green. "Jemmy's a professional trouble-maker," he said. "You want to stir things up, Jemmy'll do you, if you can find him."

"ADF?" Tischa asked.

One at a time, Jemmy shifted both eyes to focus directly on the woman. Then he rotated his right eye to look at Rust, and then at Chrome, while keeping his left steadily trained on Tischa. "Jemmy surely don't know what you speak of," he said slowly. He stared at Tischa and an uncomfortable, almost dangerous silence settled on the table.

Chrome finally broke it. "Tischa, what have you got?"

The owner of the Shadow Garden turned her attention from Jemmy to Chrome. "As Rust told you, the Commander has been a frequent patron of my establishment. Never in uniform, of course, but those tattoos are very distinctive.

"When there, he enjoys the company of my employee Maadiis, exclusively. It turns out that he also records these sessions."

Rust clicked her beak. "How did you find that out?"

Tischa shifted in her chair. "Maadiis carries themselves with significant stature and power, and has always remained aloof from many of my other employees, which generated a certain amount of tension within the Garden. But recently, they began displaying a new level of wealth that significantly exceeded what they could earn with me," she said. "Expensive clothing, elaborate accessories, that sort of thing. Other employees grew jealous, and in combination with their detached air the environment at the Garden became such that I had to confront Maadiis about it."

"The Commander?" Chrome asked. "Like I said, I don't care who he fucks or how he likes it, or what he does with his 'Claimer money."

Tischa ignored Chrome's comment and continued. "Under pressure, Maadiis told me about the recordings, and that they kept a copy, and showed me a particular recent episode. Have you brought your datacom?" Tischa held out a datastick.

Chrome made no move to take it.

"You will *definitely* be interested in who else he has involved himself with, and what else they discussed. I recommend keeping the sound low as you watch."

Slowly, frowning, Chrome reached out and took the stick, then inserted it into a port on her datacom. At first, the video appeared no different than any other cheaply-made jollypix found at one of the booths along Blindlemon Street. Maadiis was quite the imposing figure, tall and broad-shouldered with a narrow waist and supple curves, long hair and long tail. They engaged in an intense session with the Commander, whose tattoos covered every part of his body.

Then the Commander's other companion appeared from behind the recorder, sleek, slender, tall—and dappled gray. Chrome paused the playback and looked up at Tischa. She opened and closed her mouth several times before being able to speak. "That's... Minister Cloudbearer," she said at last.

"*What?!*" Rust exclaimed. "You've got to be kidding." Chrome showed her datacom screen to the urstacean, who recoiled in her chair. "I *voted* for her!" Jemmy snorted and shook his head.

"Indeed it is," Tischa said. One of the advantages of Chrome's inset lenses was that no one could read her eyes, especially when she was trying to read theirs. But the owner of the Shadow Garden gave no hint as to what she thought.

Chrome drummed her fingers on the table as the video continued to run. "This is embarrassing from a political point of view," the musicmancer said as she watched. "But it couldn't really run him off, could it?"

"Watch until the end."

The assignation continued, then the trio reclined in sweaty bliss, one on either side of Maadiis. Chrome could see that Lillioka and Cloudbearer were speaking, and she carefully raised the volume until she could understand what they were saying. It was beyond anything she could have imagined.

* * *

Chrome shut down the playback.

"This is devastating," she said to Tischa. "But why haven't you gone to the Prefect with it?"

"Don't bother," Jemmy spat. He'd watched the whole video from beside her. "Durgavati's nepotistic nest's just as bad as the Project. Jemmy says burn it *all* down."

Tischa stared at Jemmy. "No, you're not ADF," she said. "You're something far more dangerous. But I can't take this to the Prefecture," she said to Chrome. "Not myself, directly. The Shadow Garden has a reputation as the most discreet of the discreet, and I need that protected."

"Collaborator," Jemmy muttered.

Tischa frowned. "I am as eager to stick a finger in the eye of the Reclamation Project as anyone else in Ambara Down," she said while trying to ignore Jemmy. "Without this you've got nothing on the Commander. With it…"

"Why shouldn't *I* just take it to the Prefect?" Chrome asked.

Tischa spread her hands. "You could. That's the only copy of the video I had, so it's literally out of my hands, now."

Jemmy opened his mouth, but Chrome held up a hand to silence him. "I know your opinion." The reptile slouched back in his chair.

"You can't trust the government to get anything done in time," Chrome said. "And I would so enjoy publicly embarrassing that 'Claimer martinet." She put her datacom away and pulled the PPD belt in front of her on the table. "So here's what I want to do..."

* * *

By early evening, Chrome was back in the market square. Besides its usefulness as a tax dodge, the Nine Coins was a fantastic rumor mill, so on her way out Chrome had casually mentioned to Rust that despite the 'Claimer presence she was still going ahead with her show. In the few hours since, that rumor had spread throughout Old Ambara exactly as she'd intended, and the square was slowly filling with people again.

The Reclamation Project security forces still occupied the Damselfly, and had erected portable spotlights that cast harsh white light on the building's facade and on the square around its entrance. Troopers atop the transport fidgeted with their weapons as they nervously watched the locals coming back to their canceled festival. Obviously, the 'Claimers had not heard the rumor.

At least one pair of Prefect's Guards in red and yellow stood near every trooper in blue, but Rust was right, the constabulary wasn't equipped with anything that could match up with the 'Claimers. More concerning was that despite the presence of both Lieutenant Premanayanat and Commissioner Cloudbearer in the Damselfly, the Reclamation Project was still here. What had been happening for the past few hours?

As she pushed her way towards the Damselfly, Chrome recognized an ADF member. The Ambara Defense Front was committed to active resistance against the 'Claimers, and if there was one ADFer here there were more—all primed for a confrontation.

Despite the summer heat, Chrome wore a loose jacket with its hood up to disguise her multi-colored hair, dark goggles over her mirrored lenses, and gloves over her chromed hands. Getting recognized before her plan got into motion would be a disaster.

She stopped where she had a clear line of sight to the balcony. It appeared empty, but the light of the spots showed a 'Claimer standing guard just inside the building. That complicated her plan slightly, but might also work in her favor by keeping anyone else from the balcony. She watched the building, activating the infrared feed from her lenses.

Three stories above the square, a heat signature appeared on the Damselfly's roof: Jemmy. The naked reptile climbed head-first over the low parapet of the roof, gripping a large pipe that ran down the wall. As he did, his skin changed from green to the sandy brown of the Damselfly's facade. He edged his way down the pipe toward the balcony.

Chrome watched Jemmy's progress through the infrared as he used his powerful grip and prehensile tail to travel hand-over-hand down the pipe. It was slow going, moving slowly enough to avoid attracting attention from below while balancing the pack of equipment he wore across his chest.

Jemmy's natural camouflage, the gathering night, and the audacity of his approach all worked to hide him. Unless someone was actively searching the wall, Chrome didn't believe the reptile would be noticed.

The 'Claimer trooper stepped out onto the balcony. Jemmy stopped, only a few meters above. Chrome held her breath and watched, helpless. If the trooper looked up there was no way he could miss Jemmy.

The 'Claimer paced the balcony a few times, peered over the balustrade, then re-entered the Damselfly. Chrome let her breath out in a gasp as Jemmy resumed his descent. The entire episode had only taken a few minutes, but had felt like years.

Chrome grinned as Jemmy at last dropped the last two meters from where the pipe turned to the side, onto the balcony. The guard still had not noticed. Dangerous as the last few minutes had been, the real peril began now. If Jemmy were discovered before he could activate the PPD belt, everything would be lost.

Jemmy ducked below Chrome's rig, and the fox-kin turned her infrared off. A moment later she saw a flash from the balcony, then a slight shimmering in the air, and she knew Jemmy had activated the PPD belt.

Chrome's datacom chirped. Her bracelets clicked and rattled, muffled by her jacket sleeve as she pulled the device from her pocket. "Jemmy," she said softly into it, casually, to avoid attracting attention.

"Chrome," Jemmy replied, just as softly. "Remember to tell Brexa they got a drainpipe to inspect. Let's set this beast loose."

"Let's," Chrome replied. "Is the power still on? If it is, insert the first datastick into the control unit," she told Jemmy.

"Done."

"The touch screen should have a big red button showing," Chrome told him. "Tap it, and then hold tight."

Jemmy made no reply, but before long Chrome's hypersensitivity picked up light vibrations through her chest. Her plan was rolling.

In the hours between leaving the Nine Coins and meeting Jemmy again to give him his instructions and equipment, Chrome had programmed several datasticks with prearranged tracks. Jemmy was the only one who could reach the balcony unnoticed, and someone had to wear the PPD belt in order to activate it, so he would have to operate the rig as best he could. It wouldn't be the most imaginative set Chrome had ever performed, since there'd be no improvisation, but she trusted that after this show her audience would forgive her.

The subsonic beat intensified, and now others in the crowd could feel it. Even one of the 'Claimers standing atop the transport placed a hand on her chest, then leaned over and spoke to her colleague, who only shrugged in response. The beat shifted, from a steady drone to the bass thump of "Down Ambara Down," one of Chrome's earliest hits. The buzz of chatter rose as the crowd recognized the beat, and knots of people drifted toward the area immediately below the balcony.

Now all the 'Claimers could feel it, and they looked from the apparently empty balcony to the crowd and then back to the balcony. Chrome whispered to herself, "Three... two... one." The melody roared to life, layer upon layer of carefully crafted harmonics. The crowd roared in response and surged forward.

* * *

As the melody began, Chrome watched as a handful of 'Claimers gathered by the doorway to the balcony, appearing to discuss this turn of events. One of them stepped out onto the balcony into the shimmering PPD field—and immediately collapsed in a spasmodic heap.

The "PPD" in the PPD belt that Jemmy wore stood for "Personal Protection Disruptor," a battlefield protection device that emitted a field capable of scrambling any creature with a nervous system. It wasn't fatal, but when waking up after getting pasted by a PPD you might wish it had been; a cascade breakdown was nothing by comparison. Even if Jemmy dropped his camouflage, the field could be set wide enough that so long as he stayed out of a direct line of fire he could keep the 'Claimers stuck inside without danger to himself.

Lillioka might have countermeasures in his transports that could nullify a PPD, but Chrome planned to take advantage of every second of confusion before such measures could be brought to bear. The fact that Lillioka could have brought a heavier 'Claimer presence and the predominance of crowd-control weapons argued that he wasn't interested in a massacre. Chrome was counting on this—and on the 'Claimers treating the sudden commencement of music as a problem to be solved rather than as an excuse to open fire. A shootout with the Reclamation Project was not part of the plan, but humans could be unpredictable.

The pre-programmed music continued, and "Down Ambara Down" gave way to the rapid-fire bass and skyrocket melody of "Pawprints Across the Sky." Here and there, people were beginning to dance, and someone had commandeered one of the spotlights, angling the beam high and swinging it across the sky. Chrome grinned. Normally she had an elaborate light display at her shows, but the projectors were all up on the balcony, unusable. The spotlight would do, for now.

From her vantage point in the square, Chrome could clearly see a commotion brewing at the balcony doorway, but not whether the Commander presided. Could they get so lucky that the pompous clod would fry himself on the PPD? How would the 'Claimers react? Better to not find out.

She spoke into her connection with Jemmy. "How's it going up there? I saw one fool get taken out."

"Just the one, yeah?" Jemmy replied. Chrome had to strain to hear his soft reply over the music and crowd noise. "There's a few milling about with their thumbs up their holes. Jemmy don't think their boss is here, yet."

"Good. I need you to slot in the second stick and get ready to activate it. Can you do that?"

There was a long pause on the other end. "Gonna be tricky," Jemmy said at last. "The pattern of your rig is chaotic, impossible to match. Jemmy'll be putting himself out in the open, but too late to back out now, yeah?"

"Think of all the trouble you're making. For a professional troublemaker, you're doing well." Jemmy chuckled, but said nothing. "Slot the stick," Chrome said, "then get back to where you're safe. Let me know when you've done that."

Jemmy didn't reply, but there was another commotion on the balcony, and another 'Claimer dropped after encountering the PPD field. "Done," Jemmy said. "Can't believe these yahoos was ever the dominant species on this planet. They can be so *stupid*."

"To the Far Peaks" now played, and a large portion of the crowd was dancing. More of the spotlights had been appropriated, and the harsh beams flashed across the crowd, the sky, the Damselfly, and the surrounding buildings. The square was continuing to fill, as the music proved the rumor true. One of the 'Claimer transports was surrounded by townsfolk, and being rocked back and forth. ADF work? The troopers looked close to panic, but did not seem poised to retaliate. Not yet, at least.

"Time for the next move, Jemmy," Chrome said into her datacom. "Punch the button again."

Chrome waited for "To the Far Peaks" to fade into "Earthquaker Heartbreaker," then walked toward the Damselfly's door. This was an especially popular song of hers, with a thunderous, apocalyptic lower end coupled with raging minor chords. During her preparation, she'd made some edits to this version. In counterpoint to the bass line, she'd inserted samples from Tishca's video.

Specifically, she'd edited in samples of Commander Lillioka and District Minister Cloudbearer at the height of their passion. This was a technique common among other—less creative, in Chrome's opinion—DownBeat artists, and popular in the clubs, but not one Chrome had used before. She considered the use of the moans and grunts of coitus a cheap gimmick that allowed any would-be musicmancer who employed it to get away with sub-standard music.

The crowd understood what a change this was from Chrome's typical style, and a collective gasp rippled across the plaza before thousands of voices roared their approval. Chrome shook her head even as she smiled to herself. Cheap thrills always wowed the crowd. By now she was at the base of the wide set of steps that led up to the Damselfly's front door. In the chaos, it had been left unguarded. Chrome dashed up the steps and through the open door.

* * *

Inside, Chrome discarded her disguise. The barroom was still filled with patrons, though not as crowded as before. Her music rattled the walls and floor, still punctuated by cries of pleasure. Reclamation Project troopers shouted at each other, rushed back and forth, and ignored what was shouted at them. Damselfly staff danced around the 'Claimers, trying to do their jobs while avoiding interaction with the humans.

Chrome smirked. These naked monkeys *could* be astonishingly stupid. She weaved between the bodies until she reached the base of the stairs, then stopped to look for the Commander.

"*You!*" Commander Lillioka shouted at her from at the top of the stairs. His sleek hair was tousled and mussed and his face had grown puffy, rendering his facial tattoos far less fierce. He stomped down the staircase, jabbing a finger out at Chrome. "What have you to do with this? Such *insolence!*"

He stopped on the last step, where he was closer to eye level with the musicmancer. Beneath his tattoos, Chrome could see his flushed cheeks. He obviously recognized the voices. "Instruct your confederate on the balcony to deactivate their disruptor field, or serious repercussions will result!" he said, waggling a finger at her.

"Get that out of my face before I bite it off," Chrome said with a snarl. "And I'm not telling my 'confederate' anything. Not until we've had a talk."

The Commander snorted derisively. "There are no discussions to be had. Cease this absurd and obscene display immediately!" He crossed his arms across his chest and tried to look down his nose at the fox-kin, but he still wasn't tall enough to do so and could only glare at where he thought her eyes might be behind her lenses.

"Commander, why does this outrage continue?" Minister Cloudbearer said from behind Chrome. The mare appeared more composed than the Commander, but her ears flicked constantly and her nostrils flared.

Chrome bobbed her head to the mare. "Minister. A better question is why are the 'Claimers still here, when they have no right to be?"

Cloudbearer glanced at the ceiling as a sample of her voice dropped into the beat. "As the Commander announced, it was a matter of public safety. The Reclamation Project has recently discovered weaknesses along the border fence between their territory and Old Ambara here at the market square."

Chrome shook her head. "Then why not warn us? Why storm over, acting like they own the place?"

"The structural issues are severe," the Commander said. "The danger of injuries due to a collapse is too significant, and the decision was made to act immediately. Even now, repair crews are working to address the situation."

"As a representative of the Prefecture," the Minister added, "I am empowered to enter into preliminary negotiations on behalf of the city government. That has been underway since earlier this afternoon."

Chrome grinned at the mare. "Negotiations. Yes, speaking of that, we may as well begin them. I have something to show you both." She stepped away from the secret lovers, toward the entrance to the casino behind the barroom. "Come," she said.

Hesitantly, Cloudbearer trailed after Chrome. The Commander made no move until the Minister turned to look for him, and then Lillioka reluctantly followed. "I come," the Commander said. "Be quick with it." Beneath his bluster, Chrome thought he looked exhausted. Behind the Commander, a trio of 'Claimer troopers trailed.

The fox-kin pointed to the troopers. "Send them away," she said. "This is between the three of us."

The Commander shook his head. "Never," he said. "They are my personal guard, and shall remain."

"Commander," the Minister said. For a moment Chrome could see something very close to love peek through her mask of serenity and composure. "We are in no danger here. Do as the young lady asks."

Lillioka looked up into Cloudbearer's large brown eyes. "Very well," he said softly to her. His troopers were reluctant to retreat, but they eventually backed away to stand clustered near the bar.

The casino was mostly empty, but Chrome still led the Commander and the Minister across the foyer, where dark doorways opened into small, private rooms. Both officials wore nearly identical expressions of angry suspicion despite their very different faces. "I presume the nonsense being broadcast is your doing," the Minister said to her.

Chrome shrugged. "I know why you're here," she said to Lillioka. "Part of it is some stupid 'Claimer power play that I won't even bother to try to understand. The other part—" and here she turned to Cloudbearer "—involves betrayal and corruption. But you're going to pack up your soldiers and leave, now."

The Commander sneered at her. "I think not," he said. "You have not the slightest inkling of the workings of the Reclamation Project. Our considerations and morals are as elevated above yours as our flying cities are above the ground you mongrels scratch about in, and our justifications are our own. Is that all you wanted to tell me? A poor threat, but what else is a savage such as you capable of?" He made to leave, but Chrome held up her datacom and began to play the video.

The Commander stopped, then slowly turned back to face Chrome. His exhaustion had evaporated, and his eyes blazed with unbridled rage, transformed by his tattoos into a truly fearsome visage. He drew himself to his full height, one fist clenched, tight at his side. *"How did you get that?"*

Chrome paused the playback. "It hardly matters," she replied, casually as she could. The Commander seemed on the verge of tipping over some emotional ledge, and she wanted to make sure he stayed on this side. If he went over, anything could happen.

He looked up at Cloudbearer, who stared at Chrome's datacom with her lips peeled back from clenched teeth, her eyes and nostrils wide, her ears flattened against her skull. "What do you know of this?" he asked her, each word soaked with the soul-searing venom of a betrayed lover.

"*Nothing!*" the Minister brayed. "How... ?" she stammered. "Where did this come from?"

Lillioka relaxed his stance, and released his fist, though he lost none of his fury. "It matters not," he said, "for there will be punishment enough meted out."

Chrome could not keep from laughing. "You talk such nonsense," she said. "You *know* what follows, both of you. And what follows will ruin you if I broadcast it, which I'm prepared to do unless the 'Claimers leave."

The human and the mare stared at the fox-kin, who waited with her datacom ready. In the background, the slewing, slurred melody of "Mindsmear" played, punctuated by the Commander's and Minister's sounds of pleasure. Finally, Chrome restarted the video and together they watched Lillioka and Cloudbearer in their assignation with Maadiis. Chrome watched the Commander as the video played. He tried to maintain his haughty fury, but as the scene progressed his anger grew into an incandescent wrath. "Let's skip the rest of this," Chrome said. "I don't think it's that interesting, anyway."

She advanced the video until the trio reclined, spent and sleepy, on Maadiis's large bed. "My delicious berries," Maadiis rumbled, an arm around each lover. "Of all my patrons, you are my favorites."

The Minister traced a hand through the chestnut fur of Maadiis's flat belly. "We can soon be your only patrons, if you wish," she said, smiling. "We will be in a position to lift you into an opulence and wealth which you cannot imagine."

Maadiis moved Cloudbearer's hand lower. "Tischa treats me exceptionally," they said dreamily. "How will you treat me?"

Lillioka turned his face into Maadiis's shoulder, nuzzling them. "I have discovered something," he said. "It will catapult me into the highest echelons of the Project, if I can claim it."

Maadiis purred at what Cloudbearer was doing to them, and moved their own hand down Lillioka's tattooed body. "How will you do that, my berries?" they asked.

Lillioka gasped, then moaned before being able to continue. "You are a treasure," he said. "Second only to what I suspect lies beneath the Damselfly. Once I control that—" Lillioka snatched at Chrome's datacom, but she easily dodged his grasp. Then he was clawing at the pistol on his hip.

Rust appeared out of one of the dark private rooms where she'd been waiting, listening, and caught Lillioka's gun arm with an enormous upper hand while pinning his his free hand with a lower. The Commander's guard rushed forward, but stopped short when Rust raised a long, wide-barreled gun in her free upper hand. With her fourth hand she plucked the Commander's pistol from its holster and jammed it into Cloudbearer's face. Chrome could see muscles twitching in terrified tics beneath the Minister's dappled hide.

Lieutenant Premanayanat and his bulky adjutants pushed their way past the troopers and hemmed in Chrome and the others. The urstacean lowered her long gun at the ape's approach but still held the Minister at gunpoint. The mare stood stock-still, staring down at the discharge node of the plasma pistol. The Commander squirmed and struggled against Rust's grip, but could not escape.

"I suppose someone will tell me what all has led to this?" the Lieutenant said in the same implacably hard voice he'd used against the 'Claimers when he'd first arrived at the Damselfly, while staring directly at Chrome. She found Premanayanat's intense attention much less amusing when directed at her than at a hapless 'Claimer, but she said nothing.

"I am an agent of the Reclamation Project and have diplomatic immunity within the self-styled Prefecture of Ambara Down!" the Commander said to the Lieutenant.

"Perhaps," Lieutenant Premanayanat said. "But that doesn't answer my question. So I'll ask again, what's going on here?" Still, no one answered him.

The ape's serious features hardened into a scowl. "If I hustle everyone here out the back door," Premanayanat said, "who will be around to worry about where any of you have gone?"

Jemmy's comments about the integrity of the Prefecture government echoed in Chrome's thoughts. Did he really have the best handle on things, after all?

To Chrome's surprise, Rust answered the Lieutenant. "I think Minister Cloudbearer could clear everything up, couldn't you?" The urstacean's solid black eyes were almost as difficult to read as Chrome's, but she stared at the mare as intently as Cloudbearer stared at the pistol.

Cloudbearer whickered and her ears twitched as they lay folded back. A muscle quivered on her neck. She flicked her eyes from Rust's pistol to Lillioka, then to the Lieutenant. "Yes," she said slowly. "I can. There is a structural issue with the Fence in this area, and the Reclamation Project has come to secure the area so that it might be repaired."

The ape stared at the Minister. "I see," he said in a tone that indicated he did not believe a word Cloudbearer had told him. "And that is how you came to be held at gunpoint?"

The Minister laughed, a shrill, unconvincing whinny. "Yes," she said. "It is of course a disappointment to have the Founders Festival canceled. Emotions are running high."

"Yes, yes!" the Commander chimed in. "A misunderstanding, is all."

Lieutenant Premanayanat glowered around at all of them. "I have the statement of a District Minister and of an officer of the Reclamation Project that this is nothing to be concerned about. Would anyone else like to add anything?"

"*Yes!*" Chrome cried. "Fucking Engineers, *yes!*" She turned to Cloudbearer. "Rust gave you the chance to save yourself," she said to the mare, biting off each word"And to protect Ambara Down, but you've sided with the '*Claimers*. I don't know what you were promised, but now you can hang with them!" She cued the video back to the beginning of the pillow talk and held her datacom out to the Lieutenant. "Watch this," she told him.

Premanayanat frowned as the video began to play, but his thick, beetled simian brow ridge shot up in shock as he realized who was in the frame. Chrome turned the sound up loud enough for all those gathered, including the 'Claimer troops, to hear clearly. With every second, the Prefect Guards' expressions grew more alarmed, even Jank the urstacean's immobile face. They watched the video until the end, listening to Lillioka and Cloudbearer incriminate themselves in a scheme to expand the Reclamation Project Territory into this district of Old Ambara so that Lillioka might gain complete and unfettered access to whatever he thought he'd found under the Damselfly.

"Now I understand why you worked so hard to convince me this wasn't an emergency," the Lieutenant said to the Minister.

He turned to Lillioka, still held by Rust. "You may have diplomatic immunity," he told the 'Claimer, "but I'm sorely tempted to forget that. However, I'll give you thirty minutes to exercise it and get your sorry furless carcass back across the Fence, along with those under your command. If you ask nicely, I'll let you take your girlfriend so we don't have to put a District Minister on trial. Otherwise, we'll all be leaving by the back door. Have I made myself clear?"

Instead of replying, the Commander kicked out at the ape with a grunting shout that turned into a surprised squawk when Rust lifted him off his feet. Chrome took this opportunity to call Jemmy. "Slot in the third stick," she told him, "but don't play it until I tell you to."

Lieutenant Premanayanat thrust a finger the size of a sausage at the fox-kin. "Not so fast," he told her. "I'm not letting you start a riot."

He turned his attention back to the Commander. "You have *fifteen* minutes, now."

The human hung from Rust's hands, in equal parts furious, mortified, and terrified. He looked back and forth from Chrome to the Lieutenant, then to his soldiers, who stood dumbfounded. Finally, he looked at District Minister Cloudbearer, who stared intently at him. She leaned forward slightly, pleading with her eyes. "Please, Marcel," she whispered. "*Please.*"

"Yes," Lillioka spat, looking at the floor. "Yes, and damn you all. Enough! Let me down, I will go."

The Lieutenant straightened. "He's agreed, miss," he said to Rust. "Let him go." Rust dropped him, and he fell to the floor, landing upon his hands and knees. "The clock has started," Premanayanat told him.

Cloudbearer took a hesitant, hopeful step forward as the Commander climbed to his feet, but the 'Claimer did not even look at her as he pushed past the Lieutenant's deputies. "*NO!*" she screamed as Lillioka led his troops away. "Marcel, no, please! Take me with you! *PLEASE!*"

The 'Claimers did not look back, and the Minister collapsed to her knees with a wailing whinny as Jank and Creana took hold of her arms.

* * *

Outside the Damselfly, tension between the 'Claimers and the locals in the square had risen steadily as the music played. The troopers had quickly recognized the voice of their officer in the samples, both amused and alarmed at what it might mean. While most of the crowd continued to dance to the music, rings of locals with large teeth, hard eyes, and conspicuous bulges beneath their clothing surrounded the remaining troopers and their equipment. These had first appeared when the 'Claimer transport was overturned by the crowd, and even though no other violence occurred, the threat of it hung heavy over the square. The Guard, still present in pairs, made no move to interfere.

When the front door opened and a handful of blue-uniformed troopers spilled out, their Commander in their midst, the tone of the crowd shifted almost instantly, from an anxious but joyous chatter to an angry burr. The rings of toughs stiffened and hands reached beneath shirts and into jackets.

The 'Claimers braced themselves in response, preparing for Lillioka's direction. But instead of an order to charge, his coterie struggled to push through the crowd toward the remaining transport. "To me!" he called. "Eighth Cohort to me! We return to our quarters." The crowd exploded, cheering the victory over the arrogance of the Reclamation Project and jeering at the retreating humans. The rings dissipated, and the troopers trapped within them rushed to join their comrades.

From where they stood at the front doors of the Damselfly, Chrome and Rust watched Lillioka find his overturned transport. He turned and glared back at them, but Chrome only waved to him. "Keep going," she said, although there was no way he could hear. "Even if some of you have to walk."

The Commander climbed into the remaining transport, other 'Claimers filled it, and the rest formed up alongside. "There's fewer leaving than arrived," Rust said.

"Hopefully some just decided to go native and didn't get disappeared by the ADF," Chrome replied as the column began to force its way back out of the market square. "They can stay, if they behave."

Behind them, the door opened and Jemmy came out. He had put on a pair of shorts, but still wore the PPD belt. "That's it, then?" he asked, holding out the datasticks to Chrome.

"For you," she said, taking the sticks. "*I* have a show to put on!"

* * *

After a half-hour of adjustment, Chrome finally stood before her rig. All the spotlights abandoned by the 'Claimers had been directed towards the balcony, and everything around her was bathed in bright white light. Her metallic crest and forearms gleamed. The square below was packed tight from edge to edge, people of every color and kin cheering and whistling for her.

She punched at the sequencer, and the thumping bassline of "Down Ambara Down" roared forth. The crowd roared back in response. "Ambara Down, my love!" she shouted, grinning madly. Her voice rang out across the square. "We have our city, so let us *celebrate* it!" Somewhere out there, on the other side of the Fence, was Lillioka and his troops. She hoped they could hear her.

The crowd was waiting, waiting, waiting for her next move. She punched at sequencer again, releasing the melody, then swiped at the mixer, sending a tremolo through the music. This was so much better than sex, riding the wave of the music and the crowd's reaction to it. She trembled at its power, its intoxicating effect upon her. The music approached a crescendo, and Chrome initiated her chromium maneuvers.

Her coxcomb lit up, each section from the red fur at the nape of her neck to the violet forelock cresting over her muzzle glittered with bioluminescence, then began to flash in sequence, back to front. Other patches on her fur burst forth in bright whorls that swirled and moved around her body. She nodded to the intensifying beat and her crest bobbed and danced. Then she raised her chromed arms and cast out light from the fiber-optic furs, spangling the sky.

The crowd loosed their own excitement, jumping and dancing and howling and singing, exorcising their anxieties and fears through the music. The 'Claimers might always be a threat, trying to retake their fallen city from those who had taken it in turn, but they would *always* be resisted.

ABOUT THE AUTHORS

John R. Robey, also known as "The Gneech" in fandom circles, is the creator of *The Suburban Jungle* webcomic, a writer of furry and fantasy literature, and a creativity and writing coach. *The Reclamation Project* is his first outing as an editor. You can find more of his work and some pictures of his cat at http://johnrrobey.com.

Indagare lives at home with his family. He works at a local historical house that's also a museum. He likes reading, writing, and drawing as well as hanging out with friends. His work can also be found in the *Altered States* anthology edited by Ajax B. Coriander.

L. Rowyn is the penname the author chose because it was too much work to change all of her existing social media to use a different name. At the time of this writing, she has ten published books, although mysteriously this number keeps growing and so may have changed. Most of her work is fantasy romance: please visit ladyrowyn.com for details.

Nenekiri Bookwyrm is a dragon that loves writing and making games. He's also been known to paint and play the ukulele on occasion. He's been published in Anthrocon's 2018 conbook with *The Wyrm in the Mountain of Apples* and in Tiny Paws's 2018 conbook with *The Great Snipe Sighting of '92*. He's had his game, *Gasu, The Hugging Dragon* featured in an art exhibit in New York City. This is his first time getting published in a book anthology and he's more than a little excited about it! You can find more of his writing and other projects on https://www.nenekiri.com, find his game projects at https://nenekiri.itch.io, and support him monthly at patreon.com/nenekiri. Curl up with a good book and be kind to yourself.

Graveyard Greg has been through the very fires of hell and back, only to discover he forgot his keys.

Bryan Osborne, whom many in the fandom know as "StarryAqua," or just "Starry" for short among friends, has been a member of the furry fandom since 2007. While he had always had an interest in anthropomorphic characters since childhood, it wasn't until he became familiar with the furry fandom that he felt so welcomed and gained so many friends. A fondness for storytelling has always been a lifelong passion; from books to video games to tabletop games to whatever else exists. If there's a good tale to be had, you can always find Bryan front and center.

When not writing or supporting the fandom however he can, you can always find Bryan on the bowling lanes. A bowler since the age of 3, Bryan is a member of the Professional Bowlers Association and hopes to make a lasting career doing the two things he loves: writing and bowling.

Follow him on Twitter @Starry_Aqua

Royce "Sir Talen" Day is the fifty-something author of the popular *Red Vixen Adventures* sci-fi romance novellas. Day also created the *For Your Safety* science-fiction series, described by Baen Books author Ryk Spoor as "The most unique, heartwarming conquest of humanity I've ever read." Day lives in Maryland, along with his wife, two children, and a pair of obligatory cats.

If you wish to purchase his works, they can be found at Amazon. com. Alternatively, you can support him at Patreon: patreon.com/ RoyceDay or Ko-fi: https://ko-fi.com/royceday

Kayode Lycaon (Kay·o·deh Lie·kay·on) is a gregarious painted wolf living in the questionable habitat of southwestern Ohio. By day, he pretends to be a human, writing software. At night, his paws weave stories from threads spun from the fertile grounds of his imagination.

He writes stories filled with hope and hardship. The ending may be joyful, bittersweet, or tragic but it will always bring the rich inner lives of his anthropomorphic characters to life on the page. He hopes that his passion and creativity will inspire others to tell their own stories. He can be found on twitter as @kayodelycaon.

Dan Leinir Turthra Jensen Dan, or Leinir as they are more commonly known, hails from the tiny country of Denmark, but resides in England, where they live with their partner of many years writing science fiction and making food that some people have described with a variety of superlatives. Since leaving university, they have worked for several companies as a software developer, working primarily on free and open source software. They have also been known to dress up as a fluffy cat type thing, and a blue bird type thing, and enjoys spending a relaxing time and a bottle of wine shared with friends.

With his den in northern Colorado, **Juan C. Moreno** (*Vulpes vulpes moreno*) works as a marketing copywriter while moonlighting as a fiction author for anthologies like the *Werewolves Versus* 'zine series. His stories are inspired by the places he's traveled to and the cast of characters he's shared adventures with along the way.

When he's not pawing at a keyboard or raising his hackles in defense of the Oxford comma, Juan can be found hiking ancient pathways, exploring modern trails, or finding new tracks with his significant otter. You can visit Juan online by searching for WanderingGoose on DeviantArt or QuickBrownFoxWrites on Tumblr.

Ferric the Bird has been writing short stories for over ten years, and furry stories for about seven of those. Most can be found on Sofurry and FA, but recently he's started to get a few published whenever possible. He enjoys writing in his spare time as it allows him to be creative, and his head is full of too many crazy things to ever stop.

Huskyteer's short stories have been published both in and out of the fandom, and have won two Cóyotl Awards, two Ursa Major Awards, and one Leo Award. She rides a motorcycle, has a black belt in karate, and is much less cool than that makes her sound. Find her at huskyteer.co.uk, or as @Huskyteer on Twitter.

James L. Steele is a writer in Ohio. He is often asked to sum up his life's story in a single paragraph. James is very depressed by how easy this is. He is the author of the Archeon series, published by KTM Publishing, about a raptor and a fox traveling to different planets to save civilization from collapsing after their homeworld was destroyed by some unknown force. Visit his blog at DaydreamingInText. blogspot.com, and his twitter @JLSteeleAuthor.

Matt Trepal has been writing fiction on and off since his early years. From those same early years he was drawn to animal characters, furry before he even knew what furry was. He writes science fiction, fantasy, and crime fiction, mostly furry but sometimes not, and has dabbled in webcomics. He enjoys blending genres, such as fantasy noir and sword-and-planet space opera. He has previously been published in *Species: Foxes*. A faceless bureaucrat by trade and training, he lives in southwest Florida with a retired racing greyhound and lots and lots of books. Books are the best. He can be found on Twitter at @trpeal.

www.ingramcontent.com/pod-product-compliance
Lightning Source LLC
Chambersburg PA
CBHW071158020726
47502CB00002B/456